MURDER IN A SMALL TOWN

Kaden abruptly turned, pacing across the cramped space as he considered what Lia had told him. He didn't look upset, but there was a tightness to his features that suggested a part of him was disappointed to discover that Vanna was as ruthless as he'd always feared. Or maybe he was wishing his brother had never gotten involved with her.

Finally, he turned back to face her, his disappointment replaced with a grim determination.

"If she was using her power as an EPA inspector to blackmail local businesses, that might explain why no one wants her identified." He deliberately paused. "Including the mayor."

Lia slowly nodded. "It would certainly be awkward."

"It might be more than awkward."

He didn't have to spell out his suspicion that whoever was being blackmailed had murdered Vanna. Either to hide the evidence of their violations or to avoid paying the bribe. Or both.

An ancient regret sliced through her heart. "I can't wrap my mind around the thought I might have seen Vanna running from her killer."

"And that whoever killed her is still in town . . ."

Published by Kensington Publishing Corp.

DESPERATE ACTS

ALEXANDRA IVY

ZEBRA BOOKS
KENSINGTON PUBLISHING CORP.

www.kensingtonbooks.com

ZEBRA BOOKS are published by

Kensington Publishing Corp.
119 West 40th Street
New York, NY 10018

All Kensington titles, imprints, and distributed lines are available at special quantity discounts for bulk purchases for sales promotion, premiums, fund-raising, and educational or institutional use.

Special book excerpts or customized printings can also be created to fit specific needs. For details, write or phone the office of the Kensington Sales Manager: Kensington Publishing Corp., 119 West 40th Street, New York, NY 10018. Attn. Sales Department. Phone: 1-800-221-2647.

ZEBRA BOOKS and the Z logo Reg. U.S. Pat. & TM Off.

First Printing: March 2023
ISBN-13: 978-1-4201-5550-1
ISBN-13: 978-1-4201-5551-8 (eBook)

10 9 8 7 6 5 4 3 2 1

Printed in the United States of America

Prologue

Pike, WI
December 14, 2007

Tugging her coat tight around her shivering body, Lia Porter scurried down the dark pathway. It was past midnight, and the late December air was cold enough to burn her lungs as she sucked in deep breaths. This was so stupid. She should never have crept out of her house to attend the party. Even at fifteen years old she knew that a gathering of kids in an old barn in the middle of winter was a lame idea. Some of her friends might enjoy shivering around a small fire, listening to country music and drinking cheap beer, but she'd been bored out of her mind.

So why had she allowed herself to be cajoled into going?

Lia wrinkled her nose. She'd told herself that she was tired of being called Lia-Killjoy by her classmates. Okay. She liked to follow the rules. She wasn't a maverick. Or a risk-taker. She didn't cheat on tests or skip classes. She didn't even go skinny-dipping at the local lake. In fact, if she wasn't at school, she was helping her mother at the family-owned grocery store in the center of town. But that didn't mean she couldn't have a good time, right?

But deep in her heart she knew that wasn't why she spent

an hour straightening her strawberry-blond hair until it fell in a smooth curtain down her back. Or added a layer of mascara to the long lashes that framed her green eyes. Or why she'd snuck out of her room and trudged two miles to the middle of the frozen field.

She'd been hoping to attract the attention of Chuck Moore, the guy she'd nursed a secret crush on for an entire year. He wasn't the most popular boy in class. Or the cutest. He had frizzy black hair and an overbite that was prominent despite his braces. But he was one of the few guys who at least pretended to listen when she spoke. That was far more attractive to a girl who'd spent her school life in the shadows than perfect features or bulging muscles.

Unfortunately, she'd had to wait until her mother was asleep before sneaking out. They lived above the store and she couldn't just climb out a bedroom window. She had to creep down the squeaky stairs at the back of the two-story brick building. By the time she arrived at the barn the party was in full swing, and Chuck was already in the hayloft with her best friend, Karen Cranford.

Calling herself an idiot, she'd forced herself to stay long enough to drink a beer and pretend to laugh at the antics of the guys who thought it was a great idea to try to push one another into the fire. As if nursing second-degree burns was a hilarious way to spend the evening. Then, assuring herself that she'd proved whatever stupid point she'd come there to make, she'd slipped out the door and headed across the dark field.

Lia muttered a bad word as she slipped on a patch of ice. Pike, Wisconsin, wasn't the best location to take a midnight stroll. Especially in the middle of winter. If she fell and broke a leg, she was going to be in so much trouble.

The thought of her mother made Lia grimace. Trina Porter had only been sixteen when she'd given birth to Lia. That had been tough enough, but Lia's father had disappeared just months after she was born, and her grandparents had died in a tragic car accident eight years later. Trina was forced to work endless hours to keep a roof over their heads and food on their table. She'd sacrificed everything to give her child a warm and loving home.

Lia felt the constant weight of those sacrifices pressing down on her like an anchor. If she knowingly added to her mom's daily struggle, she would never forgive herself.

Rounding a bend in the pathway, Lia breathed a sigh of relief. Ahead, she could see the soft glow of streetlights. Soon she would be back in her room, tucked in her warm bed with one of the books she'd borrowed from the library. Exactly where she wanted to be.

Lost in the fantasy of being curled up beneath her thick comforter with a cup of hot cocoa, Lia came to an abrupt halt. She heard a sound in the distance. Not a car. Or an animal. It sounded like . . . like running footsteps.

More curious than alarmed, Lia watched as a shadowed form appeared from the shadows. It didn't occur to her that she might be in danger. This was Pike. Nothing bad ever happened here. The figure neared, moving down the path toward her. As she grew closer, Lia could make out the delicate features of a woman with long, black hair that flowed behind her. She was wearing a heavy leather jacket and pants that looked like some kind of uniform. Lia could also see the glitter of gold in the moonlight. The woman had a large badge pinned to the upper shoulder of her jacket. Like a cop.

Oh no.

Lia sucked in a sharp breath. Had her mother awakened and found her missing? Had she called the sheriff's office? No. She sternly squashed the urge to panic. She would recognize anyone local. Pike was too small to have strangers. This woman was from somewhere else.

So why was she running from town in the middle of the night?

It was a question that was to haunt Lia for the next fifteen years, as the woman suddenly spotted her standing in the middle of the pathway. She'd just reached the bridge that spanned the railroad tracks.

A scream was ripped from her throat, as if Lia was a monster, not a fifteen-year-old girl sneaking home from a party. Then, with a shocking speed, the woman turned toward the edge of the bridge, climbing onto the stone guardrail.

What the heck was she doing? Lia took a startled step forward, lifting her hand as the woman wobbled. It was at least twelve feet to the tracks below. Not even the local boys were stupid enough to jump from there.

"Wait!" she called out, but she was too late.

With a last, terrified glance toward Lia, the woman leaned forward and disappeared into the darkness.

Chapter 1

It was mid-December and the town of Pike, Wisconsin, looked like an image on a postcard. The ground was coated in pristine layers of snow and the trees sparkled with Christmas lights. The town square was draped in garland that filled the crisp air with a scent of pine. There was even a miniature North Pole set up in the park where Santa perched on a chair from six to seven in the evenings for the kids to take pictures.

The downside to the winter wonderland, however, was the brutal windchill that whipped through the narrow streets despite the clear blue skies and bright morning sunlight. The cold kept most sensible people snuggled in the warmth of their homes. A shame for the local businesses that depended on the holiday season to pad their yearly income, but for Lia Porter, the quiet was welcome. The grocery store was never a hot spot in town, not even during Christmas, but she was there alone and she didn't want to be disturbed.

Seated at her desk in the private office she'd claimed at the back of the building, Lia kept one eye on her computer and the other on the surveillance monitor that kept guard on the front of the store. She wasn't afraid of shoplifters. The four short aisles with wooden shelves were stocked with basic supplies. Flour, sugar, bread, and canned goods. There was also a cooler with dairy products and a section for frozen foods. If someone was desperate enough to steal food, she would be happy to hand it over to them. She just wanted to keep watch in case a customer entered and needed her help.

Something that wouldn't be necessary if Wayne had arrived on time. With a sigh, Lia returned her attention to the computer screen, where she'd downloaded the portfolio of an online retailer who was trying to attract new investors. Lia was interested. She preferred putting her capital in businesses just starting out. Getting in on the ground floor meant she would make the most profit. But she was still reviewing the business model and debt-to-equity ratio before she agreed to meet with the founder.

High risk/high return didn't mean recklessly tossing her money around. She devoted weeks and sometimes months in research before she agreed to invest. That had been her motto since she'd taken the trust fund she'd inherited from her grandparents at the age of twenty-one and invested it with a local carpenter who wanted to flip houses. Her mother had been horrified, but soon she was making a profit, and she'd taken that money to invest in another company. And then another.

Within five years, she had tripled her trust fund and proved that she could not only support herself but could build a large enough nest egg that she didn't have to worry about her future. It'd also given her mother the opportunity to concentrate on her own life. Within a few months, the older woman had married a man who'd loved her for years and whisked her away to a secluded cabin in Colorado.

Lia had been delighted that her mom could find happiness, and she hadn't minded taking over the store that had been in their family for over a hundred years. It was as much a part of Pike as the surrounding dairy farms and the stone courthouse down the street. It rarely made a profit, but the store wasn't about creating money. It was keeping the tradition that her great-great-great-grandfather had started, as well as providing much-needed provisions for the older citizens who didn't feel comfortable driving to the larger town of Grange. Not to mention offering the necessities during the winter months, when the roads could be closed for days at a time.

Scribbling a few notes she wanted to double-check before continuing her interest in the potential investment, Lia heard the familiar tinkle of a bell. Someone had pushed open the front door. She glanced toward the monitor, watching the tall, lanky boy with short, rust-brown hair and a narrow face enter the store.

Wayne Neilson was a seventeen-year-old boy who'd asked for a job the previous summer. Lia already had a part-time helper who'd been there for forty years, but Della was getting older and her health wasn't always the best, so Lia had agreed to give Wayne an opportunity. He was being raised by a single mother just like she had. She understood the need to earn extra money.

He'd proven to be remarkably dependable, arriving right after school to put in a couple of hours and on Saturday and Sunday mornings.

Until this Saturday morning.

Rising from the desk, Lia headed out of the office and firmly shut the door. Only her mother knew about her investment skills. And that was how she wanted to keep it. Pike was a small town where everyone was always snooping into everyone's business. It was even worse for someone like her. She'd always been different. She didn't have a father. She didn't mix easily with the other kids. And now she'd vaulted past her scary thirtieth birthday with no marriage proposal in sight. It made people study her as if she was a puzzle that needed to be solved. Or maybe fixed.

She wanted something that was just for herself.

She entered the main part of the store and walked toward the front counter, where Wayne was hanging his heavy parka on a hook drilled into the paneled wall.

"Hey, Ms. Porter. Sorry about being late," he said, his narrow face flushed and his blue eyes sparkling with an intense emotion.

"Is everything okay?"

"Fine." He shifted from foot to foot, as if he was having trouble standing still. "At least for me."

Lia studied him with mounting concern. Usually he was shy and subdued to the point she could barely get more than two words out of him. This excitement was completely out of character.

"What's going on?"

He glanced around the store, as if making sure it was empty. Then, he sucked in a deep breath.

"Drew and Cord found a body."

"A body of what?"

Wayne leaned toward her; his voice lowered to a harsh whisper. "A human body." He grimaced. "Or at least a skeleton."

Lia snorted. She knew both Drew Hurst and Cord Walsh. They were known around Pike as the local bullies. Clichéd but true. And their favorite target was usually Wayne.

"Are you sure they weren't messing with you?"

Wayne grimaced, no doubt recalling a thousand different

insults, humiliations, and even physical blows he'd endured over the years.

"Yeah. They're usually being jerks. Especially to me," he conceded. "But they aren't smart enough to set up an actual prank. They just shove people into lockers and steal stuff out of backpacks." He shrugged, the bones of his thin shoulders visible beneath his T-shirt. "Besides, they couldn't fake looking pale as ghosts when they climbed over the bridge railing. Or Drew puking up his guts when he told me what they'd seen. For real, I thought he was going to pass out."

Lia jerked, as if she'd just touched a live wire. And that was what it felt like as the shock zigzagged through her.

"What bridge railing?" She had to force the words past her stiff lips.

Wayne was thankfully oblivious to her tension. Like any teenage boy, he rarely noticed anything that didn't affect him directly.

"The one over the railroad tracks."

"The railroad bridge," she breathed, battling back the image that had haunted her for the past fifteen years. "I thought the whole area was closed off while they put in new railway tracks."

"It is. That's why they were there. It's a perfect time to sled down that steep hill without worrying about a train coming by and squashing them."

Lia shook her head. Both Drew and Cord had to be eighteen, or close to it. They were seniors, after all. But neither bothered to use their brains. Assuming they had one.

"So what happened?"

"Drew said he hit an icy patch that threw him off his sled and he rolled into a ditch next to the tracks. That's when he saw something under a bunch of old branches."

Lia shoved away her opinion of Drew and Cord. Right now, nothing mattered but the wild claim they'd made.

"And you're absolutely certain they found a body?"

"I can show you."

Lia took an instinctive step backward, as if he was about to pull a rotting corpse out of his pocket.

"What?"

Wayne held up the phone that was a constant fixture in his hand. "I had to see for myself."

"You went down to look at the body?"

"Of course." He swiped his finger over the screen, seemingly searching for something. "Nothing ever happens in this town. I wasn't going to miss the one nanosecond of excitement." He turned the phone around, a hint of pride on his narrow face. "Even if it was a little gruesome."

Lia glanced at the screen, realizing he'd pulled up a photo. She sent him a sharp glance.

"You took pictures?"

"Yep. And I posted them on my Instagram account. I'm hoping they'll go viral."

"Wayne."

He hunched his shoulders in a defensive motion. "Like I said, It's my one nanosecond of excitement. And it's not hurting anyone. Whoever the skeleton belongs to is dead and gone." He continued to hold out the phone. "Look."

Lia didn't want to look. She wanted to scurry back to her office and shut the door. Maybe then she could pretend it was just another day. A regular, boring day like every other regular, boring day.

A strange compulsion, however, had her leaning forward, studying the image Wayne had enlarged. Her gaze went immediately to the skull that peeked out of a layer of ice. It didn't look real. Instead, it appeared to have been carved from aged ivory, with empty eyes sockets that were shadowed, as if hiding unbearable secrets, and perfectly intact teeth that appeared too large and weirdly threatening.

With a shudder, Lia forced her gaze to take in the rest of the skeleton. Or at least what was visible.

The upper torso was covered by what appeared to be a weathered leather jacket. She hissed, enlarging the picture until she could see the gold badge that had dulled over the years but remained unmistakable.

"Oh my God." Lia pressed a hand to her heaving stomach. Any hope of returning to her office and acting as if everything was normal was replaced with a burning urgency to take some sort of action. She didn't know exactly what that action was going to be, but she couldn't sit around and do nothing. "I need you to cover the store for an hour or so," she muttered.

"Okay." Wayne climbed onto the stool behind the cash register. "But if you want to take a look at the skeleton, it's too late. The mayor is there and he won't let anyone near the place. He's such a jerk."

Lia bit her lip. The mention of the mayor jolted her sluggish brain. That was what she needed to do. Speak with a law official. Unfortunately, Zac Evans, who'd proven to be an outstanding sheriff, had left Pike a week earlier to take his wife on an overdue honeymoon. He refused to tell them where he was going, only that it involved a cruise ship and that he was shutting off his phone and refusing to think about work until after the holidays.

Good news for him. Awful news for her.

For now, Pike was without a full-time sheriff, and until Zac returned, the local mayor was filling the position. Tate Erickson was barely capable of performing his duties as mayor, let alone taking on the sheriff's job.

Still, what choice did she have?

"I'll be back later." She scurried to the back of the narrow building, using the private staircase to head up to the apartment above the store.

It was a wide-open space arranged with a living room and kitchen and bedroom with an attached bathroom. The furniture hadn't changed since her mother moved out. The leather couch and chairs were worn and sagging in places, but they were comfortable, and that was all that mattered. Grabbing her purse, Lia slid a heavy parka over her casual jeans and bright red sweater before pulling on a thick stocking hat. She'd cut her strawberry-blond hair into a short, pixie style that was easy to take care of but did nothing to keep her warm. Then, heading back down the narrow staircase, she left the building to climb into the SUV with PORTER GROCERIES painted on the side. Once a month she delivered groceries to the customers who were housebound.

Driving out of the alley, she turned away from the center square and headed toward the outer road. The streets were slick from the most recent snowfall, but she was too impatient to creep along at a cautious pace. She slid past the old drive-in, where the framework of bare wood from the screen had managed to survive. Next to it was an indoor skating rink that hadn't been so lucky. It had collapsed years ago. Farther on was the bowling alley, which had been converted into a charity shop.

At last, she turned onto a narrow path that led toward the rolling fields that surrounded Pike and drove until she reached a curve in the road. She parked the SUV and switched off the engine. Ahead, she could see the barricades that had been put up along with glowing yellow police tape. A shiver raced through her as she watched the thin plastic flap in the stiff breeze.

Climbing out of the vehicle, Lia headed toward the short, heavyset man in a brown uniform standing guard against the gathering crowd.

Anthony was the same age as Lia and had been a sheriff's

deputy for several years. He'd never been overly ambitious in school. He was the kid who sat in the back so he could sleep. At least, when he bothered to show up for school. Most days he skipped to go hunting or fishing. But she assumed that he was decent at his job.

She halted directly in front of the man. "Hey, Anthony. Is the mayor here?"

"Unfortunately." He nodded toward the steep bank behind him that led down to the railroad tracks. "He's down there."

"I need to talk to him."

"Can't. He's busy right now."

"This is important."

"Sorry, but it's going to have to wait."

"Anthony—"

The deputy held up a pudgy hand, interrupting her protest. "Trust me, Lia, this isn't the time." He glanced over his shoulder, making sure the mayor wasn't lurking behind him. "Erickson's been pissy since he became a fill-in for the sheriff, but today he's off the charts. He's been storming and stomping around ever since he caught sight of the skeleton. I assume he finally realized that being sheriff is more than getting free coffee at the diner."

Lia ground her teeth, not bothering to argue. Anthony might not have displayed ambition when he was young, but he'd always been stubborn as a mule. There was no point in beating her head against a brick wall.

"Thanks."

Turning away from the barrier, Lia stepped off the pathway and headed toward the snow-packed ridgeline. There was more than one way to get down to the tracks.

"Lia!"

Lia halted at the sound of her name being called out, glancing to the side to see a woman hurrying toward her.

Bailey Evans was Lia's best friend, and the sheriff's cousin. She was thin with brown hair pulled into a messy bun on top of her head. She was currently wearing a thick coat, but as usual she'd forgotten a hat and her gloves. Bailey was a fantastic caregiver at the local nursing home, but she could be remarkably absentminded. As if she was so occupied with tending to others that she didn't have time to worry about herself.

"Did you hear the news?" Bailey asked, halting next to Lia.

"Just that they found a skeleton."

"It's thrilling, isn't it? Horrible, of course." The flecks of gold in Bailey's dark eyes sparkled with eager curiosity, her cheeks flushed. "But absolutely thrilling."

Lia hid her grimace. She couldn't blame Bailey for being excited. Although Pike had endured more than its fair share of murders over the past five years, there was something morbidly intriguing about a mysterious death.

"Do they know who it is?"

"I don't think so." Bailey wrinkled her nose. "Tate is being more of an ass than usual. I miss Zac."

Lia sighed. "Who doesn't? He's the only decent sheriff we've had since Rupert retired." Lia was still in school when Rupert Jansen was forced to leave his position after being shot on the job, but everyone knew he'd been legendary. "Did Tate say anything?"

"He told me to keep my nose out of his business." Bailey made a sound of disgust. "Idiot. I'm the town gossip. My nose belongs in everyone's business." She glanced toward the nearby field, which was crammed with emergency vehicles. "I did hear one of the EMTs call it a 'her' when they loaded the body bag into the ambulance. Other than that, it's a complete mystery."

"A woman," Lia breathed.

"I've been trying to imagine who it could be." Bailey reached up to push back her thick hair, which was being tossed by the breeze. "I don't know any missing women. Not unless you count my Aunt Misty, who traveled to Paris thirty years ago and never came home. Really, who could blame her? Sipping café au lait in a cute little bistro certainly beats sucking down a cup of joe in a local dive, am I right?"

Usually Lia would smile at Bailey's chatter. The fact that they were complete opposites was what made their relationship so much fun. This morning, however, she was too tense to appreciate her friend's humor.

"It could be one of Jude's victims," she pointed out.

Bailey's amusement died at the mention of the monster who'd lived in Pike nearly thirty years before.

"That was my first thought as well. There's always a chance that one slipped through the cracks," she agreed, her tone doubtful. "But Zac was pretty certain they'd located all of them. Otherwise, he would never have left town."

It did seem doubtful. Zac had spent endless months searching through the stacks of evidence left behind by the serial killer. If there'd been any hint of a missing victim, he would never have closed the case.

Which meant the woman she'd seen that night hadn't been fleeing a madman. At least not a madman who'd already faced justice. Honestly, that only made things worse.

"I need to talk to Tate," she muttered.

Without warning, Bailey reached out to grasp her arm. "I wouldn't if I were you."

"Why not?"

"He not only snapped at me. The jerk." Her jaw tightened at the memory. "He's been on a rampage with everyone, including the deputies. Last I heard, he was screaming about 'crime scenes' and 'preservation of clues.' I'm guessing he's been watching reruns of *Law & Order*. Or, more likely, *The Andy Griffith Show*. He certainly has a Barney Fife vibe."

Lia bit her lower lip. She hated confrontations. It didn't mean she didn't have a spine. She could be ruthless when necessary. But she preferred to avoid messy arguments. Maybe she should wait until . . .

No. Lia squared her shoulders. The last time she'd decided to avoid revealing what she'd seen, a woman obviously had ended up dead. She wasn't going to risk letting anything bad happen again. Not if revealing the truth could prevent it.

"He'll just have to scream," she said in grim tones. "I need to talk to him."

"Fine." Bailey nodded, easily sensing Lia's determination. Still, she kept a tight grip on her arm. "Don't forget we're having a Friends of Pike meeting Tuesday night. We need to discuss the Fourth of July festival. Jolene already sent me an email." Bailey rolled her eyes. Jolene was married to Tate Erickson. Her position as the mayor's wife meant she considered herself an authority on everything Pike. Or what she envisioned Pike should be. And while Tate possessed a brash, outgoing sort of charm that had allowed him to keep getting reelected for the past twenty years, Jolene was just the opposite. She was a soft-spoken woman with deep dimples and a cloud of blond hair. But in her own way she was just as ruthless. She used her supposedly fragile health to avoid unpleasant confrontations or to manipulate others into giving in to her every demand.

"Now what does she want?" Lia asked.

"She suggested that we replace the greased pig run with an afternoon tea and cakewalk. She's afraid we might get in trouble with the PETA people." Bailey did more eye-rolling. "As if anyone would know what's happening in

Pike. We can barely interest the locals in noticing the events, let alone attract the attention of anyone else."

"I doubt PETA would be showing up to complain," Lia agreed. "But then again, I'm not opposed to getting rid of the greased pig. It's kind of disgusting."

"Agreed, but it's been a part of the Fourth of July celebrations for a hundred years. The rest of the committee is going to have a cow." Bailey heaved a sigh. "Greased pigs and cows. That's my life."

Lia managed a small smile of encouragement. "I'll be there."

"Thanks, Lia." Bailey gave Lia's arm a squeeze before dropping her hand and stepping back. "I can always depend on you."

Lia swallowed a sigh as she turned away. That was her. Dependable Lia.

Tate was frantically pulling aside the dead branches and chunks of frozen snow that were piled near the skeleton. He ignored the destruction of his expensive leather gloves. Jolene was going to bitch when he went home and she saw them, but what the hell? If it wasn't his gloves, she'd find something else to bitch about. She was nothing if not consistent. And right now, he didn't have time to worry about anything except making sure there was nothing around he didn't want found.

When he'd first gotten the call that a bunch of boys had found a skeleton by the railroad tracks, he'd been more annoyed than concerned. This sheriff thing was a short-term gig. Just until Zac Evans returned to Pike. He assumed it would be an easy way to add an accomplishment to his résumé as mayor. It was never too early to start thinking about his reelection. And claiming he'd stepped in as sheriff to keep his citizens safe was going to make a great headline. He hadn't anticipated having to climb through the ice and snow to look at a bunch of stupid bones. And certainly not on his day off.

Reluctantly, he'd wrangled into layers of thick clothing and pulled on a pair of heavy boots. Then, driving to the location, he'd slipped and cursed his way down the steep incline to where a group of gawkers were gathered around the bones.

He'd been on the point of ordering one of his deputies to take charge of removing the skeleton when he'd caught a glimpse of gold on the faded leather jacket.

It was a badge. One he recognized.

His chest tightened and his mouth went dry, and just for a horrifying second, he feared he was having a heart attack. This couldn't be happening. Not after all these years.

Forcing himself to step forward, Tate ordered everyone to leave, including his own deputies. Unfortunately, the police photographer continued taking pictures of the scene, while the EMTs fussed and argued over the best means of removing the bones without disturbing evidence. Tate was ready to scream in frustration before he was finally alone.

Now he searched for a purse or briefcase or a computer memory stick that might have survived. Anything that might reveal why the woman had been in Pike.

Rolling aside a large rock, Tate was abruptly interrupted by the sound of boots crunching through the thin layer of ice. Muttering a curse, he spun around to confront the young woman who was closer than he expected. Dammit. Had she seen him scrambling through the brush?

"No one is allowed down here," he barked out. "How many damned times do I have to say it?"

Lia Porter acted as if she hadn't heard him, continuing

forward until she was standing just a few inches from where the body was found.

"I have some information."

Tate frowned. Lia was thirty. Give or take a year. He had a vague memory of handing her a diploma when she'd graduated. Too young to have any actual information. At least none that could affect him.

"I don't care if you have the Holy Grail," he retorted, his tone harsh. "Not now."

"It's about the skeleton you found."

A small niggle of concern wormed its way through Tate's heart. Maybe he should find out what she knew.

"Make it quick."

Lia licked her lips. "I think I saw her the night she died."

Tate hissed in shock. "What?"

Lia glanced up the steep hill, her gaze locked on the nearby bridge.

"Fifteen years ago I was walking home from a party in the middle of the night and I saw a woman up there."

Tate forced himself to take a deep breath. No need to panic. "You risked contaminating my crime scene to tell me that you stumbled home drunk in the middle of the night fifteen years ago and thought you'd seen something in the pitch dark?"

Her green eyes flashed with outrage. "I wasn't drunk, and there was enough moonlight to know it was a woman."

"Did you talk to her?"

"No. When she caught sight of me, she turned and jumped off the railing."

Tate's momentary urge to throw up vanished at her clipped words. She knew nothing.

"Sounds like a figment of your imagination."

"I know what I saw."

Tate clicked his tongue, not having to fake his surge of

impatience. "Even if it wasn't a drunken illusion, we don't know if this woman jumped off the bridge or off a passing train or if she was wandering along the tracks and tripped over and broke her neck. We don't even know how long she's been here. She could have died a hundred years ago. So, if you don't mind . . ."

"I recognize the badge."

The nausea returned. "What?"

"The woman I saw jump from the bridge was wearing a leather jacket with a gold badge pinned on the front." She pointed to a place over her left breast. "Right there."

Tate's brows snapped together. "How do you know about the jacket?"

"Wayne Neilson showed me a photo of the skeleton."

"Shit." Tate knew those stupid kids were going to be trouble as soon as he caught sight of the skeleton. "I told those boys to erase any pictures they took."

Lia shrugged. "By now they're being shared around social media."

She was right, of course. And worse was the knowledge that once the pictures started circulating, the local interest story would quickly become a shit show.

"Damned Internet," he muttered.

"Do you want to hear what I saw that night?" the woman stubbornly demanded.

"Not now, Lia," he snapped. "If you want to make some sort of formal report, you can come to the office on Monday. Right now, I'm too busy."

"This is ridiculous."

She threw her hands up in the air, but thank God she turned to climb up the steep incline. He couldn't deal with Lia Porter. Not now.

After waiting until she was out of sight, Tate pulled his cell phone out of the pocket of his coat. He'd sent a quick text the moment he recognized who had been found. Now he needed to share that this was going to be more than a passing inconvenience.

He pressed a familiar number and grimaced when his call was answered with a sharp demand to know where he was.

"I'm still at the scene," he said. "The EMTs just took away the body." He listened a second. "Of course I'm sure. There wasn't any identification, but she had the badge on her jacket. It has to be her." Another pause. "No. I couldn't destroy it. Those dumbass kids had already taken pictures. You don't think people would ask questions if it magically disappeared?" He blew out a heavy breath, the puff of icy vapor reminding him that he was freezing his ass off. "And it gets worse. Lia Porter came charging down here claiming she'd seen the woman the night she died." He flinched as a sharp reprimand drilled into his ear, as if he was somehow responsible for Lia being in the wrong place at the wrong time. "I don't know. She was babbling about a woman jumping off the bridge and recognizing the jacket. She'd seen a picture one of those inbred brats took. I told her I'd talk to her later." He made a sound of impatience as the reprimand continued. "How was I supposed to distract her? I'm cold, I'm tired, and I'm done playing sheriff for the day. I'll deal with Lia after I've made sure there's nothing out here that can point back to us." He held the phone in front of his face, his tone sarcastic. "Oh, and you're welcome. Once again I'm stuck trying to clean up your messes."

Chapter 2

The sprawling collection of buildings outside the city limits of Vegas looked more like a compound for a large cult than a business. Set in the middle of an acre of barren desert ground, the long, sprawling buildings were constructed out of thick adobe, with solar panels on the roof and basins in the back to recycle the rare rainfall. The large windows were tinted and double-paned to keep out the scorching heat and the floors were recycled bamboo.

The obvious attempt to be environmentally sensitive wasn't usually associated with a pawn shop. Or even a motor garage. But there wasn't anything usual about Money Makers. Or the owner.

Kaden Vaughn had left Madison, Wisconsin, when he was eighteen. He'd traveled to Hollywood with no plans in mind beyond enjoying the warm weather and beautiful women. Within a few weeks he'd managed to land a gig as a stunt driver for an ongoing series. It wasn't supposed to be a career, but somehow he'd found himself taking offers from big budget movies. Eventually he'd been asked to do his own reality show, *Do or Die*, performing daring stunts that not only provided him the adrenaline rush he constantly craved but an obscene bank account.

Five years ago, however, he'd left Hollywood to build his own business. A combination of a pawnshop in one of the long buildings that was managed by his best friend, Dom Lucier. And a separate structure for his shop, where he created custom-built motorcycles for those who could afford his services, as well as a space that housed his collection of rare and antique motorcycles. To save time and the bother of driving back and forth to work, Kaden had an open loft built above the shop, where he lived.

He didn't have any interest in fancy houses or a splashy display of his wealth. A comfortable bed, a large kitchen where he could cook his meals, and a gorgeous view of the nearby Vegas skyline was all he needed.

Currently he was rummaging through his built-in closet, grabbing jeans and the few heavy sweaters he had folded on the top shelf. He turned to toss them into the open suitcase he'd placed on his king-size bed. For the first time in nearly five years, he wasn't packing for a quick trip to Hollywood. He was headed to Wisconsin.

The place he'd fled only minutes after receiving his high school diploma.

"Yo, Kaden!"

The sound of a male voice echoing from the shop below had Kaden spinning away from the closet and heading toward the distant railing. His heavy boots squeaked against the polished wood floor. Most of the customers assumed he wore them, along with his faded jeans and khaki Henley, to look the part of a motorhead. As if his long dark hair, piercing silver eyes, and multiple tattoos scattered over his lean, tightly muscled body wasn't enough. The truth was, he wore the clothes because they protected him when he was welding or working with searing-hot motors.

Reaching the edge of the loft, he gripped the steel railing

and glanced over the edge to discover his partner, Dom, standing in the center of the shop.

"I'm up here."

Dom nodded, moving toward the steel staircase at the end of the building. He was an inch taller than Kaden and several inches broader, with short blond hair and black eyes. The two had met in Hollywood shortly after Kaden arrived in town. He'd discovered it was going to cost him triple what he'd expected to rent an apartment and he'd gone to the nearest pawnshop to trade in his motorcycle for the cash he needed.

Thank God, Dom had been working there. He'd convinced Kaden to keep his bike and given him the telephone number of an acquaintance who was looking for a driver willing to do the sort of stunts most people would consider insane. The two had been best friends since that day.

Dom reached the upper loft and crossed to stand in front of Kaden. "I got your message saying you were headed to Wisconsin. I had to make sure it wasn't a mistake."

"Is there a problem with me taking off a few days?"

"Christ, no. But you haven't wanted a break in the five years since we opened Money Makers." Dom folded his arms over his chest. Like Kaden, he was wearing casual jeans, although Dom had chosen a flannel shirt. Neither felt the need to pretend to be something they weren't. The business was flourishing. In fact, most of the time they were busier than they ever wanted to be. "So, what is it?" Dom asked. "A disaster? A woman? A midlife crisis?"

Kaden arched a brow. He'd just turned thirty-five. "Midlife?"

"Hey, you ain't getting any younger."

Kaden casually flipped him off, not bothering to point out they were the same age. Instead, he turned to head back to his waiting suitcase.

"None of the above."

"There's no way in hell you're taking time off for a vacation." Dom followed behind him. "Not to Wisconsin."

"No."

"Talk to me, Kaden."

He grimaced. Dom could be as stubborn as a mule. No, more stubborn, he silently acknowledged. Once the man had stood in front of a bulldozer for over forty-eight hours to keep a local basketball court from being ripped out and replaced with a high-rent apartment building.

He wasn't going to get off Kaden's back until he revealed why he was headed to Wisconsin. A place no one in their right mind would choose to visit in the middle of winter.

Leaning forward, Kaden grabbed his phone from the mattress, pulling up the online image that was sent to him by his cousin who lived in Green Bay.

"Here."

Taking the phone, Dom read the lurid headline beneath the picture. Skeleton Found Near Railroad Tracks. Is the Tiny Town of Pike, Wisconsin, Cursed? He handed the phone back to Kaden. "Creepy," he said, studying Kaden with a narrowed gaze. "And confusing. Are you thinking about starting a new reality show?"

"Absolutely not."

Kaden had walked away from his show five years ago, and while he occasionally agreed to film a special when he had a famous client wanting a specialized motorcycle, he had no interest in being back in the limelight.

"Then what's your interest?" Dom asked.

"You remember I told you about my older brother?"

Dom took a second to search his memories. "Darren, right?"

"Yep. He was seven years older than me."

"You always said he was the smart one in the family."

"Without question," Kaden agreed. "He was a lawyer with the EPA."

Dom nodded slowly. "You were driving back from Darren's funeral when you called and asked if I wanted to go into business with you."

"I needed a new challenge." Kaden struggled to keep his tone light. He'd told his friend about his brother's death and the desire to move to Vegas and start a new business, but he'd never talked about the soul-deep pain that was driving him.

"Was the challenge building our empire or working with me?" Dom teased.

"Both."

"Fair enough." Dom pointed toward the phone. "You think the picture in the article has something to do with your brother?"

Kaden used his fingers to enlarge the image before turning it toward his friend. "Look."

Dom leaned forward, studying the fuzzy image. "It's some sort of badge." He read the words engraved on the badge. "Office of Inspector General Special Agent."

Kaden pointed to the top of the badge "Environmental Protection Agency," he added.

Dom straightened, his dark eyes widening. "Wait. I remember. You told me there was a woman who went missing."

"Vanna Zimmerman." He had to push the name past his stiff lips. He'd spent endless years blaming her for everything bad that had happened to Darren. "My brother's fiancée."

"You think the skeleton might be her?"

"I do." Kaden tossed the phone back on the bed and moved to the low, sleek dresser to pull open the top drawer.

"Why? There's no name mentioned," Dom pointed out, as if logic had any place in the conversation. "They don't even say if it's a male or a female."

Kaden grabbed a handful of underwear. His days of going commando had ended when he moved to a place that could get up to 110 degrees. Nothing sexy about chafing.

"The badge."

Dom snorted. "How many people work for the EPA? There must be thousands of badges handed out every year." He nodded toward the phone. "Not to mention the fact you have no way of knowing if the skeleton is even real. People pull pranks on social media all the time. Especially kids."

Kaden moved to toss the underwear into the suitcase. "There aren't that many EPA special agents," he argued. "And the town is just two hours north of Madison. I have to check it out."

"Check what out?"

"My brother spent years and a small fortune trying to discover what happened to Vanna after she disappeared."

"That's rough."

"I had no idea how rough." Kaden shuddered. He'd been in Hollywood when his brother called to say his fiancée had vanished. Kaden had met Vanna a handful of times, but he hadn't been overly impressed. She was pretty enough, but she had a hard-edged ambition that reminded him of the desperate actors who littered the streets of Hollywood. Willing to sell their souls to get what they wanted. That might help explain why he hadn't been more concerned when the woman had gone missing. Or considered how it was affecting Darren. "Not until I went through his stuff after he died. He must have hired a dozen private detectives to search for her."

Dom looked confused. "Did he believe she was still alive?"

"Not after the first few years." The stacks and stacks of paperwork Kaden had found in Darren's study had concentrated on searching for a body, not a living person. "When there was no sign of her, I think he accepted she was dead."

"Then why hire private detectives to search for her?"

"Because he had to know what happened." Kaden's voice was harsh. "Not only for his own sanity but to silence the whispers behind his back."

"Whispers?"

Kaden leaned down, slamming the suitcase shut with a loud bang. "Most people—including the cops—assumed Darren killed her and dumped the body."

"Oh . . ." Dom's mouth opened and closed, as if he was considering the impact of spending ten years being the prime suspect of killing the woman he loved. "Hell."

"Exactly." The air felt heavy with the weight of Kaden's regret. He could tell himself it was his dislike for Vanna that had made him oblivious to the torment her absence was causing his brother, but deep inside he'd known he'd been a selfish SOB, so caught up in building his career he'd ignored the tragedy swirling around Darren. "My brother drank himself into an early grave, driven there by the cloud of suspicion that haunted him."

"Okay." Dom cleared his throat. "Let's say the skeleton was your brother's fiancée. What do you intend to do?"

Kaden reached into the closet to grab his heavy leather jacket. "First, I'm headed to Pike."

"Why?"

Kaden turned away, as if ensuring he hadn't forgotten anything. He didn't want Dom to see his troubled expression. His friend knew him all too well.

"I want to be there when the body's identified," he said.

"And then?"

"Then I'm going to find out what the hell happened to her."

Dom stepped toward him, as if considering whether or not Kaden needed a good shake to clear his brain.

"You can do all of that from here," he finally pointed out. "It's not like you can perform the autopsy, or whatever it is you do to ID a skeleton. And you're certainly not qualified to investigate a suspicious death."

Kaden turned back to meet his friend's worried gaze. He didn't have a good answer, so he offered the truth.

"I ignored my brother's cries for help when he was alive. I'm not going to fail him again."

Dom flinched at the bleak words, his hands clenching at his side. "You still haven't told me what you intend to do."

"Get answers. One way or another."

Kaden grabbed his suitcase and coat before heading toward the staircase. He'd worry about getting a ticket once he got to the airport.

For now, it was enough to feel as if he was one step closer to giving his brother the peace in death he'd never had in life.

Kaden hadn't spent much time in small towns. Madison might not be a bustling metropolis, but it was a city with all the usual amenities and a large university. Driving down Main Street in the center of Pike, Kaden frowned at the empty streets and businesses that were locked tight despite the fact it was after ten in the morning. It wasn't until he pulled into the parking lot next to the courthouse that he realized it was Sunday.

Damn.

He studied the building, which looked like a solid, square

box with large windows. It'd been late when he arrived in Madison last night, and for the first time in five years he was relieved he'd continued to pay rent on Darren's fancy condo. It didn't matter that the place was a tangible reminder that he still hadn't accepted his brother's death. All he wanted was a bed to tumble into so he could fall into an exhausted sleep.

He was still in a tired stupor when he'd roused himself this morning and dragged himself to the shower. Less than half an hour later he was dressed and plugging the directions for Pike into his phone as he climbed into the Jeep he'd rented at the airport the night before. Now the caffeine from the coffee he bought at a gas station during his two-hour drive north was finally kicking in and, squaring his shoulders, Kaden climbed out of the Jeep and headed up the shallow steps to tug on the front door.

Locked. Kaden frowned. The government offices were obviously closed on the weekend, but when he googled the address of the sheriff's office, it showed it was located in the courthouse. That surely had to be open, right?

No matter how sleepy the town might appear, there had to be a law official on duty.

"The place is closed until Monday," a voice called out from behind him.

Kaden turned to see a teenage boy bundled in a heavy parka and a ski cap. The stranger was studying him with a curious expression and Kaden guessed the town didn't have many visitors.

"Where can I find the sheriff?"

"Sheriff's out of town."

Great. Kaden resisted the urge to stamp his feet. The motorcycle boots were great for working in his shop, but they didn't offer much protection against the cold weather. His toes were starting to freeze.

"Is there a deputy around?"

"Maybe." The boy wrinkled his nose, as if considering his answer. "They're probably all at church. If it's an emergency, you should call . . . hey, wait." The boy blinked, his mouth parting in shock. "You're Kaden Vaughn."

Kaden hid his grimace. Although it was five years since he'd had a regular series, *Do or Die* remained popular in reruns and on the Internet. Enough to gain the attention of a younger audience. It meant he ran into fans almost everywhere he went. Not his favorite part of the job. Especially when he preferred to remain anonymous. Then again, his fame might help him get the information he needed now.

"I am," he admitted, strolling down the steps. "And you are?"

"Wayne. Wayne Nielson." There was a flush on the thin face that had nothing to do with the brisk morning breeze. "What are you doing in Pike?"

"Actually, you might be able to help me."

"Cool."

Kaden grabbed his phone from the pocket of his leather jacket, pulling up the picture of the skeleton. He turned it to show the image to the boy.

"I'm looking for whoever uploaded this picture."

The pale eyes widened in shock. "No. Way."

Lowering the phone, Kaden belatedly wondered if he'd rattled the kid by showing him the gruesome image. He looked to be sixteen or seventeen years old, but the small community might keep people around here a lot more protected from the evils of the world.

Kaden shifted uncomfortably from foot to foot. "Sorry."

"I mean," Wayne nodded toward the phone, "that was me."

"Excuse me?"

"I'm Waino2006," the boy clarified. "I'm the one who

uploaded the picture." He released a nervous laugh. "This is crazy. I can't believe you saw my post."

Kaden's mind was reeling. It seemed like fate was stepping in to lend him a helping hand. How else could he explain nearly stumbling over the very person who'd brought him to Pike?

"Do you mind if I ask you some questions?"

"Seriously?" The boy beamed with excitement; then, without warning, the sparkle in his eyes faded. "Oh."

"Is something wrong?"

"I'm late for work." He hunched his shoulders beneath his heavy parka. "It wouldn't matter, but I was late yesterday, after I found the body."

"You were the one who found the skeleton?"

"Practically." Wayne kept his answer vague. "Anyway, Ms. Porter is really nice and I don't want to disappoint her."

Kaden hesitated. Did he continue his conversation with the boy or look for a law official? It was the distant sound of church bells ringing that made up his mind. He had no idea where one of the deputies might be located, and he had no intention of dialing 911.

"Where do you work?" he asked.

"Porter's Grocery Store." The boy pointed toward the south. "Just a few blocks from here. I won't be long. On Sundays I just go in to sweep and mop the floors. If you want to wait around, I can—"

"Do you mind if I walk with you?"

"'Course not." The boy offered an eager smile, nearly bouncing as he walked down the icy sidewalk. Kaden, on the other hand, took far more care. The last thing he needed was to fall and break a hip. Dom would never let him hear the end of it. "Man, I can't believe you're here." Wayne abruptly dug into the pocket of his jeans, pulling out a phone. He waved it toward Kaden. "Do you mind? I need proof."

Kaden swallowed a curse, pinning a smile to his lips as they halted long enough for the boy to stand close beside him and lift the phone to take a quick selfie. Seconds later, they were continuing their journey down the frozen street.

"Thanks." Wayne shoved the phone back into his pocket.

"Tell me about the picture you posted."

Without warning, the boy shot him a worried glance. "I'm not in trouble, am I?"

"No trouble." Kaden held up his hand. "I promise."

"Okay." Wayne blew out a relieved sigh, a plume of vapor circling his youthful face. "I was headed to work yesterday morning when a couple of friends—" He grimaced, as if the word threatened to stick in his throat before he continued his story. "Before they climbed up from the old railroad tracks and said they'd found a body. Honestly, I didn't believe them. They're jerks most of the time. But when I crawled down there, I could see the bones. They were just there. Frozen in the ice, like something out of a horror movie. That's when I took the pictures."

"It's odd that no one had ever noticed them before."

"Not really," Wayne protested. "None of us ever went around the tracks. There was no reason to. There was nothing down there but thornbushes and a bunch of broken bottles kids used to throw off the bridge. It wasn't until they shut down the tracks to replace them that the guys decided they could use the steep hills for some sledding fun."

Kaden offered a grudging nod. He supposed the explanation made sense. Unfortunately, it did nothing to help establish when the person had died, or how they'd gotten to such a strange location.

Had it been a tragic accident? Or something more sinister?

"Did you see anything else?"

"Like what?"

Kaden cautiously avoided a slick patch in the middle of the sidewalk, not entirely sure how to frame his question. He wanted to know why Vanna might have been in Pike.

"Anything the person might have had with them. A purse or a briefcase?"

"Oh." Wayne scrunched up his face, as if he was struggling to recall anything that might impress Kaden. "Nope," he finally conceded. "I didn't really notice anything but the skeleton. I was pretty freaked out."

"I don't blame you." Kaden offered a sympathetic smile. "What about your friends? Did they happen to notice anything?"

Wayne snorted. "They were even more freaked out than I was. Especially Drew. He puked his guts out. 'Course, he still went back down to show me the skeleton. He even moved aside some of the branches so I could get a clearer view. Cord wouldn't. He flat out refused to go."

"Drew?" Kaden kept his tone casual, even as he tucked away the fact that the boy had not only found the skeleton, he'd also touched it. He seemed like someone Kaden needed to meet.

"Drew Hurst," Wayne said.

"He lives around here?"

"Yep. He's a senior along with me at Pike High School."

"I might have a word with him."

Wayne looked disappointed. Was he hoping he'd be the only one in town to talk to Kaden? Then he suddenly perked up.

"I can set up a meeting if you want. You know . . . introduce you. Oh, and you might want to talk with Cord Walsh. He was there too, you know. He might have noticed something."

Kaden smiled. "That would be great."

Wayne came to an abrupt halt in front of a red-brick building with a glass door set between two large windows. Just above his head was a heavy sign with the name PORTER etched into the wood.

"This is the place." Wayne shoved open the door, releasing a welcome blast of warmth. "We can talk more inside."

"Great." Kaden eagerly followed the young man into the narrow space that was lined with shelves. It felt dark and cramped, but there was a warm smell of cookies that drifted through the air and a gleam on the planked wooden floor that revealed it had recently been mopped and polished.

Wayne took off his parka and tossed it on a nearby counter. "You know, you haven't said why you're interested in the skeleton."

Chapter 3

Lia was busy scrubbing the coolers when she heard voices outside. Assuming Wayne was chatting with one of his friends before coming in to work, she headed toward the front of the store. Sundays were usually slow and it was the best time to stock the shelves and get the cleaning done. Wayne was a good worker, but he needed supervision. If she didn't give him specific directions, he'd spend the next three hours staring at his phone.

When the teenager stepped into the store, however, it wasn't a friend with him. It was a mysterious stranger.

The sort of mysterious stranger who belonged on a movie screen, not in an aging family store in the middle of Wisconsin.

Lia sucked in a sharp breath, her gaze roaming over the dark hair that fell to the man's broad shoulders. Usually she disliked long hair on men, but his was thick and glossy, framing his starkly chiseled features in a way that only emphasized his male beauty. He had high cheekbones and a proud nose that might have been broken in the past. It was his eyes, however, that made her feel as if the air was being squeezed from her lungs.

They were pure silver. The precise shade of mercury. And probably just as lethal. The thought was still whispering through the back of her mind when she heard Wayne ask the stranger about his interest in the skeleton. Her odd fascination was shattered and with a muttered curse, she hurried toward the counter.

She didn't know who the man was or why he was interested in the skeleton, but she wasn't going to allow him to abuse Wayne's innocent trust in people.

"What's going on?" she demanded, coming to a halt directly in front of the man.

It was at that point she noticed the stranger was a good six or seven inches taller than her, with hard-packed muscles that were visible beneath his soft leather jacket. That was also when she noticed the tattoos that crawled up the side of his neck. A shiver raced through Lia. She told herself it was only natural to be afraid. This stranger could easily break her in half. But deep inside, she knew it wasn't fear that was prickling down her spine. It was . . .

Nope. She wasn't going to finish the thought. Instead, she turned to study her employee with raised brows.

"Wayne?"

"Hey, Ms. Porter." A wide grin split the teenager's face. He nodded toward the stranger. "Look who's in town. Can you believe it?"

Lia hesitated. Was she supposed to recognize the man? "Is he a relative?"

"I wish." Wayne sent her a chiding glance, clearly disappointed in her less-than-insightful guess. "This is Kaden Vaughn. The best motorcycle stuntman of all time."

Stuntman. That fit the stranger. He looked like the daredevil type. "Oh."

Wayne rolled his eyes. "Don't you remember his TV show? *Do or Die*?

Lia avoided the question by turning to stretch out her hand. "I'm Lia Porter."

The man's lips twitched, the silver eyes silently telling her that he was well aware she didn't have the faintest clue who he or his seemingly famous TV show were.

"Kaden." He firmly gripped her hand.

A jolt of electric pleasure zapped through Lia. His fingers were chilled from the frigid winter air, but that didn't keep them from scorching her skin. Crap. Lia yanked her hand away and took an instinctive step back, battling against Kaden's magnetic charisma.

"Kaden saw my picture of the skeleton," Wayne intruded into her deranged musings. "I told you it was gonna go viral."

Lia narrowed her eyes. "What does the picture of a skeleton have to do with a motorcycle stuntman?"

"That's what I just asked," Wayne admitted, visibly bubbling with joy at meeting a real-life celebrity.

The boy would clearly say or do anything to impress this man.

Lia stepped between Wayne and Kaden, facing the teenager. "I drove over to Grange yesterday to restock our canned goods." It was a routine she'd started years ago. Delivery to the small town cost a fortune. It saved money for her to drive to the food wholesale warehouse and pick up the merchandise. Not the most exciting way to spend a Saturday afternoon, but it wasn't like she had anything better to do. "Would you mind getting them out of my vehicle and putting them in the storage room?"

Wayne scrunched his face into a disappointed expression. "Now?"

"Yes, please. Then you can start sweeping."

"Okay." Heaving a deep, dramatic sigh, Wayne glanced toward Kaden. "I'll be around if you have any more questions."

"Good to know," the man assured him.

Dragging his feet, Wayne plodded his way between the

aisles and out of the main section of the store. Still, Lia waited until she heard the back door slam before she turned to send her companion a suspicious frown.

"Wayne is only seventeen." She didn't bother to mention the boy would be turning eighteen next month. "And very naïve."

Kaden blinked, as if blindsided by her fierce defense of the teenager. "I don't mean him any harm." He held up his slender hand. "I swear."

"So why are you here?"

He hesitated. Was he reluctant to disclose his reason because he didn't trust her? Or because he knew she wouldn't approve?

"I think I might know the identity of the skeleton," he finally revealed.

It was Lia's turn to be caught off guard. She stared at him in disbelief, belatedly realizing she'd been distracted by the revelation that he worked in television. Was it any wonder she'd assumed he intended to sensationalize the skeleton in some sick way?

Now she struggled to accept that he might have an actual connection to the victim.

"Are you joking?"

He arched a dark brow. "I've been told I have an odd sense of humor, but not that odd."

Lia grimaced. It'd been a stupid question. She glanced around the empty store. She'd gone from wanting to get rid of the stranger before he could lure Wayne into doing something stupid to wanting to discover exactly what he knew about the skeleton.

"Follow me." Without waiting to see if he would obey her sharp command, Lia marched down the center aisle and into the narrow hall. Then, entering her office, she turned to watch Kaden cautiously step in behind her. He looked mildly surprised as he glanced around, no doubt comparing the sleek, modern furniture and expensive computer system with the cozy shabbiness in the front of the building. She waved a hand toward one of the steel-and-leather chairs set in the corner. "Have a seat."

He paused, then with a faint shrug, he moved to settle on the chair that was designed for comfort as well as function. She occasionally held business meetings in the office and she wanted to make sure that no one was in a hurry to leave.

"It's my turn to ask what's going on," he said, eyeing her with a curious expression.

Lia perched on the edge of her desk. "First, I need to be certain you aren't here to exploit that poor woman," she said, still not convinced she could trust this man.

"Exploit her? What are you talking about?"

"Wayne mentioned you have some sort of television show."

His jaw tightened, as if he was offended by the suggestion he was there to take advantage of the situation.

"No longer. Nowadays I'm just a mechanic in Vegas. My presence in Pike is strictly personal."

She studied his starkly beautiful face. She didn't think he was lying to her, but she wasn't sure he was telling her the whole truth. At last, she shrugged. Right now all that mattered was discovering the identity of the woman she'd seen all those years ago.

"You said you think you might know who the skeleton is." She grimaced. "Or who she was."

He tapped one slender finger on the arm of the chair, the silver gaze moving around the office before returning to study her with unnerving intensity.

"Do you work with the police department?"

"No."

"Then what's your interest?"

"The same as yours."

He made a sound of annoyance at her vague response. "I feel like we're talking in circles. Frankly, I'm getting dizzy."

Lia sighed. He was right. Neither of them wanted to be the first to reveal what they knew. Like poker players trying to disguise what cards they held.

"I saw the woman the night she died," she abruptly confessed.

She heard Kaden suck in a startled breath. "Where?"

"She was on the old bridge that spans the railroad tracks just outside of town."

Kaden leaned forward, his brow furrowed in puzzlement. "The place she was found?"

"Yes," she agreed, although it wasn't the exact spot.

"Describe her."

A sick sensation clenched Lia's stomach, but she forced herself to answer. "It was after midnight and I couldn't see her clearly, but I don't think she was old. Probably in her twenties or thirties. Her hair was long and dark, although I'm not sure if it was brown or black. She was wearing a heavy leather jacket and pants that looked like it was a uniform. And she had a large gold badge." Lia pointed toward a spot just below her shoulder blade. "It was pinned here on her jacket. At first I thought she was a cop."

"Vanna," he breathed.

The sickness at dredging up the disturbing memory was forgotten as she clutched the edge of the desk in a tight grip. She'd waited fifteen years to put a name with the woman who'd haunted her dreams.

"You knew her?"

He nodded sharply, his tension humming through the air. Absently, she wondered if being near Kaden Vaughn always felt like standing in the middle of a thunderstorm.

"Vanna Zimmerman," he explained. "She was engaged to my older brother. When did you see her?"

"Fifteen years ago." Lia's breath caught in her throat as she realized what day it was. "Almost exactly."

His jaw tightened. "Vanna disappeared December 14, 2007."

"The same night I saw her."

"And the same date her body was found fifteen years later."

They shared a glance, both wondering if it was a coincidence or fate. At last, Lia shook her head, breaking the strange connection she felt with this stranger.

"She disappeared from where?" she asked.

"Madison. She worked as an inspector for the EPA."

That explained the badge, Lia silently acknowledged. But nothing else. "Why would she be running away from Pike in the middle of the night?"

He looked equally baffled. "She was running?"

"That's what it looked like." Lia dredged through the memories of walking along the dark lane on that fateful night. "She appeared out of the darkness, and when she saw me on the pathway, she suddenly stopped." Lia could recall the precise expression on the woman's face. Terror. "I don't know if I startled her or if she thought I was someone else, but she climbed onto the railing of the bridge and jumped."

"That's . . ." Kaden shook his head. "Crazy."

"That's exactly what I thought."

His brows drew together, as if he was trying to figure out a reasonable explanation for his brother's fiancée to be running through the dark and jumping off railroad bridges. At last, he appeared to concede defeat.

"Did she injure herself when she landed?" he instead asked.

Lia lifted her hands in a bewildered gesture. "I really

don't know. I called out for her and even went down the slope to search in case she needed help. It was dark, but there was enough moonlight to know she wasn't lying on the tracks. At least not anywhere I could see her. As far as I could tell, she'd simply vanished."

Thankfully, he didn't press her for whether or not she'd searched through the heavy brush that crawled along the edge of the tracks. She didn't want to admit she'd been too scared to do more than make sure there wasn't a body beneath the bridge before racing back up the slope and scurrying home.

"Was there anyone else around?"

She shook her head, knowing what he was asking. If Vanna was running, it was quite possibly because she was being chased.

"Not that I could see. I walked the rest of the way into town without encountering anyone." Lia grimaced. "That doesn't mean they weren't there. They could easily have been hidden in the shadows."

With a restless surge, Kaden pushed himself out of his chair to pace her small office.

"What was she running from?"

"And why was she in Pike?" Lia added.

Both questions had to be answered if they were going to figure out what happened to Vanna Zimmerman.

Kaden continued to walk in a circle, his expression distracted. Lia remained perched on the desk. There was only room for one pacer at a time in the cramped space. Plus, she didn't want to risk brushing up against his hard muscles. The touch of his hand had been enough to send tingles through her. She was afraid if she had full-body contact, she might self-combust.

Thankfully unaware of her absurd thoughts, Kaden came to an abrupt halt, turning to face her.

"I wonder if it's possible she was here in her official capacity."

"As an EPA agent?"

"Yes."

Lia had never encountered an EPA official in town, but she assumed they made yearly inspections in every community. The city water supply, landfills, maybe even the local dairy farms. It seemed doubtful, however, they would do their inspections in the middle of the night.

"Can you ask your brother if there was a reason she might have been in Pike?"

His jaw tightened. "Darren died five years ago."

The words were carefully devoid of emotion, which only made them more painful. This man was still mourning the loss of his brother.

"I'm sorry."

"He never stopped searching for Vanna." Kaden clenched his hands into tight fists. "He was certain her disappearance wasn't an accident."

Lia felt an odd urge to reach out and offer him comfort. She sensed this man didn't easily share his emotions. Even his grief. With an effort, she resisted temptation.

"He thought someone deliberately hurt her?"

"Yes."

"Who?"

"He didn't say. At least not to me." Kaden shrugged, but Lia didn't miss the pain that darkened his eyes. As if the memory of his brother was still an open wound. "But if she was running down the road in the middle of the night, it seems possible he was right."

Lia wrinkled her nose. "I don't remember hearing any rumors of anyone in trouble with the EPA."

"It was a long time ago. You couldn't have been more

than . . ." He tilted his head to the side, studying her with open curiosity.

"Fifteen."

"Fifteen. What were you doing out in the middle of the night?"

She snorted at the hint of reprimand in his voice. "You never snuck out when you were a teenager?"

"Constantly. But I was a rebel. I doubt you were."

She stiffened, offended by his words. Even strangers assumed she was a follow-the-rules, always-dependable bore.

"Why do you doubt I was a rebel?"

"Because you look like an angel."

Oh. Her heart fluttered. Really and truly fluttered. Like a butterfly trapped in a net. Good grief. She cleared her throat, battling back the urge to blush.

"Did you come here to ID the body?"

His lips twitched, but he allowed her to return the conversation to the reason he was in Pike.

"No. I assume Vanna's foster parents will have dental records or whatever they need to prove the skeleton is hers. They'll be the ones to do the ID."

Lia tucked away the knowledge that Vanna had come from a foster home. It didn't seem relevant, but who knew? Right now all they had was questions.

"Then what are you doing here?"

"To find out what happened," he said without hesitation. "For my brother."

Lia nodded. She understood. Not knowing was like an aching tooth that gnawed at her year after year. They both obviously needed closure.

"Have you spoken with the sheriff?"

He rolled his eyes. "Apparently there are no officials on duty during church hours."

Lia grimaced. "Our real sheriff is out of town. And our best deputy, Lindsay, just took a job in Green Bay. We're down to Anthony and a couple new deputies who work part-time."

"When will the real sheriff be back?"

"I don't know. Not until after the holidays."

Lia swallowed a sigh. No one begrudged Zac his time off after what he'd gone through the past few months; then again, it was a pain in the ass when they needed a lawman with an actual brain.

"So who's in charge?" Kaden demanded.

"For now it's the mayor, Tate Erickson. Unfortunately."

"Why do you say 'unfortunately'?"

"He's barely capable of being mayor." She ground her teeth, still angered by Tate's rude dismissal of her eyewitness account. It was as he if wanted to pretend the skeleton was tossed off the train with no connection to Pike. And maybe he did. God knew the town didn't need any more bad press. "There's no way he can be a decent sheriff."

Kaden shook his head in disbelief. "I feel like I wandered into *The Twilight Zone*."

"More like *The Dukes of Hazzard*. Complete with Boss Hogg."

Drew Hurst shivered, cursing as the icy wind cut straight through his letterman jacket. It was his bright idea to meet at the graveyard. It was not only on the edge of town, but the tall cedar trees that framed the cemetery made sure no one could see him from the road. The perfect spot when he wanted some privacy.

Unfortunately, it was also cold enough to turn his balls blue.

At long last he heard the gruff rumble of a pickup that

echoed loudly enough to wake the dead. That had to be his best friend, Cord Walsh. He'd inherited the piece-of-shit truck from his grandfather his freshman year and hadn't bothered to replace the muffler. Or the tires. Or the sketchy brakes. The thing was a rolling death trap. The engine cut off and a few minutes later, Cord pushed his way through the trees.

Like Drew, his friend was almost as broad as he was tall. And he was wearing a matching letter jacket that barely fit over his broad shoulders. They were raised in farming country where they spent the summers tossing around hay bales and hammering fence posts. Their size and strength made them perfect linemen for the high school football team.

"Dude, where have you been?" Drew stomped his feet against the frozen ground, trying to get some feeling back in his toes. "I said to meet at eleven."

Cord hunched his shoulders, spitting a stream of tobacco juice through his front teeth. "I had to wait for my mom to head out for church."

"Why?"

"She's decided you're a bad influence on me. I'm forbidden to see you."

"Forbidden, eh?" Drew chuffed out a breath, pretending he found the idea funny as hell.

Mothers had been forbidding him to be around their precious kids since he was in preschool. What the hell did he care?

"That's what she said."

"Bitch."

Cord frowned. "Hey, that's my mom."

"Whatever."

Perhaps sensing Drew wasn't completely indifferent to being considered a pariah, Cord changed the conversation.

"Why did you want to meet?"

"Did you see what Neilson just posted?" Drew shoved his hand into the pocket of his jacket, pulling out his phone.

"What?" Cord moved to stand next to Drew, watching as the image of a smiling Wayne popped up on the screen. Next to him was a tall, stern-faced man who was easily recognizable to any male who owned a television. "Kaden Vaughn in Pike? No friggin' way," Cord breathed in disbelief. "This must be some sort of trick."

"The twat isn't smart enough to Photoshop."

"I don't know." Cord reached up to wipe the snot running from his nose before it froze. "He always gets good grades."

Drew shook the phone in front of his friend's face. "This is real."

"Why would Vaughn be in Pike? There's nothing here but snow and cows."

"Have you forgotten the skeleton?"

"What about it?"

Drew rolled his eyes. Cord wasn't the sharpest tool in the shed. Most of the time he used his head for running into things, not actual thinking.

"Vaughn does reality shows, dumbass."

Cord ignored the insult. "Yeah. He does stunts and rebuilds awesome bikes. He doesn't do old bones."

"Maybe he's trying a new gig." Drew shrugged. As far as he was concerned, the only reason a cool dude like Kaden Vaughn would be in Pike was because he thought he could make money off the skeleton. There wasn't any other reason for a stranger to come to this frozen hellhole. "He's getting kind of old to be racing around on motorcycles."

Cord's eyes brightened. The guy was no doubt going to be stuck on his family farm, milking cows for the rest of his life, but he loved anything with an engine. Race cars, motorcycles, four-wheelers. Even tractors.

"I don't care why he's here. I just want to meet him. How long do you think he'll be around?"

"That's what I want you to find out. If he is in town to do a show on the skeleton, I have a couple of items he's going to be interested in."

"Items?" Cord blinked at the unexpected revelation. "What items?"

Drew smiled. After he nearly landed on top of the skeleton, he'd panicked. He'd scrambled up the hill, screaming like a girl, and then promptly upchucked in front of that jerk, Wayne Neilson. It was almost as humiliating as the time he'd pissed his pants in kindergarten. That was the only reason he'd agreed to take Wayne down to see the bones. And why he forced himself to reach out and touch the thing. He wanted to prove he wasn't a pussy. He hadn't expected to discover a potential treasure while his companion was busy digging out his phone and taking pictures.

"A little something I found on the body," he murmured in mysterious tones.

Cord spit another string of tobacco. "Liar."

"It's true." Drew held up his hand. "Swear to God."

"Show me."

"No way. You'd blab about it all over town and it ain't going to be worth shit."

"Blab what?"

Drew shook his head, impatient to get going. The day wasn't getting any warmer and he was going to have to walk. The sooner he could get to his destination, the better.

"Just find out where Vaughn is and how long he's going to be in town."

Cord jutted out his lower lip. He looked more like a baby than a guy who'd just celebrated his eighteenth birthday.

"Why don't you do it?"

"First I'm going to see if I can make some money. I'd rather be rich than famous."

Chapter 4

Kaden dismissed any hope of locating the sheriff on a Sunday. He would have to return later to speak to the man. And there was no use trying to track down anyone in the coroner's office. It would take time to properly ID the body and determine the cause of death. Something he probably should have thought of before jumping on a plane and then driving to Pike like a bat out of hell.

That didn't mean that he was willing to return to Madison and sit on his ass, however. He might not have any detective skills, but that wasn't going to stop him from poking his nose into the investigation.

But where did he start?

He glanced toward the woman watching him with a steady gaze. His heart did a crazy zigzag in his chest. He'd spent the past seventeen years surrounded by the most beautiful women in the world. But there was something about Lia Porter . . .

She was a tantalizing combination of small-town girl with an elusive hint of mystery that challenged him on a primitive level. As if she was daring him to discover the truth beneath her easy smile and bright green eyes.

With a shake of his head, Kaden dismissed his bizarre

fascination. "Can you give me directions to where the skeleton was found?"

She nodded, almost as if she'd been expecting the question. Probably because there was nothing else he could do. Not until the temporary sheriff decided to open his office.

"I can take you."

He arched a brow, caught off guard by the offer. "What about your store?"

"It's always slow on Sundays. I just keep it open in case someone needs something on their way home from church. Wayne can lock up whenever he's done mopping the floor."

Kaden hesitated. Not because he didn't want her company. Just the opposite. He very much wanted to prolong his time with her, but having her around was no doubt going to cause all sorts of distractions. Still, she was a potential eyewitness to Vanna's disappearance.

Who better to show him where and how it happened?

"Actually, that would be great."

"I'll let Wayne know I'm leaving." With brisk movements, she grabbed her purse from the desk and headed out of the office. Kaden followed behind, waiting in the narrow hallway as she disappeared into what he assumed was the storage area. A couple of minutes later she reappeared and moved to the coatrack next to the back door. Choosing one of the heavy parkas, she pulled it on and bundled herself in a heavy knit cap and matching gloves. She was clearly prepared for the weather. Unlike him. "My SUV is parked in the alley."

Opening the door, she revealed the large vehicle with the words Porter's Grocery Store painted on the side.

"I rented a Jeep, but I left it next to the courthouse," he told her, grudgingly climbing into the passenger seat as she slid behind the steering wheel and started the engine. It wasn't often he rode shotgun. Like never.

"I don't mind driving." She put the SUV in gear and bumped her way out of the snow-packed alley. "It's not far."

Kaden settled back in his seat, studying her delicate profile as she turned onto Main Street.

"Why do I get the impression you prefer to be behind the wheel instead of me?"

"You're from Hollywood. How much driving do you do in the snow?"

"I'm in Vegas now," he reminded her.

"Same thing."

That was true enough. Hollywood and Vegas had a lot in common, including a lack of ice-coated roads. In his mind, however, they were worlds apart.

"But I'm originally from Madison. I've had plenty of practice driving in the snow."

She shot him a glance that revealed she wasn't impressed with his argument. "How long since you've lived there?"

He took a second to do the mental calculations. "Seventeen years."

"That's a long time."

"Maybe, but I'm a professional driver."

"*Stunt* driver."

"Is it the stunt part that bothers you?"

"No comment."

Kaden chuckled. He wasn't sure why he was teasing her about her opinion of his skills behind the wheel. Probably to keep himself from dwelling on the fear that he was wasting his time in Pike. When he'd arrived in town, he'd been certain he was about to put the past behind him. Now he realized there was a chance he would never have the answers he needed.

Lia maintained a slow, steady pace as they drove through the heart of town. He caught sight of Bella's Restaurant, which apparently sold Italian food, and on the other side of the street was a bar called the Bait and Tackle. It was squeezed between a dentist's office and a laundromat. Small-town America.

"Have you always lived in Pike?"

Her fingers tightened on the steering wheel. Was she bothered by his question?

"Always."

"I suppose you have a husband and children?"

She sent him an annoyed frown. "Why would you suppose that?"

He hid his smile. That had been his less-than-subtle attempt to discover if she was single.

"It's what most people do." He waved a hand toward the couple who were scurrying into the laundromat with a child in a stroller. "Grow up. Get married. Produce kids."

"Not me."

Satisfaction blasted through him. Obviously single. "Me either."

She turned onto a side street, weaving past the small, tidy homes, with their Christmas decorations on full display. Did everyone in town have a cedar tree in the front yard?

They turned onto yet another road. This one barely more than a dirt pathway and layered with snow. She slowed to a mere crawl. A speed he fully approved of as the back wheels fishtailed on a patch of ice.

"What made you run off to Hollywood?" she abruptly asked. "Did you want to be a movie star?"

Kaden had a dozen answers to the familiar question: He'd jumped on his motorcycle and hadn't stopped riding until he hit the ocean. He'd gone to meet the legendary stunt driver, Buzz Bundy. He'd been touring the country and ran out of money when he hit Hollywood . . .

Shockingly, the truth spilled out of his mouth. "I wasn't running *to* anything. I was running *from* something."

He heard her suck in a sharp breath. "Oh."

"Nothing dramatic," he hastily assured her. "My father was a horse's ass and I was too stubborn to keep my mouth shut. Putting several hundred miles between us seemed like the sensible solution."

"Your brother stayed in Madison?"

"He had more brains and a higher tolerance for my dad's drunken outbursts."

"And a fiancée."

Kaden's heart missed a beat. He'd never cared personally for Vanna Zimmerman, but Darren had been head over heels in love.

"And a fiancée."

Silence filled the SUV as Lia inched around a curve and then pressed on the brakes. She shoved the gear into Park, but she left the engine running.

"This is the place."

Kaden studied the empty surroundings with a frown as he climbed out of the vehicle and crunched through the snow to the edge of the bridge. He wasn't sure what he expected. Emergency vehicles with flashing lights? Uniformed deputies lining the path? Barricades and police tape? Instead, there was some trampled snow, a few bits of trash left behind by the gawkers, and an eerie sense of isolation.

Kaden grimaced. He better than anyone knew that what he saw on television wasn't real. This was a small town with limited resources. Besides, it wasn't as if it was a recent death. The bones had been lying there for fifteen years. Discovering what had happened so long ago would be a low priority for any law official.

Squaring his shoulders, Kaden determinedly focused on

the reason he was standing in the middle of the frozen landscape.

"You were walking along this road?" He pointed toward the other side of the bridge, waiting for Lia to nod. Then he glanced over his shoulder in the direction they'd just come. "And Vanna was coming from town?"

"Yes." Lia crossed to stand next to him. "I spotted her as she came around the bend."

He glanced toward the empty fields that were divided by the sharp slope that led down to the railroad tracks. There was nothing for miles in that direction. On the other side, there was a thick layer of trees that made it impossible to see what was there. Even in the daylight, someone could hide in the shadows without attracting attention.

"You're sure she came along the road and not out of the trees?" he asked the woman standing next to him.

The seconds ticked past as she tried to dredge up her memories. Finally, she shrugged. "At the time I assumed she was coming from Pike, but I suppose it's possible she might have been somewhere else."

"Are there any homes close by?"

"Nothing on this road. There's an old hunting lodge that was converted into a rental space for weddings and family reunions. I think it was empty back then." She frowned, glancing around as if mentally mapping out the area. "The Walsh farm is on the other side of the trees, but it would be a hike to get from there to here. Especially on such a cold night."

Kaden glanced at her in confusion. "Why is the name Walsh familiar?"

"Their son, Cord, was one of the boys who found the skeleton."

Kaden abruptly recalled his conversation with young Wayne. He'd tucked away the names in the hopes of talking to them at some point. Now he wondered if the proximity of the Walsh farm to Vanna's body had any connection.

"A coincidence?"

Lia sent him a startled glance. "What else?"

Kaden didn't press the issue. He would check out the Walsh family and the hunting lodge when he returned to Madison. There were plenty of online services you could use to investigate people and businesses.

There was no such thing as privacy.

He turned back to the road in front of him. "You said you saw the woman jump off the bridge?"

With a sharp nod, Lia moved to the very center of the bridge, reaching out to grasp the steel railing.

"Right here."

Kaden joined her, not missing the edge in her voice. He couldn't tell if it was fear or anger. Perhaps a combination of the two.

He gazed over the railing at the long pieces of steel and broken wooden ties that had been dug up to make room for the new tracks. It looked like a bulldozer had gone through and ripped out everything in its path.

"And that's where they found the skeleton?"

"No." Without warning, Lia spun around and moved to the other side of the bridge. She pointed toward a spot that had been cleared of snow and undergrowth to leave a large, bare patch of raw earth. "It was there."

Kaden softly cursed. He understood this wasn't like a fresh murder scene, where everything might be a potential clue. But the damage that had been created around the spot where the body had been found seemed like overkill. Almost as if someone deliberately wanted to destroy the crime scene.

He shook his head. Maybe later he would come back to

look around. But not until he had a thick parka and a pair of insolated boots.

With a shiver, Kaden shoved his hands into the pockets of his leather jacket, trying to imagine how the body had gotten so far from the bridge.

"Obviously, she couldn't have landed in that spot. She must have survived the jump."

"That's what I assumed after I went down that night and didn't find her. Otherwise I would have gone for help." Lia made a choked sound, as if tortured by her memories. "Now, I'm afraid she might have been seriously injured but managed to stumble far enough away I didn't see her. If I had gone to the sheriff that night, I might have been able to save her."

Kaden felt an unexpected urge to wrap her in his arms. As if it was his right to offer her comfort. He took a step back, making sure he didn't do anything stupid.

"Or whoever killed her was waiting in the dark to make sure no one found the body. If this was murder, you're lucky to be alive."

Her lips parted at his blunt words, a visible shiver racing through her body. "Is there anything else here you want to see?"

"Not today."

"Good. Let's get back in the SUV."

They hurried to the vehicle, climbing in and holding their hands toward the vents that were blasting warm air. Kaden sighed in relief. His years on the West Coast had thinned his blood. Or maybe he was just getting old. Whatever the case, he felt as if he was frozen to the bone.

Lia put the engine in gear and did a careful U-turn before heading back to town. They rode in silence until they were once again within the city limits of Pike.

"You can drop me off at the courthouse if you don't mind," he said.

She turned toward the center of town, driving past an old funeral home and then a cemetery before she was back on Main Street.

"Where are you staying?"

Lost in his thoughts, Kaden answered the question without thinking. "At my brother's condo in Madison."

"Oh, I thought you said . . ."

Kaden's heart clenched with a familiar sense of loss as her words trailed away.

"I've been paying the rent since he died."

She pulled into the parking lot next to the courthouse, sending him a sympathetic glance.

"I'm sure it's hard to let go."

Kaden grabbed the handle of the door, clenching it until his knuckles turned white.

"I keep telling myself I don't have the time to box up his things and clear them out of the place, but you're right. I'm not ready to admit to myself that he's gone and never coming back."

Drew patted the wad of cash in the pocket of his letterman jacket, allowing a sneer to twist his lips. Honestly, he hadn't really expected to get a dime. He thought they'd look at the stuff in the rotting leather pouch and tell him they didn't give a damn if he told people what he'd found. Or even threaten to call the sheriff for tampering with a body or something stupid. Still, he'd been willing to take a chance he could get something. The worst thing that could happen was having the door slammed in his face. Wouldn't be the first time.

And now he was walking away with a nice payout that

would cover the cost of the new game system his mom was too cheap to buy him. He might even have enough for a bag of weed. He'd be all set for Christmas vacation.

Oblivious to the chill in the air, Drew ambled past the red-brick church with the soaring steeple that had emptied of its congregation and cut through the graveled parking lot. Unlike most of his friends, he didn't have a car or a truck. Not even a clunker like Cord. His mom could barely pay rent on their trailer with the shit wages she earned at the meatpacking plant. And his dad was a waste of human space. The creep hadn't worked in years. 'Course that might have all changed now. He had five hundred dollars in his pocket. Who was to say he couldn't turn that into five thousand? Maybe more?

If people paid once, they would pay again, right? And if they wouldn't, he would track down Kaden Vaughn and see if he was in the market for some secret information. If he was doing a show for television, he should have a big budget he could share with an enterprising young man. Thankfully, he'd already turned eighteen, so he wouldn't have to share anything with his parents. To hell with them.

Busy contemplating which badass truck he should buy to get out of this crap town, Drew didn't bother to glance around when he heard a vehicle behind him. It would be one of the old farts headed home from lunch at the diner. The place was packed on Sundays. Or maybe it was the preacher, returning to the church to say an extra prayer or whatever they did when they weren't on stage, lecturing people about the evil of their ways. As if they weren't twice as evil in private.

It was probably a good thing he hadn't turned around. He thankfully had no idea that death was barreling toward him. Not until the grill of the vehicle smashed into him with enough force to drive the breath from his lungs. He could hear the snap of his ribs and feel his inner organs being crushed, but oddly, there was no pain as he flew through the frozen air like a deflated football.

Dizzily, he wondered if he was in shock. He probably was. Not that he had to worry about it. Gravity was doing its thing, and as quickly as he was launched into the air, he was hurtling toward the ground. He squeezed his eyes shut, belatedly trying to move his arms. They refused to cooperate. Was something wrong with his spine? Had he been paralyzed? The horrifying fear was still forming when he smacked headfirst against the frozen ground.

A loud crack echoed through his brain, as if his head had been shattered like the shell of an egg.

His last thought was that his mom had been wrong all these years. Turned out his skull wasn't as thick as a stump.

Chapter 5

The hospital in Grange was bustling despite the early hour and the threat of snow in the low, sullen clouds. Pulling her SUV into the visitors' lot, Lia hurried toward the front entrance.

She wasn't entirely sure why she was there. When Bailey called to tell her that Drew Hurst had been injured in an accident, she'd just been stepping out of the shower and was pulling on a pair of jeans and a bright yellow sweater. It was Monday morning and, as always, she had a dozen things on her to-do list. And honestly, she barely knew the boy.

But without thought, she grabbed her coat and headed for her vehicle.

A part of her was genuinely worried. Drew might be an aggravating bully at times, but he was just a kid. It was horrifying to think the poor boy had been hit by a car and then abandoned in the empty lot. He might have frozen to death if someone hadn't driven by and seen him crumpled on the snow.

Another part of her couldn't ignore a nagging fear that this was somehow connected to the skeleton the boy had discovered. It didn't make any sense. What could a death that happened years ago have to do with a teenager now? Especially if the skeleton did belong to Vanna Zimmerman. A woman who wasn't even from Pike. But whether it made sense or not, she couldn't dismiss the odd unease.

Walking down the brightly lit hallway, she entered the public waiting room, blinking at the sight of the dozen or so people stuffed in the cramped space. Most of them were high school kids, but near the table at the back of the room was a clutch of adults huddled around the coffee maker.

Lia came to a halt near the doorway, absorbing the hum of frenetic energy that was weirdly combined with the muffled whisper of voices. It was an atmosphere that was unique to hospitals.

"Ms. Porter."

Weaving his tall, slender form through the crowd, Wayne moved to stand directly in front of her.

"I just heard about Drew." She studied the boy's pale yet flushed face. She didn't think he was glad Drew had been injured, but the shocking event provided an exciting distraction. "Do you know how he's doing?"

"He's still unconscious." Wayne shook his head, glancing around the packed waiting room. "I can't believe this happened. Someone just ran him over like a dog."

Lia winced at the blunt words. "Do you know where it happened?"

"Next to the church, off Maple Street."

Maple Street. She visualized that area of town. It had seen better days, like most of Pike, but it was a quiet residential neighborhood. Not the sort of place where teenagers raced up and down the streets in their cars, or drug dealers hung out on street corners.

Then she blinked. "Oh. That's not far from where you live, is it?"

"A few blocks away. I was walking home when I heard

the sirens." His flush faded away, revealing the pallor that had been hidden beneath the rosy color. He was more bothered by the accident than he wanted to admit. "By the time I got over there, they were loading Drew into the ambulance."

"So terrible. Who would be heartless enough to hit a child and drive away?"

"He's not really a child," Wayne protested. "He's eighteen and as big as an ox."

"You know what I mean."

"Yeah. It's pretty sick." He shrugged. "I suppose someone might have panicked."

Lia slowly nodded. What other explanation could there be? Unless . . .

Unless it had been a deliberate attempt to kill Drew.

A shiver traced down her spine and Lia was forced to clear a lump from her throat.

"Did you talk to Drew yesterday?"

"Naw. It's not like we're besties."

"And no one saw it happen?"

"Not that I heard." Wayne leaned forward, dropping his voice to a mere whisper. "There's a rumor going round that Burke did it, but that's just crazy."

"Burke?" It took a second for Lia to realize Wayne wasn't referring to another classmate. "Ryan Burke?" She waited for Wayne to nod before making a sound of disbelief. Ryan Burke was the owner of the local meatpacking plant and one of the wealthiest businessmen in Pike. Not that money made him a decent person. Usually it was just the opposite. But while Lia had heard he was a pain-in-the-ass to work for and regularly cheated on his taxes, there'd never been rumors he had homicidal tendencies. Especially not toward school-children. "Why would he try to run over Drew?"

"I guess because Drew's mom works at the meatpacking

plant. Someone said they saw the two of them outside the plant screaming at each other a couple of days ago."

Lia paused. Okay. If Ryan Burke had a personal grudge against the Hurst family, it might make sense there was gossip swirling about him. But it certainly wasn't proof.

"Screaming about what?"

"Who knows? Drew's mom is always screaming about something. She's at the school once a week, storming up and down the hallways like a psycho."

Lia glanced across the waiting room where the adults were gathered in a tight circle.

"That's Barb over there, isn't it?" she asked in a low voice, nodding toward the tiny woman who dyed her hair to a weird, orangish shade and had a narrow face that was already deeply wrinkled. Years of tanning, smoking, and no doubt stress had obviously taken their toll.

Wayne glanced over his shoulder. "Yep, and that's his dad standing next to her." He turned back to Lia. "I don't know his real name. They always call him Cap. Drew says it's because he was captain of the Pike football team that won state."

Lia studied the large man who towered over his wife. He had broad shoulders beneath his coat, but they were hunched forward and he was carrying a cane. His face was broad, and his eyes were sunken, while his dark hair was already threaded with gray.

"I don't think I've ever seen him around town." Lia wasn't surprised not to recognize the man. Pike was small, but there were people who worked in Grange, or even Madison, and rarely participated in local events.

"From what I've heard, the dude never leaves the house. He was in some sort of accident when Drew was just a kid. He was working construction out at the meatpacking plant when a pile of steel pipes rolled off the back of a truck and smashed into him. Now he does nothing but eat painkillers and watch TV."

Lia grimaced, feeling a pang of sympathy. It was no wonder Drew acted out on occasion. His homelife seemed to be a mess.

"That's . . ." Lia forgot what she was going to say as someone stepped through the doorway and entered the waiting room. It was a teenage boy in a letter jacket and a stocking hat. "Oh," she breathed out, her heart racing.

Wayne sent her a puzzled glance. "What's wrong?"

"Just for a second I thought that was Drew walking through the door," she confessed, her pulse returning to normal as she belatedly recognized the boy. "I never realized how much Cord and Drew look alike."

"It's the matching coats and lack of necks," Wayne said.

"Maybe." Lia turned her attention to the girl who was holding Cord's hand as they walked across the room to talk to Drew's parents. She was tall and slender, with long dark hair and pale skin. "Is that Sunny Erickson?"

Wayne nodded, his features tightening into an odd expression. "Her and Cord go out when she can get away from her mother."

Lia pursed her lips. Sunny was the same age as Wayne, but she wasn't in the same class. Mayor Tate and Jolene had insisted the girl be homeschooled, as if they were afraid she might be tainted by spending time with the other kids. Even worse, Jolene treated the poor girl as if she was her pampered pooch on a leash, constantly having her next to her whenever she left the house.

Not that Sunny seemed to mind. Like her parents, she treated people with a condescending attitude that made sure to let everyone know she was far superior.

Lia glanced back at Wayne. "I can't imagine the mayor's very happy with his daughter dating Cord Walsh."

His lips pinched, as if he'd tasted something sour. Or maybe it was his thoughts that were sour.

"The only reason she goes out with Cord is to piss off her parents."

Lia hid her smile. Obviously, Wayne had a crush on Sunny Erickson. A shame. Sunny wasn't going to settle for a penniless boy who had never been outside of Pike. She would eventually find a nice, rich guy with a big brick home to marry.

She turned the conversation away from the sensitive subject. "Shouldn't you be headed to school?"

"They decided to start Christmas break a couple of days early. Between the skeleton and Drew's accident, they didn't think the kids would be able to concentrate."

"Probably a good idea." Lia glanced around, accepting that this wasn't the place to try to discover the truth of how or why the accident had happened. She would never have come to the hospital if she'd taken the time to think through her decision. "I'm headed back to Pike. Let me know if you hear anything about Drew."

Lia turned toward the door. The store was closed on Mondays, but she always had work to do.

"Hey." She glanced back at Wayne as he called out. "Are you going to see Kaden Vaughn today?"

The question came without warning and Lia sucked in a sharp breath. It was stupid. Why did the name Kaden Vaughn send a hot sizzle of excitement shooting through her? *Because he was smoking hot*, a treacherous voice whispered in the back of her mind.

"No." She stopped to clear her throat. "Why would I?"

"I thought he might be back in town."

Wayne was attempting to act nonchalant, but it was clear he was eagerly hoping he'd have another opportunity to spend time with his idol. And no doubt get another selfie to share with the world.

"It's possible, I suppose," she assured him, not bothering to add that it was doubtful either of them would see the man again.

"Okay. I might stop by to pick up a few extra hours. I could use the money."

"Sure. See you later."

For the second day in a row, Kaden climbed the shallow steps to the front door of the courthouse. And for the second day in a row, the wind cut through the frigid air like a knife. This morning, however, he'd stopped by a store in Madison to buy a thick parka and insolated boots. They weren't particularly stylish, but at least he wasn't in danger of freezing his ass off.

Carrying the heavy leather satchel he'd brought from his brother's condo, he entered the front office to discover a middle-aged woman seated at a wooden desk.

"How can I help you?"

"I need to see the sheriff."

Her lips turned down. It was impossible to know if she was annoyed with him. Or the sheriff. Maybe both.

"I'm sorry. He isn't in his office."

Kaden forced himself to count to ten. "Is there a deputy I can speak to?"

Without warning, a heavyset man in a brown uniform and a baseball cap appeared behind the woman. He looked to be in his early thirties, although he had one of those baby faces that made it hard to be sure. He was studying Kaden with a narrowed gaze. Or was that a squint?

"I'll deal with this, Monel," he assured the woman.

"Thank God someone can," Kaden muttered.

The deputy waved for Kaden to follow him. "It's a little stressful around here right now." He stopped to push open the door to a connecting office. "Come in here."

Kaden stepped inside, instantly hit with the scent of old wood. It was oddly soothing, as if it was a silent reassurance that the place had stood in this spot for a hundred years and would be there for another hundred. He grimaced, telling himself to be more impressed with the high-tech monitors that were mounted on the wall over the old wooden filing cabinets. That was the sort of thing that could solve cases, right?

His gaze moved toward the large window that offered a view of the town square. He had to admit it looked stunning. A perfect backdrop for a Hallmark Christmas movie.

"I'm Anthony." The deputy interrupted his wandering thoughts.

Kaden turned back to discover the man leaning against the heavy desk, which looked as if it'd been around as long as the courthouse.

"I'm—"

"I know who you are," Anthony interrupted Kaden's attempt to introduce himself. "The whole town is buzzing about you showing up yesterday. Are you here to do a show about the skeleton we found?"

"Absolutely not."

The deputy grimaced. "I knew it was too good to be true. Why are you here?"

Kaden swallowed his annoyance at the locals' hope of using the recently discovered skeleton to grab a bit of fame. He hadn't liked Vanna, but she deserved better.

Drawing in a deep breath, he forced himself to speak in a calm voice. "Fifteen years ago, my brother's fiancée, Vanna Zimmerman, went missing." He reached into the satchel to pull out the eight-by-ten photo of Vanna in her official uniform. Stepping forward, he handed it to the deputy. "This is her picture. You can see her jacket. It looks exactly like the one that was posted on the Internet."

In the blink of an eye, Anthony went from casual curiosity to a man on duty. "You think the skeleton belongs to her?"

"I do."

"If you want to write down her name and any other information you have on her, I can pass it along to the coroner."

Kaden breathed out a sigh of relief. Finally. He started to reach back into his satchel. "My brother passed away five years ago, but he left behind a stack of files. I have them here if you would like—"

His words were cut short when the door slammed open and a man in his midfifties with thinning dark hair combed straight back and a nose that was too large for his narrow face stormed into the room. He was wearing a dark suit with a red tie that looked like it had Christmas trees printed on the silk and he had a metal flag pinned to his lapel.

Kaden didn't have to guess who the intruder was. He had the smug look of a man who'd been given a tiny bit of power that had gone straight to his head.

Tate Erickson. Mayor of Pike and acting sheriff.

The man came to an abrupt halt at the sight of Kaden. Or maybe it was Anthony, who was still leaning against his desk.

"What's going on?"

Anthony straightened, his expression settling into defensive lines. "This is Kaden Vaughn. He thinks he might be able to ID the skeleton."

Tate visibly stiffened. "What?"

"Her name is—"

Kaden was once again interrupted. It was a trend that was starting to piss him off.

"I don't care," Tate snapped, his gaze never straying

from his deputy. "The bones have been shipped off to the medical examiner in Madison and the railroad company is up my ass to get back to work. As far as I'm concerned, the case is closed."

"How can it be closed?" Kaden stepped forward, towering over the smaller man. "You don't know who she is or what happened to her."

Tate took an instinctive step backward, reluctantly tilting his head to glare up at Kaden.

"That's the job of the coroner. I have too much on my plate to worry about a random death from years ago. Especially since it was probably some whack job jumping off a moving train. Happens all the time. People kill themselves without concern about the mess they leave behind."

Kaden blinked. That was a very specific hypothesis. "You think it was suicide?"

"What else?" the mayor snapped, reaching into the pocket of his suit jacket to pull out his phone. Glancing at the screen, he muttered a curse. He dropped the phone back into his pocket and returned his attention to Anthony. "I'm going to . . . to see if there are any of those camera thingies around where the accident happened."

"CCTV?" the deputy helpfully supplied.

"That's it." Tate inched his way toward the open door. "It's a long shot, but worth a try."

"I can do that," Anthony offered.

"I got it. Just take care of . . ." Tate waved a vague hand that included Kaden and the nearby desk. "This."

Darting out of the office, the mayor slammed shut the door. Kaden glanced toward Anthony, who was glaring at the disappearing mayor with a deep scowl. The deputy didn't appear to be particularly impressed with his temporary boss, but that wasn't what interested Kaden. He was more concerned with the odd sense of premonition niggling at the edge of his mind.

"What accident?"

"Hit-and-run yesterday afternoon." The man paused, his jaw suddenly tightening as he glanced back at Kaden. "It was weird."

"Why do you say that?"

"The victim was Drew Hurst."

Kaden's breath hissed between his clenched teeth. His premonition had been right.

"The boy who found the skeleton?"

"Yep."

"How bad was he injured?"

Anthony looked grim. "Right now they don't know if he's going to make it."

"Damn."

Chapter 6

Lia pulled into the alley behind her store and shut off the engine. She'd briefly considered driving to Green Bay to check out a potential investment in a microbrewery, but the overhead clouds were low and heavy with the threat of snow. She could wait a few days to make the trip.

Climbing out of the SUV, Lia heard the crunch of tires on the ice behind her. Her heart lodged in her throat as she whirled around. She had no idea what she was expecting, but the fact that Drew had just been run down put her on edge. She released a shaky breath at the sight of the Jeep parked behind her.

Not that her heart slowed its racing at the sight of Kaden Vaughn crawling out of the vehicle. She'd truly believed she'd never see him again. Which might explain why she'd allowed him to play the central role in her dreams last night. For several delicious hours she'd imagined tracing each and every tattoo with her tongue.

He'd changed into a sensible parka, but he was still dangerously sexy as he moved to stand directly in front of her.

"Lia."

Knowing her cheeks were flushed with awareness, she pressed a hand to her chest and acted frightened.

"You startled me."

"Sorry. I tried to wave you down, but you seemed distracted."

His words reminded her of how she'd spent the early part of her morning. Regaining command of her composure, she turned to unlock the door to her building.

"I went to the hospital to check on Drew."

"I just heard he'd been in an accident."

She nodded. "A hit-and-run."

"Did he notice anything about the car?"

"He's still unconscious." She studied the gorgeous male face that had haunted her dreams. "Did you need something?"

"I'm not sure." He reached up to impatiently push his hair out of his face as a gust of wind whipped through the alley. "I came to Pike to talk to the sheriff."

That explained how he'd known about Drew's accident. She tilted her head to the side. "And?"

"And he's not interested."

"Predictable. He doesn't seem to be interested in anything."

He shifted from foot to foot, as if he wasn't entirely sure what to do with himself. "I know you're probably busy, but . . ."

"The store is closed on Mondays," she assured him, pushing open the door. Then, without allowing herself to consider whether it was a bad idea to spend more time with Kaden Vaughn, she motioned for him to join her. "Would you like some coffee?"

"That would be great." He surprisingly turned back toward his Jeep. "Let me grab something right quick." Opening the passenger door, he pulled out a leather satchel before he turned back to face her. "I brought a few of my brother's files with me. I intended to give them to the sheriff."

"But he wasn't interested."

"Exactly."

Lia stepped inside the building and removed her coat to hang it on the wooden rack. Once Kaden was inside, she hurriedly slammed shut the door. It was colder now than it had been when she'd awakened at the crack of dawn.

Kaden followed close behind her as she headed down the hallway to her office. She wasn't foolish enough to take him upstairs to her apartment.

"Now I'm hoping there's something in the files that might jog your memory," Kaden admitted.

"I've told you everything I saw that night."

"I just meant in general. Maybe you noticed something around town or heard something that didn't mean anything at the time."

"It wouldn't hurt to try." She unlocked her office and waved him toward the chairs at the back. "I'll get the coffee going. There are cookies on the table."

She headed toward the corner where she kept a fancy, barista-quality coffee maker. Behind her was the sound of Kaden removing his coat and settling in one of the leather chairs. A few seconds later, he released a low groan that sent shivers of pleasure through her.

"These are dangerous," he growled. "Did you make them?"

"Yes." She switched on the machine and within seconds, the scent of brewing coffee filled the air. "I'm a stress baker."

She didn't add that she often had important business meetings in the office. And that fresh chocolate chip cookies were a remarkably effective tool in negotiations. That was her secret weapon.

Along with massive amounts of research.

"I tear apart engines when I'm stressed," he confessed.

"Less fattening."

"I doubt you have to count calories." Kaden made a choked sound, as if he was shocked he'd said the words out loud. "Sorry."

Lia pretended she hadn't heard. Just as she was trying to pretend she didn't notice the awareness that sizzled between them.

"Cream or sugar?"

"Black."

No surprise there. Lia filled two heavy ceramic mugs with the steaming coffee and headed to where Kaden was seated. Handing him one of the mugs, she took the chair directly facing him.

He took a sip, eyeing her with an expression that was difficult to read. "Do you know anything about Drew's accident?"

"Not really. Apparently, he was walking through an empty parking lot next to the church when a car lost control on the ice and hit him from behind." She wrapped her fingers around the mug, trying to absorb the heat into her chilled body. "So far, there hasn't been anyone willing to admit they were responsible. And there were no witnesses."

"The sheriff is supposedly looking for any potential video of the crime."

She blinked, briefly assuming he was joking. Then she shook her head in disbelief. "Tate is actually out in the cold, investigating a crime?"

"That's what he said. My guess is he was headed for the diner."

"That would be my guess as well."

As far as Lia could tell, Tate spent his days strolling around town, convincing the citizens what a good job he was doing without actually *doing* his job.

Kaden took another sip, his eyes a dark, smoky gray as he churned through his inner thoughts.

"It seems odd," he at last murmured.

"The mayor?"

He flashed a quick smile. "That too, but I was talking about Drew's accident. Don't you think it's strange he discovered a hidden body one day and nearly was killed the next?"

She wasn't surprised this man shared her suspicions. The question was why no one else seemed to be concerned.

"I do. But what connection could there be?" She met his steady gaze. "If the skeleton is Vanna Zimmerman, Drew would have been a small child when she died. No more than three or four years old."

"Do his parents own a farm or a business?"

"No. His mom works at the meatpacking plant and his dad is unemployed. Why?"

"I thought maybe Vanna was investigating them."

"Even if they were being investigated, what would that have to do with Drew?"

"A warning? Retribution?" He heaved a frustrated sigh. "To be honest, I'm grasping at straws."

"None of it makes sense."

Setting his mug on the small, round table between them, Kaden reached into his satchel to pull out a stack of files.

"Let's see if these will shed any light."

Tate entered the sleek, contemporary home he'd personally designed a few years before. The rooms were all large and open, with a gray and silver décor and modern furniture that was perfect for entertaining. Most importantly, it was constructed on the highest point in town with large windows that allowed him to overlook Pike. Like a king surveying his kingdom.

And that's exactly what he felt like.

Most of the time.

Today? Today, he felt like the court jester trying to avoid complete disaster.

Entering through the front door, he pulled off his coat and tossed it on a silver table before heading into the formal sitting room. He intended to have a quick shot of the ludicrously expensive cognac he had imported from France, but he was interrupted by a short, curvaceous woman with glorious blond hair and pale blue eyes. Jolene Erickson had been the prettiest girl in town when he married her. He'd been aroused every time he saw those flashing dimples and mouthwatering boobs. It hadn't bothered him that she'd always been fragile. He liked to know she depended on him. But over the years, he couldn't deny there'd been times when he'd had to search out a woman who offered him some raw, bang-it-together sex. He was a man. It happened.

Jolene drifted into the center of the room, still wearing a frilly robe despite the fact it was past ten in the morning.

"Oh, it's you."

Tate swallowed a sigh, accepting his cognac would have to wait. Jolene didn't like him to drink before noon.

"Who were you expecting?"

"Sunny."

Tate felt a stab of surprise. His daughter rarely left the house during the day. She was not only busy with her online classes, she was very protective of her mother. She didn't like to leave her alone.

"Where is she?"

Jolene sniffed. "She insisted on visiting that horrible boy who was hit by a car yesterday."

Tate sucked in a sharp breath. "Wait. Is he awake?"

"She didn't say. All I know is that she refused to eat the breakfast I cooked for her, then dashed out the door when

Cord Walsh pulled up in his truck." Her tone was peevish. "Really, love, you should start giving people tickets for noise disturbance. The racket was enough to cause one of my migraines."

Tate was instantly distracted. "Sunny is with Cord Walsh?"

"He was driving her to the hospital in Grange."

Anger bubbled through Tate. He did his best to shield his family from the less desirable citizens of Pike, but he couldn't be everywhere all at once. He needed some help.

"Why did you let her go?" He sent his wife a frustrated frown. "I don't like that kid. He's nothing but trouble. And she needs to stay away from that Hurst boy as well. Both of them should be in jail."

Jolene lifted her hand to her throat, her eyes glittering with unshed tears. "I tried my best to keep her home, but lately she has developed a mind of her own." They both glanced toward the long window at the rumbling sound of an approaching vehicle. "That's her now."

Tate didn't bother to watch the rusty truck come up the steep driveway. He already felt guilty for snapping at his wife. He'd wait until he had his temper under control before confronting his daughter.

"I'll have a word with her later."

"Why can't you do it now?"

"I have a meeting in my office." Tate sent one last, longing glance at the decanter of cognac before he crossed the silver carpet to brush his lips over his wife's cheek. "Make sure I'm not interrupted."

Jolene clicked her tongue, stepping back. "I don't understand why you can't have your meetings at the courthouse. This is my home, not a public building."

"Because I don't want anyone overhearing what I have to say."

She blinked at his sharp tone. "Tate. What's going on?"

"Nothing you need to worry yourself about." He forced a stiff smile to his lips. "I just have a few loose ends to tie up."

With a determined stride, Tate left the sitting room and crossed through the vast kitchen that was Jolene's domain to push open the door to the four-car garage. He'd deliberately separated his office from the rest of the house to ensure privacy. Something a mayor needed on a regular basis.

Pulling the keys from the pocket of his slacks, he unlocked the connecting door and stepped into the small but comfortable room that was completely different from the main house. He'd chosen heavy wood furniture and a dark crimson carpet that matched the drapes. It was a masculine space that suited his position of authority.

He glanced out the window, grimacing at the sight of the power-blue Cadillac parked in the private driveway. He'd told everyone to meet at ten, but he'd had a personal errand to take care of before he could return to the house.

Tate unlocked the front door of his office and pulled it open, gesturing to the older man who was waiting for him.

With slow, cautious movements, Judge Leon Armstrong slid out of the Cadillac and shuffled his way up the frosty driveway. The judge had recently celebrated his seventy-second birthday, but he looked ten years older. The tall, barrel-chested frame that had always seemed to take up more than his fair share of space was now stooped forward, as if gravity was trying to bend him in two. His round face sagged to a flap of loose skin beneath his chin and his dark hair had thinned to wisps of silver that he kept firmly plastered to his scalp. Even his eyes were sunken and bloodshot, and his wool overcoat was at least two sizes too large.

Tate remembered him as being a loud, brash man who terrified anyone stupid enough to defy him. Now, his threats were nothing more than bluster.

A shame.

Tate could really use someone who had the power to keep the past buried.

"About damned time you got here," Leon groused as he entered the office. "I've been sitting in my car for a half hour."

"Do you know how many fires I'm trying to put out?"

"The only fire I care about is that Zimmerman woman."

Tate didn't have a chance to reply as the door was shoved open and a short, heavyset man with a round, ruddy face and dark hair buzzed close to his scalp charged inside.

Ryan Burke was a couple of years younger than Tate and the owner of the Pike Meatpacking Plant.

"Shit." Ryan held his hands up to his mouth to blow hot air against his chilled skin. "It's cold out there."

Tate frowned as he glanced toward the window. There was only one car in the driveway.

"Did you walk here?"

"No. I parked around the corner. I don't like having this meeting in broad daylight."

Tate snorted. Ryan was always paranoid. He'd been that way from the beginning.

"You don't think it would cause any suspicion if we were skulking around in the middle of the night?"

The businessman glared at him with annoyance shimmering in his pale blue eyes. "Then let's get this over with."

"Agreed." Tate deliberately moved to stand behind the cherrywood desk he'd had hand-carved from a local shop. It put him in a position of power. "We all know why we're here. Vanna Zimmerman."

Ryan's heavy brows snapped together. "Has there been a positive ID?"

"Not yet. But it's just a matter of time."

"Christ." The judge reached up to rub his nearly bald head. "This is a disaster."

Tate lifted his hands, trying to project an image of calm. No need to share that his nerves were shredded and he hadn't slept since the body was discovered.

"Not necessarily. There's no reason for the bitch to be connected to us."

"Easy for you to say," Ryan growled. "I guarantee you, if the truth leaks out, I'm not going down alone."

The judge tried to draw himself up to his full height. "You can't pin any of this on me. I have friends in powerful places."

Tate rolled his eyes. What was that saying? *No honor among thieves.*

"No one is going down," he assured them. "Not unless we panic."

The judge shifted from foot to foot, as if standing in one place was making his knees ache. "Then why did you call us here?"

"There's been a . . . complication," Tate grudgingly admitted. "I managed to get the autopsy on the skeleton put on the slow track. The medical examiner's office has enough to do trying to keep up with its current caseload without worrying about what happened years ago. I'm sure the good people of Pike will soon lose interest if there's no new information."

Ryan folded his arms over his chest. "So what's the complication?"

"Kaden Vaughn."

"Who?"

Tate and Ryan ignored the old man. Of course he wouldn't recognize the name. He still watched reruns of *Columbo* and *M*A*S*H*.

"I heard he was in town," Ryan said. "What's he doing here?"

"His brother was engaged to Vanna Zimmerman."

Ryan stared at Tate in disbelief. "Holy shit."

That was Tate's reaction. How bad did his luck have to be for the bitch to have a world-famous television star looking for her?

The judge looked peevish as he glanced from Tate to Ryan. "What's going on?"

Once again, they ignored him.

"He doesn't know anything, but having him around is going to keep people talking," Tate pointed out the obvious. "The sooner we can convince him to return to Hollywood, the better."

Ryan shrugged. "It's a small town. It won't be hard for you to make a stranger feel unwelcome. And I can make some calls to Grange. I have enough influence to make it hard to remain in the area."

"Good." Tate paused, dreading the need to reveal the second part of his bad news. Being the messenger sucked. Unfortunately, it had to be done. "And then there's the matter of Lia Porter."

Ryan had started to turn away, obviously assuming the meeting was finished. Slowly, he turned back.

"What about her?"

"She claims she saw a woman running through the dark one night on her way home from a party." Tate kept his tone nonchalant, as if it was no big deal. "Now she's convinced the skeleton is the remains of that woman."

Ryan made a strangled sound, his beefy face turning red as he glared at Tate in disbelief.

"She saw Vanna the night she died?"

"It might have been Vanna, but who knows if it was the same night? The woman was in and out of Pike a dozen times. She was always sticking her nose in where it didn't belong."

"Yeah, but if Lia starts talking about what she saw,

people are going to wonder who she was and why she was running. And if it was Vanna . . ."

Tate ground his teeth together. When he was young, he'd been short and chubby and dirt poor. The kids had teased him mercilessly until he developed the ability to charm them with sappy compliments and empty promises. People were utter schmucks. He used that talent for manipulation to earn a place on the student council and, later, to run for class president. He'd become addicted to power at an early age and by the time he was thirty, he was mayor of Pike.

Still, there were times when he considered the pleasure of packing his bags and disappearing to a small island with lots of sand and sun.

"We need to convince Lia that what she saw had nothing to do with Vanna Zimmerman." He allowed his companions a glimpse of his ruthless inner core. "Got it?"

"I don't like this." The judge looked like a petulant child.

Tate swallowed a curse. "Do you think any of us do?"

"I have to go." The older man stomped to the door and disappeared from the office. A few minutes later, they could hear his Cadillac reversing out of the driveway.

"I don't trust him." Ryan strolled to the window to watch the judge drive away. "He'll do whatever is necessary to save his own ass."

Tate snorted. He didn't trust either of the men. But it was too late for regrets.

"We stay strong and all of this will blow over."

Chapter 7

Leon Armstrong drove home at the speed of a snail. Not only was he more cautious as he grew older, he frankly couldn't see a damned thing without his glasses. And worse, he'd made the stupid decision to stop by the electric department to inform them they could shove his bill up their asses. He wasn't paying a late fee. Not when his utilities were already ungodly expensive. They'd get his money when he was damned well ready to give it to them.

The impulsive decision meant that by the time he was headed home, the snow that had threatened all morning was swirling from the heavens in a blanket of white. He struggled to make out more than a blur as he inched his way through the icy streets.

Aging was a bitch.

Of course, there was no need to hurry, he reminded himself. He'd retired from the bench six months ago and he had nothing but time on his hands. Which gave him plenty of opportunity to consider the looming disaster.

Leon tapped on the brakes as he turned the large Cadillac onto the private lane that led to his house. He grimaced as his back end fishtailed on the ice. He wished he'd stayed home. There hadn't been any point in being at the meeting. Years ago he wielded the sort of power that could have squelched the investigation into the skeleton before it could even get started. But now . . .

Now he could do nothing more than regret ever getting involved with Tate Erickson and Ryan Burke.

It had nothing to do with morals. He'd discovered early in his career as a judge that there was nothing black and white in this world. A smart man understood there was a plethora of opportunities in the gray areas. Especially if he was ambitious.

But he was accustomed to working with professionals. They understood the necessity of hiding evidence in a way that couldn't be traced back to them. And they most certainly didn't allow their dead bodies to be discovered.

"Sloppy amateurs," he muttered, pulling into the driveway in front of the massive brick house at the end of the lane. It was three-storied, with arched windows and a full conservatory on one side and a pool in the back. It'd cost a fortune, of course. But he'd made sure it was the largest house in Pike. He'd never been a man willing to settle for second best.

He just had to hope his ambitions weren't going to cause his ruin—

Leon's dark thoughts were abruptly shattered as he belatedly realized the garage door was shut. What the hell? He pressed his foot on the brake, frowning in confusion. He always left the door open when his driveway was covered with snow. It made it easier to pull into the garage if he could drive straight in without being concerned about stopping and spinning on the ice. Besides, it wasn't like he had to worry about crime in Pike. No one was stupid enough to break into his house.

With a grimace, Leon pushed the button on his visor and waited for the garage door to glide up. No doubt he'd simply forgotten he wanted it left open. Things like that were happening more and more often. Lost keys, burned dinners, laundry abandoned in the washer . . .

Tapping his fingers, gnarled with arthritis, on the steering wheel, he returned his thoughts to his more pressing troubles. He wasn't completely defenseless, he staunchly reminded himself. There were still a few old pals he could contact this afternoon.

Debating which favor he needed to call in first, Leon carefully eased his car into the garage. He was nearly blinded by the darkness that swallowed him as he pulled inside. Like Jonah being sucked into the belly of the whale.

Snorting at the ridiculous image that formed in his mind, Leon put the car in Park and switched off the engine. Then, reaching up, he pushed the button to close the garage door.

The electric motor hummed overhead as Leon shoved open the car door and started to push out his aching body. That was as far as he got before a shape that was darker than the shadows suddenly appeared.

"Who's there?" Leon called out in a rough voice. There was no answer as the blurry form continued to move toward him. "Dammit, if this is a joke, it isn't funny."

He thought he heard a muffled laugh, as if the intruder found the situation hilarious. Bastard.

"Fine. You think this is a game? I'll teach you not to play with me."

Plopping back into the car seat, Leon grunted as he tried to turn to the side. He had a gun in the glove compartment. If only he could loosen his stiff muscles enough to reach it. He'd just managed to stretch his arm backward when he heard the whoosh of wind.

Something was being swung through the air. A knife? A tool? A baseball bat?

Whatever it was, it hit him in the face with enough force to bust his nose and shatter his front teeth.

The second blow crushed his skull.

He was dead by the third.

Kaden settled back in his seat as he watched Lia work her way through the stack of files. Unlike most people, she didn't quickly scan the thick stacks of official forms or the detailed reports that had been gathered by the private detectives Darren had hired. This was a woman who didn't offer her assistance lightly. If she agreed to do something, she was going to do it to the very best of her ability.

He wondered if she approached everything in her life with such unwavering devotion. He was going to guess she did.

When she reached the thick binder filled with Vanna's official reports, however, she lifted her head to send him a rueful smile.

"I have no idea what these mean. They might as well be written in Greek."

"I think they are. It will take a scientist to decipher them." He grabbed the binder and shoved it into his satchel. "I brought them because I hoped the sheriff would hand them over to an expert."

"Seems doubtful he'll bother."

"No crap." Kaden had already reconciled himself to the fact that the local law enforcement was going to be zero help. "Which means it's up to us."

She nodded. "Agreed."

"I read through the files last night, and it seems to me that most of my brother's notes are detailed accounts of what *didn't* happen to Vanna," Kaden admitted, ticking a finger for each dead end. "No one fitting her description was taken to a hospital in the area. No Jane Doe was found in the nearby morgues. No one touched her bank accounts after the day she disappeared. There was no record of her buying tickets for an airplane or train or bus. And her passport was left in my brother's condo, along with her clothes and engagement ring." He quit when he reached the end of his fingers.

"What about her car?"

"Gone."

Lia looked grim. They both knew a woman didn't disappear for fifteen years without some trace she was still alive. A text to a friend. A withdrawal of cash from her account. A picture on social media. She at last shook her head, returning her attention to the files stacked on the table between them.

"Well, the files at least revealed that Pike was in the district Vanna investigated in her regular duties for the EPA," she pointed out. "And her official travel logs have a record of her visiting the town several times during the month before she died."

"There was also this."

Kaden reached into the side pocket of the satchel to pull out the folded paper that had been kept in a locked drawer in his brother's office at the condo. He assumed it meant it was important. Or at least Darren had thought it was important. Smoothing out the paper, he handed it to Lia.

She studied it in confusion. "A map of Wisconsin?"

Kaden leaned forward to point toward the heavy outline that included several counties in the middle of the state. "Vanna was responsible for this district. I don't know exactly what she did, but my brother marked five spots in red."

"Pike is one of them."

"Yes." His finger moved to the corner of the map. "And in the margin he scribbled the words 'water pollution.' I don't know which location he meant. Maybe all of them."

"Were there any other notes that mentioned this map?"

Kaden shook his head. After finding the map, he'd searched through the files, but he hadn't found anything that might connect to the five towns circled or the mention of water pollution.

"Nothing, but he wrote something on the back."

Lia turned over the paper and read the first line out loud. "'TXT. DO 18 BAGR 05119016912453611324. Seventy-five thousand dollars.'" Her brows drew together as she glanced up at him. "What is this?"

Kaden shrugged. It'd been difficult to try to decipher the strange list. Not only because he had no idea what the hell any of it meant but his brother's handwriting was so painfully familiar. It was a stark reminder of all the years he'd stayed away from Madison and the brother who'd so desperately needed him.

He flinched at the sharp-edged guilt that sliced through him. Then, with fierce determination, he shoved aside his futile regret. He couldn't change the past. But he could make damned sure his brother could finally rest in peace.

"If I have to guess, I'd say they were a list of fines for EPA violations."

"It's possible." She tapped her finger against the paper. "But why would he have these routing numbers?"

"What do you mean?"

"These look like international bank routing numbers. Specifically, from the Dominican Republic." She sent him a puzzled glance. "Was Vanna a forensic accountant for the EPA?"

"I don't think so." Kaden shifted through his memories of the woman who'd become such an important part of his brother's life. "I'm sure Darren told me she had a degree in chemistry. And I know she spent most of her time working outdoors, not behind a desk. I heard her complaining that she could never have a decent manicure with her job. And that's why she didn't wear her engagement ring when she was working."

Lia shook her head. "Strange."

It *was* strange. When Kaden decided to open a business in Vegas, he'd been wise enough to bring in his old buddy, Dom. Not only because he knew everything about running a pawn shop but because he was a genius with numbers. Kaden might have bankrolled Money Maker, but it was a success because Dom had taken over the accounts.

Unfortunately, that meant he knew very little about international banking or routing numbers. Or why his brother would have written them on the back of the map.

"Are the letters at the start of each line a part of the routing number?"

She shook her head. "It could be an abbreviation for the company." She ran her finger over the top line. "The company. Followed by their IBAN number. And the amount they had to pay."

"Do you recognize any of the abbreviations? Could one of them be a business from Pike?"

She studied the list before heaving a sigh. "It's like they're written as ticker symbols for the stock market. I might be able to track them down, but it's going to take time."

Kaden narrowed his gaze, studying her with a burst of curiosity. He'd sensed there was something mysterious about this woman from the moment he stepped into this office yesterday. The space was a sharp contrast to the worn, almost shabby public area. Plus, why would the owner of a small-town market need two state-of-the-art computers with massive monitors? Or a seating area that clearly doubled as a meeting room? Or a coffee maker that looked like it came from NASA?

"You know a lot about international banking and ticker symbols."

"I took a few online global business and investment classes." The words were tossed out in a casual tone. Too casual.

"To run a small store in Pike, Wisconsin?"

She stiffened, as if annoyed by his soft question, then abruptly rose to her feet. Whatever the reason for her fancy office, she didn't want to discuss it with him. He ignored his small stab of disappointment as she made a sound of surprise.

"Oh."

Kaden shoved himself out of the chair, on instant alert. "What?"

"It's started snowing."

Kaden glanced toward the small window, where he could see the heavy swirl of snowflakes. Any relief that there wasn't an immediate enemy about to crash into the office was quashed by the realization that the weather could be just as dangerous.

Winter in Wisconsin was no joke.

"Damn. I forgot to look at the forecast this morning."

"You've been gone from Wisconsin too long if you didn't check out the weather as soon as you crawled out of bed."

"Obviously. How much snow are they predicting?"

"Three to five inches."

Not a blizzard, but if the wind picked up, it could make any traveling a hazard. "I should get back to Madison."

Lia held up the paper she held in her hand. "Can I keep this for now?"

He nodded, reaching into his pocket to pull out a business card with his cell phone number.

"Let me know if you figure out anything."

"Of course."

She took the card and placed it on her desk with the map. Then, opening the door, she waited for him to grab his satchel and led him out of the office. Kaden followed her, reluctantly acknowledging he wasn't ready to leave. He was convinced Lia would be able to discover something about the businesses written on the back of the map. Not to mention he'd only had one cookie. He could easily eat a dozen more.

And . . .

Nope. He didn't want to consider what came after "and." He was sure it was directly connected to sharing more time with Lia Porter in the cozy privacy of her office.

"Thanks for the coffee."

He forced himself to open the door, bracing himself for the blast of frigid air. It hit him like a punch, knocking the air from his lungs. With a shiver, he carefully crossed the graveled alleyway that was now layered with a fresh dusting of snow. He had a long list of reasons why he hated winter in Wisconsin. He didn't intend to add falling on his ass in front of Lia Porter.

Opening the door to the Jeep, Kaden was about to step in when he realized something was wrong with his front tire. It was completely flat. Annoyance flared through him. Great. It was just what he needed in the middle of a snowstorm. Thankfully, there was a spare.

He turned toward the rear of the vehicle, his gaze narrowing as he caught sight of the back tire. Flat. An ugly suspicion curled through the pit of his stomach and slowly, he walked to the opposite side of the Jeep. Just as he'd expected. They were both flat.

"Shit."

Bending down next to the back tire, he reached to grab

the wooden handle that was sticking out of the rubber. He yanked it out to reveal a three-inch blade.

"What's wrong?" Lia called out, smart enough to stay inside the building to avoid the cutting wind.

"My tires are flat." Straightening, Kaden moved back to the open door, holding out the pocketknife so she could see what caused the damage. "This was no accident. I don't suppose you have a security camera?"

Her lips parted in shock, but with a visible effort she quickly shoved aside her disbelief that someone would vandalize his Jeep in broad daylight and considered his question.

"I have one inside, but it wouldn't cover the alley. Do you want me to call Ray Sykes?"

Kaden swallowed his disappointment. He very much wanted to know who was responsible for slashing his tires. And why.

"Who's Ray Sykes?"

"He runs the local automotive shop."

Kaden shook his head, pulling his phone out of his pocket. Another shiver raced through him as he scrolled through his emails.

"No need. I'll call the rental company. It's insured." He pressed in the number and held the phone to his ear. A few minutes later, he was shoving it back into his pocket. He was used to living in the city. He hadn't taken into account the fact he was two hours away from the rental office and that the snow was swiftly piling up. "They can't get a replacement here until tomorrow."

She grimaced. "I doubt Ray would be any quicker. He usually has to order his parts. Even tires."

Kaden considered his options. He had a couple of cousins who lived in Madison and one in Green Bay. He could call any of them and they would be happy to come and pick him up. But it didn't make sense to leave town when they would be bringing the replacement car tomorrow, did it? And he still had to make a police report for the insurance to pay for the damages.

"Is there a hotel in town?"

She hesitated, her nose wrinkling before she answered. "Yes."

"You grimaced."

"It's not a five star."

Kaden's lips twisted. Over the years, he'd slept on the streets of Hollywood, in the back of a van on a movie set, and in a tent in the Mojave Desert while his business was being constructed. A cheap hotel was nothing.

"No problem. It's just for the night."

"I can drive you there." She nodded toward the nearby SUV. "I'll grab my coat and purse."

"Thanks."

Kaden moved to the vehicle, not surprised to discover it was unlocked. People in a town like Pike didn't expect bad things to happen. Hopefully, the events of this morning would encourage Lia to be more cautious. Knocking the snow off his boots, he climbed into the passenger seat and pulled the belt across his body. A couple of minutes later, Lia joined him and started the engine.

"Someone really hates Jeeps," he murmured as they inched past his disabled vehicle. "Or they were sending me a message." He glanced down at the knife he held in his hand. There was nothing special about it. In fact, he would guess half the men in town carried one that looked exactly like it. Which meant there was no reason to hand it over to the sheriff. The idiot would probably toss it in the trash.

"A message?" Lia broke into his thoughts, driving through a maze of snow-packed streets with the confidence of someone who'd lived in Pike her entire life.

"You don't have a jealous boyfriend lurking around town, do you?"

"No boyfriend. And if I did, he wouldn't be the sort of guy who would go around slashing tires."

He turned his head to study the pure lines of her profile. There was something utterly unique about Lia Porter. It was no wonder he found her so fascinating.

"What sort of guy would he be?"

She shook her head, refusing to take the bait. "We're discussing who vandalized your vehicle."

"If it wasn't done out of jealousy, it could be a disappointed fan of my latest special."

"Doubtful."

"You'd be surprised." Kaden was shocked by the messages he received after he started his reality show. Then there were the uncomfortable confrontations when he just wanted to have a nice meal or enjoy a movie. "I've had death threats from mothers who are angry their kids tried one of my stunts. And men who think I should be shot for restoring a Vincent Black Lightning motorcycle instead of leaving it a rusting pile of junk."

She sucked in a sharp breath. "That's awful."

It was, but Kaden wasn't so self-centered that he didn't understand it was a small price to pay for living his dream.

"It comes with the territory. My show and the occasional television specials allow me to do what I love."

Her expression softened. "Yeah, I get that."

He sensed she truly did understand. So what were her dreams? And what was she paying to achieve them? Kaden shook his head. If she wanted him to know her secrets, she would share them.

"But you're right." He returned the conversation to his vandalized Jeep. "I doubt anyone in Pike feels strongly enough about my career to slash my tires."

"Then why?"

"A warning. Someone—or maybe more than one someone—doesn't like me asking questions."

Lia lightly pressed on the brakes, pulling into the narrow parking lot attached to a long building with a row of doors and a sagging metal canopy. They parked in front of a door with the word *Office* hand-painted in red. Kaden hid his grimace, hoping the place was at least clean.

Turning in her seat, Lia sent him a worried glance. "If it's a warning, maybe you should go back to Vegas."

He arched a brow. "Are you trying to get rid of me?"

She hesitated, glancing toward the swishing wipers that struggled to keep up with the thickening snow. "This is starting to feel dangerous."

"I'm not leaving." Kaden clenched his teeth, mentally visualizing the bastard creeping through the alley to slash his tires. He was either desperate or brashly confident in his ability not to get caught. Leaving the knife behind made it feel like sheer arrogance. "Not until I have answers."

She rolled her eyes. "How did I know you were going to say that?"

He allowed his gaze to trace the delicate lines of her face, lingering on the smattering of freckles that dusted her nose. Everything about her was familiar. As if they'd known each other in another life.

"Because we're partners." The words felt eerily right as they left his lips.

"Partners?"

"That's how it feels to me."

Her lips parted, but no words came out. Were they stuck in her throat? At last, she turned away, her hands clenching the steering wheel until her knuckles turned white.

"If you get hungry, you can order takeout pizza from

Bella's. They don't deliver, but it's just a couple of blocks away and it's the best food in town."

He was being firmly dismissed. Something that hadn't happened in a long time. It didn't matter if people loved or hated him, he was famous. And that meant he was usually given star treatment. Now he struggled to hide his smile.

"Good to know." He shoved open the door, holding on to the satchel and knife. Climbing out of the SUV, he turned back to send Lia a warning glance. "Be careful. I'm not the only one who's asking uncomfortable questions."

Chapter 8

It was precisely eight o'clock the next morning when Lia climbed into her SUV to drive to the motel. Kaden didn't strike her as the sort of guy who would sleep until noon. Not with that barely leashed energy that hummed around him like a force field. But he was from the West Coast and he might not have adjusted to the time difference yet.

Plus, she had to wait for Della to arrive to watch the store.

Della Kramer had been a friend of Lia's mother and had worked at Porter's for over forty years. The older woman was widowed, with a son who rarely remembered to visit his mother. Lia considered her a part of her family and one of the many reasons she was determined to keep the store open. Della not only needed the income she earned, it gave her a reason to get up in the morning.

Lia pulled into the parking lot, realizing for once she'd had perfect timing. Kaden was not only up, he was also currently standing in an open doorway being handed a set of keys by a young man dressed in a pair of blue coveralls. Apparently, the rental company had gotten on the ball bright and early to bring the new black Jeep that was parked near the office.

She waited until the younger man had jumped into the

passenger seat of a waiting tow truck before she switched off the engine of the SUV and climbed out. The snow had stopped, but the lot hadn't been plowed and Lia was glad she'd been sensible enough to pull on a heavy pair of snow boots, along with her thick parka. The middle of winter was no time to worry about fashion. Even if she had spent yet another night fantasizing about Kaden Vaughn.

Closing a mental door on the delicious dreams that had kept her warm, Lia battled through the snow to stand in front of Kaden. He was wearing the same clothes as yesterday, but she caught the fresh scent of soap clinging to his skin, as if he'd just stepped out of the shower. Awareness tingled through her as her gaze lingered on the stubble that darkened his chiseled jawline. The shadow only added to his dangerous appeal.

With an effort, Lia forced her attention toward the shiny Jeep. "You should give your rental company five stars. I thought it would take them all day to get out here with a replacement."

"Me too. They must have been up at the crack of dawn." He shoved the keys he'd just received into the front pocket of his jeans. "I still need to stop by the courthouse to make an official police report for the insurance."

"One of the deputies can probably help."

"Let's hope." He stepped back. "Come in."

She stepped past him to enter the small room, her eyes widening. It wasn't so much the cheap furniture, which included a narrow bed and one dresser with a portable TV bolted to the top. This was Pike, not Beverly Hills. But she hadn't been prepared for the orange shag carpeting, or the wallpaper that had splotches of brown and green with big yellow flowers. Or the Styrofoam beams glued to the ceiling.

It all swirled together to create a psychedelic nightmare.

"Oh. This is . . ." Words failed her.

"Groovy?" Kaden supplied, closing the door to protect what little heat was in the room.

She turned to face him. "That's one way of putting it."

He glanced around. "Weirdly, it's not that bad to me. I have friends who've paid serious cash to get this retro vibe."

"Some people have too much money."

"No argument from me." He returned his attention to her with a curious expression. "Did you have a specific reason for stopping by?"

She reached into the pocket of her parka and pulled out a piece of paper. Unfolding it, she turned it so Kaden could see the list that was written on the back.

"I spent yesterday trying to locate these businesses."

He stilled, his body suddenly tense with anticipation. "Did you have any luck?"

"Yes and no."

"I'm not sure what that means."

Lia grimaced. She was nearly as confused as Kaden. She didn't consider herself an expert in business, but she'd acquired a few skills over the years. It was frustrating and more than a little baffling to spend so many hours only to hit one dead end after another.

At last, she concluded it couldn't be mere coincidence. There was a pattern that had to mean something.

"I discovered that each of the companies mentioned on this paper were legally incorporated."

"Okay."

"But none of them exist today."

"None of them?" He frowned, as if considering the likelihood of five separate companies with overseas bank accounts being shuttered in the local area. "Were they closed by Vanna?"

That had been her first thought as well. But a closure by the EPA would have made big news in such a small community. If nothing else, the companies would have hired lawyers to fight the penalties. She'd found nothing to indicate a problem.

"As far as I can figure out, each of these were shell companies with no tangible assets that were opened and shut down in less than a year."

"I thought shell companies were for avoiding taxes."

"Sometimes, or they can be used to hide assets during a divorce or a hostile merger." She ignored his curious gaze. Eventually, she might reveal that she was interested in more than a grocery store. Right now, they had more important things to discuss. "Unfortunately, I can't access the names of the owners or even the location of the businesses. They were all incorporated overseas."

"Damn." He stepped forward, taking the list from her hand. "I was hoping this might hold the answers."

The scent of warm skin and a tangy aftershave that clung to his clothes teased at her nose, sending shivers down her spine. Lia breathed in deeply, allowing herself to savor the sensation. It'd been a long time since she'd been so fiercely attracted to anyone.

No. She'd *never* been this attracted before.

"I was thinking last night." She was forced to halt and lick her lips. How did they get so dry? "And I have a theory."

"Tell me."

"I suspect the corporations were created to pay Vanna."

"Why would they need a shell company?"

That question was what had driven Lia crazy as she searched the Internet for hours. It just didn't make sense that a corporation would be opened and then closed just a few months later. Two of them had only been open a couple of weeks.

"At first, I considered the possibility that it was to hide the fact the company was in trouble with the EPA. Violating the environment is never good for public relations. Especially in an area where people depend on the land for their livelihood." She shrugged. "If they could pay the fine through a separate account, they might have hoped it wouldn't be traced back to them."

"But you don't think that's the answer?"

"If it was all legit, I should have been able to find something online that showed the payment had been made to the EPA. Plus, your brother would have the reports listing the violations Vanna discovered, along with the paperwork for the penalties. Even if he hadn't noticed them while he was working with the EPA, it's in the public domain and his private detectives would easily have located them."

He shook his head. "I didn't see anything in the files."

She hadn't seen anything either when she glanced through the stacks of papers Kaden had shared with her. There had been a few minor violations that were cited, with a date for the company to make the necessary changes to prove they were compliant. And even a couple of tickets handed out to two separate landfills had been paid. But nothing in the amounts that were written on the back of the map.

"That's what makes me suspect the payments were made off the record."

"Off the record?" It took Kaden a second to realize what she was implying. Then he flinched. "Bribes?"

Lia held up her hands in a silent apology. "I'm sorry. I know Vanna was going to be part of your family."

"No." He made a sound of impatience. "I mean, yes, she was engaged to my brother, but there's no need to apologize. Honestly, I never liked her."

Lia was caught off guard by his blunt confession. "Why not?"

He answered without hesitation. "She seemed shallow. When they visited me in Hollywood, all she could talk about was her new Porsche and flash around the diamond ring that must have cost my brother a fortune. I even said something to Darren about her obsession with material things."

"He didn't mind?"

"Darren was convinced it was a result of being raised in a series of foster homes. He said she constantly needed to prove to herself that she'd succeeded despite her rough childhood." Kaden scowled, making no effort to disguise his opinion of his soon-to-be sister-in-law. "He also swore that beneath her hard exterior was a soft heart. If that was true, she kept it well hidden."

Lia would always feel sympathy for the woman she'd seen climb onto the railroad bridge and jump. She'd obviously been driven by some intense emotion. But assuming it had been Vanna Zimmerman, Kaden's impression of a money-hungry woman would fit into her theory of bribery.

"She had a Porsche? On a government salary?"

He nodded, easily following the direction of her thoughts. "Yeah. I wondered at the time if Darren had bought it for her, but he said she had it before they met."

"My guess is she was making money on the side."

Kaden abruptly turned, pacing across the cramped space as he considered what Lia had told him. He didn't look upset, but there was a tightness to his features that suggested part of him was disappointed to discover Vanna was as ruthless as he'd always feared. Or maybe he was wishing his brother had never gotten involved with her.

Finally, he turned back to face her, his disappointment replaced with a grim determination.

"If she was using her power as an EPA inspector to blackmail local businesses, that might explain why no one wants her identified." He deliberately paused. "Including the mayor."

Lia slowly nodded. "It would certainly be awkward."

"It might be more than awkward."

He didn't have to spell out his suspicion that whoever was being blackmailed had murdered Vanna. Either to hide the evidence of their violations or to avoid paying the bribe. Or both.

An ancient regret sliced through her heart. "I can't wrap my mind around the thought I might have seen Vanna running from her killer."

"And that whoever killed her is still in town."

Lia shivered at his blunt words. If it was hard to imagine she'd seen Vanna in the final moments of her life fifteen years ago, it was even more difficult to imagine the person who'd murdered her was still walking the streets.

It didn't matter that Pike had recently endured a rash of murders. The deaths hadn't touched Lia on a personal level. Those horrible crimes happened to other people, right? She lived a quiet, simple life; how could she be touched by darkness?

Lia shoved her hands into the pockets of her parka, battling back the surge of genuine fear. She was going to be totally freaked out if she allowed her imagination to run wild.

"You know, it's still possible the bones don't belong to Vanna Zimmerman and we're jumping to conclusions about what any of this means," she forced herself to remind him.

He jutted his jaw to a stubborn angle. "My slashed tires indicate we aren't too far from the truth."

She didn't have a comeback for that. With a grimace, she headed for the door. "I should get back to the store."

"Are you there alone?"

She sent him a startled glance. Was he worried about her?

"No, Della will be there all morning. And I think Wayne plans to come in later this afternoon."

"Good."

Lia pretended she didn't feel a warm glow at his concern. She'd been taking care of herself for a long time.

"Are you headed back to Madison?"

"Actually, I think I might stay around for a few days," he surprised her by saying. "I have some questions I want answered."

Something fluttered in the pit of her stomach. Lia told herself it was unease as she left the motel room, even if it did feel perilously close to anticipation.

Kaden placed his hands flat on the Formica countertop, leaning forward to glare at the middle-aged man in disbelief. He'd strolled into the small office that smelled of coffee, cigarettes, and musty carpeting with every confidence he'd quickly have his room for another night.

He'd rung the silver bell and watched the manager step out of a back room, waving his hand as if hoping to hide the smoke from the cigarette he'd just stubbed out. Once he noticed who had entered the office, however, the man appeared less than happy. In fact, there'd been an obvious reluctance as he moved to stand behind the counter.

Kaden assumed the sour expression the manager's narrow face was caused by being caught sneaking a cigarette. Instead, he gruffly informed Kaden there was no possibility of extending his stay.

Now Kaden allowed his gaze to run down the man's dress shirt and slacks, which hung loosely on his gaunt frame before, returning to study the deeply lined face. He didn't look like he was joking, but Kaden refused to accept he was serious.

"What do you mean, there aren't any rooms?" he demanded.

The manager hunched his shoulders. "We're fully booked through the holidays."

Kaden deliberately glanced out the window at the empty parking lot. "There's no one here."

"It's early."

"Fine." Kaden had no way of knowing whether or not there was a busload of visitors about to descend on Pike. With an effort, he turned back to the man with a tight smile. "I'll stay in . . ." He furrowed his brow as he struggled to recall the name of any nearby towns. He drew a blank. "Can you give me directions to the nearest hotel?"

The man shifted from foot to foot, his jaw twitching as if he was struggling to come up with an answer to what should have been a simple question.

"It's a busy time of year," he finally burst out. "I doubt you'll find any rooms available in the area. In fact . . ." He paused, then cleared a lump from his throat. "I'm almost certain of it."

Okay. This had gone from suspicious to outright unbelievable. There was no way in hell every hotel room in the area was suddenly filled with eager guests. Unfortunately, there was no way he could force the man to let him stay. And there seemed little point in driving around the county hoping he could find a place. Someone was going to a lot of effort to get rid of him.

He ground his teeth together. "Astonishing."

"Best you go back to Madison."

With a shake of his head, Kaden headed out of the office. "So much for small-town hospitality."

He climbed into the Jeep and started the engine. It had the smell of a new vehicle and he wryly wondered if whoever had put out the word that he was unwelcome in Pike had also contacted the rental company to replace his vehicle at record speed.

But then, if that was the case, why slash his tires in the first place?

None of it made any sense.

Absently latching his seat belt, Kaden reversed out of the parking lot and headed toward the center of town. If he was going to have to return to Madison today, he needed to fill out the police report before leaving town. They were forecasting more snow tonight and it might be a couple of days before he could get back.

He turned onto Main Street, passing the pretty park that was layered in snow that shimmered in the morning sunlight and the storefront windows that were brightly decorated for the holidays. Even annoyed with the local innkeeper and whoever was trying to force him out of town, he couldn't deny he found the place oddly charming. There was a sense of home that even an outsider could appreciate.

Swerving to park next to the curb, Kaden climbed out of the Jeep and headed up the stairs. There was a real possibility he was in a no-parking zone, but the snow was plowed high enough to hide any signs and what he couldn't see couldn't hurt him, right? And honestly, it was too damned cold to worry about a ticket.

Halting at the front door, Kaden pressed the intercom and waited to be buzzed in. A couple of minutes later, he was standing in the reception area of the sheriff's office.

There was no one seated at the front desk, but at his

entrance, a familiar deputy in a brown uniform appeared through a side door. What was his name? Anthony? Yes, that was it.

The deputy halted next to the desk, eyeing Kaden with mild curiosity. "You're back."

"Like a bad penny."

"We haven't heard anything from the medical examiner if that's why you're here."

Kaden shook his head. "I need to report a vandalism."

Anthony blinked, as if he'd never heard the word before. And maybe he hadn't. At least not in an official capacity.

"Seriously?"

"My tires were slashed yesterday."

"Damn. Did you see who did it?"

"No. I was parked in the alley behind Porter's Grocery Store."

"Sorry 'bout that." Anthony pulled out the chair of the desk and sat down to tap his password into the computer. "When school's out, stuff like that happens. Kids have too much time on their hands. It shouldn't take long to fill out the form." He searched through the computer to pull up the necessary screen before glancing up at Kaden. "Is Kaden Vaughn your real name?"

Kaden nodded. He'd never considered the possibility his job as a stuntman would make him famous or that he might want to use a stage name. Anthony typed it into the computer.

"Address?" Kaden parted his lips to answer, but before he could say anything there was a loud ring and Anthony reached for the landline on the desk. "I have to take this," he muttered, pressing the receiver to his ear. "Sheriff's office." Anthony frowned as he listened to whoever was on the other end of the line. "Wait. Slow down. An accident?"

Anthony shoved himself to his feet. "Where?" He made a choked sound. "Did you say Judge Armstrong? Is he hurt?" Anthony grimaced. Obviously, the news wasn't good for Judge Armstrong. "No. Don't touch him. I'm calling the ambulance and I'll be there in a few minutes." Anthony disconnected the caller before he punched in a number and waited for the other person to answer. "Britt, we need the ambulance at Judge Armstrong's place. ASAP." He once again disconnected, tossing the receiver on the base as he rounded the desk and headed for the coatrack in the corner. "I gotta go."

"Is there a problem?"

"Judge Armstrong slammed his car into the back of his garage." Anthony pulled on a thick brown coat and his cap with the sheriff logo. "Damned fool should have had his license taken away years ago."

"Is he hurt?"

Anthony scowled, as if realizing he was saying more than he should. "Wait here. Monel will be back in a few minutes to finish the report."

"No problem."

Kaden watched the deputy scurry out of the office with a narrowed gaze. It was an effort not to race after the man. He wasn't sure why. An accident involving some unknown judge had nothing to do with him or his reason for being in the courthouse, but he couldn't deny an urgent desire to find out exactly what happened.

Impatiently tapping his fingers on the edge of the desk, Kaden forced himself to wait for Monel to saunter out of the break room with a doughnut and coffee in her hands. Thankfully, Anthony had been right about the form. It didn't take more than ten minutes to complete and with his task finished, Kaden headed out of the courthouse and jumped in his Jeep.

It wasn't until he pulled away from the curb and headed down the street that he realized he'd already made the decision of where he was going. He needed help. And he knew exactly who to ask.

He was parked in the back alley when he heard the sirens screaming down Main Street. Leaving the Jeep running, he crossed the short distance to knock on the back door of Porter's Grocery Store. It didn't occur to him that Lia might be in the front, dealing with customers, or in her office with the door closed. Not until a minute ticked past, and then another. Just when he was about to return to his Jeep and drive around to the public entrance, the door was pulled open to reveal Lia.

She was wearing a casual pair of jeans and a red cable-knit sweater with a white snowflake on the front. Her short hair was spiky, as if she'd been running her hands through it, and her green eyes were bright with curiosity as she stared at him. A growl rumbled in his chest.

She looked like a sexy elf he'd very much like to find on his shelf.

"Kaden," she murmured.

He skipped over the pleasantries. "Something's happened. Get your coat."

Chapter 9

Lia had no idea why she readily obeyed Kaden Vaughn's command to get her coat. Maybe because she was intrigued by what had happened. Or because she was bored with her latest research. Or because she simply wanted to spend more time in his company.

Whatever the reason, she didn't hesitate. Plucking her coat from the peg, she hurried into the store to tell Della she would be gone for a while and then grabbed her purse before she stepped out of the back door to join Kaden in the alley. It wasn't until he started moving toward his Jeep that she dug in her heels.

"I can drive."

He glanced over his shoulder with a wry smile. "You're going to have to trust me at some point."

It wasn't a matter of trust. He was a professional driver who had far more experience than she did behind the wheel. She just didn't want to be a passenger. Not when it meant allowing someone else to determine where they were going, how long they would be gone, and if anyone else was going to join them.

Control issues . . .

That's what her last boyfriend claimed, and Lia hadn't argued.

Kaden continued toward his Jeep and, swallowing a sigh, Lia grudgingly followed. It didn't make any sense to insist on taking her SUV. She had no idea where they were going and his Jeep was already running. Climbing into the passenger seat, she slammed shut the door and pulled on her seat belt.

"You see, that wasn't so hard."

She glanced toward him, meeting his teasing smile. "If you end up in a ditch, I can promise you that Wayne will have it posted all over the Internet."

He didn't appear particularly worried. "I'll keep that in mind."

He put the Jeep in gear and drove to the end of the alley.

"Where are we going?" she asked.

"Judge Armstrong's home. I hope you know where it's located."

"Turn left." She studied his profile, absently noting it was perfectly sculpted. Like everything else about him. "Why are we going there?"

"I was at the courthouse when a call came in saying the judge had driven his car through the back of his garage."

Lia sucked in a sharp breath. "Oh no. Was he hurt?"

"I'm not sure, but it sounded pretty serious."

"That's terrible." She paused. It was awful to think the older man had been injured, but she'd never been very close to the judge. In truth, she didn't really like him. "Why are we going there?"

His jaw tightened. "Right now, I'm not willing to accept anything is a random accident."

"Okay, but honestly, Judge Armstrong is seventy years old and a terrible driver." She'd seen the man take out a mailbox, back into a dumpster, and nearly destroy the local bakery when he put his car in Drive instead of Reverse. He never slowed until he smashed into the building. "Even when the streets aren't covered in ice."

"It's probably a waste of time, but I think we should check it out."

"Okay." Lia shivered at the sound of sirens that echoed through the streets. They were becoming all too familiar. "Take another left at the corner. We'll circle around to the back. I'd rather not get trapped by the inevitable gawkers."

He nodded, turning onto the narrow dirt path that would lead to the empty lot behind the judge's house. Years ago, there'd been a laundromat, but the judge had the place condemned and torn down when he built his new house.

Parking the Jeep next to the curb, they climbed out of the vehicle and headed toward the massive brick home.

Kaden muttered a curse as he struggled through the snow that was up to his knees. "Good thing I bought some decent boots."

She wisely followed his trail. There was no use in both of them forging a path through the heavy drifts.

"The judge's house is built on a dead-end street. It will be packed with emergency vehicles, not to mention half the town wanting to discover what's happened. This will be the easiest way to get close."

He nodded as they neared the large, built-in pool that was covered with a tarp and the patio edged with an outdoor kitchen, complete with a brick pizza oven. It looked like a home you would find in Hollywood, not Pike, Wisconsin. His attention, however, appeared to be on the pristine blanket of snow that covered everything in sight.

"No one's been back here," he said.

"Not since it snowed," she agreed.

"Does the judge live alone?"

"Yes. As far as I know, he never married." She paused.

"And I don't remember him dating anyone from around here. Which is kind of weird." Until that moment, Lia had never realized how secretive the judge was about his private life.

"Is he retired?"

"Just recently." The entire town had furtively celebrated when Judge Armstrong stepped down from the bench. "Unfortunately, he's still the president of the Chamber of Commerce for Pike."

"A man with some influence."

"And good buddies with the mayor."

"Interesting."

"Kaden."

Without thought, she reached out to grab his arm, nodding toward the paramedics she could see pushing a gurney toward the ambulance that was parked at the side of the house. Even from a distance she could see the body was zipped in a bag. That could only mean one thing.

"He's dead." Kaden spoke the words out loud.

"Looks that way."

He gently tugged his arm out of her clinging grip, his expression grim. "I'm going to try to get closer. If you want to wait in the Jeep—"

"No," she interrupted. "I'm going with you."

He looked like he wanted to argue. Instead, he shrugged as he glanced back at the house.

"Fair warning. I have no idea what I'm hoping to find."

"Me either."

Together, they waded their way past the pool and stepped onto the patio. Then, circling around the massive, built-in BBQ and pizza oven, they at last had a clear view of the back of the garage.

"Yikes." Lia's eyes widened at the sight of the busted wall and bricks smashed on the ground. The front of the

Cadillac was peeking through the carnage, revealing the shattered windshield and crumpled bumper.

"Damn." Kaden looked shocked at the gaping hole in the garage. "He must have had his foot fully on the gas to cause that kind of damage."

Lia had to admit it was a lot worse than she was expecting. Dozens of people in town had fender benders during the winter. It was impossible not to occasionally slide on the ice. But this was a violent collision that had taken a lot of force. She struggled to imagine what could possibly have happened.

"If the snow drifted across his driveway, he might have gotten stuck and gunned the engine to get out," she offered at last. It was a lame explanation, but it was the only one she had.

"Possibly." He looked dubious. Lia didn't blame him. "Let's take a look out front."

Kaden walked toward the corner of the house, where the ambulance was backing out. He paused, as if waiting for the vehicle to disappear before he continued. It wasn't until Lia was standing next to him that she realized he was watching the two men who appeared from the front of the house.

Anthony was in his deputy's uniform and Tate Erickson was in an expensive wool trench coat and fur cap. The mayor had a hold of Anthony's arm as he pulled the younger man to a spot out of sight of the gathered crowd.

Kaden sent her a quick glance, waiting for her to nod in understanding, before they crept forward to hide behind a fir tree loaded with Christmas lights. It was close enough to overhear the conversation between the men.

"Stop arguing, Anthony," Tate was saying, his voice edgy and his narrow face flushed. "Just write the report like I told you."

"I know what I saw," Anthony stubbornly insisted.

"What you saw was an old man who hit the gas when he should have hit the brakes and smashed into the back of his garage. It happens. Hell, the judge did it before. Don't you remember the bakery? He took out the front window."

"Why wasn't he wearing a seat belt?" Anthony demanded. "And why was his airbag switched off?"

Kaden and Lia exchanged a silent glance. Anthony clearly didn't believe the judge's death was a random accident.

"Because he thought he was above the laws he enforced on everyone else," Tate snapped. "You know that better than me. How many times did you complain he parked in handicapped spots without the proper tags?"

Anthony folded his arms over his chest. "He looked like he'd been beaten."

"He was just in a car wreck, for Christ's sake."

"I still say it should be investigated. That's what Zac would do."

Lia silently applauded Anthony's dogged determination to stand his ground. And the deputy was right. If Zac Evans were here, the sheriff's office would be investigating a lot of stuff. Starting with her belief that she'd seen a woman jump from the railroad bridge fifteen years ago to Kaden's insistence the skeleton was Vanna Zimmerman to this latest accident.

"Zac isn't here and I'm in charge."

"It should be investigated."

Tate stomped his feet, his gaze flicking toward the nearby house, as if searching for inspiration. Then, a strange smile twisted his lips.

"Listen, Anthony, I didn't want to share this with anyone until I had a chance to decide what to do."

"Share what?"

"Leon came to see me yesterday."

Anthony frowned, as if it took him a second to recognize

that Leon was the dead man's first name. Everyone in town called him "Judge."

"He came to the office?" he at last asked.

"No, he called and wanted to meet at my house. He said he wanted privacy to tell me something."

"What was it?" There was a long silence. "Well?" Anthony prompted.

The mayor cleared his throat, glancing from side to side before he spoke. "He confessed that he hit that boy. What's his name? The one with no neck?"

"Drew Hurst?" Anthony hesitantly offered.

"Yes." Tate snapped his fingers. "That's the one. Leon said he hit him and drove away."

Anthony's mouth hung open as he visibly struggled to accept what the mayor was saying. Lia was battling the same stunned sense of disbelief. Of all the things she thought the mayor might say, that was at the very bottom of the list.

"Judge Armstrong hit Drew Hurst with his car and drove away," Anthony said, as if he needed the words repeated.

Tate shrugged. "He told me that he slid on the ice and didn't even see the kid until it was too late. A tragic accident." He shrugged again. "Unfortunately, he panicked, and instead of staying to face the consequences, he returned to his house and tried to pretend it didn't happen."

Anthony's brow furrowed, a sudden anger tightening his features. "Why didn't you arrest him?"

"Don't be ridiculous. He's an old friend and a respected member of this community."

"If what you just said is true, he nearly killed Drew and then fled the scene of a crime."

Tate clicked his tongue, as if to indicate that Anthony was completely overreacting to the situation.

"I was in the process of negotiating for him to turn himself in. It would have been fine."

"It's not fine," Anthony growled. "You don't negotiate with criminals. You handcuff them and drag their ass to jail."

Tate squared his shoulders, clearly annoyed by his deputy's refusal to concede he'd done what was necessary. But instead of a cutting response, the mayor glanced toward the house and heaved a dramatic sigh. "I'm the acting sheriff; I took care of the matter as I thought best. I never dreamed he would . . ."

"He would what?" Anthony asked.

Tate waved his hand in a vague motion. "End things like this."

Anthony's eyes widened. "You're . . .you're saying he rammed his car on purpose?"

"Why else would he take off his seat belt and make sure the airbag wouldn't work? Clearly he couldn't bear the shame of what he'd done." The mayor released his hold on Anthony and stepped back. He was obviously done with the conversation. "Still, we can't be sure what happened. Or why. Just write the report to say it was an accident. It's the best ending for everyone."

"But . . ."

"Do it."

Anthony's protest died on his lips as Tate disappeared around the front corner of the house. For a second, the deputy stood staring into space, as if debating how to handle the latest debacle the sheriff had tossed in his lap. Then, with shoulders stooped with weariness, Anthony trudged in the direction of the street.

Waiting until both men were out of earshot, Lia slowly shook her head. "I can't believe Judge Armstrong ran over Drew."

Kaden turned to send her a puzzled glance. "You did say he was an awful driver."

"Yes, but . . ."

"Something's bothering you."

He was right, but it took Lia a second to sort through her tangled thoughts and pinpoint her unease.

"The mayor was right when he said the judge considered himself above the law." She battled through her reluctance to speak ill of the dead. Midwest manners weren't nearly as important as a potential murder. Besides, the man hadn't earned the right when he was alive to be treated with respect after his death. "He never paid his city taxes, he ruled on cases where he had a clear conflict of interest, and he put 'no trespassing' signs on public land so he would have a private place to hunt. There were even rumors that he shot stray dogs."

Kaden snorted. "Sounds like a classy guy."

"He was an arrogant bully, but he wasn't a coward." Lia could easily picture the judge losing control of his car and hitting an innocent trespasser. That could happen to anyone. But she could never imagine the man being so racked with guilt that he couldn't bear to continue living. No way. "If he'd hit Drew, he would have stayed and dared anyone to blame him," she explained. "Not only that, he would also have convinced everyone in town it had been entirely Drew's fault. The Hursts don't have any power or money and Drew has been in and out of trouble since he was a young boy. Most of the sympathy in town would have gone to Judge Armstrong."

Kaden's jaw tightened, easily following her line of reasoning. "And if he didn't have any fear of repercussions, why kill himself?"

"Exactly." She shuddered as the wind whipped around the corner of the house. "So why did the mayor lie?"

"Let's ask him."

Chapter 10

Not for the first time, Kaden was happy he'd followed his intuition to find out more about the accident. It was the same intuition that had urged him to leave Wisconsin and head out west. And, eventually, to leave Hollywood to open his business in Vegas.

Of course, suspecting Judge Armstrong's death was no accident didn't mean it had anything to do with Vanna. He was guessing the older man had managed to acquire a number of enemies over the years. Many of them right here in Pike. And even if it was connected to the fifteen-year-old murder, he still had no idea who was behind the crimes.

Keeping close to the house, Kaden battled his way to the front of the garage. There was no way to be graceful in the thick snow, but at least he didn't fall on his ass. He was taking that as a win.

At last reaching his destination, he peeked around the corner, not surprised to find a crowd gathered in the street. It was human nature to be curious about what was happening. Especially in a place where everyone knew everyone. He turned his attention to the deputy who was keeping people from trespassing on the property. It wasn't Anthony.

This man looked as if he was barely out of high school, with a spotted face and a nervous expression.

He frowned, wondering if the mayor had already managed to slip away, when he caught sight of him approaching a couple of teenagers who were standing on the sidewalk. Assuming he was going to urge them to leave, Kaden sucked in a shocked breath when Tate reached out to shove the boy wearing a letter jacket, knocking him off balance. Next, he grabbed the young girl by the arm and tugged her toward his shiny black car, which was parked in the middle of the street.

Kaden glanced toward Lia, who was standing next to him. "What was that about?"

"Sunny is his daughter. He doesn't want her dating Cord Walsh."

"Cord." Kaden recognized the name. "The boy who found the body?"

"Yes."

"I want to talk to him."

Knowing there was no point in urging Lia to return to the Jeep to wait for him, Kaden crossed the front yard toward the boy. At the moment, Cord was distracted as he glared at the black car backing down the street. Good. It made it simple to pretend this was nothing more than a chance encounter.

The snow crunched loud enough to attract the boy's attention as Kaden passed along the sidewalk. On cue, Cord rushed to stand directly in his path.

"Dude," he breathed, a puff of mist forming in the frigid air. "You're Kaden Vaughn."

"I am."

"Awesome." The boy bounced from foot to foot, unable to contain his excitement. "I'm a huge fan. When you flipped your bike over that fountain in Vegas . . ." His words trailed away as if he was too overwhelmed to speak. "Man. Epic."

The jump had been arranged to celebrate the opening of Money Makers as well as a spectacular ending to his career as a stuntman. It'd been one of his biggest, most elaborate jumps, and when it was over, Kaden had accepted that he was well and truly done with the surge of adrenaline and the screaming crowds that had once driven him.

He'd reached the age when he didn't want to face death on a daily basis.

Still, he was willing to use his fame from the event to get Cord chatting.

"Thanks. A lot of people worked to make the stunt a success."

"Just you on the bike, though." The teenager stuck out his hand in an awkward motion. "I'm Cord, by the way. Cord Walsh."

"Cord." Kaden shook the offered hand, lifting his brow, as if surprised by the name. "Oh right. I think Wayne Neilson mentioned you when he was telling me about finding the skeleton near the railroad tracks."

"Crazy, right?"

"You were the one to find it?"

"Yep." The boy coughed, shifting from foot to foot. He looked nervous. Was it because he was still bothered by finding the skeleton? Or was it because he was talking to a famous television star? "We were sledding down the hill when Drew blasted through a patch of thornbushes. I thought he screamed because he was hurt. It wasn't until I ran down there that I saw the bones."

Kaden nodded, as if fascinated by the story. "Tell me about them."

"Just bones, man." He forced a shaky laugh. "And a skull staring up at us without any eyes. Creepy."

"Did it have on clothes?"

"Oh, yeah. It did. A leather jacket. Everything else had just . . ." Cord waved his hands as if there'd been a tiny explosion. "Poof."

Kaden studied the boy. Cord was trying to act casual, but there was a brittle tension just beneath the surface. A part of Kaden knew he should walk away. It didn't matter that the kid was eighteen and legally an adult. It felt like he was manipulating him.

Then again, if there was someone out there willing to hurt, and even murder, to keep their secrets, how could he not do whatever was necessary to get the answers? Cord might very well be in danger.

"And there was nothing else laying around the area?"

"I didn't really look. Drew went back down with Wayne, but I'd seen enough." Cord shuddered, his face paling at the memory. "I could show you where we found the bones, but I doubt there's anything left behind."

"No. That's okay." Kaden conceded. If Cord had any information about the skeleton, he wasn't going to share. Time to try a different tactic. "I was just curious."

"Is that why you're in town?"

Kaden flashed a meaningless smile. "It's personal reasons."

"Oh." A hint of curiosity rippled over the boy's face. "Okay."

"Nice to meet you, Cord." With a nod, Kaden stepped forward, as if he intended to continue down the sidewalk, only to abruptly halt. "Oh. I almost forgot. I found this." Reaching into the pocket of his coat, Kaden pulled out the pocketknife and held it toward the boy. "Maybe you'll recognize it so I can return it to its owner."

Cord grabbed the knife out of his hand before Kaden

could stop him, holding it up as he studied the faux wood handle. "This is Drew's."

Kaden narrowed his eyes. He'd expected Cord to deny any knowledge of the knife. Instead, he'd quickly identified it. Too quickly?

"Drew Hurst? You're sure?"

"Positive. His dad gave it to him when he was a kid." Cord pointed toward the gold end cap. "Drew engraved his initials. See?" Kaden leaned forward to detect the faint scratches in the gold. He supposed they might have been a "D" and a "H." "He never went anywhere without it," Cord continued, lifting his head to meet Kaden's suspicious gaze. "Where did you find it?"

"In the alley behind Porter's Grocery Store."

"Seriously?" Cord shook his head, as if baffled by Kaden's answer. "What was it doing there?"

"I'm assuming it must have dropped out of his pocket," Kaden smoothly lied.

If Cord was responsible, he'd know exactly what the knife was doing there. If not . . . Kaden didn't want to give away why he was interested. Not until he could identify the culprit.

"Oh, I remember. He said he'd found something and he wanted to—" Cord snapped his lips together, as if he regretted his words.

"Wanted to what?"

"Nothing. Just that he had some stuff to take care of."

"Did it have anything to do with the skeleton?"

Cord's face flushed. Either Drew had found something that was connected to the skeleton or Cord was more cunning than he appeared.

"I really gotta get home and help my dad with the chores." Cord nodded toward the knife. "I can take this to

Drew if you want. I'm heading back to the hospital later today."

"That's okay." Kaden plucked the knife out of the boy's hand before he could shove it in his pocket. He had an unshakable feeling Cord intended to toss the small weapon into the nearest dumpster. Guilt? Fear? Protecting someone else? "I can take it to his family," Kaden assured him.

"No problem." Cord waved his hand in an uncomfortable motion as he backed away. "See ya around."

Kaden watched as the boy turned to hurry down the street, his hands shoved in the pockets of his letter jacket and his head bent forward as he battled against the stiff breeze.

"If that's Drew's knife, someone else used it to slash your tires," Lia said from directly behind him.

Kaden turned to face her. She was right. Drew had been lying unconscious in the hospital when his tires were being destroyed.

"Did it seem like Cord was being cagey?"

She nodded in agreement. "But why? Because he's guilty?"

"Or he knows who is."

Lia parted her lips, but before she could speak a gust of wind scooped up the snow coating the yard and swirled it through the air. The tiny tornadoes hit them with icy pellets that made Lia shiver.

"Let's get out of the cold."

"Good idea."

Kaden led the way past the swelling crowd of gawkers toward the side of the house and around to the backyard. He might return to snoop around after the crowd had wandered away, but for now he needed to get the blood flowing again. It felt as if it'd been frozen in his veins, leaving his toes and the tips of his fingers completely numb. Never a good thing.

They didn't speak until they were back in the Jeep with the heater blasting on high. Carefully, Kaden backed onto the frozen street and headed toward the grocery store. He hadn't forgotten Lia's warning that Wayne would have his picture plastered all over the Internet if he ended up in a ditch. She'd been teasing, but he had enough pride to want to avoid that humiliating fate.

"Now what?" Lia asked once he hit Main Street.

"I'll drop you off at your store and then I'm not sure," he admitted. "I've been kicked out of my hotel."

"Kicked out?" She repeated his words as if she thought he was joking. When he didn't laugh, she stared at him in confusion. "Why?"

"Apparently, the owner is expecting a mad rush of holiday guests."

"In Pike?"

"That's what he claimed."

She snorted in disbelief, proving he'd been right to question the sincerity of the manager's refusal to offer him a room.

"There might be a few visitors for Christmas, but I wouldn't call it a mad rush. More like a slow trickle."

"Not only is the motel full, but there's not one room available in the entire county," he continued.

"That's impossible."

He sent her a quick glance as they passed by the park. She was truly baffled.

"I'm guessing it's deliberate. Someone doesn't want me hanging around town."

Kaden didn't mention the mayor, although Tate Erickson was the obvious choice. He would have enough leverage to force the local businesses to do what he wanted, and he was obviously reluctant to have anyone digging into the past. But while he wasn't a real investigator, Kaden knew it would be a mistake to leap to conclusions. It was always possible it was someone else pulling the strings.

Lia seemed to agree as she turned the conversation away from who was responsible for the change in his plans.

"What are you going to do?"

"I'll drive to a few of the nearby towns. There has to be at least one hotel that isn't overrun with guests."

Lia hesitated; then her words came out in a short burst. "If it's just for a night or two, you can crash at my place."

Blindsided by the offer, Kaden pulled into the alley and parked behind Lia's SUV. This was a conversation he wanted to have face-to-face. Not only because he feared she felt obligated to make the offer but because he needed to be sure he could accept without making an idiot of himself.

He couldn't explain the intensity of his attraction to Lia. Without false modesty, he knew he could have his pick of women. Hundreds, sometimes thousands, sent him messages through social media on a daily basis. But he'd never experienced such an immediate sense of connection. Not with anyone.

The thought of staying beneath the same roof was creating all sorts of dangerous fantasies.

Unlocking his safety belt, he turned in his seat. "I wouldn't want to intrude."

"You wouldn't be." She offered a stiff smile. "I live above the store, but I have a bedroom attached to my office with a full bath. It's pretty cramped, but it's a place to sleep."

He quashed the tiny pang of disappointment they would be on separate floors, sternly reminding himself that they were virtual strangers. He was lucky she trusted him enough to let him stay in the same building.

"That's quite an office you have," he teased, letting her

know he didn't see her offer as anything more than kindness toward a stranded traveler.

Her tension seemed to fade as she accepted she hadn't made a huge mistake.

"I had the rooms upstairs opened into a studio apartment, which is great when I'm on my own, but it makes it awkward when my mother and her new husband come to stay."

"You don't like her husband?"

She blinked in surprise at his question. "I like him very much. My mother devoted her life to taking care of me and keeping a roof over my head when I was young. I was thrilled when she started taking bus tours to see the country. She'd never been out of this area before then. And I was even more thrilled when Everett started to join her on the tours. He loves to travel and read and cook. All the stuff my mom loves."

There was no doubting the sincerity in her voice and Kaden hid a wry smile. His own parents had been . . . a challenge. His father was a violent drunk and his mother had abandoned ship when he was still a kid. She'd randomly show up, bringing presents and promising they could come and live with her just as soon as she got settled. Both he and his brother knew it was a lie, but a part of him had harbored a futile hope.

"Where are your mother and stepfather now?"

"Everett bought a cottage in Colorado where they spend most of their time. But he also has an RV they take to Arizona during the winter months."

Kaden glanced toward the sky, which was beginning to cloud over with the threat of more snow.

"Smart man."

"Mom does insist on flying home to make sure I'm taking care of myself." She rolled her eyes, as if being able to take care of herself was a running joke between her and her mother. A sure sign they were close. "And it's nice for them to have some privacy when they stay with me."

He studied her delicate features. She'd gone to a lot of trouble to make sure her mom was comfortable, but he suspected it wasn't just for the older woman.

"And for *you* to have some privacy."

"That too."

"Will they be home for Christmas?"

"Not until the end of December. Everett has a son who lives in Denver, with three small kids. They want to be there when Santa brings their presents."

"Ah. The magical pull of grandbabies."

She nodded. "Exactly."

"So what do you do for Christmas?"

Her tension returned at his casual question. As if she didn't like to discuss the holidays.

"I volunteer to help serve dinner at the local shelter in Grange." She shrugged. "And I have friends who invite me to their parties. I'm never alone."

"But you can leave whenever you want, right?"

She frowned, instantly on the defensive. "Are you implying something?"

He reached out to brush his finger down her cheek. "Just that we have a lot in common, Lia Porter."

Chapter 11

Lia's mouth was suddenly as dry as the Sahara Desert. What prompted her to offer her spare room? She'd been raised with good manners, but Kaden Vaughn was a virtual stranger. Her mother would be horrified if she found out.

Of course, he wasn't actually staying in the loft, and she could lock the door at the bottom of the stairs, along with her bedroom door if she was worried. And honestly, she wasn't. Not at all.

She had no idea why she felt as if she'd known this man her entire life. As if she'd sensed he was out there and she'd been waiting for the moment he would arrive and change her world.

Shoving away the strange and frankly scary sensations, Lia glanced out the passenger window toward the sky that was slowly being obscured by a bank of low, sullen clouds.

"Do you want to come in now?" she asked.

He sent her a quick smile, patting his stomach. "I think I'll grab some lunch first. That pizza you suggested from Bella's was delicious, but it's long gone."

"I have some chili in my slow cooker. There's plenty if you want some."

The offer escaped before she could halt the words. Just

like they'd done when she asked him to stay in her spare bedroom. Had her mouth disconnected from her brain?

"It sounds perfect."

He was pushing open his door and was out of the Jeep before she could change her mind. She followed behind, silently telling herself it was too late for regrets.

Not that the flutters in the pit of her stomach felt like regret. Just the opposite. They were perilously close to excitement.

She reached into her purse to pull out her keys, unlocking the back door and stepping into the hallway. Then, shuffling for yet another key, she unlocked the door that led to the narrow steps heading to her private apartment.

Taking the lead, she climbed the stairs, which creaked in protest. Thankfully, the wood-planked floor, which she'd had refurbished at the same time she'd removed most of the walls, was sturdy and there were no embarrassing squeaks or moans as she led Kaden through the living room to the kitchen.

"Nice." Kaden pulled off his heavy coat, placing it on the back of her worn sofa as he turned in a slow circle. "I had my place built into a loft above my shop. I like the feeling of space. Plus, it's convenient."

She slid off her own coat and tossed it on the counter. "Sometimes too convenient."

"No crap."

The dry edge in his voice assured her that he was all too familiar with the urge to spend an extra hour working in the evening. Or using the early morning hours to take care of tedious tasks instead of enjoying a cup of coffee.

Kaden had said they had a lot in common, and maybe they did. Hard as it was to believe.

She waved a hand toward the small kitchen table. "Have a seat."

Lia busied herself with grabbing two bowls and scooping out the chili she'd put into the Crock-Pot the night before. She never knew when she was going to have time to eat. It made sense to have something ready and waiting. It wasn't like they had fast-food places all over town even if she did want something easy.

Placing the bowls and silverware on the table, she poured two large glasses of ice-cold water and grabbed a crusty loaf of bread she'd bought at the local bakery.

At last, she settled in a seat across the table from Kaden, watching as he bent forward to take a deep sniff of the bowl in front of him.

"It smells delicious."

"I hope you like it spicy."

He glanced up, his eyes a smoky gray as he allowed a wicked smile to curve his lips. "Is there any other way?"

Awareness sizzled in the air, hotter than any peppers in her chili. For a breathless moment, Lia savored the tingly sensations. Why not? It wasn't like tall, dark, deliciously sexy men landed on her doorstep every day. More like never ever ever.

Then, feeling a blush stain her cheeks, she lowered her head and concentrated on eating her lunch. Kaden followed her lead with a gusto that warmed her heart. She wasn't a fancy cook, but she liked to think she could make a decent meal. Waiting until he'd polished off his chili along with a large hunk of bread, Lia pushed aside her bowl and put her elbows on the table.

She was too distracted to be hungry. And not just because Kaden was creating all sorts of intoxicating sensations. Deep down, there was a nagging unease that the sins of the past had created a cancer in the very heart of Pike.

"You don't think Judge Armstrong's crash was an accident, do you?" she asked, although she already knew the answer.

"No."

"I don't either." She wrinkled her nose in confusion. "But I don't know how you could force the man to smash his car into the back of his garage. Not without risking a serious injury."

"The deputy said the judge looked like he'd been beaten."

Lia shrugged. "The mayor did have a point when he reminded Anthony the judge had just been in an accident. The windshield was smashed like he'd hit it with his head."

"Yeah, but what better way to cover a murder than a car crash?" He settled back in his seat, his expression distracted, as if he was considering the best way to commit the crime. "That's how I would do it."

"How?"

"I'd wait in the garage until he pulled in. You said yourself that he lives alone and doesn't have any close neighbors. Who would be around to notice someone sneaking inside? Plus, he would be going from the bright morning light to darkness. He would be momentarily blinded. It would be easy to catch him by surprise."

Lia nodded. "That makes sense."

"As soon as he opened his car door, I'd use a weapon to knock him unconscious," Kaden continued. "He was an old man. I doubt he would be hard to overpower, especially if he wasn't expecting the attack." Kaden paused, his expression grim. "Once he was dead, I would wedge a heavy object against the gas pedal and put the car in gear. After the crash, it would be easy to remove the object and walk away."

Lia shuddered. It was terrifying to imagine the old judge

pulling into his garage with no idea that a killer was lurking in the shadows.

"It sounds like something from a movie."

He sent her a wry glance. "It was a lot riskier than a choreographed stunt. One mistake and the killer could have been run over by the Cadillac. Or the garage could have collapsed before they escaped. Someone is either desperate or arrogant enough to believe they're impervious to danger."

Lia was ready to accept his version of events. It was the logical conclusion. Still, it would be better if they had proof. She tapped a finger on the edge of the table, trying to figure out how to discover exactly what had happened.

"I wonder if we could find it."

He arched a brow at her abrupt words. "Find what?"

"The heavy object that was wedged against the gas pedal. Whoever killed the judge might have left it behind."

"You're right. Once the crowd leaves, we should have a look around."

"Probably best to wait until tomorrow." She knew her fellow citizens well enough to predict there would be people trying to get a peek at the spot where the judge died for the rest of the day. Probably into late evening. "Although even if we do find something, I'm not sure what it would tell us beyond your theory being right."

Frustration smoldered in the smoky depths of his eyes. "There has to be a connection between him and Vanna."

Lia considered the limited opportunities the two could have crossed paths. The judge obviously traveled to Madison for his job. It was possible they met there. It seemed more likely, however, that their relationship was based in Pike.

"He was the local judge at the time she would have been visiting the area," she finally pointed out.

Kaden nodded. "The most logical answer would be that

he used his influence to keep her from filing an official report against a local business."

Lia didn't have any trouble imagining the older man storming his way into the EPA headquarters to threaten them with legal action if they didn't drop their investigations. He always seemed like the sort of man who took pleasure in throwing his weight around.

Then she furrowed her brow as she realized the explanation didn't make any sense.

"But if he managed to prevent any violations, why would anyone pay her bribes? Unless we're mistaken about the meaning of the numbers on the back of the map."

"The money could have come from companies in other towns," Kaden suggested. "Not all of them would have a local official with enough power—or the lack of morals—to hide their sins."

"True. Or . . ." Lia's words died on her lips as she was struck by a sudden thought.

Kaden studied her with a faint frown. "What?"

"Or it might not have been a local business that was in trouble. The EPA inspects city water and landfills and waste management, right? The judge was the president of the Chamber of Commerce for years. He would do anything to protect the reputation of Pike."

"So would the mayor. If he was hiding a toxic danger in town, it might have endangered his chances of getting re-elected."

"That explanation would tie Vanna with both Judge Armstrong and the mayor." Her heart picked up speed at the possibility that they might be making progress in solving the mystery of Vanna's death. If she was a threat to the town of Pike, it would make sense that the judge and even Mayor Erickson would do whatever was necessary to prevent her from . . .

She abruptly blew out a resigned sigh. "If the judge managed to get the violations dismissed, there was no need to kill Vanna."

Kaden considered her words. "Maybe she offered him the same deal as the other companies. The city of Pike could pay the bribe or be exposed. The judge might have decided it was simpler to get rid of her than try to use his influence to stop the report."

"Maybe." It seemed a lot easier to blackmail the owner of a company than an entire town, she silently conceded. Plus, there was something else bothering her. "None of this explains why someone would want to hurt Drew Hurst."

Kaden shook his head, his expression annoyed. "Being a detective isn't as easy as I hoped."

"Does that mean you're keeping your day job?"

"For now." His gaze swept over her face, lingering on her mouth. "You, however, should consider changing careers."

Lia shifted in her seat, battling against the odd urge to lick her lips. "To a detective?"

"To a chef. Anyone who can cook chili like this needs to share it with the world."

She smiled as a burst of pleasure raced through her. "It's my grandpa's recipe."

"I'd ask you to share it with me, but it would be as Greek as Vanna's reports."

"You don't cook?"

"Not unless it's throwing something on a grill."

A silence descended. It wasn't uncomfortable. It was . . . loaded. Yes, that was the word. As if there was a pressure building between them that was destined to explode. Shoving herself to her feet, she stepped away from the table.

"I should go down to the store," she babbled. "It's time for Della to take off."

He straightened, appearing far more graceful than she had. "I'm going to drive around town to see if anything catches my attention." He glanced down at his sweater. "I don't suppose there's someplace I can get some clothes around here?"

She resisted temptation to take a survey of his lean, muscular body. "There's a thrift shop, but if you want something that actually fits, you'll have to go to Grange."

He grabbed his jacket and pulled it on. "Gotcha."

Oh." She turned toward the counters and pulled open the drawer where she tossed all the weird items that collected in the various corners of her apartment. Notepads, pens, small flashlights, batteries that might or might not be dead, and several screws that appeared randomly. She had no idea where they came from or if something was about to fall apart without them. She reached in to grab a small item at the very back. Turning to Kaden, she held out her hand. "Here's a spare key for the back door. I'll leave the office unlocked so you can get in if you're late."

Something flared in his eyes. An emotion that was impossible to read. Then, stepping forward, he plucked the key from her palm.

"Thanks."

Kaden aimlessly zigzagged his way out of town. He was supposed to be looking for . . . well, he wasn't quite sure what he was looking for, but he assumed he would know when he spotted it. Instead, his thoughts were consumed with Lia Porter.

He'd been amazed when she'd offered him the use of her spare room. But he truly hadn't considered the trust she'd placed in him until she'd held out the key. The hint of vulnerability in her expression had stirred a fierce urge to prove he was worthy of her faith in him. Not only that he was a decent guy but a dependable partner to share their on-going investigation.

Realizing he'd reached the railroad bridge where Vanna's body was found, Kaden pulled the Jeep to the side of the road. He left the engine running as he stepped out and glanced around.

Last time he was here, his mind had been focused on the possibility that he'd finally located Vanna. Now, with the clouds hanging low and the wind sheering through the pine trees, he concentrated on the remote location.

Why the hell was Vanna in this precise spot? And how did she get there? Her car was never found. And if the kids who discovered the skeleton were telling the truth, there wasn't a purse or cell phone with her. So where had they gone?

It was possible, of course, that she'd been killed some-where else and dumped there. Or jumped off the bridge to kill herself. But why was her body found so far away from the road? She couldn't have accidentally rolled that dis-tance.

No. For now, he was going with the hypothesis that she'd had a particular reason to come here. Or that she'd been lured to this area by her killer.

With a shiver, Kaden shoved his hands in the pockets of his jacket and plowed his way through the snow toward the road that cut through the thickly huddled trees. Lia had said the Walsh farm was in this general area. Was it possible Vanna was there that night? He was certain Cord was hiding something.

But if she was fleeing from the farm, why would she turn toward the bridge? It would make more sense to try to reach town. Especially if she'd lost her phone. Of course, it was late at night. Maybe she'd become lost in the darkness?

Trying to picture Vanna tromping through the woods in the middle of the night, Kaden stiffened as he heard the unmistakable crunch of someone or something walking through the snow.

"Hello?" He glanced over his shoulder. It sounded as if it'd come from near the bridge. "Is someone there?"

Silence. A thick, unnerving silence that sent chills down Kaden's spine. He'd faced death more times than he could count, but suddenly, he wanted to be away from this spot.

It felt . . . cursed.

Indifferent to the knowledge there was nothing rational about his urge to leave, Kaden returned to his Jeep and drove down the road leading through the trees. He had more important matters to think about. Starting with the fact that it was possible there was something besides the Walsh farm that had attracted Vanna to this area.

Someone dumping trash? Cows roaming on public land? A meeting with someone who had agreed to pay her bribe?

He bumped over the icy track, clearing the far end of the wooded area. Over the rolling hills, he could see the distant outline of peaked roofs. Presumably, that was the Walsh farm. There was another snow-covered road, however, that veered off toward town.

Kaden hesitated. He had four-wheel drive, but it was impossible to judge the depth of the drifts. The last thing he wanted was to get stuck. Tapping his fingers on the steering wheel, Kaden at last planted his foot on the gas pedal and plowed his way down the narrow lane. He had his phone with him and plenty of gas in the tank. If he got stuck, he'd call for help.

Inching his way around a sharp curve, Kaden widened his eyes in surprise as he caught sight of the large, cement-block building off to his left. It was just one-story, but it extended in an L shape, with large chimneys belching out white smoke. There were no windows he could see, but there was a cement parking lot that was cleared of snow for forty or so cars. This was obviously one of the larger businesses in the area.

Intent on figuring out what the place was doing out in the middle of nowhere, Kaden nearly missed the figure that stepped out of a small wooden shack across the road to flag him down.

With a muttered curse, he took his foot off the gas, but he didn't slam on the brakes. It'd been years since he'd driven in snow, but he hadn't forgotten the dangers of fishtailing. Slowing to a stop, Kaden rolled down his window as the short, heavyset man in a thick coat and stocking hat trudged around the front of the Jeep to stand next to Kaden's door.

He was younger than Kaden had first assumed, maybe in his late twenties, with a round face and brown eyes. His expression was more curious than threatening, and Kaden released the breath he hadn't realized he was holding.

"Sorry," the man said as he reached the window. "This is private property . . ." His mouth fell open and his eyes widened as he got a good look at who was driving the Jeep. "You're Kaden Vaughn."

"Yep." Kaden smiled, relieved to be recognized. It made it much easier to ask complete strangers intrusive questions. "And you are?"

"Manny Boren." The man beamed in blatant pleasure at the unexpected encounter. "I heard you were in town."

"I got turned around on my way back to Pike," Kaden lied smoothly. "I didn't realize this area was off-limits."

"Not really off-limits. It's just that Mr. Burke doesn't want anyone roaming around back here."

"Are you building something secret back here? Government weapons? UFOs?" Kaden teased, his tone light.

"I wish." Manny chuckled. "That's just the meatpacking plant. Mr. Burke is worried about the gun club over there." The younger man pointed toward the empty field, where there was a row of hay bales set several feet apart. "The members come out whenever they want to do some target practice. It could be dangerous for strangers."

It wasn't an unreasonable explanation, but Kaden found it hard to believe anyone would pay for a full-time guard at a place that was empty 99 percent of the time.

"You get a lot of strangers back here?" he asked.

Manny glanced around. There was one set of tire tracks from the Jeep and another set coming from the opposite direction that Kaden assumed had come from Manny's truck, parked next to the wooden shack. The entrance to the meatpacking plant had to be on the other side of the large building. Clearly this wasn't a main thoroughfare.

"I think he meant reporters and folks from other places snooping around," Manny finally explained.

Kaden blinked. "Reporters?"

"Because of the skeleton."

"Ah." Kaden was instantly intrigued. "Have you had to run a lot of people off? I mean, besides me."

"Actually, this is my first day."

"Your first day back here?"

"Nope, my first day on the job." Manny shrugged. "I'm usually driving the school bus, but Mr. Burke asked if I wanted to make some extra bucks during Christmas break and I said hell yeah. I got three kids."

Manny's first day on the job. There had to be something around here that Mr. Burke didn't want discovered by any potential reporters. But what?

"I don't blame you." He kept his smile firmly in place. "That's a lot of Christmas presents."

"Exactly."

Kaden had a thousand questions gnawing at him. What was Burke's connection to the skeleton? Was he keeping people away from the gun range? Or the meatpacking plant? What secrets was he trying to protect?

Unfortunately, it was doubtful Manny had any answers. He was a man trying to make a few extra bucks to buy Christmas presents for his kids. Unless he was a hell of a lot better actor than he appeared.

"Where does this road go?" Kaden finally asked. If Manny was a local, he surely knew every back road in the area. "Just so I don't stumble across it again."

"It goes past the gun range and the back of the meat-packing plant before cutting through the Walsh place." Manny paused, his nose scrunching as he mentally mapped out the pathway. "I think it ends at the reservoir. Honestly, it's been years since I've driven down there."

Kaden stiffened. Reservoir? Now, that was certainly a place Vanna would have visited. And a potential reason for her to be out this way. He needed to check it out.

"Is that a place to go fishing?" Kaden pretended to be dumb. It was an easy act. People always expected stuntmen to be a few bricks short of a full load. "I wouldn't mind having a look around."

"Nah. I think it's where the town's water comes from."

"So, it's not open to the public?"

Manny shook his head. "They have it all fenced off. But if you're interested in some ice fishing, I have a couple of spots I'd be happy to show you."

Kaden offered a vague nod. He'd have to come back later. It seemed doubtful Mr. Burke would pay a guard to stand out there at night.

"I'll keep that in mind. Thanks, Manny."

"No problem."

Manny reluctantly stepped back as Kaden rolled up the

window and performed a cautious U-turn. He hated the thought of leaving without checking out the reservoir. It felt like his first actual clue in discovering Vanna's reason for being in Pike. But for now, Manny seemed ready to believe Kaden's excuse that he was lost. He didn't want to do anything that might reveal he was interested in the place.

Besides, he still needed to get over to Grange to buy a few clothes before the snow started again.

Chapter 12

Lia was up bright and early the next morning to open the store. It was Wednesday, which meant Della would be attending the weekly prayer breakfast at her church. Lia had never been, but she suspected it served up more hot pancakes and the latest gossip than actual prayers.

Lia didn't mind, especially this morning. She'd slept remarkably well considering she had a strange man in the office below her. Not that she'd seen Kaden after lunch. He was gone until late last night. She was upstairs baking cookies when she heard him open the back door. But the sound of his return hadn't bothered her. In truth, with the disturbing events plaguing Pike, it was a comfort to know she wasn't alone in the building.

Lia had just unlocked the door and turned the sign to "OPEN" when Bailey was shoving her way past her to enter the store.

She was wearing a heavy coat and work scrubs, with her hair pulled into a messy bun. Her cheeks were rosy, either from the chilled wind or from excitement. Hard to tell. It didn't take much to get Bailey agitated.

"Is it true?" she burst out.

Lia closed the door and eyed her friend with a faint smile. "Good morning, Bailey."

"Good morning." She waved an impatient hand. "Is it true?"

"You're going to have to be more specific."

"Is Kaden Vaughn staying with you?"

Lia's mouth dropped open. She didn't know why she was shocked. Rumors spread like wildfire through Pike. But . . . damn, this was supersonic speed.

"Where did you hear that?"

"Della came to the nursing home last night to visit her aunt." Bailey watched the heat stain Lia's cheeks. "So, is it true?"

Lia silently cursed herself for sharing the information with the older woman. She should have known Della would tell everyone in town about Lia's temporary guest.

"I let him spend the night in my office."

Bailey made a strangled sound. "You made that gorgeous man sleep in your office? What's wrong with you?"

Lia felt her blush deepen. A part of her agreed with Bailey. For the first time in forever she had a man under her roof and she'd kept a locked door between them. It did seem a wasted opportunity.

Another part, however, knew she needed more than a physical attraction to take a lover.

"I barely know him."

"So?"

Lia rolled her eyes. "Did you need anything? Milk? Bread?"

Bailey glanced around the store, as if making sure they were alone. "I wanted to tell you that during my shift last night, I passed by the break room and overheard Kari Wentz talking to Megan Griffin. They're both aides at the nursing home."

Lia held up her hand, trying to stop her friend. "If this is gossip—"

"Gossip you're going to be interested in," Bailey insisted.

"Why?"

"It involves your Kaden Vaughn."

"He's not mine," Lia protested, even as the words sent a thrill of pleasure down her spine.

Bailey winked, obviously aware she was rubbing a raw nerve. "Whatever you say."

"Tell me."

"Kari's mom is a maid at the Pike Motel. She told Kari that the mayor showed up at the crack of dawn yesterday to tell the manager that he wanted Kaden Vaughn out of town."

It was exactly what they'd suspected, but having it confirmed was unnerving.

"Did he say why?"

"The mayor is putting word around town that Kaden Vaughn is here to make a documentary."

"What sort of documentary?"

Bailey lifted her hands to make an air quotes gesture. "'Pike, Wisconsin, is the murder capital of the world.'" She paused, wrinkling her nose. "Or maybe it's the murder capital of America. Anyway, he claimed we're all going to be portrayed as savage beasts who kill each other on a regular basis."

"That's ridiculous."

"Not really. We've had more than our fair share of murders here."

That was true enough, but Lia didn't think for a minute that the mayor was worried about Kaden embarrassing the city of Pike. He was worried that Kaden was going to expose something from the past. Something that was a danger to him, or one of his cronies.

"Kaden isn't here to do any documentary." She sent her friend a stern frown. "Period."

"Then why is he in Pike?"

"It's personal." It was quite likely that Kaden's interest in the skeleton had already spread through town, but she wasn't going to add to the rumors.

Bailey waggled her brows. "Personal with you?"

Lia parted her lips, but before she could chastise her friend, the door was pushed open by a small woman with golden hair that was ruthlessly styled in a knot at the back of her head and a curvaceous form outlined by a designer jacket. Lia blinked in shock at the sight of Jolene Erickson. She couldn't remember the mayor's wife ever shopping at Porter's Grocery Store. Not even to grab a loaf of bread or a carton of eggs.

"Good morning, Jolene," she managed to choke out.

"Lia. Bailey." With a vague smile, Jolene drifted down the nearest aisle.

Bailey leaned toward Lia, whispering in her ear, "I have a feeling you're going to have a lot of customers today, checking to see if you really are living in sin with Kaden Vaughn. I'll see you later."

With a finger wave, Bailey headed out of the store and down the street. Lia slowly turned, squaring her shoulders. Unlike her friend, she didn't think Jolene Erickson was there to discover if she was sleeping with Kaden Vaughn.

Lia would bet money the mayor had sent his wife there to try to discover why Lia had allowed Kaden to stay in Pike. And, hopefully, find a way to convince her to get rid of him.

Slowly, she strolled down the aisle to where Jolene was pretending to study the loaves of bread.

"Is there something I can help you with?"

Jolene turned, flashing her deep dimples that gave the illusion she was half her age. "You have a lovely store, Lia. I'm sorry I haven't visited before."

Lia arched her brows. Lovely? It was functional. A few customers might consider it charming. In an old-fashioned, nostalgic way. But never lovely.

"It's not fancy, but if you need a basic supply, we should have it."

Jolene waved a hand in a dismissive gesture. "I'm not really here to buy anything. I prefer to order my groceries from shops that sell organic food. I have to be cautious of my health, you know."

Shocker. Lia's lips twitched. "Then I suppose you want to discuss the greased pig contest at the Fourth of July celebration?" she asked in overly sweet tones. "Don't worry, I can guarantee you have my vote to get rid of it."

Jolene's smile tightened, but it never faltered. "Perhaps you haven't heard, the planning meeting has been postponed."

"Postponed?"

"After Judge Armstrong's accident, I decided we needed a few weeks to adjust to his loss. He was such an important member of the committee. It won't be the same without him."

"Yes, such a tragedy." Lia studied the woman's expression. It was impossible to read. "If this visit isn't connected to the greased pig contest, can I ask why you are here?"

"You've never been married, have you?"

Lia hesitated. The question had come out of the blue, reminding her that she wasn't nearly as skilled as Jolene in manipulating others.

"No."

"I fell in love with Tate when we were schoolkids. He was chubby with an overbite and was ruthlessly teased by the other boys, but I saw something special in him. I knew he was destined to become a leader." There was a self-satisfied expression on her face, as if being the wife of a small-town mayor had been her ultimate goal in life. "We've been married twenty-five years, and he's always been a wonderful husband and father. But he can be ridiculously overprotective."

"Overprotective of you?"

"Of me. Of Sunny." She nodded toward the front window, where the morning sunshine was shimmering against the fresh layer of snow. "And this town. He takes his job as mayor very seriously. Sometimes too seriously."

"I'm not sure I understand."

Jolene stepped closer, lowering her voice as if sharing a secret. "I heard the rumors that Tate has been attempting to . . . to urge your friend to leave town."

"You mean Kaden Vaughn?"

"Yes, I believe that's his name."

Lia felt a surge of anger. Kaden had not only been kicked out of the motel but his tires were savagely slashed. That wasn't a harmless urge. It was a blatant threat.

"I've heard the same rumor." Lia allowed the words to come out in a cold voice. "The mayor has been spreading vicious lies about Kaden."

Jolene parted her lips, pretending to be shocked by the accusation. "Hardly vicious," she protested. "And it's only because he's worried that the discovery of the skeleton will stir up our town's recent unpleasantness. No one wants a pack of reporters returning to write endless stories about another victim of the Pike serial killer. We all just want to return to our quiet, peaceful existence."

Ah. So that was how Jolene was going to dismiss any need to investigate the skeleton. No doubt she'd also try to pin the death of the judge and Drew's accident on the killer if he wasn't already dead. Again. It seemed unlikely he'd crawl out of his grave a third time.

"Zac was convinced they'd found all the victims," she reminded the older woman.

Jolene clicked her tongue. "He closed the case so he could leave town to be alone with his wife."

Lia scowled. "No one can question Zac's loyalty to his job."

"That doesn't mean he can't make mistakes."

Lia quashed the urge to continue to defend her friend. Or to point out that the Pike killer hadn't been in the area at the time Vanna disappeared. Jolene wasn't there to debate the truth of what happened. She was there to convince Lia to get rid of her temporary houseguest.

"Kaden isn't in Pike to make a documentary," Lia said. "So there's no need to worry."

Jolene clicked her tongue. "It doesn't matter why he's here. His presence is disruptive."

"To you? To your husband?"

Jolene turned away, her profile tight with frustration. "I don't watch much television, but according to my daughter, Kaden Vaughn is something of a star. The fact he's in this small town is certain to attract attention. Especially with those nasty tabloids that are always looking for some scandal. It would be better for all of us if we could avoid publicity. At least for now."

"Even if Kaden left Pike, that wouldn't mean we won't have reporters around. The boys did find a skeleton."

"Ancient history that is best forgotten. It's time for healing, not dwelling on our unfortunate past."

"What if it isn't connected to the Pike serial killer? Don't you think we should discover what happened to the poor woman before we dump her bones in an unmarked grave?"

"If it wasn't the Pike killer, I'm sure it was nothing more than a tragic accident. Or, more likely, a suicide."

Lia briefly wondered if Jolene was coached by her husband

on what to say, or if she'd come up with her own version of dismissing the potential murder of a young woman.

"An accident just like Drew Hurst and Judge Armstrong?"

"Exactly."

Before Lia could respond, the door was shoved open and Sunny poked her head into the store.

"Mom, are you coming?" Her dark curls were tumbled from the morning breeze and her cheeks were rosy. She was wearing a red designer coat that must have cost a small fortune. "I want to finish up our errands so I can go visit Drew this afternoon."

Jolene's lips pinched in disapproval. "I thought you went yesterday?"

"I did, but he's still fighting for his life, Mother. Don't you care?"

"Of course I care, but I need the car this afternoon and your father is busy."

The girl shrugged. "It doesn't matter. I'll find a ride."

Obviously outmaneuvered by her daughter, Jolene returned her attention to Lia.

"It was good to see you, Lia. And think about what I said." She reached out to pat Lia's arm. "This store has been a part of Pike history. It would be a shame to see it closed."

With her warning delivered, Jolene strolled toward her impatient daughter and out of the store. The door closed with a sharp bang, and a few seconds later, Jolene and Sunny disappeared from view.

"That sounded like a threat."

Lia wasn't startled to hear Kaden's voice. She'd sensed him enter the store a few minutes before. It wasn't the sound of footsteps or even the rich, musky scent that was so much a part of him that alerted her. It was the electric buzz in the air. As if he carried around his own force field.

Or maybe it was because she was so acutely aware of him.
An unnerving thought.

Pressing her hand against her stomach to ease the sudden flutter of butterflies, Lia turned to watch Kaden stroll toward her. He'd recently showered and his long hair was still damp as it brushed his broad shoulders. He'd shaved and he was wearing a new flannel shirt and jeans, proving he'd spent at least part of the day before shopping. Not that it mattered what he was wearing. He would be drop-dead gorgeous in an old sweatshirt and jogging pants.

Lia sucked in a slow, deep breath, battling back the heat that threatened to stain her cheeks.

"Yeah, not a very subtle one," she said as he stopped next to her.

He gazed down, his expression oddly tense. "I never thought I might be putting you in danger when I agreed to stay here."

"Danger?" She snorted. "I'm not afraid of Jolene Erickson."

"Maybe not Jolene, but I'm sure the mayor has some influence in this town. He could make things very difficult for you."

"I have some influence of my own."

Lia wasn't bragging. Watching her mother struggle, however, had taught her that money provided a sense of security. Not just because she never had to worry about bills or a roof over her head, but it protected her from bullies. If Tate Erickson wanted a fight, she'd give him one. She could fund a candidate to run against him for mayor. Or hire a lawyer to sue him for harassment . . .

"I don't have any trouble believing that." A smile touched Kaden's lips before it quickly faded. "But it's not just about the threat to your store. There's someone out there who doesn't want me poking into the past." He reached out to brush his fingers down her cheek. "I would never forgive myself if something happened to you."

Pleasure inched down her spine, tiny sparks of electric bliss, but Lia refused to be distracted. "If I'm in danger, it's not because of you. Before you ever arrived in town I was insisting the skeleton belonged to the woman I saw fifteen years ago."

Lia didn't add that she was safer with him staying in the same building.

Before she could change the subject, Della rushed into the store, her face flushed. She was a short, solidly built woman with a square face that was deeply wrinkled around her brown eyes. Her hair was dyed coal black and tightly curled against her head, giving her the unfortunate impression that she was wearing a helmet. She could never be called pretty, but she was kind and dependable and utterly devoted to Lia.

Pulling off her wool coat, she moved around the counter and hung it next to the window. Then she turned to Lia with an overly innocent expression.

"Sorry I'm late." Her dark gaze moved to take in the silent Kaden. "We had extra prayers to say this morning."

"I bet." Lia rolled her eyes, resigned to the knowledge she was the center of local gossip. "I'll be gone this morning, Della, but Wayne should be here by noon. Call if you need anything."

Not waiting for the older woman to answer, Lia walked down the aisle and into the narrow hallway. She'd reached the back door when Kaden caught up with her.

"Are you busy this morning?" he asked.

Lia grabbed her parka, which was hanging on the wall. "I want to check out Judge Armstrong's garage while it's still early."

"You read my mind." Kaden stepped into the office,

slipping into his jacket before he followed her out the door and pressed the key fob to start his Jeep. "And then I want to stop by the meatpacking plant."

Lia hesitated, her instinctive need to be in charge vying with the acceptance that Kaden would insist on taking his vehicle. He not only had his own control issues but he was a professional driver. Being a passenger was clearly painful for him.

Climbing into the Jeep, Lia pulled on her seat belt and glanced toward Kaden's profile.

"Why do you want to go to the meatpacking plant?"

Kaden turned out of the alley. "Yesterday I tried to drive behind the plant, but the owner recently hired a guard to keep people from using the road. I want to know what he's hiding. And whether it's connected to his business or the local reservoir."

Ryan Burke had hired a guard? Lia frowned. The man was notoriously cheap. What could be so important that he was willing to pay an extra salary?

"Okay."

Chapter 13

Kaden managed to reach the one-way street leading to Judge Armstrong's house without needing directions. He had the overall layout of Pike memorized, although it was like a lot of small towns: a maze of narrow lanes that often led to dead ends.

Pulling into the driveway, he left the engine running as he glanced around. He was prepared for a quick getaway if necessary.

"No one's here." Lia pushed open the door of the Jeep and hopped out.

Kaden quickly joined her, staring into the empty space. Someone had removed the car, revealing the gaping hole in the back wall. He stepped forward, catching sight of the snow that had swirled into the once immaculate garage, adding to the sense of chaos.

"They left it open." He released a sound of sheer disgust, his hands on his hips. "Sloppy. They should have at least tried to cover the hole in the back with plyboard and shut the garage door. Even if it wasn't a crime scene, someone could easily break into the house."

He nodded toward the flimsy door that connected the garage with the interior of the main house. One strong kick and he could bust the thing open.

"Maybe that's what the killer wants."

Kaden nodded. "You have a point. The more people tromping around the area, the less likely they'll be caught. And even if a miracle occurred and someone did decide to investigate the judge's accident, nothing could be used in a trial. Not after being left abandoned for anyone to stroll by and contaminate the crime scene."

Lia squared her shoulders, as if gathering her courage. "Let's take a look."

"Careful, I'm not sure how much structural damage was done," Kaden warned as she headed into the garage.

She nodded, but her expression was distracted as she halted and bent down to study a large stain on the cement.

"This looks like blood."

Kaden joined her, gazing down at the dark spot that was starting to flake. He wasn't an expert, but if he had to guess, he would say Lia was right. It did look like a pool of blood that had dried and frozen to the cement.

"Yes." He stepped back, judging the distance from the entrance to the garage. He wasn't an expert on blood, but he was an expert on cars.

"If the judge pulled into the garage, this would be the general spot he would be getting out of the car."

Lia straightened. "Only he was attacked."

"And probably shoved back into the car before it was smashed into the back wall." He glanced around the large space. "You look for a potential weapon and I'll see if I can find something that could have been used to wedge the gas pedal."

She headed across the garage as he searched closer to the attached house. It quickly became obvious that the judge hadn't been a man who worked on his own vehicles. Or even his house. There were no shelves, no toolboxes, no metal cabinets to hold the typical junk people collected over the years.

"I don't see anything obvious." Lia crossed back to stand next to him. "Honestly, there's nothing out here."

"Which means they probably brought their own weapon."

Lia grimaced. "Premeditated."

"Yeah, whoever was waiting in the garage didn't come here to talk. They came here to kill." Kaden was turning in a slow circle, his gaze sweeping over the shadowed corners until he spotted something beside the screen door that opened onto the back patio. He noticed it because it should have been hidden beneath the shattered debris that littered the floor in that area. Instead, it was lying on top of the busted drywall. As if someone had tossed it there. He walked forward, glancing up at the ceiling to make sure it wasn't about to collapse on his head.

Once he reached the object, he bent down to pick it up. He didn't bother to be careful about preserving fingerprints or DNA. There were a dozen people tromping through here yesterday. Anyone might have touched it.

"What is it?" Lia asked.

He turned to show her the iron statue that was cast in the shape of Lady Justice. It was around eight inches tall and surprisingly heavy.

"It looks like an old-fashioned doorstop," he told her. "My grandfather had one." He held up the object, eyeing it with the expertise of a stunt driver. "This would be the perfect size and weight to wedge against the gas pedal."

Lia grimaced. Was she picturing the killer leaning over the brutally murdered judge to arrange the doorstop? It was a disturbing image.

"Should we drop it off at the sheriff's office?"

"Nope. I'm taking this with us."

"Isn't it evidence?"

"Probably, but who's going to care?"

She glanced around the garage that had been left open to the elements. It felt as if the memory of Judge Armstrong was being swept away by the brutal wind.

"No one," she admitted.

"Besides, if we leave it here, there's a chance it might be stolen." He continued his list of reasons to keep the doorstop. "And if we take it to the sheriff's office, it's going to end up in the nearest trash can. Even if Erickson wasn't involved in the death of the judge, he's doing his damnedest to cover it up."

"Okay," she conceded, a visible shiver racing through her body. "Are you done? We should probably move along before anyone notices us poking around."

Kaden led her out of the garage without hesitation. There was nothing left to see there. And it was obviously upsetting to Lia to stand in the spot where a man she'd known her whole life was killed. Hell, it was upsetting to him.

His years in Hollywood were filled with special effects that had included graphic accidents and death scenes. But seeing an actor pretending to be dead was nothing at all like seeing a real corpse.

Pulling out of the drive, Kaden headed away from the grimly silent house.

"We don't have tangible proof," he said, glancing over his shoulder at the doorstop he'd placed on the back seat. "But I'm one hundred percent certain the judge was murdered."

"I agree. But why?"

It was a question that had plagued Kaden during his long, restless night. He'd only been able to come up with two plausible explanations.

"Either he has a connection to Vanna's disappearance. Or he was a witness to whoever ran over Drew Hurst."

"Oh." Her eyes widened at his mention of Drew. "I didn't even think about that. It's certainly possible he saw who hit Drew. And if he did, he would have confronted that person. He wasn't the sort of man to turn a blind eye."

Kaden grimaced, a frustration that was becoming all too familiar churning through him.

"I feel like I'm lost in a whiteout. Everything is obscured, but I keep stumbling forward, hoping to find a pathway. It's no wonder my brother became obsessed with this mystery."

She sent him a sympathetic smile. "Maybe Ryan Burke can give us some answers."

"You'll have to direct me to the plant. I found it yesterday by a back road."

"Turn right at the corner and drive until you reach the cemetery, then you'll take a left."

He slowed the Jeep without stepping on the break and made a wide turn around the corner. The streets hadn't been cleared. Probably because there would be more snow before they could get it all plowed.

"Were you close to your brother?"

Lia's question blindsided him, and Kaden clenched the steering wheel tight enough to turn his knuckles white.

"Not in the way most brothers are." His voice was harsh, but he couldn't help that. "Darren was several years older than me and he spent most of his time with his nose stuck in a book."

"Not your style?"

A portion of his tension eased at her deliberate teasing. "Not back then. I was more interested in finding trouble."

"I'm guessing you were good at that."

"The best." His lips twisted at the memory of adolescent pranks and brushes with the law. Looking back, he could only be thankful his stupidity hadn't landed him in jail. Or the morgue. "My dad was convinced he could beat some sense into me, but it only made my behavior worse. The more he hit me, the more I was determined to show him that I couldn't be controlled. Thankfully, Darren kept him from doing any permanent damage." He paused, forced to clear the lump from his throat. "Darren was more of a father to me than Dad. At least I would occasionally listen to him."

"And your mother?"

Kaden concentrated on the slick road as he caught sight of the cemetery. "She was smart enough to bail when we were just kids."

He braced himself for the gush of sympathy. There was nothing that prompted pity like being abandoned by your mom

But Lia was never predictable. She studied him in silence before she asked an unexpected question. "Do you resent her?"

Kaden considered his answer as he turned left and drove toward the edge of town.

"I did, but honestly, she had to save herself," he finally confessed, not bothering to share the terror that had filled his young heart when he first realized she was gone and never coming back. Lia already knew his father was a violent asshole. It was obvious any kid would be horrified to be left alone with him. "If she'd taken us with her, there would have been no way to get my dad out of her life. He might not have loved us, but he considered us his personal property. And eventually he would have hurt her. Maybe even killed her."

Lia absorbed his words, thankfully not pressing for any more details. The last he'd heard, his mother had remarried and had a new family. As far as he was concerned, she was a ghost who no longer had a place in his life.

"What happened to your dad?" she asked instead.

"He drove his car into a tree not long after I left home. I didn't even go to his funeral."

She reached out, touching his arm before quickly withdrawing her hand. "When something's toxic in your life, you have to remove it. Otherwise it spreads like cancer."

He wondered if she was speaking from experience.

"I'm not sorry I left. But I wish I had paid more attention to my brother," he admitted. "After our childhood, I never dreamed he would follow in my father's destructive footsteps. If I wasn't so self-absorbed with my career—"

"He was an adult, right?" she firmly interrupted. "He made his own choices."

"Maybe." Kaden shrugged, unable to dismiss his duty to his brother so easily. "I failed him once. I won't fail him again."

Lia pointed out her window at the narrow lane that was built parallel to the nearby highway.

"Take the outer road. There's a sign that shows the turn for the meatpacking plant."

Kaden released a small sigh. He usually shut down anyone digging into his past. It was no one's damned business who he was before arriving in Hollywood. But he'd wanted Lia to know where he'd come from and how it'd made him a man who was willing to risk everything. Not just because they were currently partners in the quest to discover the truth about Vanna, but because . . .

Because he was starting to think of having Lia in his life long after they solved the mystery.

As Lia promised, the sign for the Pike Meatpacking Plant was placed at the edge of the turnoff, large enough to be seen from the highway. He followed the bumpy lane that ended in a small parking lot in front of the L-shaped building. He pulled into a spot nearest the glass door, glancing around. There were no other buildings in the area and he was assuming the majority of the workers parked in the back lot he'd seen yesterday. It gave the feeling of being isolated from the rest of the world.

He shook off the strange desire to turn around and leave. It was his idea to come here in the first place.

Forcing himself to shut off the engine, Kaden unhooked his seat belt and glanced toward the silent Lia.

"Are you ready?"

She looked as uneasy as he felt about going inside. "I'm not sure."

"Me either. Let's go."

Kaden exited the Jeep and waited for Lia to join him at the door before pulling it open to enter a cramped reception area. A woman with curly brown hair and a long face sat behind a bare desk that looked as if it was found in a thrift shop. The carpeting was worn and the walls were in dire need of a fresh coat of paint. Not that Kaden cared about the shabby appearance. He was just happy he couldn't see the inner workings of the plant. It might make him a hypocrite, but he didn't want to see the sausage being made. Even if he did love eating it.

The receptionist looked bored as they entered, but catching sight of Kaden, her eyes widened in surprise. She straightened in her seat, her dark eyes sparkling with a sudden excitement.

"Lia," she breathed, reaching out to straighten the name plaque that read 'Marla Walsh, Office Manager'. Kaden tucked away the information, silently wondering if she was related to Cord Walsh. "I haven't seen you around forever."

Lia curved her lips in a stiff smile. "Hi, Marla."

"What are you doing here?"

"We're here to see Ryan Burke. Is he around?"

The receptionist's excitement was replaced with confusion. "He's in his office. Do you have an appointment?"

"No, but this won't take long," Lia promised.

"He doesn't like to be interrupted." Marla Walsh reached for the receiver of a nearby phone. "Let me check to see if he can squeeze you in." She swiveled in her seat, speaking into the receiver. "Mr. Burke, Lia Porter is here to see you with . . ." She cleared her throat, shooting Kaden a quick glance. "With a friend." She listened for a second before grimacing. "Of course. I'm sorry." She replaced the receiver. "He doesn't have time today."

"Hi, Marla. I'm Kaden Vaughn." Kaden flashed a smile, moving to stand just inches from the desk. "I hate to be a bother, but could you tell Mr. Burke that we're here to talk about Vanna Zimmerman? I think that will change his mind."

Marla blushed even as she tried to remain professional. "Zimmerman?"

"Yes." He offered another smile. "Vanna Zimmerman."

Holding Kaden's gaze, Marla reached for the phone and pressed the intercom. "Sorry, Mr. Burke, but they said they're here to talk about a Vanna Zimmerman." She listened, her mouth dropping open at whatever Burke was telling her. "Okay." She replaced the receiver. "He said he'll give you ten minutes." She pressed another button on her phone and there was a loud buzz from the door behind her. "The office is at the end of the hallway."

"Thanks, Marla," Lia murmured as they rounded the desk and headed into the narrow hall.

"No problem," the woman called out. "Good to see you."

Kaden closed the door and they walked forward. "He knows something or he wouldn't have let us through," he said.

"Yes, but I have no idea what to ask."

Neither did Kaden. When he was confronted by the guard yesterday, he was determined to discover why Burke had hired him. The man had to be trying to hide something, right? But now that he was here, Kaden was reconsidering his approach. Manny had quite likely reported seeing him on the back road, and Burke would be prepared with his lie about keeping away reporters. He wanted to catch the man off guard.

"Tiptoeing around hasn't worked," he muttered.

Lia swallowed a choked laugh. "You've been tiptoeing?"

"For me. From now on, I intend to be more direct."

"Why now?"

He halted as they reached the door at the end of the hall, glancing down at her curious expression.

"Because I'm afraid you might be in danger."

Before she could respond, he pulled open the door to expose Ryan Burke's private office.

If the rest of the plant looked worn down and in need of repairs, this space had been spared no expense. It was twice the size of most offices, with a thick white carpet and sleek black leather furnishings. The lighting was muted and the white walls plastered with numerous oil paintings that weren't to Kaden's taste but were obviously expensive. There was a fireplace with a black marble mantel and a long row of windows that overlooked a distant lake. The reservoir? Possibly.

"Lia." Ryan Burke lifted himself from his chair and rounded the glossy black desk. He was wearing a white dress shirt with the sleeves rolled to his elbows and gray slacks. The clothes should have made him appear professional, but instead, they emphasized the crude features and his bulky form. There was a smile on his lips, but it didn't reach his pale blue eyes. "I'm surprised to see you here."

"This is Kaden Vaughn," Lia said, pointing toward Kaden.

The man didn't bother to glance in his direction. "I'm really very busy today—"

"My older brother was engaged to Vanna Zimmerman."

The silence that followed Kaden's abrupt words was tense. As if someone had just tossed a live grenade into the center of the room. And he supposed that was exactly what he'd done.

At last, Burke turned his head to stab Kaden with a fierce glare. "Is that supposed to have some sort of meaning for me?"

"My brother was Darren Vaughn. A lawyer for the EPA in Madison. His fiancée, Vanna Zimmerman, worked as a special agent."

"Okay." Burke forced a strained chuckle. "They sound like a wonderful couple."

"They're both dead."

There was another awkward silence before Burke cleared his throat. "I'm sorry."

Kaden waved aside his faux sympathy. This man knew something. Kaden could read the fear in his pale eyes.

"Vanna disappeared fifteen years ago in this area."

"Disappeared?"

"Vanished without a trace," Kaden said in a hard voice. "My brother spent years and a small fortune searching for her before he died."

The ruddiness drained from the man's face, but he clenched his hands and maintained a grim ignorance.

"It's a very sad tale, but again, I don't know why you're in my office."

"Because your name was in one of my brother's files."

Lia made a choked sound at his blatant lie. Thankfully, Burke didn't seem to notice. He was staring at Kaden with a wide gaze.

"Excuse me?"

"This meatpacking plant was in Vanna's territory." Kaden didn't actually know if the EPA would have any interest in this plant. He was just trying to rattle the man. "She was here."

Burke scowled. "We have a lot of inspectors. USDA. OSHA. FDA. I can't remember them all."

"You would remember Vanna," Kaden insisted. "She was a gorgeous brunette with a bitchy attitude. Oh, and she threatened you with several violations."

"You're mistaken."

"I don't think so."

"Enough." Burke sliced a beefy hand through the air. "I run a clean, by-the-book operation here. If anyone says otherwise, they're lying. So unless you're here to try to squeeze money out of me—"

"Why would you think we would want money?" Lia interrupted abruptly.

Burke flushed, obviously afraid he'd given away more than he intended. "We're done here," he growled.

Kaden ground his teeth together. He had a dozen questions he wanted to ask, but Burke's stubborn expression warned him that he wasn't going to answer any of them. Not now. Kaden could only hope he could discover a way to put pressure on the man and make him talk.

"I'm still going through my brother's files," Kaden warned, giving Burke something to consider after they left. It might give him a few nights of heartburn. "When I'm done, I plan to hand them over to the FBI. No one around here seems interested in investigating Vanna's potential connection to the skeleton, but I have no doubt I can find someone willing to listen."

The man's lips twitched, but they refused to form a smile. "I wish you luck."

"Do you?" With a shrug, Kaden turned toward the door. "We'll see."

They were about to step out of the office when Lia paused and glanced over her shoulder. "Oh, Mr. Burke."

"What?"

"I heard you were having a loud argument with Barb Hurst a few days ago."

"It wasn't an argument," Burke groused. "It was a discussion."

"A discussion about what?" Lia pressed.

Burke scowled, clearly annoyed by the question. "Not that it's any of your business, but the bitch is trying to organize a union."

"And that makes you angry?" Kaden asked, silently acknowledging that this man had a reason to want to punish the Hurst family. And what better way than running down their son?

"After all I've done for my employees, not to mention the town of Pike? Yeah, it makes me angry." The man sent Kaden a defiant glare. "So sue me."

Kaden held his smoldering gaze. "I intend to do more than that."

Chapter 14

Burke waited until he heard his unwelcome visitors leave the building before pulling his phone out of his pocket and punching in a number. A second later, he heard the sound of a familiar voice, and he angrily shared his encounter with Lia Porter and Kaden Vaughn. He'd expected sympathy for what he'd endured. Or even fury that he was being harassed.

Instead, he was told to settle down and not overreact.

"Don't tell me I'm overreacting," he snapped. "That man knows something." He scowled as the voice once again tried to calm him. "Bluffing? Kaden Vaughn knew the bitch was here. And he claims he has files he's going to turn over to the FBI." The urgent words floating through the speaker only intensified Burke's fury. "I'm not panicking, I'm protecting my ass. This shit is getting out of hand." He sucked in a harsh breath, trying to regain control of his shattered nerves. "Get rid of Vaughn and clean up this mess."

He ended the connection and was about to toss the phone on his desk when a text popped up. What now? Skimming the message, he felt a stab of surprise. He sent back a text that was just as quickly answered. Well, well. It seemed he might have a way out of this shit show after all.

That was one disaster he could put on the back burner.

Unfortunately, he still had to get rid of the barrels of bio-hazardous sludge that were buried beneath the hay bales at the gun range. He was a man who knew the benefit of cutting corners when necessary, and it was damned expensive to have that stuff carted off by a legitimate treatment facility. He'd already had to spend a fortune to deal with his wastewater. It'd seemed a simple solution to use the empty land that surrounded his property to dump it.

The last thing he'd expected was for Vanna's bones to be discovered. . . .

Christ, if it wasn't one thing, it was another.

Lia walked out of the building with Kaden, her thoughts still focused on their meeting with Ryan Burke. She wasn't sure they'd learned anything that could reveal what had happened, but she was absolutely certain the older man had lied when he said he didn't recognize Vanna Zimmerman's name. There'd been a tightness in his features he couldn't disguise. She also believed he suspected the skeleton belonged to Vanna. But there was still no answer to why Vanna had been in Pike in the middle of the night. Or why someone would want her dead.

The only thing they knew for certain was that he was furious with Barb Hurst. Perhaps furious enough to hurt her son.

She was climbing into the Jeep when she felt her phone buzz. Pulling it out of her purse, she glanced at the screen and swallowed a sigh.

"Shoot," she muttered, shoving the phone back in her purse and pulling on the seat belt.

Kaden settled behind the wheel and fired up the engine. "Something wrong?"

"Wayne sent me a text to say he's giving a friend a lift to

the hospital and can't work this afternoon. I need to go back to the store."

Kaden pulled out of the parking lot and retraced their route to the main road. "Is his friend worse?"

She shook her head. If Drew had taken a downhill turn, Wayne would have told her.

"I'm guessing Sunny Erickson asked him to drive her over to Grange." Lia hadn't forgotten the girl's determined expression when she was in the store that morning. "She mentioned wanting to visit Drew and looking for a ride. Wayne would drop everything to spend time with her."

Kaden turned onto the outer road. "Cord and Wayne and Sunny. A lover's triangle?"

Lia snorted. "The usual agony of teenage years. You either want what you can't have or what you shouldn't have."

"Who was your crush?" Kaden asked as they slowly bumped their way over the snow-packed roads back into Pike.

"Chuck Moore. He was the reason I snuck out of my house fifteen years ago. And the reason I left the party in time to catch sight of Vanna jumping off the bridge."

"Where is he now?"

"Married with four kids."

"Do you regret that the two of you didn't get together?"

"God no." Lia tried and failed to imagine herself married to the man who'd once made her heart flutter. It wasn't just that he'd packed on a hundred pounds and was in the process of losing his hair. Or even that he was still employed at the local gas station where he'd been working during high school. It was his habit of flirting with her whenever he came into the store. As if he was still a teenager and not a grown man with a wife and kids. "Don't get me wrong, I'm sure he's a great guy. Just not for me."

A smile curved Kaden's lips, as if he was pleased with her answer. They drove past the graveyard, and he turned onto the road that would lead to her store.

"I know about your mother. What about your father? Does he live in Pike?"

The question came without warning, and Lia flinched. It wasn't that her past was a secret. She lived in a town where everyone knew everyone's business. But she never discussed her father.

"No," she eventually forced herself to say. She'd rather he hear the story from her than the town gossips. "He was my mother's high school sweetheart, but when she told him she was pregnant, he swore he couldn't be the father." She shrugged. The truth no longer had the ability to hurt her. "And his parents stood by him, insisting my mom was . . ." She wrinkled her nose, trying to recall what her mother had told her. "I think their precise words were 'gutter trash' who was sleeping with every guy in town."

Kaden hissed in disgust. "Jerks."

"My gramps called them much worse than jerks when he paid them a visit."

"I hope he insisted on getting support for you and your mom?"

"No." Lia smiled. Donald Porter had been a kind, gentle man who believed the best in people. He was also generous to anyone in need. Most people in Pike adored him, but there were always those who mistook his compassion for weakness. A mistake for anyone stupid enough to mess with his family. "He showed up on their doorstep and made them sign a document giving up any legal claims to me. He was convinced my life would be better without any contact with them. At least until I was old enough to decide for myself if I wanted a relationship."

"You didn't?"

Lia shook her head. "My dad left town when he turned eighteen and never came back. I'm sure I could track him down, but I never had any interest."

Kaden slowed as they neared Main Street. "I'll ask you the same question you asked me. Do you resent him for leaving?"

"Not really. He was young, probably scared. He panicked. I consider it his loss, not mine." She paused, realizing she wasn't being entirely honest. There were times in her life when she'd fantasized about finding her father just to tell him that she'd had a fabulous life without him. Thankfully, she'd been so smothered in love she'd never bothered to act on the spiteful impulses. "It would probably have been different if I hadn't had a fabulous mom and doting grandparents when I was young," she conceded. "They made sure I never felt as if anything was missing in my life."

He pulled next to the curb in front of the store. "You were lucky."

She was. Kaden was not only abandoned by his mom, he'd been left in the hands of an alcoholic father. The fact that he'd not only survived but actually thrived was a testament to his fierce drive to succeed. Along with the support of his brother.

Resisting the urge to trace the beautiful tattoo on the back of his hand—or better yet tangle her fingers into the long strands of his hair—Lia concentrated on the fact that Kaden hadn't put the Jeep in Park.

"You're not coming in?"

He shook his head. "First, I want to visit the local diner. I think Burke lied to us. I want to ask a few questions of people who might be able to give us a clue what he's hiding out there."

If he was just another stranger in town, she would have

warned him not to bother. The locals were polite, but they were wary of people who didn't grow up in Pike. Kaden Vaughn, however, wasn't just another stranger, and she didn't doubt for a minute the men would fall over themselves to tell him whatever he wanted to know.

Quashing the regret that she couldn't join him to hear what they might have to say, she pointed toward the nearby corner.

"Turn left at the stop sign. It's four blocks east of here, next to the real estate office." She unhooked her belt and pushed open the passenger door. "Try the apple pie. It's the best in town. Probably the best in the state."

"Can I bring you anything?"

"No, thanks."

"I won't be long," he promised.

Slipping out of the passenger seat, Lia closed the door and walked into the store without allowing herself to glance back. She wasn't a teenager with a crush on the new, cute boy in town. Or an obsessed fan who drooled over the mere sight of Kaden Vaughn.

She was a grown woman who had better things to occupy her mind than the silver beauty of Kaden's eyes or the chiseled perfection of his features. Or at least she should, she sternly told herself.

Pushing open the door, she stepped into the store and glanced toward the woman behind the counter.

"You can take off, Della. I'll be around to take care of any customers."

Della readily grabbed her jacket and pulled it on before collecting her purse. "I'll be on time in the morning, I promise." She winked in Lia's direction as she strolled toward the door. "Feel free to sleep in."

Lia shook her head as the older woman left the store.

Della had spent the past few years urging Lia to find a nice, decent man to marry. Now it appeared she was willing to accept a steamy one-night stand.

The question was, was Lia equally willing to accept a one-night stand?

Heading to her office, she slipped off her coat and tossed her purse on her desk. She would worry about her reaction to Kaden later. For now, she needed to get caught up on the work that was accumulating at an alarming rate.

She'd updated the store accounts, including the payroll and the monthly bills and was skimming through a business prospectus she'd requested when the sound of shattering glass destroyed her concentration. With a muttered curse, Lia shoved herself to her feet and marched out of the office. The sound had come from the back alley where she kept her dumpster. It wasn't uncommon for one or more of her neighbors to use it as their personal trash can. A habit she was attempting to curb since she'd gotten a ticket for someone throwing paint cans into the stupid thing.

Lia shoved open the door, but she was careful to remain inside the building. She wasn't charging blindly into any situation. Not until they'd discovered who ran over Drew and murdered the judge.

She glanced toward the dumpster, frowning when she didn't see any sign of movement. Had someone driven past and tossed out a bottle? She turned her head, absently glancing in the direction of her SUV. That was when she realized the back window was busted.

Damn. Had it been deliberately smashed? Or was it the result of an unseen crack and the frigid cold? It wouldn't be the first time she had a shattered window.

Lia leaned forward, trying to get a better look at the damage, already assessing what she needed to do to get it repaired. She'd have to call to make a police report, contact her insurance, make an appointment with Sykes Automotive . . .

She was running through the mental list when she caught a movement out of the corner of her eye. She had no idea what it was, but she instinctively jerked backward.

That quick reaction saved her from a cracked skull as a heavy object scraped over her temple, taking a layer of skin before it thudded heavily to the ground. Pain stabbed through her head and the world went dark for a brief moment, but Lia, thankfully, didn't pass out. With a strangled sound, she slammed shut the door and locked it before scurrying toward the front of the store to bolt the main entrance. Then, heading back to the office, she closed the door and locked it before grabbing her phone and sending a frantic text to Kaden.

I need you

The diner was exactly what he'd expected. A long, narrow room with Formica tables and tiled floor that was worn by years of wear and tear. A high, wooden shelf that held a collection of black-and-white ceramic cows ran the length of the walls. There were hundreds of them, in all sizes. Obviously, a reference to the numerous dairy farms that surrounded the town.

As he entered, Kaden caught sight of the long table near the back counter, where a half dozen men were sitting together, sipping coffee and no doubt sharing gossip. They were dressed like men who worked with their hands in thick flannel and coveralls. Their faces were ruddy from days spent in the sharp wind and they had various amounts of hair that were flattened by their hats. They fell silent as

Kaden entered, their brows lifting when they realized he intended to join them at the table.

He smiled toward the hovering waitress before taking a seat and introducing himself to the locals.

Thirty minutes later, Kaden felt a stab of satisfaction as he glanced around at the men who watched him with rapt expressions as he shared yet another memory from his days on movie sets. He didn't really like to talk about his years as a stuntman because it always sounded like he was bragging. Or implying he was best buds with famous actors. But over the years he'd developed a few stories that centered on his occasional disasters. Like the time he destroyed a hundred-thousand-dollar Lamborghini. And when he'd forgotten to close the curtains on the trailer that was set up for him on the movie lot and a group of tourists were standing at the window watching him step out of the shower stark naked. And when the director asked him to fill in a small role and he kept screwing up the lines until the actress threatened to have them tattooed on her forehead.

As he finished the last story, the men burst out laughing, and Kaden leaned back in his seat, sipping his coffee. He'd already consumed two slices of pie. Lia wasn't lying when she said it was the best. Now he judged the time was right to get to the reason he'd come to the small diner.

"Are all of you from Pike?" he asked, his tone casual.

They nodded in unison, but it was the heavyset man with a broad face and dark eyes who answered. He had told Kaden his name was Rex and he had a remarkable resemblance to Deputy Anthony. He also seemed to be the unofficial leader of the pack.

"Yep, born and raised."

Kaden leaned forward. "I was wondering if you might answer a few questions for me."

The men exchanged glances, suddenly wary.

"About the skeleton?" Rex demanded.

Kaden sensed the hesitation. This diner crew would shut him down if they suspected he was there to exploit their town. He had to let them know his interest was personal, not professional.

And the only way to do that was to be honest.

"My brother's fiancée disappeared in this area over fifteen years ago. When I heard about the skeleton, I decided to travel here to see if it might be her."

"Lots of girls have disappeared in these parts," one of the men muttered.

Kaden grimaced. "So I've heard."

"Any luck?" Rex asked.

"Not so far. I've been poking around in the hopes I could retrace her footsteps before she died."

"Why do you think she would have been in Pike?" one of the younger men with a heavy beard and dark eyes demanded.

"Vanna worked for the EPA and this town was located in the area she investigated."

"EPA?" Rex furrowed his brow. "That's some sort of government watchdog, ain't it?"

"Yes. I assume she was here to inspect the town's reservoir, or maybe the landfill." He paused, as if considering his words. "And, of course, the local businesses. I wanted to check out the meatpacking plant."

The bearded man gave a sage nod of his head. "That's where I'd start. Everyone knows Burke runs a shoddy business."

"Shoddy?" Kaden prompted.

The man waved a gnarled hand. "There's been a dozen workers injured because he doesn't care about safety, and I heard there was talk of shutting the plant down when they found rats on the property a few years ago. Nasty."

Kaden kept his tone casual. "I tried to drive out there on the back road, but I was turned away by a guard."

Rex shook his head, his expression one of disgust. "Yeah, I heard Manny saying he was hired by Ryan Burke to keep people away from the gun range."

"Bullshit, if you ask me," the bearded man muttered. "That's a public road."

"When did Burke ever care about anyone but himself?" a thin man with an impressive nose and a bald head chimed in.

Kaden hid his surge of satisfaction. He wasn't the only one who found Burke to be a first-class prick.

"He doesn't sound like the most popular guy in Pike."

"He doesn't even live in town, but everyone around here bends over backward to kiss his ass," Rex groused.

"What kind of ass-kissing?" Kaden prodded.

Rex shrugged. "There were rumors going around when he first opened the plant that our taxes paid for the swimming pool he installed when he built his fancy new house over in Grange. And I know for a fact it was our taxes that built him a new lagoon and parking lot and replaced his roof after part of it collapsed."

Kaden considered his words. It was one thing to use incentives to lure a new business to town, but it seemed excessive to continue handing out tax dollars.

"Why?"

Rex shrugged. "It's tough times for the local dairy farms and God knows there's no new businesses moving in. The meatpacking plant is about the only place to work. I suppose the local officials are afraid if Burke leaves, this town will collapse."

Kaden wasn't convinced. Okay, there might be some ass-kissing to keep the meatpacking plant in Pike, but building a new parking lot and replacing the roof? That was above and beyond the call of duty.

"Is the mayor included in the local officials?"

Rex nodded. "Erickson and Burke are thick as thieves."

"Yeah. And Judge Armstrong. They're all golfing buddies," the large-nosed man added, grimacing, as he remembered the fatal accident that happened just twenty-four hours ago. "At least they used to be."

"Did . . ." Kaden's question died on his lips as the phone he'd laid on the table buzzed with an incoming text. He glanced down, his heart squeezing in fear as he realized it was from Lia. *I need you.* Surging to his feet, he grabbed his coat from the back of his chair. "Sorry, guys. I'm going to have to take off. Great to meet you." He reached into his pocket to pull out a twenty-dollar bill. More than enough to pay for the pie and several rounds of coffee. "Let me get this."

"We're here every morning," Rex assured him.

"I'll try to stop by."

Kaden forced himself not to run as he hurried from the diner and hopped into the Jeep. He even managed to drive at a reasonable speed. He wasn't going to be any help if he crashed before he could get to the store. But once he pulled into the alley, he barely remembered to put the Jeep in Park and shut off the engine before he was charging toward the back door. He cursed when he discovered it was locked and fumbled to find the spare key. Once he managed to get into the back hall, he halted, listening for any sounds that might indicate what was wrong.

When he heard nothing but the pounding of his own heart, he called out, "Lia!"

There was the sound of a click before the door to the office was pulled open. "I'm here."

"What happened?" Kaden moved to join her, his gaze skimming over her pale face. His breath lodged in his throat as he noticed the blood on her forehead. "You're hurt."

"I'm fine."

"I see blood. That's not fine."

She wrinkled her nose. "It's a graze."

Kaden reached out to lightly touch her forehead, a surge of fury racing through him as he realized it was more than a scrape. Had someone hit her? The mere thought caused a red mist to cloud his brain.

"I feel a lump."

She pulled away, looking oddly embarrassed. "A graze and a lump. I've had worse hitting my head when I'm stacking the shelves."

"You should still see a doctor," he insisted.

"Kaden. I'm fine."

With an effort, Kaden forced himself to leash his need to insist on rushing her to the hospital. Lia wasn't stupid. If she was seriously injured, she would seek out medical attention. Releasing the breath he'd been holding, he forced himself to turn his attention to how she was hurt.

"Tell me what happened."

She paused, as if gathering her thoughts. Or maybe just finding the necessary words.

"I was working at my desk when I heard glass shattering in the alley," she finally said.

Kaden glanced toward the window, making sure it wasn't broken. Which meant it had to be something outside.

"I'm guessing you didn't lock the door to the office and call 911?"

"I didn't know what had happened." She jutted out her chin, looking defensive. "It could have been someone throwing something into the dumpster. They do it all the time."

He scowled, his gut twisting into knots at the thought that she'd put herself in danger.

"Lia," he rasped.

She held up a slender hand. "I heard a noise and opened the back door. I didn't leave the building."

He closed his eyes, counting to ten. He was overreacting, but he didn't know how to stop himself. If something happened to this woman, it would shatter something inside him. It didn't make any sense. They were barely more than strangers.

But he knew it beyond a shadow of a doubt.

Once he managed to regain his composure, he opened his eyes and gazed down at her troubled expression.

"Did you see anything?"

Her features tightened. "The back window of my SUV is busted."

Kaden wasn't surprised he hadn't noticed. When he pulled into the alley, he'd been so focused on getting to Lia that an elephant could have been standing there.

"Do you know who did it?"

"No." She lifted her hand to touch the wound. "I leaned forward to get a better look at my vehicle and I felt something hit my head. I jumped back and locked the door. Then I bolted the front door and sent you the text."

Kaden stepped forward to wrap his arms around her, pulling her close. He needed to feel the warmth of her slender body. It was the only way to assure himself she was truly unharmed. Plus, there was a secret part of him that was smugly pleased at the knowledge that she'd reached out to him when she was in danger. It proved she trusted him.

Breathing deeply, he caught the hint of her shampoo.

It was fresh, with a sharp tang of lemon. A scent far more enticing than the most expensive perfume. He swallowed a groan, his hands skimming down the curve of her back, pressing her even closer. She fit against him with sheer perfection. Two halves of one whole.

Cheesy. But true. There'd been a sense of destiny nestled in his heart since he first stepped into the store and caught sight of Lia Porter.

Savoring the much needed moment of peace, Kaden rested his cheek on the top of her head, smiling as Lia wrapped her arms around his waist. They both needed a second to gather their strength. And remind each other that not everything in the world was awful.

A minute passed, and then another, before Kaden reluctantly lowered his arms and stepped back. Someone had deliberately attacked Lia. This was no longer just an attempt to discover what had happened to Vanna. Now it was a quest to destroy whoever had dared to hurt Lia.

"I'm going to have a look around the alley. I'll be right back."

She nodded, thankfully not insisting on joining him. "I'll be upstairs."

They left the office together, Lia crossing the hallway to open the door to the stairs while Kaden headed out of the building. His jaw tightened as he easily caught sight of the busted window on the SUV. Making a slow circle around the vehicle, he assured himself that there wasn't any other damage before peering into the back compartment to see a brick on the floorboard.

Straightening, Kaden felt a stab of frustration. It seemed like such a petty crime. Like slashing his tires. But he sensed there was more to it than mere vandalism. He turned, glancing back at the door where Lia had leaned out.

Next to the building, he could see a brick that matched the one that had busted the window.

A shiver raced through his body. This had been a deliberate trap. He was sure of it.

With a grim determination, Kaden walked down the alley, his gaze sweeping from side to side. He found what he was looking for a few minutes later. A stack of bricks were tossed in a haphazard pile behind the dumpster.

Standing next to the bricks, Kaden realized this would be the perfect spot to hide after busting the window. It would give the assailant a perfect view of Lia as she stepped out of the door while remaining in the shadows. And it was a short enough distance to make it easy to hit her with the brick.

So, the question was whether they'd intended to scare her or actually do physical damage? Perhaps even kill her?

Gritting his teeth, Kaden continued to search the alley, looking for anything that might give a clue to the attacker. He could see footprints and tire tracks, but the frozen snow meant there was no way to tell if they were fresh or not. And even if they were, it wasn't much help to Kaden. He was an amateur sleuth, not a professional. He needed a clue that came complete with a name and a phone number.

He headed back inside, locking the door behind him before climbing the stairs. Lia was in the kitchen, pouring hot water into a cup. The scent of tea filled the air, and Kaden suppressed a smile. He was going to suggest a shot of whiskey, but whatever calmed her nerves.

Turning at his entrance, she leaned against the counter and took a sip of the steaming liquid.

"Anything?" she asked.

He crossed the wooden floor, halting next to the table. "There were bricks piled around the dumpster. That's what broke your window and hit you on the head. I'm guessing they threw the first brick to lure you out to the alley so they could attack you there." He folded his arms over his chest. "Who knows there aren't any security cameras out there?"

"Everyone." She shrugged when he sent her a frown of disbelief. "My mother went to the city council to complain about the feral cats getting into the dumpster a few years ago. The council refused to do anything to help because she didn't have video proof of the damage or what had caused it. It was a public hearing, so anyone could have heard her admit she didn't have surveillance back there."

Kaden sighed. That was . . . unhelpful. "That means anyone in Pike might have been hiding behind the dumpster."

She grimaced. "Why would they throw a brick at me?"

"I'm guessing it was a warning."

"For me? Or you?"

"Both of us, probably."

"I find it hard to imagine the mayor hiding in the alley in the freezing cold to lob bricks at me."

Kaden had to agree. Tate Erickson reminded him of the power-hungry wannabes in Hollywood. They were willing to sell their souls to achieve their goals, but they didn't have the balls for a fair fight. They would cheat, lie, and manipulate to get what they wanted.

"That doesn't mean he's not responsible," Kaden said. "He's not a man who gets his hands dirty. He hires someone else to do it."

Her lips parted, but before she could respond, her eyes widened as if she'd just thought of something. "Oh."

"What is it?"

"I just remembered. After I slammed shut the door, I heard someone gunning an engine. It was loud. Like a jet taking off."

Kaden tucked her words in the back of his mind. One

good thing about Pike being such a small town was that anything distinctive would stand out.

"That should be easy enough to track down." He studied her, attempting to keep his expression casual. "But not today. Do you feel up to packing an overnight bag?"

She blinked in surprise. "I'm fine. But why do I need an overnight bag?"

"We're going to Madison."

Lia was shaking her head before he finished speaking. "I can't leave the store."

"Okay." He was wise enough not to push. Lia was a control freak. Like him. She had to feel like she was making the decision, not being forced into it. "I have a meeting set up with Vanna's foster mom early tomorrow morning. I thought you might want to be there."

She narrowed her eyes, easily sensing she'd been outmaneuvered. "You know I do." She hesitated, then, turning, she set aside her teacup to grab her phone from the counter. "I'll let Della know the store will be closed for a day or two. I don't want her or Wayne here alone."

"No one should be here alone."

His stern tone held a warning that he wasn't going to make the same mistake again. There was no way in hell he was going to leave her here without someone close by. She glanced around the loft, her eyes darkening with a pain that had nothing to do with the wound on her head.

"This isn't just a store, it's my home."

Kaden stepped forward, cupping her chin in his hand to tilt back her head. He wanted her to see the resolve in his eyes.

"We're going to discover who's behind this, Lia. Then things can go back to normal." His thumb brushed the soft curve of her lower lip. "Or perhaps there will be a new normal."

Their gazes locked, a fragile promise of what might be pulsing in the air between them.

"A new normal?" she whispered.

"That's what I'm hoping for." He bent his head, pressing a light kiss against her mouth before he straightened and stepped back. "Pack a bag and I'll meet you downstairs."

Chapter 15

Ryan Burke stood at his office window, watching the last of his employees drive out of the back lot. Earlier, he'd assured his receptionist that he would lock up and the nightly cleaning crew wouldn't arrive until midnight.

It was one of the rare times he was completely alone in the isolated plant. Ryan grimaced, feeling an odd tingle of unease snake down his spine.

"Heebie-jeebies," he muttered, repeating the words his grandma had used when she had a shiver.

He wasn't afraid. It was just a reaction to being alone in a large, empty building, he assured himself. And a distaste for the upcoming meeting he'd arranged.

Usually, he didn't mind throwing his weight around. Figuratively speaking. What was the point of having money and power if you couldn't force people to do what you wanted? And if he had to break a few of them to get to this position, he didn't have any regrets. At least he didn't have any moral regrets. He did what he had to do. But he was beginning to have doubts about the wisdom of agreeing to work with partners when he made his deal with the devil. He knew he could keep his mouth shut, but he didn't trust anyone else. And even with the judge dead, he couldn't be sure his sins would remain buried in the past.

Thankfully, he was smart enough to keep the receipts. He intended to make sure no one was going to stab him in the back. Not without having their own sins revealed.

The darkness thickened as Ryan stood staring out the window. He'd been requested to schedule the meeting to occur when most of the good folks of Pike were sitting down to eat dinner. That was fine with him. It was the one time they weren't peering out to see who was doing what and who they were doing it with. Nosy bastards.

There was the flash of headlights as a vehicle pulled into the back parking lot.

Good. Ryan wanted to be done with this so he could head home. His wife no doubt had plans to meet with friends for dinner. They rarely spent a night at home, despite the fortune he spent on their fancy brick mansion. Probably because they didn't have anything to say to each other. In fact, they rarely glanced in each other's direction. After twenty years of marriage, they stayed together because it was too inconvenient to split up.

Moving to the wall safe that was hidden behind a very fine watercolor of a tropical sunset, Ryan pulled out a faded manila envelope. It wasn't thick, but the information inside was explosive. The sort of information that could destroy the city of Pike.

He walked back to his desk, pausing to tap a button on the panel that controlled the security cameras. He'd been reminded by his soon-to-arrive guest that they didn't want any record of this meeting. Then, turning, he waited for the knock on his door.

And waited. And waited.

Ryan muttered a curse. He'd specifically said to meet in his office. But he'd also said to use the back entrance. It hadn't occurred to him how dark it would be. And how difficult it might be to navigate through the maze of conveyer belts and long, overhead rails where the carcasses moved through the plant on massive hooks. Obviously, he was going to have to locate his missing visitor before they got spooked and left.

With the ease of years spent keeping a close eye on his operation, Ryan crossed to the inner door that opened directly into the heart of the plant. He shoved it open, grimacing as he realized it was even darker than he'd expected. Only the glow from the exit light provided a dim glow.

"Hello?" Ryan took a few steps forward, his brows pulling together when there was no answer. "My office is this way." There was nothing but silence. "What the hell?"

Accepting that he was going to have to turn on the main lights even though he'd hoped to avoid anyone realizing he was hanging around at this hour, Ryan reached toward the nearby wall. Before he could locate the switch, however, he sensed a movement beside him. Confused that his companion hadn't bothered to answer when he called out, Ryan whirled around, intending to express his desire to make this meeting short and sweet.

The words never left his lips.

Instead, there was a violent shock wave that started at the back of his skull and blasted toward his eyes.

Grunting at the explosion of agony, Ryan fell to his knees, his hands lifting to cover his face. Was he having an aneurism? A stroke?

It wasn't until he caught another movement next to him that he realized whoever was standing beside him had attacked him with some sort of weapon. And that they were about to strike again. Ryan tried to duck, but his brain was fogged with pain and his body refused to cooperate. He knelt there like a willing sacrifice as the second blow connected with the back of his skull, shattering his consciousness into shards of darkness.

He didn't know how long he was out, but he was sure it couldn't have been more than a few minutes at most. He shivered, sensing it was the icy air that had revived him. Was he outside? He struggled to open his eyes. They felt swollen, but he managed to pry them open far enough to see he was still inside the plant. He recognized the stainless-steel ceiling above him. This was one of the massive freezers that were attached to the side of the building.

This was weird. What was he doing there? He couldn't have walked this far. Not with his head aching and his limbs so numb he couldn't feel them.

He was still trying to figure out what was happening when a shadowy form bent over him.

Ryan released a sob of fear, desperately trying to form the words for mercy. They remained stuck in his throat as the intruder bent down and he felt a hand shoved into the front pocket of his slacks. He grunted in shock, baffled by what was happening until there was a glow of light as his phone was pulled from his pocket. A futile pang of hope that he could snatch the stupid thing and call for help bloomed and withered as he watched it tossed onto the cement floor and then crushed beneath the ruthless heel of a heavy boot.

The light flickered and died. Just as Ryan's consciousness flickered and died.

He was sucked back into the darkness as the freezer door slammed shut. His last thought was that the envelope he'd been clutching was gone.

Early the next morning, Kaden returned to his brother's condo and quietly made his way to the living room. It was a long, elegant space with black leather furniture and a polished marble floor. It'd always felt cold and impersonal to Kaden, but the view of Lake Mendota visible through the floor-to-ceiling window that ran the length of the wall more than compensated for the lack of warmth.

Placing the pink pastry boxes he'd collected from a nearby bakery on the coffee table that stood in the center of the floor, he crossed into the kitchen and switched on the coffee maker.

Only then did he slip out of his coat and smooth back his hair, which had been ruffled by the morning breeze. He stretched his arms over his head, feeling oddly energized by his walk. Or maybe it was the fact that since they'd arrived in Madison the gnawing worry that he'd put Lia in danger was temporarily tucked into the back of his mind. He'd been careful to make sure they weren't followed when they left Pike. Better yet, Darren's condo was in a gated community that had a full-time guard. No one was getting in without him knowing. For the moment, they were safe.

Or maybe it was because he'd slept in a bed knowing that only a thin wall separated him from the woman who was rapidly becoming his obsession.

As if his thoughts had conjured her, Lia strolled out of the guest bedroom. She'd recently showered, and the short strands of her hair were damp, her cheeks flushed. Dressed in jeans and a soft, green sweater, she looked like a pixie stepping out of the woods.

Desire spiked through Kaden, as hot and fierce as a bolt of lightning. But that was to be expected. What was unexpected was the sweet satisfaction that settled in the center of his being at having her walk into the room. As if something had been missing until she appeared.

Dangerous . . .

He ignored the warning that whispered through the back of his mind. It was too late to take precautions. At least when it came to Lia Porter. Besides, he was more concerned with the hint of bruising that surrounded the cut on her temple. It wasn't as bad as he feared, but it was enough to make his gut twist with anger.

"How are you feeling?"

She lifted a hand to touch her injury. "Good."

"Are you sure? Did you sleep okay?"

"Actually, I slept like a log." She smiled wryly. "I think I must have been more tired than I realized."

"It's because of the rush of adrenaline," he assured her. "After I completed one of my stunts, I used to go home and pass out on the couch. It was like my body used up all my energy in one big rush and I had to replenish it."

She sniffed the air. "Do I smell coffee?"

"Yep." He poured out two mugs, handing one to Lia before pointing toward the boxes he'd placed on the coffee table. "Along with fresh bagels, muffins, doughnuts, and fruit."

She wandered toward the bounty, checking out each box before grabbing a blueberry muffin and taking a bite. "Yum."

"I can't cook, but I can smell a bakery from a mile away."

She licked a crumb from her lip. "That takes talent."

Kaden swallowed a groan. "Indeed."

Lia moved to enjoy the view, thankfully unaware of the hunger that vibrated through him. A hunger that had nothing to do with muffins or bagels.

"Where are we going to meet with Vanna's foster mom?"

"She asked to come here this morning." Lia turned to send him a surprised glance. "I think she has kids home for Christmas vacation and she didn't want them to overhear what she has to say."

Lia arched a brow. "Interesting."

"Let's hope so." On cue, there was a clicking sound from

the intercom and Kaden crossed the room, assuring the guard he was expecting a guest. Then, heading to the front door, he pulled it open. A few minutes later, a well-used van pulled into the driveway and a short, solid woman climbed out. She had dark hair peppered with gray pulled into a ponytail and a no-nonsense expression on her broad face.

He smiled, holding out his hand. "You must be Sharon Bradly."

"Yes." Her grip was firm as they shook hands. "I recognize you, of course."

"Come in." He stepped back, allowing her to enter the foyer before he closed the door and led her into the living room. He waved a hand toward Lia, who was standing near the window. "This is my friend, Lia Porter."

"Lia," Sharon murmured.

Kaden stepped behind his guest. "Let me take your coat."

"Thanks." Sharon struggled out of the heavy jacket. "There are days I wonder why I don't pack up and head south."

"This weather is brutal," Kaden agreed, placing the coat on a chair in the corner. "But there are times when I actually miss the snow."

"Are those times when you're sitting next to a pool with the sun beating down on you?" Sharon asked.

Kaden chuckled at the woman's dry tone. He suspected you needed a good sense of humor to be a foster parent. And the patience of a saint.

"Probably." He nodded toward the long, leather couch. "We can sit in here. There's coffee and muffins if you're interested."

"None for me, thanks." She settled on the edge of the cushion, patting her stomach, which filled out the bright red sweater. "I've started my baking for Christmas. I think I've already put on five pounds."

Her words reminded Kaden of his brother telling him that Vanna's foster parents volunteered at a dozen charities. No doubt this time of year was a mad dash from one task to another.

"I'll try to keep this short," he promised, sitting next to her. "Have you heard from the coroner's office yet?"

Sharon nodded, her dark eyes shadowed with grief. "They contacted me to get the name of Vanna's parents for possible DNA matches, along with the names of her dentist and medical doctor. I'm assuming they intend to use the X-rays if they can't locate anyone from Vanna's birth family to help them identify the skeleton." She paused, clearing a lump from her throat. "They warned me it could take a while to give me a firm yes or no."

Kaden grimaced. He'd been so focused on getting answers that he hadn't considered the old wounds he was ripping open. Sharon had raised Vanna as if she were her own daughter. Of course she was still mourning her loss.

"I realize this must be a tough time for you. I appreciate you coming over this morning to talk to us."

Sharon nodded, but her expression was set in lines of determination. "It's tough, but honestly, I've been praying for answers for the past fifteen years. The not knowing is the worst."

"It was the same for my brother," Kaden agreed.

"You said you had some questions for me?"

Kaden turned so he was fully facing Sharon. Out of the corner of his eye, he could see Lia standing next to the window, as if she was trying to avoid distracting them.

"Vanna never really talked much about her past. I was hoping you might give me some background on her."

Sharon appeared confused. "Anything in particular?"

"I'm just trying to understand who she was. I moved to California not long after Darren started dating her, so she was pretty much a stranger to me."

The woman's lips twisted into a wry smile. "Well, if you could ever understand Vanna Zimmerman, you're way ahead of me."

"Complicated?"

"That's an understatement."

"How did she end up with you?"

"The usual story." Sharon hunched her shoulders. "Her parents were junkies. Her dad overdosed when she was just a baby, but her mom, Lisa, tried to clean up her act a few times. Unfortunately, she always ended up back on the streets."

"That must have been hard on Vanna."

"A lot harder than she ever wanted to admit." Sharon glanced down, her hands clenching as she allowed the painful memories to return. "If her mom had just abandoned her and walked away, Vanna could have hated her. But Lisa would get herself sober once a year or so and come to the house. She'd promise to do better and beg for forgiveness. At least until Vanna turned fifteen. As far as I know, Vanna never heard from her mom after that. I assumed she died of an overdose. Or was killed."

Kaden felt an unexpected pang of sympathy for Vanna Zimmerman. He understood the convoluted, gut-wrenching roller coaster of having a parent who was an addict. The love/hate was so deeply entwined, it was impossible to know where one began and the other ended. Eventually, it became a toxic brew that could destroy a person.

"Did Vanna resent her?"

"I don't think so. It was more like she was . . . " Sharon searched for the exact word. "Resigned. She loved her mom, but she had no expectations that Lisa would ever be more than a fleeting stranger who appeared and disappeared from her life. It made her jaded."

Kaden nodded, considering the young woman who was abandoned by her parents. It would have been easy for Vanna to end up on the streets. Instead, she went to college and created a respectable career. Well, respectable on the surface.

"She was obviously smart," he said.

"Yes. And driven," Sharon added, lifting her gaze. "I think she decided at a young age her life was going to be the complete opposite of her parents'. She detested any hint of weakness. I don't think I ever saw her cry. Sometimes I worried she had hardened her heart to the point she could never care about anyone."

"It seems odd that she would decide to become an EPA agent. It's not the sort of glamorous, high-paying job that would attract most women with ambition."

"I'll admit I was surprised. She always loved science, so I hoped she would become a doctor. Or maybe a pharmacist." Sharon shrugged. "When she told me she intended to work for the EPA, I assumed it was because it wouldn't demand a graduate school degree. Unlike a lot of kids, she didn't have parents to help with college expenses and she was drowning in debt."

Kaden arched his brows. Vanna had only been out of school a year or so when she became engaged to Darren. So how had she managed to achieve a lifestyle anyone would envy?

"If she was drowning in debt, I'm surprised she could afford a Porsche. And her apartment must have cost a fortune."

"I never visited her apartment—we'd usually meet at a restaurant or my house—but she did come by to show me the car."

"Did she say how she paid for it?"

"I did ask. She claimed she'd gotten a fellowship her senior year that wiped out her loans." Sharon lifted her hands, something that might have been regret rippling over her face. "Honestly, I assumed some man bought her the car and she didn't want to admit the truth."

"Was it usual for her to have people buying her stuff?"

Sharon hesitated before heaving a sigh. "Vanna was a beautiful girl and she leveraged it to her advantage. I think she had the philosophy of using people before they could use her. Like I said . . . she was jaded." Clearly, the older woman knew about her foster daughter's habit of getting what she wanted by whatever means necessary. But Kaden doubted she knew about the blackmail. She might accept Vanna having her quirks, but she didn't seem the type to turn a blind eye to illegal activities. Then, abruptly, her expression softened. "At least until she fell in love with your brother. That was different."

Kaden was instantly distracted. "Different how?"

"It was the first time I'd ever seen her truly happy. As if she discovered whatever it was she was seeking and was suddenly content with her life." She sent Kaden a small smile, as if sensing his need to believe Vanna hadn't been using Darren for her own selfish reasons. That she'd loved him. "That's why I didn't believe for one second she simply disappeared."

"Neither did Darren. He was convinced something happened to her."

"And now . . . maybe . . ."

The older woman's words hung in the air as they both considered the potential end of the fifteen-year-old mystery. It was bound to change both of their lives.

Of course, nothing was solved yet. There were still more questions than answers. Kaden took a second to consider what he'd learned from Sharon, trying to decide what might be relevant to Vanna's murder.

"Did Vanna say anything about the fellowship she received?" he finally asked. It seemed odd she would get enough money to pay off her debts her senior year.

"She called it the Burke Fellowship Award," Sharon said without hesitation.

Kaden grunted, as if he'd taken a blow to the gut. "Burke? You're sure?"

"Yes." Sharon gave a firm nod of her head. "I remember the name because I looked it up after Vanna left and couldn't find any information about the fellowship. I even contacted the college. They couldn't give out any private information, but they did say they didn't have a fellowship by that name. The next time Vanna visited me, I asked for more information. I was worried she was being lured into some con. After all, if something seems to be too good to be true, it usually is."

Kaden clenched his hands. "What did she say?"

"She claimed it was a private fellowship that was given by some man named Burke to a worthy student going into the EPA." Sharon's eyes dimmed. "That's when I began to suspect a man bought the Porsche for her and she didn't want to admit it. At least not to me."

"Do you know how much the fellowship was supposedly worth?"

Sharon pursed her lips. "If Vanna was being honest and she really did pay off her loans, it had to be at least twenty-five thousand dollars. Plus whatever the car and her apartment cost."

Kaden whistled. He hadn't expected such a large number. "That's a big fellowship."

"Yes." Sharon grimaced, then, with a brisk movement, she was pushing herself off the couch and walking to retrieve her coat. "I really should be getting home. I have a couple of teenagers who need hands-on supervision."

Kaden rose to his feet, holding up his hand. "Just one more question."

"What?"

"Did Vanna ever mention the town of Pike?"

Not really expecting the older woman to have an answer, Kaden was surprised when Sharon nodded as she pulled on her coat.

"Since I was contacted by the coroner's office to say that a skeleton had been found near that place, I've been trying to figure out why she might have been there. Her work took her all over the area, of course. But there was something about Pike that seemed familiar."

"Did you figure it out?"

"Yes. I think it was the summer after her sophomore year that she did an internship at the University of Wisconsin Extension Office near Pike."

Kaden's gaze flicked toward Lia, watching her eyes widen. It hadn't occurred to either of them that Vanna's connection to Pike would have started before the EPA job had taken her there.

He returned his attention to Sharon. "Do you know what she did?"

"A lot of it I didn't understand, but basically, she helped develop plans to protect the waterways from the animal waste produced at the dairy farms."

Kaden nodded. That sounded legit. "How long was she there?"

"For several weeks." A sad smile touched Sharon's lips. "At first, she came home every weekend, complaining that she was stuck at the ends of the earth. She was truly convinced there was nothing in town but aging farmers and cow manure."

"She wasn't entirely wrong," Lia muttered.

"After a week or so, she must have made a few friends," Sharon continued. "She stopped coming home."

Kaden made a mental note to check out the extension office once they returned to Pike.

"Did she ever talk about her time there? Or mention any names?" he asked.

"No, but when she came back after her internship was over, she was different."

"Different?"

"Distracted. Even . . . restless. Like she had something on her mind."

"Did you find out what was bothering her?"

"No. She went back to college and we barely spoke for months." Sharon lifted her arm to glance at her watch. "I really need to go."

Without warning, Lia stepped forward. "Do you know any friends she might have from college?"

"Not really." Sharon turned and started out of the room. At the door she paused, glancing over her shoulder. "There was a professor. What was her name?" She paused before snapping her fingers. "Professor Sanders . . . no, Sanderson. Yes, Sanderson. That was it. I think the two of them were close. Vanna talked about her all the time."

"Thanks," Lia murmured.

Sharon glanced toward Kaden. "Let me know if you discover anything. I'd like to have a proper funeral for Vanna. She deserved that."

"I will."

Chapter 16

Lia waited until she heard the car drive away before she broke the silence. "Burke Fellowship. That's not a coincidence."

"My thought exactly." Kaden slowly turned to face her, his expression troubled. "Then again, Ryan Burke doesn't strike me as the philanthropic type."

Lia rolled her eyes. She'd never spent much time with the businessman, but she'd known plenty of people who worked at the meatpacking plant. According to them, Ryan Burke was cold and ruthless and willing to cut any corner to save a buck. Certainly not the sort of man to hand out thousands of dollars to anyone, let alone a college student he barely knew.

"No. He would more likely make up the fellowship for a tax break and pocket the money."

"So, did Vanna discover something about the meatpacking plant while she was an intern?"

"I used to visit the extension office with Mom," Lia said. "They had a large greenhouse where the students tested hybrid seeds for the university ag program. In the fall, they would donate the vegetables and fruits. We put out crates in front of the store for the locals to grab." She struggled to think of the last time she'd been there. "I'm pretty sure it shut down at least ten years ago." Her breath caught in her throat as she pictured the dilapidated building. "Oh."

"What is it?"

"The old office isn't too far away from the railroad bridge where Vanna jumped."

Kaden arched his brows. "We should check it out. But while we're in Madison, we should see if we can track down Professor Sanderson. She might know more about the supposed fellowship."

They were both potential leads in discovering Vanna's various connections to Pike, but Lia was hoping to find something more tangible. Didn't the cops always say to solve a crime you had to follow the money? That seemed like the most straightforward way to discover who might have the motive to murder her. And, just as importantly, who might have profited from her death.

"What happened to Vanna's belongings after she died?"

"My brother donated most of her clothes, although he kept a few of her personal items." Kaden nodded toward a door across the room. "I have them packed away in his study."

"Are there financial records?"

"There were some bank statements my brother gave to the private investigators."

"Can I see them?"

"Sure."

Kaden crossed the floor and pushed open the door, leading her into a large, distinctly masculine room with heavy wooden furniture and walls lined with bookshelves. It was surprisingly cozy compared to the sleek starkness of the living room, and Lia silently wondered if Vanna had chosen the décor for the public area of the condo, while Darren stamped his own personal taste in here.

Kaden headed directly to the walnut desk. He touched a

button and one of the shelves swung open to reveal a hidden closet. It was all very 007, but Lia was too distracted to appreciate the craftsmanship. Vanna's foster mother had revealed that Vanna had a habit of manipulating the people around her for monetary gain. It confirmed their suspicion that the woman was capable of blackmailing someone—or several someones—in Pike.

Kaden stepped out of the closet carrying a box he placed on the desk. Flipping open the lid, he pulled out stacks of files and handed them to Lia.

"These are the originals, along with the private investigator's report. He didn't find anything."

Lia offered an absent nod, quickly scanning the private investigator's notes. It was thorough, but it wasn't what Lia was interested in.

"He didn't find anything because he was searching for evidence of Vanna being alive. Or if someone had killed her and was drawing money from her accounts."

Kaden positioned himself so he could glance over her shoulder as she sorted through the bank statements.

"What are you looking for?" he asked.

"Her cash flow." Lia read through one statement after another, all the way up to when they abruptly stopped in December 2007. She blew out a frustrated sigh. "It's not here."

"You'll have to explain. Numbers give me a brain cramp."

She turned to meet his wry smile. "If Vanna was bribing companies or towns for large sums of money, there should be some evidence."

"Maybe she stashed her ill-gotten gains in a secret bank deposit box," he suggested. "That's what they do in the movies."

"The numbers we saw on the back of the map indicated

she was receiving electronic transfers into an account, not cash." Lia considered the various ways a person could hide such large amounts of money. "She might have another savings account for the bribes, but you said she had expensive tastes."

"She did."

Lia held up the top statement so he could see the transactions. "This appears to be a woman who lived a very modest lifestyle. Two thousand bucks or so for rent, utilities, and groceries. Easily within her monthly salary."

Kaden reached to take the statement, his brows snapping together. "This can't be right. Vanna spent more than this on her weekly spa treatments. And her rent had to be triple what this shows."

Lia placed the statements on the desk, accepting she wasn't going to learn anything from them. There were no unexplained deposits, no large influxes of cash, nothing beyond her monthly paycheck.

"Which means she must be using two separate checking accounts." She shook her head. "Risky."

"Why do you say that?"

"Regulators start to wonder why you need your money spread around to multiple places. Especially if you have funds coming from shell companies based overseas. That's how drug lords launder their money, and foreign countries pay off spies. Add in the fact that she works for a government agency and it wouldn't take much to trigger an investigation."

"How could she hide the money?"

A good question. Unfortunately, Lia's expertise was in assessing the financial viability of a prospective company, not hiding bribe money. She did suspect, however, that it wouldn't be easy.

"It's possible she had an accomplice," she suggested.

Kaden stiffened, his brows snapping together. "Not my brother."

She reached out to lay her hand on his arm. She hadn't known Darren, but she knew Kaden. No matter how much he loved his brother, he wouldn't ignore his faults. He didn't believe for a second that Darren had any knowledge of his fiancée's blackmail scheme.

"Or she set up a fake identity," Lia hastily suggested. "You don't have her tax returns, do you?"

Kaden glanced toward the boxes stacked in the closet. "I don't think so."

"We need to find out where she hid the money and what happened to it." Lia considered their limited options. "I'll do some snooping when we get back to Pike. Vanna must have left some kind of trail."

Without warning, Kaden stepped close, wrapping her in the heat of his body. Like a warm blanket.

"How?"

Lia tilted back her head, her heart lurching as she watched his eyes soften to a silver mist.

"How did she leave a trail?"

"How do you have the skills to trace a fifteen-year-old account? Most people wouldn't know where to start."

She knew what he was asking. He wanted to know what she did in the privacy of her office. She found herself instinctively trying to deflect his question. "I'm not making any promises—"

"Lia," he interrupted, tracing the line of her jaw with the tips of his fingers. "There's no pressure. You don't have to talk about it if you don't want to."

"It's not that. . . ." She allowed her words to trail away with a sigh. "I suppose I am a little uncomfortable. I never talk about my real career."

"You're not a superhero in disguise, are you?"

Her lips twitched at his teasing. "I wish. I'm just an investor."

His brows arched at her revelation, but he didn't look particularly surprised. "Like a day trader?"

"No, I invest directly in businesses, not the stock market."

"You're a bank?"

"In a way," she conceded. She'd created her business with nothing more than gut instinct and a good head for numbers. Certainly, there was nothing traditional about it. "I loan money to start-up companies or help existing ones expand."

"And they pay you back with interest?"

"Most of the time. Once in a while I remain a silent partner because I have a personal connection to the business. Either because I know the owners or I'm interested in what they create."

A mysterious smile curved his lips. "I assume you've done well?"

"Yes," she admitted without false modesty.

This man wouldn't be intimidated by her wealth. And he certainly wouldn't be one of those jerks who tried to con a woman out of their money. He had built his own empire.

"So why the secrecy?"

"Pike is a wonderful place to live, but sometimes it's annoying to have everyone in town discussing my business. This is one part of my life that I'm not willing to share."

"How did you get started?"

"It was a fluke, really." Lia recalled the sleepless nights when she made her first loan. She'd not only worried she would lose all her money but the first few clients were people she knew. The destruction of their friendships would have been worse than the debt. "I inherited my grandparents' trust fund and used it to help a friend open his construction business in Grange. It just sort of snowballed from there. I invest in businesses all over the world now."

It wasn't exactly a boast, but Lia was honest enough to admit she was proud of the career she'd created. And it felt astonishingly good to share her accomplishments with this man.

"I can understand keeping your investments quiet. I'm sure your clients appreciate your discretion." He studied her with a curious gaze, his thumb brushing her lower lip. "But why keep up the pretense of running a grocery store?"

Lia shivered, anticipation swirling through her body. He was barely touching her, but she felt every nerve tingle to life. It was . . . intoxicating.

"There's no pretense." Lia struggled to concentrate on forming the words. What she really wanted to do was yank his head down and kiss him until the world faded away. "That store has been in my family for over one hundred years. It's important that it stay open. For Pike." She shrugged. "And for my mother."

"Ah." His eyes held a tenderness that threatened to melt something deep inside her. "She doesn't know you use your own money to pad the store accounts, does she?"

Lia wrinkled her nose. "It's been limping along for years. My mother and I barely scraped by. It got worse after she retired. There are stores in Grange that will deliver to Pike. And, of course, there's online shopping."

His hands cupped her face as he stepped closer, the warm scent of him filling her senses.

"You're a fraud, you know, Lia Porter."

Her heart pounded, her palms damp as he smiled down at her. "Excuse me?"

"You pretend to be this quiet, down-to-earth woman who spends her days baking cookies and stocking shelves."

She blinked. "That's exactly what I am."

"Liar." He bent his head, brushing his lips against hers as he spoke. "You're a risk-taking entrepreneur who thrives on living on the edge. Just like me."

Like him? Daredevil, stuntman, sex idol? No way. She was boring Lia, who always did the right thing and didn't know how to have fun. *Except for when she was with Kaden Vaughn*, a voice whispered in the back of her mind. When she was standing close to this man, she didn't feel boring. And most certainly didn't want to do the right thing.

She wanted to be a risk-taker.

"You're trying to make me seem a lot more exciting than I am," she whispered.

"Trust me, there's no way you could be more exciting. Feel." He grabbed her hand and pressed it to the center of his chest. Directly over his pounding heart. "You have me . . ."

"What?"

"I don't have the words." He pressed a kiss against her lips. "Let me show you."

"Kaden."

"Just this." He nibbled a warm path along the line of her jaw. "That's all I ask. Just this."

Lia groaned, lifting her arms to wrap them around his neck and arching against his hard body. His lips returned to her mouth, kissing her with a passion that sent jolts of pleasure searing through her. She went on her tiptoes, tangling her fingers in his hair as she silently encouraged him to deepen the kiss.

There was a fluttering excitement in the pit of her belly that made her toes curl in her boots. She'd never had a kiss that felt so . . . monumental. As if she was no longer the same Lia Porter. She was different. Special.

A fierce hunger ignited and spread through her body She wanted more than this man's kisses. Much more. Lia parted her lips, inviting his tongue as his hands cupped her backside to tug her tight against the hard thrust of his arousal.

Yes . . .

A buzzing sensation raced up her arm. At first, Lia assumed it was part of her intense reaction to Kaden's kiss. There were dozens of shivers racing through her. As the buzzing continued, she frowned. This was different from her tremors of pleasure. It took a few seconds for her passion-dazed brain to recognize it was her watch, signaling an incoming call.

Reluctantly, she untangled herself from Kaden's warm grasp and glanced at the screen on her watch.

"Strange."

Kaden flashed her a frustrated smile, shoving his fingers through the silky strands of his hair.

"'Strange' is not a word a man wants to hear after he kisses a woman."

"Sorry. The sheriff's office is calling. I should get this."

Turning, she hurried out of the office, through the living room, and into the spare bedroom she'd used the night before. She'd left her phone charging on a dresser. She snatched it up and managed to connect the call before it could be dumped into her voice mail.

"Hello." Her brows snapped together as she heard a familiar voice. "Hi, Anthony. Is anything wrong?" She listened to his breathless words, her mouth falling open in shock. "Oh my God. I'm in Madison now, but I can meet you at the store in a couple of hours."

She disconnected the call and glanced toward Kaden, who had followed her into the bedroom.

"What's going on?" he demanded.

"They found Ryan Burke in a freezer at the meatpacking plant."

Kaden looked puzzled. "Was he hurt?"

"He's dead."

Chapter 17

Kaden grabbed his suitcase and the files from his brother's office and bundled Lia into his Jeep in record time. They were both silent on the drive back to Pike, trying to process the thought that the man they'd just spoken with the day before was dead.

It was unnerving.

And worrisome.

Both Drew Hurst and Judge Armstrong had been strangers to Kaden. Just names of people who had been attacked. This death was a lot more personal.

Pulling into the alley behind Porter's Grocery Store, Kaden shut off the engine and studied the empty space where the SUV was usually parked.

"Your vehicle is gone," he pointed out the obvious.

"I called Sykes to have them repair the window." She climbed out of the Jeep, digging in her purse to retrieve her keys. "They'll bring it back when it's done."

Kaden joined her, holding his suitcase and her overnight bag as she jiggled the knob and the door swung open. He grimaced, knowing it wouldn't take a stuntman to easily kick through the flimsy lock. Anyone walking through the alley could force their way in.

"You need an upgrade on your security system," he

muttered as they walked into her office so he could set down the bags.

"Yes," she agreed without hesitation. "I'll have to call someone from Grange to put in new cameras and change the locks. Unfortunately, this time of year means it will take a while for them to get out here."

Kaden bit back his offer to call in one of his buddies, who could give her Pentagon-grade protection. Lia was perfectly capable of deciding what security system she wanted and had plenty of money to pay for it. She wasn't the type of woman who wanted anyone interfering in her business. Including him.

Still, he wasn't happy at the knowledge she was vulnerable while a maniac stalked the streets of Pike.

"I don't like the thought of you here alone," he muttered.

She turned to face him, a teasing smile curving her lips. "I'm not alone."

"True." Kaden struggled out of his coat before tossing it onto a nearby chair and moving to wrap his arms around Lia. His body tensed, his passion flaming to a fever pitch as her fresh, lemon scent filled his senses. His mind might whisper he needed to take things slow, but his desire for her was quickly spiraling out of control. Tugging her closer, he lowered his head. "Where were we before we were so rudely interrupted?"

His mouth had barely brushed her parted lips when the sound of a vehicle rumbling into the alley echoed through the office.

"That must be Anthony," she whispered.

Kaden muttered a curse. As grateful as he was to the deputy for contacting them about Burke's death, he could happily throttle him. His habit of interrupting them at crucial moments was as annoying as hell.

"His timing really sucks."

"We need to find out what happened."

"I know." He nuzzled soft kisses over her upturned face, savoring the satin softness of her skin.

There was a sharp knock on the back door and Lia pressed her hands against his chest.

"Kaden."

Grudgingly, Kaden lifted his head and dropped his arms. "Okay."

Lia reached up to smooth the short strands of her hair, her cheeks flushed and her eyes smoldering with a hunger that pulsed inside him. But with a brisk motion she grabbed the plate of chocolate chip cookies she'd left for him before he'd announced they were heading to Madison. He wanted to protest. He didn't want to share the treats with anyone. Instead, Kaden quickly joined Lia as she headed to the back door and pulled it open. He didn't think the deputy was involved, but he wasn't taking any chances. Anthony had, after all, lured Lia back to town with the promise of information about the recently deceased Ryan Burke. Maybe he intended to get rid of anyone who threatened his secret.

Including Lia and Kaden.

Not nearly as cautious, Lia pulled open the door and smiled warmly at the man who was wrapped in a heavy jacket and wearing a fur hat with a sheriff star stitched on the front.

"Hi, Anthony." She stepped back to wave the deputy inside with the plate she held in her hand. "How's your mom?"

"Good, thanks." Anthony widened his eyes as he caught sight of the wound on Lia's temple. "What happened to you?"

"It's just a scratch. Come in."

The deputy paused, looking over his shoulder as if he was worried he'd been followed into the alley. Only when he was sure he was alone did he step over the threshold so Lia could shut the door.

"I really shouldn't be here."

"We can talk upstairs," Lia said, leading them up the steps to her private loft. Once they were in the kitchen, she set the cookies in the middle of the table. "Have a seat. I'll make some coffee."

Kaden hid a smile, realizing what Lia was doing. Like any businesswoman, she understood the first rule of dealing with a client, which was making sure they were comfortable. Anthony was clearly nervous and she was taking swift action to keep him from bolting.

Taking his cue, Kaden moved behind the deputy and gently pressed him into the chair.

"You're worried," he said, taking a seat next to Anthony. He was prepared to tackle the man if he tried to leave.

"Yeah." Anthony cleared a lump from his throat. "I'm worried."

"So are we," Kaden assured him.

"That's why I called." Anthony grimaced, his squint more pronounced than usual. "You guys seem to be the only people in town who don't think what's been happening is a bunch of crazy accidents."

Kaden leaned forward. "There's nothing accidental about anything that's happened since Vanna's skeleton was discovered."

Anthony heaved a deep sigh and pulled off his hat, tossing it on the table. "It's been a freaking nightmare. I wish Zac was here."

Lia crossed to the table to set down a bowl of sugar and a creamer. "Tell us what's bothering you."

Anthony took a second to gather his composure. At last, he grabbed a cookie and settled back in his chair.

"Like I said, they found Ryan Burke in a freezer at the meatpacking plant."

Lia returned to the coffee maker, as if trying to make the meeting seem like a nice visit between friends. Not a discussion about dead bodies and potential murder.

"When?" Kaden asked.

"Early this morning." Anthony shivered, taking a bite of the cookie.

Kaden studied the deputy's pale face. "Do you know who found the body?"

"The morning janitor, Rio Boren."

"Boren?" It took Kaden a second to connect the name with a face. "Any relation to Manny Boren, the temporary guard Burke hired?"

"Cousin."

Kaden frowned. Was it relevant that the two were cousins? Maybe. Maybe not. In a small town, everyone was related.

"Why did the janitor go into the freezer?" he asked.

"He's part of a crew that goes in before the workers arrive to sanitize the equipment. Rio said he noticed one of the freezer doors wasn't fully closed and he went to check it out."

Kaden slowly nodded. That seemed like a reasonable explanation. "And he found Burke?"

"Yep." Anthony polished off his cookie and reached for another. Kaden didn't blame him. Those cookies were magical.

"If the door was open, he obviously wasn't trapped inside." Lia moved back to the table to place two mugs of coffee in front of them. "So what happened?"

Anthony's jaw tightened. "According to the mayor, he slipped and busted his head."

Lia continued to bustle around the kitchen, grabbing mugs and napkins. "You don't agree?"

"I did at first," Anthony confessed. "When we found Burke in the freezer, there was a layer of frost on the steel floor and a nasty gash on the side of his head, like he'd hit it on something hard. And his phone was all smashed. He could have slipped and dropped his phone before smacking his head on the floor. It made sense."

"What made you question that explanation?" Lia asked.

"It was obvious he'd been in there for several hours. I decided to ask around to see if anyone would know why he would go in there at night."

Kaden regarded the deputy with a hint of surprise. It would be easy to underestimate Anthony. He acted like a good ol' boy who sat at his desk and passed the time playing on his phone. He obviously had some investigative skills.

"A good question," Kaden murmured. "Did you get any answers?"

"I talked to Marla Walsh." The deputy glanced toward Kaden. "She's the receptionist for Burke."

"We met."

"That's right." Anthony chuckled. "She told me she almost peed her pants when you walked into the plant. She's still excited about seeing you in real life."

Kaden firmly turned Anthony's attention back to the death of Burke. "Did she have any explanation for why her boss would be in the freezer?"

"She didn't have a clue." Anthony reached for the sugar to pour a heaping teaspoon into his mug. "She claimed he kept a close eye on the floor to make sure his employees were doing their jobs, but he didn't wander around the place unless there was something specific he needed to deal with."

Lia took a chair at the table, studying Anthony with a

troubled expression. "She couldn't tell you anything that might help?"

"Actually, she did." Anthony sipped his coffee. "She said Burke came to her yesterday afternoon to tell her that he would be working late and that he would lock up."

Lia shrugged. "Was that unusual?"

"*Extremely*." Anthony emphasized the word. Presumably because the receptionist had emphasized it. "Burke also told Manny he could take off early."

Kaden jerked in surprise. Burke had just hired the man. Why would he be giving him time off?

"Did he say why?"

"Just that he had work to do and he didn't want to be interrupted."

Kaden made a sound of disbelief. "If he didn't want to be interrupted, it would make more sense to insist his receptionist and guard stay so they could keep anyone from bothering him."

Anthony suddenly leaned forward, returning his mug to the table. "Unless he didn't want anyone to know what he was doing."

"Why do you say that?" Kaden demanded.

"The security cameras were switched off."

Kaden sucked in a sharp breath. "By Burke or someone else?"

"I watched the tape," Anthony answered. "It was Burke who turned them off."

"Why?" Lia asked in confusion.

"I don't know, but there was a hidden safe in his office that was left open."

Kaden stiffened. "Was there anything in it?"

Anthony shook his head. "Empty."

That did it, Kaden silently decided. The chances that

Burke's death was nothing more than a tragic accident had gone from small to zero. There had to have been something inside that safe. Something worth killing for.

So, why was the Pike Sheriff's Department pretending nothing unusual had happened? They should be doing a full investigation. Or, better yet, calling in the state officials to take over. There had to be some department that had the resources to discover how Burke had died and who was responsible.

"Tate didn't think any of that was suspicious?" Kaden growled.

"He said it was an accident and that was that. But he looked . . ." Anthony grimaced. "Tense. Like he was disturbed by Burke's death."

"I suppose that's not surprising," Lia murmured. "They were friends, weren't they?"

Anthony was shaking his head before she finished speaking. "Not friends like I have. I think they went golfing together and showed up at the same fancy parties, but when they were together they seemed weird."

Lia blinked. "Weird?"

"Antagonistic." The deputy looked proud at being able to use such a big word. As if he'd practiced it. "Like they could barely stand to be in each other's company."

Kaden tapped a finger on the edge of the table, considering Anthony's assessment of the mayor and Burke's relationship. It sounded like two men bound by expediency rather than genuine companionship. Was it just because they were both rich and powerful? Or was it something else that held them together?

Kaden ground his teeth together. More questions without answers.

"Was there anything else?" he asked.

"Yeah. When I was examining the body, I found a scrap of paper in his hand. It looked like the corner of a manila envelope. I'm guessing he was holding the envelope and the killer ripped it out of his hand." Anthony leaned back to unzip his thick coat. Then, reaching into an inner pocket, he pulled out a stack of photos. He handed them to Kaden. "Here are the pictures I took of the crime scene."

"Thanks."

Kaden took them with a surge of surprise. It was one thing to have the deputy share information about Burke's death. After all, the mayor was writing it off as an accident. But to get official crime scene photos . . .

As if realizing he was risking his job, Anthony shoved himself to his feet and snatched his hat from the table.

"If anyone asks how you got those pictures, I'm going to claim I don't have a damned clue," he warned.

Kaden held up the pictures. "Can I ask what you hope we can do with them?"

"I know Tate is covering up something, just like I know there's a killer in Pike." Anthony shook his head in frustration. "But Zac would have my ass if I did anything that might jeopardize the perp getting convicted if there ever is a real investigation." He glanced from Kaden to Lia. "I'm a deputy, I have to follow the rules. You don't."

Tate waited until midday before returning to the meat-packing plant. As he'd hoped, most of the employees were gathered in the lunchroom for their break . . . including the receptionist.

Moving to the desk, he hit the button that would unlock the door to the inner offices. There was a buzzing sound, followed by a soft click as the door swung open, and Tate hurried through the opening and down the hall. He had every right to be there. He was the acting sheriff. It was his duty to make a thorough search of the area, even if Burke's death had been an accident.

The brave words echoed through his mind, but they didn't keep him from tiptoeing his way to the end of the hallway and pressing the door open without making a sound.

In the end, it was a wasted effort.

When he passed the empty desk in the reception area, he assumed Marla Walsh was with the other employees. It wasn't until he'd entered the large office that he realized she was standing next to Burke's desk.

Tate frowned, his gaze running over the unwelcome intruder. She looked older than her thirty-odd years, with the first streaks of gray visible in her brown curls and her waistline at least twice the size it was in high school. A shame. She'd once been attractive enough that he'd tried to get her in the back seat of his car when Jolene wasn't around. Now he wouldn't touch her with a ten-foot pole.

"What are you doing in here?"

Marla jerked, her head snapping up to reveal her startled expression. "Tate."

He stepped forward, his brows furrowed into an annoyed frown. "I asked you a question."

There was a short silence, as if the receptionist was considering her options, then she turned to face him, a defiant expression settling on her square face.

"Mr. Burke's nephew is coming in today."

Tate vaguely knew Gavin Burke. The younger man lived in Grange and ran some sort of business. Apartments? Storage units? Something like that. Nothing to do with meat.

"Why would he be coming in?"

"Mrs. Burke asked him to start sorting through the accounts."

Tate tried to keep his expression from revealing his concern. That was the last thing he wanted.

"Why?"

"Obviously, she hopes she can sell the place. If not . . ." Marla shrugged. "I suppose it will close down."

"Krystal is selling?" Tate made a strangled sound. He'd been so worried about the past, he hadn't considered the future. What would happen to Pike if the plant closed? How many citizens would lose their jobs? He didn't have an actual empathy for those who might potentially be without a paycheck, but he had enough political savvy to know that unemployed people weren't happy. And that they might blame him for their misfortune.

He cleared his throat. "You're sure Krystal plans to sell the plant?"

"ASAP." A cruel smile curved Marla's lips. She was taking pleasure in his discomfort. "Her words, not mine."

Realizing he was giving away more than he wanted, Tate squared his shoulders. "That doesn't explain what you're doing in here."

It was Marla's turn to look uneasy. She waved a vague hand toward the box set on the floor next to the desk.

"I thought I would collect Mr. Burke's things to make room for the new Mr. Burke."

Did he believe her? Not entirely. Marla Walsh was sneaky as hell. She always had been. Stealing lunch money out of desks in elementary school and telling lies to get kids in trouble. Right now, however, Tate was only interested in getting rid of her.

"You'll have to do that later."

She glared at him. "Why?"

"Because I want to look through this stuff."

"Why?"

Tate wanted to strangle the stupid woman. Unfortunately, there were at least forty workers on the other side of the connecting door who would no doubt hear her screams.

"This is a crime scene."

Marla's eyes narrowed. "I thought you said Mr. Burke's death was an accident."

"It was."

"Then why—"

"I'm the sheriff," Tate interrupted, his voice harsh. "You'll do as I say."

Marla sniffed. She'd known him too long and too well to be intimidated. "You're the *acting* sheriff and you don't have any right to be in here. Not unless you have a search warrant."

"What do you know about search warrants?" Tate sneered. "I can arrest you if you impede my investigation."

"I'd like to see you try." Marla held his gaze, her hand reaching out to grab the phone receiver from the old-fashioned landline on the desk. "I'm calling Mrs. Burke. I think she'd like to know you're in here snooping around."

Tate puffed out his chest. He was used to giving orders and having them followed. "I'm here on official business."

"You can tell her that." Marla started to dial a number.

Tate muttered a curse. She'd called his bluff and he had no choice but to back down. Dammit.

"I don't have time for this nonsense." He smoothed his hands down the expensive fabric of his trench coat. "I'll be back later to do my search."

"Bring a warrant."

Tate lifted his hand, pointing a finger in the woman's face. "Careful, Marla."

"Or what?"

"Trust me, you don't want to find out," he warned, turning to head out the door. He paused, glancing over his shoulder. "And tell that son of yours to stop sniffing around my daughter. Unless he wants to end up in a hospital bed next to Drew Hurst."

Marla's face flushed an ugly crimson shade. "You'll be sorry you threatened me, Tate Erickson."

"Doubtful."

Chapter 18

Lia leaned forward as Kaden spread the photos across the kitchen table. Her stomach clenched with horror, but she forced herself to study the gruesome close-ups of the bloody wound on the side of Ryan Burke's head and the blue tint to his face. There was no doubt she was staring at a corpse. Just as there was no doubt he'd been murdered.

But they still had no idea who or why or when the killer might strike next.

As her grandpa would have said, they didn't know jack shit.

"I can't believe he's dead," she breathed, trying to wrap her head around what she was seeing. "We were just in his office."

Kaden slid his chair closer to her, as if sensing the warmth of his body would help to ease the knot that had formed in the pit of her stomach.

"I can't believe he's not the killer," he muttered.

"Yeah." She lifted her head to meet his troubled gaze. "That too."

"Everything was starting to point toward him." Kaden tapped a finger on the nearest picture. "When I talked to the locals, they implied that Burke's business ethics have always been sketchy. Something that might have attracted the attention of the EPA. And he obviously recognized Vanna's name despite trying to act dumb. Plus, he hired a guard to keep people away. Only someone with something to hide would do that."

Lia nodded. "And he would have had the sort of money necessary to pay off student loans seventeen or eighteen years ago."

"Exactly. The Burke Fellowship ties him directly to Vanna." Kaden huffed in exasperation. "If this was a television show, Ryan Burke would be the killer. . . ." He stiffened, as if he was struck by a sudden realization. "You know, just because he was murdered doesn't mean he wasn't involved in Vanna's death."

Lia's breath caught. It hadn't occurred to her that there might have been more than one person who wanted the poor woman dead. It made the memory of that night even more disturbing. And their current investigation more dangerous.

"You're right. If he had a partner—"

"Or partners."

"Or partners," she agreed. "Then one of them might be trying to keep the others from confessing to what happened to Vanna."

Kaden studied the pictures spread over the table, his expression grim. Was he realizing they might have more than one enemy lurking in the shadows?

"The mayor seems to be the most obvious accomplice," he said at last. "But I think we should keep an open mind."

Lia nodded. It was possible the mayor was using his position as temporary sheriff to hide his crimes. It was equally possible he was covering the crimes for a friend. Or maybe he was being paid to make the deaths look like accidents.

A shiver raced through her body and she grabbed her mug to take a sip of the coffee.

It had started with a question.

Did the skeleton belong to the woman she'd seen jump off the bridge fifteen years ago?

And now Drew was fighting for his life in the hospital, Judge Armstrong was in the morgue, and Ryan Burke's head was bashed in. It felt like a bad dream. One she wouldn't wake from until they discovered the truth.

With an effort, Lia gathered her wandering thoughts and concentrated on the pictures.

No doubt a trained professional could see all sorts of clues the killer had left behind, Lia, however, couldn't get past the fact he'd been left in the freezer.

"Why would he be in there?" she muttered, grabbing a cookie. It was hours since she'd eaten the muffin for breakfast. Now her stomach rumbled with hunger.

Kaden leaned back in his seat, his eyes darkened to charcoal. "He claimed he was going to work late. Something he never did."

"And he turned off the security system." She tried to imagine Ryan Burke alone in his office. Why turn off the cameras? Was he meeting a woman? No. She instantly dismissed that idea. If he wanted to have an affair, he had the money to go to a luxury hotel. Who would want to have sex in a meatpacking plant? Then she abruptly recalled what else Anthony had told them. "Because he didn't want to record what he had in his hidden safe?"

Kaden nodded, as if he'd already considered the possibility. "Very possible. It might have been some sort of proof of what happened fifteen years ago."

That made the most sense. Ryan might have questionable morals, but he wasn't stupid. If he'd been involved in Vanna's death with a partner, or partners, he would make sure they couldn't turn on him. Not without paying a painful price.

She frowned, once again imagining Ryan in his office, pulling some mysterious item from his safe. Anthony had mentioned the corner of a manila envelope, so she assumed it was pictures or papers he had hidden away. So why go to such an extreme effort to be alone?

"But why tell Manny to leave early?" she abruptly demanded. "He was across the parking lot. He couldn't have seen what was happening inside the office from that distance."

Kaden considered the question. A few seconds later, he sucked in a sharp breath. "Damn."

"What is it?"

"Manny could see the back parking lot."

Her breath caught in her throat. "Burke was meeting someone."

Kaden nodded. "And he wanted to keep that meeting a secret."

Lia set down her mug, swallowing the last of her cookie. "It had to have something to do with Vanna. Or one of the other supposed accidents that have happened. Why else go to such lengths?"

"I'm guessing we said something to spook him and he reached out to one of his partners. Either to threaten them to keep quiet or to suggest they confess what happened."

Lia found it hard to believe Ryan Burke would ever confess, but then again, if he feared his sins were about to be exposed, he might have wanted to get ahead of the potential repercussions. What better way than pointing the finger at someone else?

"Maybe that's the same thing that happened to Judge Armstrong," she suggested.

"Okay." Kaden narrowed his eyes as he considered the various implications. "Let's assume he was meeting someone. Why not use his office? Why go to the freezer?"

Lia tried to put herself in the man's shoes. Ryan Burke was obviously comfortable enough to arrange the meeting with the mystery killer in a place that was isolated, but that didn't mean he hadn't taken precautions.

"If Ryan suspected his partner had already killed the judge, he would have been on guard," she spoke her thoughts out loud. "He might even have a gun in his office for protection."

"Yes." Kaden nodded. "If I was the killer, I would have found some way to lure Burke away from his comfort zone. Maybe they claimed they had something to show him. Or created a distraction that would lead him into the area of the freezer."

"Then the killer bashed him on the head and crushed his phone to make it look like an accident."

"And if they happened to have a temporary badge, they could stop any investigation," Kaden added. "I'm sure the freezer floor was slick. Who's going to question the sheriff?"

Lia made a sound of annoyance. It was a good theory. A damned shame it was just that. A theory.

"The problem now is how we prove any of this." She shook her head in disgust, her finger touching the nearest picture. "Whoever attacked Ryan now has the evidence. They've probably already destroyed it."

"True."

Kaden's tone was distracted, as if he had his mind on something else. She turned, belatedly realizing he had leaned forward, close enough for his warm breath to brush her cheek.

"Kaden."

The silver eyes darkened to smoke as they watched the blush stain her cheeks. "Yes?"

The room suddenly felt too hot. As if someone had cranked up the furnace. Not surprising. Kaden was big and gorgeous and indecently sexy. He would give any woman hot flashes.

"We're trying to figure out how to prove Ryan Burke was murdered."

"I know. But . . ."

"But?"

He swept his fingers through the short strands of her hair. "I keep getting distracted."

Her heart thundered so fast she could barely breathe. "Don't blame me."

"I do." His hand cupped the back of her head. "This is entirely your fault."

"What is?"

"This."

He tugged her close, sealing their lips together in a kiss that sent shock waves of pleasure to the tips of her toes. Desire blasted through her, melting away any hesitation as she wrapped her arms around his neck. She could taste coffee on his lips and something else. Something that was pure Kaden.

Magic.

Butterflies fluttered in her stomach, tiny sparks of pleasure racing through her. She tightened her arms around his neck, suddenly wishing she could freeze this moment. This was exactly where she wanted to spend the rest of eternity.

The thought had barely managed to form when it was shattered as the revving of a loud engine broke the sensual spell. It was distant enough she could easily have ignored the annoying sound. And any other day she would have. She wanted to drown in the glorious sensations that spilled through her. It'd been so long since a man had stirred her hunger to a fever pitch. She wanted to climb in his lap and forget the world outside.

But today the noise of the engine was a sharp reminder that she'd heard that sound before.

"Wait." She pulled back, trying to think through the passion that clouded her mind.

Kaden frowned, concern darkening his eyes. "What's wrong?"

With a strangled sound, she was leaping to her feet and running toward the door. "That's the engine I heard after my window was busted."

"Careful, Lia," he called out as she wrenched open the door and took the steps three at a time. "Damn."

With a burst of speed, Kaden had caught up to her as she entered the store and dashed toward the large front window. Lia pressed her face against the cold glass, her gaze sweeping the street for a glimpse of a vehicle before it could disappear. Thankfully, the driver was headed south and had been forced to stop at the corner. It gave Lia the opportunity to get the full view of the truck before it drove through the intersection and disappeared.

She sent Kaden a startled glance. "Cord Walsh."

"You're sure?"

"Absolutely. His grandfather painted a cow on the back tailgate when he used the truck to deliver milk around town. It's faded, but you can still see that outline. As far as I know, it's the only one in town that looks like that."

Kaden muttered a curse. "I've been intending to have a word with that young man. Looks like it needs to be sooner rather than later."

Lia agreed. She didn't have any idea how Cord could be connected to their investigation, but she was certain it was his truck she'd heard drive off after she'd been hit by the brick.

Together they entered the office and Kaden grabbed his

coat. He was pulling it on when Lia noticed a piece of paper on the floor beneath the table at the back of the room.

"What's that?" She moved to grab the paper, turning it over to read the words that were written in bold letters. *You're next.* "Oh my God."

"Lia?" In two long strides, Kaden was at her side. "What's wrong?"

"This."

She held out the paper and he read the words with a grim expression.

"Someone put this in here after we left for Madison," he said. "How did they get in?"

Lia forced herself to take a deep, calming breath. Panicking wasn't going to help. Even if the thought of someone creeping around her home to leave threats was sending icy chills down her spine.

Managing to maintain her composure, Lia headed toward the computers on her desk. "Let's check out the security cameras."

Kaden was quickly at her side, watching as she tapped on the keyboard to pull up the video from the cameras.

"How far does this go back?" he asked.

"Twenty-four hours." She tapped the mouse set next to the computer and scrolled backward. "I'll start at the beginning."

Two black-and-white screens popped up, one showing the grocery store and the other displaying the office. They remained steady as she skimmed through yesterday afternoon and into the early evening, but once night settled in, the view became shadowed. And worse, the flickering from the Christmas lights outside the store caused the front camera to zoom in and out of focus. The security system was installed by her mother in case someone fell in the store and tried to sue her for damages, not to capture criminals in the dead of night.

It wasn't until the video hit midnight that there was a movement as the front door was pushed open and a figure stepped into the building.

"There," Lia murmured.

Both Lia and Kaden leaned forward, as if it would help them peer through the gloom as the form moved toward the back of the store and disappeared from view.

Kaden hissed in frustration. "It's too fuzzy to make out any details."

"Fuzzy" was an understatement. The intruder appeared to be wearing a heavy coat and a fur hat with a scarf wrapped around their face. But honestly, it was nothing more than a smudge on the video.

A few seconds passed and then the door to the office was pushed open and the dark form entered. The video didn't zoom in and out, which made it easier to see what the intruder was doing, but it was still impossible to determine who it might be. Lia couldn't even be sure whether it was a man or a woman.

The mystery person stopped, as if glancing around, then with quick steps was headed toward the back of the room. Clearly they knew where they wanted to go. Halting next to the table, they reached into their pocket and pulled out something. Was it the note? Probably. There was a tense minute as the form bent forward, perhaps arranging the paper in a precise spot. Then, weirdly, the person lifted their arms, as if they were shrugging out of their coat. Lia frowned. No. It wasn't their coat.

"What is that?" she muttered.

"It looks like a backpack." Kaden leaned his palms on the desk, watching the video with the intensity of a hawk spotting its prey. Then he stiffened as they both watched the intruder shoving something into the backpack. "Shit. The files." Kaden spun around to glare at the bare table. "I didn't even notice they were missing."

Lia grimaced. She had a vague memory of catching a glimpse of the files before they left for Madison, but she hadn't noticed they were gone when they returned. Not even when she grabbed the cookies to take upstairs.

"Neither did I."

Kaden turned back to the computer. "What time did this happen?"

Lia pointed toward the bottom of the screen, where the video was date- and time-stamped.

"Just after midnight."

Lia pushed the mouse to restart the video and they watched in silence as the intruder left the office with the backpack in their hand and hurried out of the front of the store. She kept the images rolling, hoping they might catch a glimpse of a vehicle drive past the front window, but there was nothing but darkness. At last she switched off the camera and straightened.

The stranger hadn't tried to get into the cash register or searched the office for money or valuables that might have been left in the desk. They hadn't even glanced toward the computers that were worth a fortune. They'd come in with a specific purpose.

She shook her head in confusion. "Who would even know about the files? Or where to find them?"

Kaden sent her a rueful glance. "I told everyone in the diner I had information about Vanna that I intended to hand over to the FBI. By now I'm sure everyone in Pike has heard the story."

"Seriously?"

"I wanted to stir things up. Our killer—or killers—have been annoyingly clever at staying hidden in plain sight.

They managed to run over Drew and slam the judge into the back of his garage in broad daylight." His eyes smoldered, his frustration vibrating around him. "It has to be someone local. Someone who wouldn't be noticed driving around town or walking the streets."

"I agree. But why pretend you have information for the FBI?"

He shrugged. "I was hoping it might make them desperate enough to expose themselves."

Lia glanced toward the empty table. She didn't doubt the men from the diner had quickly spread the rumor of mystery files and the FBI. And no doubt embellished the story until it sounded like the government was about to sweep into Pike and start hauling off potential criminals.

"It looks like it worked."

"Too well." He crossed toward the back of the room, peering out the window into the alley. "I didn't consider the fact that anyone could have walked past and seen the files on the table." He slammed a fist into his open palm, the sound echoing loudly through the office. "Damn. That was careless."

Lia shook her head. "It wasn't your fault. Anyone could have walked past and seen the files, but not everyone has a key to get in the building," she reminded him.

He slowly turned to meet her steady gaze. "Wayne?"

"I think we should ask him."

Chapter 19

Lia left the office to head upstairs. She'd left her phone on the counter when they were talking to Anthony.

"Who do you want to talk to first? Cord or Wayne?" Kaden asked, walking close behind her.

"Wayne." Grabbing her phone, she tapped in a quick text. "I'll see if he can meet us here." Less than a minute passed before Lia had her answer. "He's on his way."

Kaden looked grim. "Let's go back to the office. I don't want him up here."

Lia readily retraced her steps to the office. She understood Kaden's caution. And honestly, she didn't want anyone in her private space right now. Well, no one except the man who was walking close enough to tease her senses with his warm, male scent. Kaden would always be welcome in her home.

Still, she didn't want to consider the possibility that the young man could ever be a threat. Not to her.

"I can't believe Wayne would be responsible for any of this." She spoke her thoughts out loud as they entered the office. "Certainly he couldn't have been involved in Vanna's death. He wouldn't have been more than two or three years old when she disappeared."

Kaden leaned against the desk, his arms folded over his chest. "What about his family?"

"He was raised by a single mother."

"Do they live in town?"

"Yes." Lia had driven Wayne home when the weather was bad or if he happened to work late. The house was rapidly decaying, with a sagging roof and a porch that tilted to a drunken angle. Amber Neilson did her best, but it was tough for a woman raising a kid on her own. It wasn't the condition of the house that made her grimace, however. It was the location. "It's just a couple of blocks from where Drew was hit."

Kaden's jaw tightened, as if her words confirmed his suspicion that Wayne was somehow involved in the crimes.

"Where does she work?"

"She bounces from job to job." Lia didn't mention the fact that Amber was often fired for not showing up for her shifts. "Last I heard, she was tending bar at the Bait and Tackle."

"Did she ever work at the meatpacking plant?"

Lia hesitated, trying to latch onto a vague memory. "I think she was working there when she was pregnant. There were a lot of people in town mad when she was fired just a few weeks after Wayne was born."

"A coincidence?" Kaden arched a brow. "Or a connection?"

"No, not Amber."

The protest was more reflexive than heartfelt. Lia didn't want to think someone she knew was responsible for the awful crimes.

"Whoever entered your store last night had a key," Kaden insisted. "It has to be Wayne or Della."

"Either one of them could have left a key laying around." Lia knew that sticking her head in the sand wasn't going to help. Just the opposite. But there was a stubborn part of her that wanted to cling to her belief in both Wayne and Della. They weren't just employees. They were a part of her family. "It's not like we ever worried about being robbed. Not in Pike."

Easily sensing her distress, Kaden smoothly turned his suspicions to a less sensitive suspect.

"Wayne and Cord are friends, right?"

Lia eagerly latched onto the opportunity to point the finger of blame in another direction. Selfish, but hey, she was human.

"Not really friends," she conceded. "But I'm sure they've been together at the hospital to visit Drew. Or just hanging around town. Pike isn't big enough for them to avoid each other."

Kaden's expression was distracted, as if he was mentally shuffling through the various bits of evidence against the young man.

"The Hurst family owns a dairy farm. Maybe they weren't happy with the work Vanna was doing at the extension office. If she confirmed that the dairy industry was destroying the environment, it could have put their livelihood at risk."

They exchanged a glance, knowing it was a stretch. Before Lia could respond, there was the sound of the front door opening, and Wayne called out, "Ms. Porter?"

"I'm in the office," Lia called back.

Kaden straightened from the desk and lowered his arms. "He still has his key."

Lia nodded, watching as Wayne entered the office. He was wearing a heavy parka, but he had on a pair of expensive sneakers. That meant he'd used his mother's car to travel the short distance. He wouldn't risk ruining his new shoes in the snow.

Belatedly catching sight of Kaden, Wayne skidded to a halt, his face flushing with pleasure.

"Oh . . . hey, man." He cleared his throat, trying to play it cool. "How's it going?"

Lia grabbed a laptop and moved forward to take control. She knew Wayne well enough to realize he had a wonderful heart, but he was like any teenager. If he thought he was being interrogated, he would shut down.

They needed information, not sullen silence.

She set the laptop on the table and took a seat, waving a hand to the chair next to her. "Thanks for coming so quickly."

"No problem." Wayne plopped down, his eyes widening as he caught sight of Lia's face. "You're hurt. What happened?"

Lia wrinkled her nose. She'd forgotten about her wound, but it offered the perfect opening.

"Someone threw a brick at me."

Wayne blinked, staring at her as if he thought she was trying to make a joke. At last, he shook his head in disbelief.

"Where? In the store?"

She waved a hand toward the window. "In the alley."

He continued to stare at her, as if lost for words. "I . . . I don't get it. Who would do that?"

"That's what we're trying to figure out." Kaden strolled to stand next to the table.

"And you think I can help?" Wayne demanded.

Kaden nodded. "That's the hope."

"I can ask around. It's hard to keep secrets in Pike." Wayne returned his attention to Lia. "When did it happen?"

"Yesterday. Around noon," Lia answered.

"You weren't in the neighborhood, were you?" Kaden's tone was deliberately casual. "You might have noticed who was driving around."

"Noon." Wayne tapped a finger on the table as he shuffled through his memory. "I wasn't even in town. I was headed to Grange to visit Drew. Sorry."

Lia exchanged a quick glance with Kaden. If Wayne was telling the truth, he couldn't have been the one who threw the brick at her.

"How's Drew doing?" Lia asked.

Wayne shrugged. "About the same."

"Do you remember who else was at the hospital?" Lia asked. Wayne might be eliminated, but it still left a long list of potential suspects.

"Not really. There were people coming and going. No one gets to go back to the room except his mother, so everyone is crammed into the waiting room. Why?"

"I thought I heard Cord's truck drive away after I was attacked."

"Cord?" Wayne released a sharp laugh. Then, realizing Lia was serious, he shook his head. "No. No way."

"It could have been a coincidence," Lia hastily added, caught by surprise at Wayne's adamant refusal to believe Cord could have been the brick thrower. She didn't think he liked the kid. "He might just have been passing the store at the same time."

"No, I mean it couldn't have been Cord," Wayne insisted.

Lia frowned. "Why not?"

"He was at the hospital with me."

Kaden leaned forward. "You're sure?"

"Absolutely." Wayne glanced from Lia to Kaden. "I gave him a ride over to Grange. Is that all?"

"No." Kaden placed a piece of paper on the table in front of Wayne. "We found this in the office this morning."

"'You're next,'" Wayne read out loud. He lifted his head to send Lia a puzzled frown. "What does it mean?"

"We're not sure. But we checked the security camera."

"So you know who did it?"

"Not exactly." Lia opened the laptop and quickly brought up the security footage. She fast-forwarded until she reached the section where the prowler entered the store. "We thought you might be able to recognize the intruder."

Wayne leaned toward the screen, his expression intent. "It's too dark to see much," he muttered as the flickering image headed into the office and crossed to the back of the room. "Looks like they took something from the table."

"Files from my brother's search for his fiancée, Vanna Zimmerman," Kaden revealed, his voice sharp.

Wayne glanced up. "The one you think is the skeleton?"

"Yes."

Returning his attention to the video, Wayne pointed at the screen. "They keep their back to the camera."

"You're right." Lia belatedly realized the mystery person managed to avoid ever looking directly toward the camera. Luck? Or knowledge of where the cameras were located?

As the footage came to an end, Wayne shook his head and sat back. "I can't tell who it is. Sorry."

Lia closed the laptop, carefully considering her words. "Did you notice how they got in?"

"You mean the front door?"

"I mean they got in with a key," she gently pointed out.

"You're right." Wayne looked puzzled. "Was it a friend of yours? Well, not really a friend, obviously. But you know what I mean."

"I have a key. Della has a key." She held Wayne's gaze. "And you."

"Yep." Wayne abruptly froze, his mouth hanging open as he realized what Lia was saying. "Hey. You don't think it's me, do you?"

Lia held up her hand as Wayne glared at her in outrage.

"I'm wondering if someone could have borrowed your key."

"'Course not." His voice was gruff. "I always keep it . . ."

Lia studied him as the words dried on his lips. Had he remembered something? "You always keep it where?"

Surging to his feet, Wayne shifted from one foot to the other, as if he was suddenly anxious to be anywhere but there.

"In my pocket, of course."

Lia frowned. Wayne was a terrible liar, and it was obvious he was trying to hide something. "Always?"

"Look, I gotta take off." He backed toward the door. "Mom needs the car to go to work."

With long strides, Kaden moved to block the boy's path to freedom. "If you know anything, you can talk to me, Wayne. I'm just trying to keep Lia safe." He gazed down at Wayne with a somber expression. "That's what we both want, right?"

"Absolutely."

"Where do you keep your key, Wayne?" Lia pressed.

Wayne looked troubled. "I don't want you to be mad at me."

Lia rose to her feet and moved to stand next to the boy. "I'm not going to be mad if you tell me the truth. That's all I want."

He remained rigid for a long moment, then, glancing toward the grim-faced Kaden, he heaved a gusty sigh.

"Okay, the truth is, I leave the key on the top of the front-door frame."

Lia stared at him in disbelief. "The front door? Are you serious?"

Wayne hunched his shoulder. "It's not like I ever use it. Either you or Della are always here when I come in after school and I leave before you lock up. The only time I need it is if you ask me to come in early on Saturday to stock the shelves or if you aren't here on Sundays when I leave, and I was always forgetting it and having to go back home, so . . ." His words trailed away as a dark flush stained his cheeks. "I'm sorry."

Lia held up her hand as Kaden's lips parted, his eyes smoldering with anger. She shared his urgent desire to reprimand Wayne for being so careless. The truth was, she wanted to tell him to leave and not bother coming back. But now wasn't the time to make any rash decisions.

"Later, we're going to have a long talk about responsibility," she said stiffly, holding out her hand. "For now, you can leave your key with me."

Wayne swallowed hard. "I put it back over the door," he confessed, then, with an unexpectedly quick movement, he darted around Kaden and scurried out of the office. "I really gotta go. Mom's boss is going to shit his pants if she's late again," he called as he dashed through the store and out the front.

Kaden swiftly followed behind the boy, his shoulders set at a tense angle as he returned to the office with the key in his hand. "Anyone in town could have seen him getting this or replacing it over the door."

"Yes." Lia grimaced. "We're back to the beginning."

"Not exactly."

"What do you mean?"

Kaden dropped the key on her desk. "We were focused on how the intruder got the key to get in, but how did they know we weren't here last night?"

Lia blinked. "I don't know."

"You called Wayne and told him that you were going to Madison and that you intended to close the store for a couple of days," Kaden reminded her. "And he said he gave

Cord a ride to the hospital. He could have mentioned it to his friend."

"True, but if he was in Grange, Cord couldn't have been the one to hit me with a brick."

Kaden sent her a worried frown. "If there's more than one person involved, it's impossible to count anyone out."

Lia nodded slowly. "Marla would be the most obvious person to be driving Cord's truck if he was at the hospital with Wayne."

"Marla Walsh. The receptionist?"

"And Cord's mother," Lia said. "She could have followed us from the plant and waited until I left to try to lure you into the alley so she could attack you. And Cord who came back to leave the note and steal the files."

"She would also be the most obvious suspect in Burke's death."

Lia wasn't as convinced as Kaden that Marla Walsh was an obvious suspect. "She has a connection to Ryan Burke, but why would she want him dead? And why steal your files?"

He considered his answer. "She could have been working with Burke and Armstrong to get rid of Vanna," he finally suggested. "She might have been bribed to turn a blind eye to Burke's shady business over the years. And if she feared the men were going to crack under pressure, she might have decided to get rid of them."

Lia still wasn't convinced, but she didn't have a better suggestion. They might as well investigate the possibility of a Hurst connection. Anything was better than sitting around doing nothing.

"The farm is close to where I saw Vanna." She headed toward the door. "Maybe we should drive out there and check it out."

"Agreed." Kaden was swiftly behind her, pulling on his coat.

"We could also stop by the extension office," Lia suggested. "I don't think there's much left, but it's on the way."

"Okay." Kaden pressed a hand against his stomach as it gave a loud rumble. "And lunch. Definitely lunch."

Lia grimaced as a queasy sensation washed over her. The mere thought of food was repulsive.

"We'll run by Bella's when we're done," she promised, unable to bear the thought of cooking.

The silver eyes shimmered in anticipation. A familiar reaction to the mention of Bella's pizzas.

"Deal."

Chapter 20

Kaden walked around the derelict structure. The wooden slates were peeling and several windows had been busted out. He planted his hands on his hips and shook his head.

"This isn't what I was expecting."

Lia remained near the Jeep, wisely avoiding the heavy snowdrifts that made each step a challenge.

"I warned you it was in bad shape."

Kaden shook his head. It wasn't the decaying state of the place that came as a surprise. It was the wide, covered porch and detached garage.

"It looks like a house, not a place of business."

"I think it was. My grandpa knew the old owners. They defaulted on their loan and the university bought it from the bank. It was before my time, but my grandpa always thought his friend got a raw deal," Lia told him. "The extension office took over the front room and dining area to use as an office." She pointed to an open field, which had several old greenhouses in various stages of decay. "There were gardens, and I think they used to do classes in the evenings in the garage."

"What kind of classes?"

"Conservation, farming, gardening . . . stuff like that."

Kaden peered into the broken window at the back of the house. "The kitchen area looked like it was converted into an apartment. There's a set of bunk beds pushed against a wall, with a dresser on one side and a desk on the other."

"It's possible it was used by visiting interns," Lia suggested.

"Like Vanna."

Lia nodded in agreement. "Yes."

Kaden found it impossible to imagine the glamorous woman living in the cramped kitchen of an old house, but back then, she might not have been so fussy about her accommodations. Especially if she was already honing her skills in the art of blackmail. She would have realized she was destined to have the lifestyle that was once just a dream.

Kaden glanced down the snow-packed road. "It's close to the railroad bridge."

"True." Lia studied the building, which was set far enough from the road that it wouldn't be readily noticeable. "She might have come back here that night for some reason."

"Yes." It was an odd place to go at midnight, but then again, there might be a new intern living in the apartment at the time. "Maybe she left something behind when she returned to the university."

"Or deliberately hidden it," Lia added.

Ah. That made sense. If she had some sort of evidence that proved a local farmer or business was violating the EPA laws, she might have left it in what she hoped was a safe location until she was in the position to use it to her advantage.

Kaden turned in a slow circle. He pointed at the road that

veered through the edge of the trees. "That's the road to the Hurst farm, right?"

"Yes."

"Let's check it out."

Kaden climbed into the Jeep and set the heater on high. The sky was starting to cloud over and there was a dull chill in the air. It wouldn't be long until the snow started to fall. The sooner they finished checking out the area the better.

He waited for Lia to pull on her seat belt before he made a shallow U-turn and headed down the side road. This time he bypassed the path leading to the meatpacking plant and veered to the right. The lane was narrow, but it was recently plowed and obviously well maintained. Kaden assumed it was Farmer Walsh who was responsible. The rest of the roads in the area were barely passable.

It took several minutes, but at last they cleared the trees and Kaden caught a glimpse of the Hurst homestead. It was beautiful. The white farmhouse, with the traditional wraparound porch and black shutters. The neatly tended paddocks and the massive barns painted a bright red. The rolling fields coated in a layer of pristine snow. It was exactly what you would expect to see if you traveled to Wisconsin.

Unfortunately, Kaden could also see the shed next to the house was empty. And unless the family parked their vehicles in the barn, there was no one around. Marla was no doubt at work. So where were Cord and his dad? It was possible they were out doing chores. Kaden didn't know what all was involved in running a dairy farm, but he assumed it would be a demanding schedule. Especially in winter.

Turning his attention from the house, Kaden studied the surrounding fields. They were on the top of a ridge that gave them a fantastic view of the area. Including the ugly sprawl of buildings below them.

"You can see the meatpacking plant from here." He wrinkled his nose at the smoke belching out of the tall chimneys. "I can't imagine the Walsh family was excited when the place was built. It can't add to the value of their land."

Lia pointed through the front windshield. "And that's the reservoir."

Kaden tapped his fingers on the steering wheel as he studied the distant lake surrounded by a high chain-link fence. It was within easy walking distance of both the plant and the farm.

"It's like the Bermuda Triangle," he murmured. "Vanna could have been coming from any of these places."

"Or the extension office."

"Or town," he added in dry tones.

"It doesn't look like there's anyone around," Lia said, shivering despite the heater being on high.

Kaden studied her pale face, which looked oddly drawn, as if she was tired to the bone.

"Are you okay?" he asked.

She grimaced. "I think I'd like to lie down for a little bit."

"No problem. It's going to take a couple of days to recover from the blow to your head. You need to take it easy."

She didn't argue. Which meant she was even more tired than she wanted to admit. Not surprising. Even if she did insist her wound wasn't bothering her, she'd been violently attacked. The adrenaline rush from that encounter would suck away her energy. Maybe for days.

Jamming the gear into Reverse, Kaden backed into the driveway and turned the Jeep in the direction of town. He pressed his foot on the gas pedal, going at a speed that felt like a crawl but was as fast as he dared on the slick road.

Lia leaned back in her seat, her eyes closed as if she was too weary to keep them open. It wasn't until they were back on Main Street that she sat up straight and glanced around.

"Kaden, look," she abruptly broke the silence, pointing toward the ambulance that was parked in front of the courthouse. "Something's happening."

Kaden had noticed the emergency vehicle, but he wasn't interested in anything but getting Lia tucked in her bed as quickly as possible.

"I'll drop you off at the store and come back to find out what's going on."

"No," she surprisingly protested, her jaw clenched. "I'm worried about Wayne. If he confronted someone about using his key to enter the store, they might have retaliated."

With a sigh, Kaden swerved to pull up behind the ambulance. He didn't care what was happening. Or even if Wayne was involved. At least not when he was worried about Lia. But he knew she would never be able to relax and get better until she was sure her young friend wasn't in trouble.

Rolling down her window, Lia leaned out, her gaze searching the crowd of spectators that had already gathered at the bottom of the courthouse steps. Finally spotting whoever she'd been searching for, Lia waved a hand.

"Bailey."

A woman with a thin face and brown hair pulled into a ponytail approached the Jeep. As she neared, Kaden noticed the green scrubs she was wearing beneath her heavy coat. She must work in some sort of health care, he silently decided, although she didn't appear to be connected with the EMTs who were closing the back of the ambulance.

Leaning her elbows on the open window frame, Bailey peered into the Jeep to inspect Kaden with a curious gaze. Then, with a faint smile, she glanced toward Lia.

"Hey, girl. No need to ask how it's going."

A hint of color touched Lia's pale face, but she ignored the teasing words. Instead, she nodded toward the courthouse.

"What happened?"

"They just loaded Anthony into the ambulance."

Lia sucked in an audible breath. "Seriously? Was there an accident?"

Bailey shook her head. "I don't think so. Someone said he felt sick."

Kaden leaned across the center console, a nasty premonition crawling down his spine. Had someone discovered that Anthony was helping them investigate the death of Ryan Burke?

"Was it a heart attack?" he asked, trying not to overreact.

Baily wrinkled her nose. "I think it's more like a stomach bug. Or maybe food poisoning."

Kaden settled back in his seat, trying to convince himself it was nothing but an unfortunate fluke. Anyone could catch a stomach bug. Especially this time of year. But it didn't feel like a fluke. It felt like a deliberate attack.

Lia obviously agreed as she started to roll up the window, her movements jerky. "Thanks, Bailey."

Bailey reluctantly stepped back, her eyes sizzling with blatant curiosity. "We should get together. Soon."

"Yeah, I'll give you a call," Lia promised as she shut the last few inches of the window.

Kaden narrowed his eyes as he watched the ambulance pull away, the lights suddenly flashing and the siren echoing through the frozen street.

"Someone wants to keep Anthony from sharing his opinion on Ryan Burke's supposed accident," he said.

"Yes."

Kaden's attention remained locked on the emergency vehicle as it zoomed away, his thoughts consumed with who might have tried to silence the young deputy. It had only been a few hours since they saw him. It should be easy to discover who he'd been in contact with . . .

"Kaden." Lia broke into his distracted thoughts. "I think we should go to the hospital."

"We will, but I doubt they'll let us in to speak with Anthony until he's been treated. It could be hours. Until then, I think you should—"

"Take me to the hospital."

There was a sharp edge in Lia's voice that had Kaden turning his head to watch as she grimaced in pain, a clammy layer of sweat beginning to coat her face.

"Shit."

Putting the Jeep into gear, Kaden slammed his foot on the accelerator, fishtailing his way down Main Street and out of town. He never slowed as he hit the highway, using every skill he developed over the years to get Lia to the hospital in Grange in record time.

He beat the ambulance to the emergency room.

Lia struggled through the darkness that threatened to smother her. She had to get somewhere . . . or maybe she had to find someone. Whichever it was, her life depended on it.

"Kaden," she breathed, instinctively reaching out her hand. If she was in danger, that was who she wanted at her side.

A second later, strong fingers grasped her hand and the mattress dipped as a heavy body sat next to her.

"I'm here."

Cautiously, Lia forced open her heavy lids, trying to study the man who was leaning over her. He was oddly blurry, as if her eyes were having trouble focusing. Strangely, she could make out the stylized tattoos that crawled up the side of his neck and the thick hair that framed his face. His features, however, remained indistinct.

"Where am I?" she rasped.

"The hospital in Grange."

Hospital? Lia frowned. It was a struggle, but she at last managed to dig up a few fragmented memories of a brightly lit emergency room and white-coated strangers who bent over her, speaking words she couldn't understand behind their masks. And pain. A ravaging pain that felt as if it was going to rip her in two.

She had a clearer memory of the frantic trip from Pike to Grange.

"Right. You brought me here." Her lips twisted. "How fast were you driving?"

"Not fast enough." He leaned forward and, abruptly, his features were sharp and clear enough to see the tension that clenched his jaw and the shadows beneath his eyes, which appeared silver in the shadowed light of the room. "The trip seemed to take an eternity. How are you?"

Lia paused, doing a silent inventory. The ravaging pain was gone. Thank God. Along with the tremors that had jolted through her with shocking force. Now she felt like a dishrag that was wrung out and tossed aside.

"Weak but better." Her lips parted as she remembered she wasn't the only one who was sick. "What about Anthony?"

"Like you. Weak but better," Kaden reassured her.

She swept her gaze over his tight expression. "It wasn't food poisoning, was it?"

"No." The word came out clipped, as if his lips were suddenly stiff. "Arsenic."

It took Lia a full minute to process what he was saying. After all, it was one thing to worry about a meal that had gone bad or a stomach bug. But arsenic? That was a deliberate attempt to take the life of another person.

"Oh my God." A shudder raced through her. "How?"

"It had to have been the cookies."

Lia frowned, considering the various possibilities. It was true both she and Anthony had eaten the cookies when he visited her store that morning. But they'd also had coffee. Of course, Kaden had coffee and he hadn't gotten sick. Plus, while Anthony had used the cream and sugar, Lia had taken her coffee black.

The cookies did seem to be the link.

"You're right." Lia remained confused. She hadn't bought the cookies. She'd baked them from scratch. And she'd made batches from the same ingredients just a few days before with no one getting sick. "Did someone switch them? Or enter the building while we were gone . . ." Her breath caught in her throat as she abruptly realized that was exactly what had happened. "The intruder?"

Kaden nodded. "That's my guess."

She tried to recall the details from the security video. "Do you think they deliberately distracted us by taking the files and leaving behind the note?"

"Yes."

"But . . ." The tape had been dark, but she basically was able to see what the person was doing. If not in detail. "There was no way they could have switched the cookies. We would have noticed that."

He lifted her hand to his mouth, pressing a kiss to the back of her fingers. "I talked to the doctor. She said it's possible someone used a liquid form of the poison. Just a couple of drops could be fatal."

Fear squeezed the air from Lia's lungs. After watching the security tape, she'd known someone had snuck into the store. Someone with a key. And they'd been rummaging around her office. That thought was horrifying enough. But the realization that the intruder was there to dump poison on her cookies without concern for who or how many people might eat them was shocking.

Whoever it was had to be a monster.

"We need to have them tested," she told Kaden.

"We will."

Lia squeezed Kaden's fingers, needing him to understand how important this was to her.

"Kaden, you can't wait. Whoever poisoned them might try to come back to get rid of them."

"Don't worry." He leaned down to press a kiss to her forehead. As if they'd somehow reached the stage in their relationship where they casually exchanged caresses. Lia didn't mind. Right now, it was more comforting than anything. "I'll go back to get them as soon as you're transferred."

Lia frowned, wondering if she'd misheard what he'd said. Her brain was still a little fuzzy.

"What are you talking about?"

He straightened, gazing down at her with an expression that was suddenly hard, as if he was anticipating an argument.

"I'm having you moved to a hospital in Madison."

Lia's heart missed a beat. "Why? Is something wrong?"

"No, it's just for observation," he hastily assured her. "You should be released tomorrow."

"Then why can't I stay here?"

"It's not safe."

Lia glanced around the room. She appreciated that Kaden was worried about her, but one hospital room was pretty much like another.

"It's as safe as anywhere."

Kaden gave a firm shake of his head. "Between you and

Anthony and Drew, the waiting room is overflowing with worried citizens from Pike. I don't trust any of them." His lips twisted in disgust. "Not to mention that the security consists of one old guard who doesn't even have a weapon. Anyone could wander in here."

Lia shivered. Okay, maybe it wouldn't be so bad to spend a few hours away from Pike and the monster who was creeping through her store at night. At least she wouldn't be so weak when she returned.

She heaved a sigh. "I'm too tired to argue."

"And you know I'm right."

She rolled her eyes. "Are you driving me to Madison?"

Kaden hesitated, as if considering his words. "No. I arranged for an air ambulance."

She waited for him to smile. That had to be a joke, right? When he simply gazed down at her with a defiant expression on his face, Lia made a sound of disbelief.

"Okay, now you're just being silly. I don't need a helicopter."

"It's the safest and fastest way to get you there," he stubbornly insisted.

"Kaden—"

"Indulge me," he interrupted, leaning down to steal her protest with a soft, pleading kiss.

Lia conceded defeat. She really was too tired to argue. "What about you?"

"I hired the services of a private security firm in Madison. They promised they'll have a uniformed officer waiting at the hospital. Only the staff will be allowed in or out of your room," he told her.

Lia couldn't imagine how much money it was costing Kaden to not only arrange an air ambulance for her trip to

Madison but to have a security guard at her room. That was a worry for another day.

Instead, she sent him a confused glance. "You're not coming?"

"I'll be there," he promised. "But first I want to stop by the store and pick up a few things you'll need. And grab the cookies before they disappear."

Sharp-edged fear sliced through her at the thought of Kaden returning to the store. "I don't want you going there alone."

"I'll be careful." He cupped her cheek in his hand, his expression somber. "I promise."

Lia glared at him. Kaden Vaughn didn't have a clue how to be careful. His whole life had been one reckless adventure after another.

"Have you considered that the poison was probably meant for you?" she said, needing him to take the threat seriously.

He seemed puzzled by her words. "Why do you say that?"

"The cookies were in the office where you were staying. You would be the most obvious person to eat them."

Kaden shrugged. "The intruder might not have known that."

"They took your files."

"Yes, but that was probably just for distraction." With a grimace, Kaden abruptly rose to his feet and paced across the cramped floor.

Lia could easily see the tense angle of his shoulders and his clenched expression. "What are you thinking?"

He spun back to send her a frustrated frown. "That none of this makes sense."

"The poisoning?"

"The poisoning. The brick throwing. The hit-and-run." He spread his arms. "If you wanted someone dead, what would you do?"

"Get a gun and shoot them," Lia said without hesitation.

"Exactly. And even if you didn't have a weapon, everyone else in town has one you could steal."

Lia agreed. There were few people in Pike who hadn't grown up hunting. Her own grandfather had a shotgun that was currently locked in her attic.

"Maybe they don't know how to load a gun. Or how to shoot," she suggested, knowing the explanation was lame as the words left her lips.

"Then they could use a knife."

Lia wrinkled her nose, forcing herself to consider the various ways to kill someone. "You do have a point."

"Thanks," he said dryly.

"A gun or a knife makes the most sense if you want to get rid of someone. And while poison is probably effective, putting it on the cookies was weirdly random," she said with a shake of her head. "There was no guarantee either of us was going to eat them." She furrowed her brow, remembering the first attack. "And it would have taken sheer luck to kill me by lobbing a brick at my head."

Kaden nodded, his expression still troubled. "I suppose those could be written off as trying to scare us rather than kill us, but even the judge and Burke's deaths were strange."

Lia shuddered. Right now, everything seemed strange. And awful. "That doesn't make them any less dangerous," she reminded him.

"That's why we're leaving Pike." He abruptly tensed and swiveled toward the door as it was pressed open. It wasn't until two men in uniform stepped in that he relaxed. "Right on cue," he murmured, moving to stand next to

Lia's bed. He leaned down to place a lingering kiss on her lips. "Behave yourself."

Lia reached up to tangle her fingers in his hair. She had a sudden fear that something bad would happen if they were separated.

"Be careful," she commanded.

"Without a doubt." He gazed at her with eyes that shimmered with silver fire. "For the first time in my life, I have too much to lose to take any risks."

Chapter 21

Kaden waited until the helicopter lifted off the ground and swooped its way toward Madison before he returned to the parking lot and crawled into his rented Jeep. A portion of his grinding tension eased at the knowledge that Lia was safe and that she would make a full recovery. But there was no way to fully relax when the killer was still out there.

Driving back to Pike, Kaden refused to dwell on the frantic drive to the hospital. Or the grinding fear that Lia would die before he could get her to the emergency room. That trip would be giving him nightmares for years to come. Instead, he concentrated on their conversation just before she was whisked away by the air ambulance.

None of the killings made sense. A hit-and-run. A staged accident. The mysterious death of Ryan Burke in his meat-packing plant. And then to add in the brick thrown at Lia and the poisoned cookies . . .

These truly felt like the acts of a madman who had no plan or purpose. Just a random desire to hurt people.

Arriving in Pike, Kaden drove directly into the alley behind the store and climbed out of the Jeep. He left the engine running. It wouldn't take long to grab a few clothes and personal belongings for Lia and toss the cookies into a plastic bag. He wanted to be in Madison as soon as possible.

Of course, his desire to be with Lia didn't make him forget that the mysterious killer might have made a duplicate key to the store and been willing to set up a nasty trap. Kaden cautiously opened the back door and stepped into the hallway. It was shadowed, but there was enough light to see it was empty. He entered the office and made a quick search before heading into the store to ensure there was no one hiding in the aisles or behind the counter. Once convinced he was there alone, Kaden made his way up to Lia's apartment.

He did another quick sweep, checking to see if anything had been disturbed since they left. And that there were no lethal surprises. Like a ticking bomb. Or a plague of rats. Who knew what might happen in Pike?

There was nothing to find. Tossing the cookies into a plastic bag, Kaden unpacked Lia's suitcase, which was still filled from her previous trip to Madison. Grabbing fresh clothes, he jogged his way down the steps. He was back in his Jeep in under fifteen minutes.

He placed the cookies and suitcase in the back compartment, locked the door, and climbed into the driver's seat. Intent on the number of things he needed to do, it wasn't until he reached down to put the Jeep in reverse that he noticed there were two manila envelopes tossed on the passenger seat.

Kaden cursed as he realized he'd been so focused on the danger that might be waiting for him inside, he hadn't bothered to worry about what might happen outside.

Which was ridiculous, of course. The killer was as unpredictable as the Wisconsin weather. Assuming he was dealing with someone who would behave like a rational person was a waste of time. They had their own agenda and their own way of achieving their goals.

Pulling on his winter gloves, Kaden grabbed the top

envelope and pulled up the flap. He wouldn't risk dumping
out the contents; instead, he warily peered inside. It took
only a second to recognize the files he'd brought from his
brother's condo.

Shit. Whoever had poisoned Lia had been creeping
through the alley while he was in the store. And they had
returned the files they'd stolen the night before. Why? Was
the killer taunting him? Proving they would always be one
step ahead?

That seemed the most logical conclusion.

Tossing the envelope on the floorboard, Kaden reached
for the second envelope. He frowned as he caught sight of
the corner that had been ripped away. Why did that send a
strange sense of dread through him? A dread that went
beyond the thought the killer had left it for him. As if there
was a voice in the back of his mind, trying to warn him that
the missing corner was important.

Kaden muttered a curse and forced himself to open the
envelope so he could see inside. He was wasting precious
time. Thankfully, there was nothing creepy. No weapons.
No bloody body parts. In fact, there was nothing more
shocking than a stack of papers. Tilting the envelope, Kaden
shook the contents onto the seat.

His brows arched as he caught sight of what looked to be
official reports. Official reports from the EPA.

With a strangled gasp, Kaden grabbed the papers and
shuffled through them. Most of it he didn't understand.
There were charts and graphs that only a professional could
decipher, but thanks to Lia and her knowledge of international banking, there were a few things he did recognize.
Certainly enough to realize he was holding what Hollywood would call a "smoking gun."

Dropping the papers on the seat, Kaden tapped his fingers
on the steering wheel. The killer had to have been the one

to leave the envelope, but why give him this evidence? It was almost as if the mystery person wanted to help him solve Vanna's death. Certainly, the papers tied the dead woman to the town of Pike. And to the men who would have wanted her dead.

Judge Armstrong. Mayor Erickson. Ryan Burke.

Ryan Burke. Kaden's fingers squeezed the steering wheel as the name seared through his mind. Not just because his was the most recent death. But because of what Anthony had told him. The deputy had been certain the businessman was clutching an envelope in his hand when he was murdered, right? And a corner had been ripped off when the killer took it from him.

For a second, Kaden struggled with what to do with the information he had. It would be easier to decide if he knew exactly who had put the envelopes in the Jeep. And why. It felt like . . . manipulation. As if the mystery person was deliberately dropping breadcrumbs for him to follow. A trap? A false trail?

Only one way to find out.

Shoving the Jeep into gear, Kaden stomped on the gas pedal and exited the alley. He turned onto Main Street and drove the short distance to the courthouse. Without hesitation, he swerved to park in a loading zone. If someone was stupid enough to give him a parking ticket, they would be very sorry.

Pausing long enough to gather the papers, Kaden stepped out of the Jeep and made sure it was tightly locked. He didn't want any more unexpected surprises. Then, jogging up the steps, he pressed the intercom set in the stone wall. A second later, there was a loud buzz, and Kaden pushed open the glass door to enter the building.

He headed directly for the sheriff's office, barely noticing the young deputy who was seated at the front desk.

"Can I help you?" The deputy shoved himself to his feet as Kaden stormed his way toward the inner office. The poor man was wearing a uniform, but he was painfully young, with a nervous expression on his face. He probably hadn't been on the job more than a few months. "Wait. You can't just go in there."

"Watch me," Kaden muttered, never slowing as he reached the door and shoved it open.

He was inside the office and had the door closed behind him before the mayor realized he was no longer alone. Jerking up his head, Tate Erickson glared at Kaden with obvious annoyance.

"What the hell? Get out of here."

Kaden moved toward the desk. "I have a few questions."

"I don't give a shit." The man continued to glare. "Leave or I'll have you shot."

Kaden held up the stack of papers in his hand. "When I leave here, I'm handing these over to the FBI."

Tate rolled his eyes, tossing aside his pen. "Yeah, I've heard that threat before," he taunted Kaden. "If you had any actual evidence, you would have gone there in the first place."

Kaden shrugged, pretending it hadn't been a direct hit. "These aren't my brother's files."

"I don't care if they're the Ten Commandments sent by God." Tate reached up to shove his fingers through his dark hair. The older man might not be worried about the papers Kaden was holding, but something obviously was bothering him.

Kaden laid the stack on the desk in front of Tate. "They're from Ryan Burke."

Tate made a sound of disbelief. "Burke wouldn't give you shit."

"He didn't give them to anyone." Kaden reached to pull

the envelope from beneath the bottom of the stack. "They were ripped from his dead hand." He nodded toward the torn corner. "See?"

Tate lost several shades of color, his eyes widening as he studied the envelope. "You," he breathed. "You killed him."

Kaden narrowed his gaze. It had to be an act. Tate Erickson was the only one who had a reason to murder the businessman.

"You claimed his death was an accident," Kaden taunted. "Now it's murder?"

Tate licked his lips. "It's still under investigation."

"Good." Kaden tapped his fingers on the stack of papers. "I'm sure this evidence will be vital in revealing the killer."

Tate leaned back in his chair, as if trying to put distance between himself and the papers.

"You have the envelope," he muttered. "You knew Burke had it in his hand when he died. Obviously, you're guilty."

A hard smile curved Kaden's lips. "I had no reason to want the man dead. You, however, would no doubt do anything to keep his mouth shut."

"Burke was my friend."

"Friend? More like your reluctant partner in crime," Kaden said.

Tate's jaw clenched. "I don't know what you're talking about."

"Let me refresh your memory." Kaden grabbed the papers from the desk, intending to go through them one by one.

Tate muttered a curse, abruptly rising to his feet. "I don't have time for this."

Kaden shrugged. For the first time since arriving in Pike, he didn't have to bluff.

"Okay. Like I said, I'm sure the FBI will be interested."

Kaden turned away. He didn't know exactly how a private citizen went about contacting the federal agency, but it couldn't be that tough.

"Stop!" Tate called out.

Kaden slowly turned back to meet the mayor's worried gaze. "You know what's in here, don't you?"

"Not . . . exactly," he hedged.

Kaden walked back to the desk. "I'm happy to share."

Tate looked as if he'd swallowed a lemon. "Just get this over with."

Kaden peeled off the papers that were stapled together. They had an EPA crest at the top to indicate they were official reports.

"Maybe you'll recognize these." He held them toward Tate.

The mayor shook his head, pretending to be confused as he glanced at the various charts and graphs.

"Nope."

"They're EPA reports."

Tate shoved them back at Kaden. "These are fifteen years old. Who cares?"

Kaden pulled out the next forms. Unlike the complicated graphs, these were a straightforward listing of the various violations. Even he could understand them.

"I'm certain the citizens of Pike would be very interested in the fact that the meatpacking plant was allowing their wastewater to be dumped into the city reservoir," he said. "Probably from the day it was built. And that you turned a blind eye to the health risks."

"Wastewater?" Tate tried and failed to sound shocked by the accusation. "I don't know anything about that."

Kaden rolled his eyes. The mayor made a habit of knowing nothing. Was it a politician thing?

"Really? It's right here in black and white." He waved a

form in front of Tate's face. "And here." He waved another form. "And here. And here." He pointed toward the bottom of the page. "Plus, that's your signature at the bottom."

Tate's expression hardened. "You can wave those around all you want. I can promise you, there was never an official report."

Kaden pulled out another paper. When he'd first glanced through the forms, he'd been puzzled by the technical terms, but the actual citation had been simple and straightforward. The Pike Meatpacking Plant had been caught dumping its wastewater into the nearby reservoir. The mere thought was enough to make his stomach churn in protest.

"Only because you paid Vanna Zimmerman not to file the violations."

"You don't have any proof of that."

"I didn't. Until this." Kaden pulled out the bottom page and turned it toward Tate.

The man paled even as he tried to act indifferent. "A bunch of numbers and letters."

"That's what I thought too. Until a very clever friend revealed they're international bank routing numbers attached to shell corporations."

"So?" Tate shrugged. "I'm sure Burke had lots of accounts spread around. He was always trying to avoid paying taxes."

"Vanna had matching account numbers."

Tate took a step away from the desk, his expression tight. "Look, if Burke was paying bribes it was none of my business."

Kaden narrowed his gaze. The forms might have been in Burke's possession when he died, but it was Tate's signature on the dotted line. He'd known all about the nasty water being dumped illegally.

Right now, however, he was more interested in the one

photo that was in the envelope, which revealed a familiar, dark-haired woman in a leather jacket with an EPA badge on the shoulder. Vanna Zimmerman. She was facing a man who was only an inch taller than her, with dark hair and a narrow face. He was wearing an expensive cashmere coat despite the fact it was snowing, along with leather shoes. There was no mistaking it was Tate Erickson. In the background, Kaden could make out the extension office, although it looked considerably different in the past. There was a fresh coat of paint on the wooden slates and a large wooden sign in the front yard directed visitors to the front door. And in the driveway was a pickup truck that looked vaguely familiar.

Kaden was assuming the photo was taken by Burke, and the businessman had kept it as insurance to maintain a grip on the mayor.

Turning the photo around, he held it toward the mayor. "What about this?"

Tate cast an impatient glance at the picture, no doubt intending to dismiss it with another claim of ignorance. Instead, his mouth fell open with unmistakable shock, as if he'd seen a ghost.

Kaden arched his brows at the intense reaction. When he showed Tate the proof he'd been paying bribes to Vanna and allowing potentially dangerous wastewater into the city reservoir, he'd been defensive but confident he could somehow argue his way out of being blamed. As if he'd been preparing to be caught for years.

Now he snatched the photo from Kaden's hand, gazing down at Vanna with a strange expression.

"This . . . this isn't what you think."

Kaden frowned. Why did the photo bother him? Because

it was visible proof he'd known Vanna? And that he'd spent time in her company?

It had to be more than that.

"It's fairly obvious to me," Kaden said slowly. "You're handing a wad of money to Vanna Zimmerman. Sloppy."

Tate's expression was wary. "Sloppy?"

Kaden pointed to where Vanna was awkwardly cradling a large stack of cash in her arms in the picture.

"You're making the exchange in broad daylight. This is undeniable proof you were paying bribes to a government official."

Tate made a strange sound. Not anger. Not even outrage. It was more like a grunt of relief. A strange ball of unease settled in the pit of Kaden's stomach.

"It never happened." The mayor dropped the photo on the desk. "This must be a fake."

Kaden frowned, ignoring the predictable claim. There was something about the picture he was missing. But he didn't have a clue what it was.

With a shake of his head, Kaden forced himself to concentrate on the obvious facts.

"When I first saw the picture, I was curious. Why hand over so much cash instead of using the overseas bank accounts? Those are a lot tougher to trace," he said, reaching to grab the photo from the desk. "I couldn't figure it out until I saw the date at the top."

Tate glanced away as Kaden held the photo toward him. "I told you, that's a fake."

"December 14, 2007." Kaden helpfully read the date out loud. "The day she disappeared."

"So?"

"You wanted to be able to take back the money after you killed her," Kaden suggested. "Something that would have been a lot more difficult if you'd transferred it to an offshore bank account. This way, you could lure her into a false sense of complacency before you bashed her on the head and grabbed the cash."

Tate's lips parted, as if he was about to laugh. Then, catching sight of Kaden's grim expression, he stiffened in outrage. "What?"

"You murdered Vanna Zimmerman."

Chapter 22

Kaden watched the emotion drain from Tate's face. He'd seen professional actors create an image of astonishment. They widened their eyes and gasped in shock. Some could make their pulses race. But not one of them had been capable of creating the image of being sucker punched.

Which meant the mayor either possessed amazing acting skills or he was genuinely stunned by the accusation.

"You think I killed Vanna?"

Kaden shrugged. "It's obvious."

With an effort, the older man gathered his rattled composure. "The only thing that's obvious is that you're trying to find some schmuck to pin the murder on." He pointed his finger in Kaden's direction. "And the only reason you would be doing that is if you were guilty."

"Don't be an idiot. I was very publicly doing a live stunt for my show on the day Vanna disappeared," Kaden shut down any possibility of the mayor trying to pin the blame on him. "Besides, I had no reason to want her dead. While you and your pals have several thousand."

Frustrated by his inability to divert the blame from himself, Tate clenched his hands into tight fists.

"You have no proof."

"For Christ's sake, cut the bullshit," Kaden ground out.

He was done with the petty games this man had spent a lifetime playing. "We both know I have more than enough proof to send you away for a very long time. If nothing else, your position as mayor of Pike will be over. A crushing blow to a man with your ego."

Tate tried to look defiant. He was accustomed to using a combination of charm and ruthless bullying to manipulate people. But meeting Kaden's unwavering gaze, he allowed his breath to hiss between clenched teeth. The world the mayor had carefully crafted was starting to crumble around him.

"What do you want from me? Money?"

Kaden resisted the urge to roll his eyes. He had the sort of money Tate could only dream about.

"What I want is the truth."

"The truth." Tate released a sharp laugh. "Who even remembers what that is?"

Kaden glanced toward the stack of files on the desk. "I'm sure there's someone in law enforcement who can jog those reluctant memories if you don't want to talk to me."

Tate pinched his lips. As if he wanted to tell Kaden to go to hell. But he wasn't stupid. He knew Kaden had the upper hand. At least for now.

"Okay. Fine," he muttered. "I met Officer Zimmerman."

"And you paid her bribes?"

"Not me."

"Ryan Burke?"

"Yes."

Kaden considered his next question. He wasn't a professional cop, with experience in interviewing a suspect. He was a stuntman and a mechanic who was completely out of his comfort zone.

"And Armstrong?" he at last demanded. There had to be

a reason the three men were reluctant friends. "Why would he be involved?"

Tate looked disgusted at the mention of the judge. "Burke paid off the bitch to get rid of the violations, but she also insisted that the meatpacking plant build its own lagoon."

Kaden arched his brows, genuinely surprised. He had no idea Vanna possessed morals when it came to her job.

"Thank God someone was concerned about the health of the citizens of Pike," he said dryly.

"Only after she bled us dry," Tate rasped

Kaden refused to be distracted. "That still doesn't explain the judge's involvement."

"Burke refused to pay for the new lagoon." There was an ancient bitterness in the older man's voice. "He threatened to move the plant to another town that would offer him better incentives if we didn't finance the changes. We couldn't allow that to happen. The plant is the biggest employer in town."

"And you were afraid you would lose your position as mayor?"

Tate sniffed. "I was thinking of my constituents."

Kaden glared at the slimeball in disbelief. "You were allowing them to be poisoned."

The mayor waved aside the inconvenient reminder. "We had to keep the plant in Pike, so the judge used the funds from the Chamber of Commerce to finance the building of the lagoon and the new parking lot."

Kaden's lips twisted at the memory of the men in the diner complaining about paying for a new pool for Ryan Burke. It was possible they weren't exaggerating.

"So why go to all that effort and then kill her?" he abruptly demanded. "Did she keep pressing for more money?"

"No one killed her."

"Obviously, someone did," Kaden snapped. "Her body was found in your town."

"Well, it wasn't any of us." Tate spread his hands in frustration. "Why would we kill her after we invested thousands of dollars to keep her mouth shut?"

It was a legitimate question. They'd gone to a lot of trouble to satisfy Vanna and her demands. There could be only one reason for them to snap.

"Like I said, maybe she wanted more."

"No." Tate sliced his hand through the air. "Officer Zimmerman made her demands. We gave her exactly what she wanted. End of story."

Kaden hesitated. Tate had reached the limit of what he was willing to admit. And in truth, Kaden wasn't nearly as convinced the man was responsible for the crime wave in Pike as he had been when he first arrived at the courthouse.

Frustration blasted through him. For once, he truly thought he had the answers he needed. Now he felt as if he was once again stumbling through the dark.

"Who else might want Vanna dead?"

"Everyone," Tate muttered. "She was a greedy bitch who took advantage of her position. There were lots of people who would want her out of the way."

"In Pike?"

Tate hunched his shoulders. "Who knows?"

Kaden clenched and unclenched his hands. Why was the truth so damned elusive? Was Vanna cursing him from her grave? She knew he didn't approve of her. Maybe her revenge was to ensure he never had the answers he needed to put the memory of his brother to rest.

He shook away his gruesome thoughts. "What happened to Burke and the judge?" he abruptly demanded.

Tate blinked. "I was about to ask you that."

"Me?"

"It's apparent you decided we were somehow guilty of the death of your brother's fiancée." Tate leaped on the chance to turn the blame on Kaden. He was nothing if not predictable. "Did you come here to punish us?"

"I loved my brother, but I barely knew Vanna," Kaden growled. "Certainly not well enough to seek revenge for her death."

"Why should I believe you?"

"I'm not the professional liar," Kaden reminded the slimy toad.

Tate flushed, but he couldn't argue. The man had made a career of lies, secrets, and empty promises. He wouldn't know the truth if it bit him on the ass.

"Fine. If you didn't hurt the judge or Burke, I don't know who did," Tate muttered. "Or why. My job was always to try to clean up Pike's messes and that's what I did."

Kaden stared at him in disbelief. If the man was telling the truth, surely he realized he was in danger?

"You should consider turning the investigation over to the professionals, Erickson," Kaden warned. "As much as you might want to cling to your position as mayor, it will be a wasted effort if you end up dead."

Tate stumbled backward. "Is that a threat?"

"Just a suggestion." With a shake of his head at the man's inability to accept his lies were about to be exposed, Kaden stepped toward the desk and scooped the papers into his arms before heading toward the door.

"Where are you going?" Tate called out.

"There's a killer out there who tried to hurt Lia," Kaden said. "I'm not waiting around for him to try again."

"What about those files?"

Kaden didn't bother to glance over his shoulder as he

left the office. "I'm done screwing around. They're going to the FBI."

Lia settled in the leather seat of the Jeep and heaved a deep sigh. She'd been ready at promptly eight o'clock that morning to leave the hospital. Not only was she feeling better, the doctor had come by to say she was being discharged that morning. Four hours later, the nurses at last appeared with a wheelchair they insisted she use until they rolled her out the front doors to where Kaden was waiting.

Pulling on her seat belt, she held her breath until they left the parking lot and veered into the heavy traffic. As if a part of her feared one of the doctors might run out and insist she return.

"At last," she muttered.

"Hospitals suck," Kaden sympathized, turning his head to send her a rueful glance. It was the first time they'd been alone since she was whisked away from Grange to Madison.

A shiver raced through Lia as she met the smoky gray gaze, excitement feathering down her spine. It was no wonder the hospital staff had fluttered around him the moment he arrived, she ruefully acknowledged. And not because he was a famous stuntman. Kaden could have been a dog walker and still been the center of attention. There was a raw, compelling energy that sucked in everyone around him. And, of course, he was outrageously gorgeous. What woman wouldn't tingle in pleasure at the sight of the fierce male features that were framed by his long hair and the hard body that was shown to perfection beneath the leather jacket and faded jeans? The intricate tattoos were just the icing on a very fine cake.

One she wanted to lick from top to bottom.

Clearing the lump that threatened to form in her throat, Lia forced her thoughts in a less dangerous direction.

"Have you spent a lot of time in hospitals?"

Kaden easily weaved his way through the lunch-hour traffic. "Far more than I want to admit. Being a stuntman has its drawbacks."

Lia tried to imagine a job where you routinely defied death to earn a paycheck. It was impossible. All she knew was that she was deeply relieved she hadn't known him back then. She would have been in a constant state of panic, terrified he was going to be hurt.

"What was your worst accident?" she asked.

"I was performing a stunt for a movie in south LA. The technical director was supposed to have cleared a six-block safe zone, but somehow a car managed to get past the barriers and drove directly onto the street where I was doing my stunt. To avoid a head-on collision, I had to lay down my bike and skidded into a nearby building. I broke my leg in two places and cracked four ribs."

She flinched. "And you continued after that?"

"For a few years." He shrugged. "The money was good and I' always knew my career would be short. I wanted to get a nice, fat retirement fund before I walked away."

"Risky," she murmured.

He sent her a quick smile. "No longer."

"Mmm." He might not crave the adrenaline rush of facing death, but he would never be satisfied with a normal life.

Not the sort of life she preferred.

The thought cast a sudden shadow over the sunny day.

As if sensing the change in her mood, Kaden stopped at a light and glanced in her direction.

"How are you feeling?"

"Weak but much better," she assured him. "Did you get the cookies from my apartment?"

"The cookies and so much more," he said.

"More? I don't understand."

Pressing on the gas as the light changed, Kaden returned his attention to the busy road as he quickly revealed what had happened when he went to the store to collect her belongings and the plate of cookies.

Lia remained silent as he shared information about his trip to the sheriff's office and the confrontation with Tate Erickson. Once he finished, she stared out the front windshield, trying to digest what he told her.

It wasn't easy.

There was a lot of information to shuffle through. The fact that Kaden now had genuine proof that the men were blackmailed by Vanna. And that they'd hidden the toxic waste being pumped into the water supply. There were also a lot of holes in the story. Gaping holes that included who killed Vanna. And why the people of Pike were currently being stalked by a crazed killer.

At last she focused on the first question that popped into her mind. "You said you went into the apartment to get my things and when you came out you discovered the files just sitting in the Jeep?"

"Yep."

She shook her head in confusion. "How would anyone know you were going to the store at that time?"

He shrugged. "I assume they were at the hospital and followed me back to Pike."

She grimaced, sharply reminded that whoever was responsible for the murders had to be a local. One who possibly had been in and out of the store dozens of times. The thought made her stomach twist with dread.

"And you're sure the files were in the envelope Ryan Burke was holding when he was murdered?"

Kaden slowed as they reached the outer suburbs. The

traffic was lighter, but the streets had narrowed, and there were several pedestrians scurrying from shop to shop. The frenetic days of the holiday season had well and truly arrived, sending a buzz of activity through the city.

"As sure as I can be," he conceded.

Lia nodded. For now, she was willing to accept it was possible they came from Ryan Burke. But that only created more questions.

"Only the killer could have those files, right? Why give them to you after they went to the trouble of murdering Burke to keep them secret?"

"It makes about as much sense as everything else connected to Vanna's death," Kaden muttered.

Puzzles within puzzles within puzzles. Or maybe something far less complicated, she silently acknowledged. Instead of a devious schemer, this could all be the chaotic results of a deranged mind. The killer might have their own twisted agenda, and who could outguess the motives of a psychopath?

Suppressing a sigh, Lia turned the conversation to Kaden's encounter with Tate Erickson.

"Do you think the mayor is responsible?"

He paused as he pulled into the private drive and waited for the security guard to buzz open the gates.

It wasn't until they were traveling through the tree-lined streets that Kaden finally answered her question.

"I think Erickson paid bribes to hide the fact he was allowing the city water supply to be contaminated. And he might even have killed Vanna," he said. "But I don't think he murdered Burke or the judge. Or that he tried to poison you."

Lia wrinkled her nose. It was impossible to imagine the fussy man with the bloated ego sneaking through a meat-packing plant to smash in Ryan Burke's skull or risking damage to his expensive car to run down Drew Hurst.

"No. I don't think so either," she conceded.

"If the recent spate of crimes has anything to do with Vanna's death, who else would know the three men were connected with her?"

Lia considered the question. The possibilities would be limited. Not only would they have to be over a certain age, they would have to have an intimate relationship with at least one of the men to know their secrets.

"Oh." She abruptly realized there was a potential suspect they'd forgotten about. "Drew's mother, Barb, worked for Burke back then."

"True," Kaden agreed, pulling into the driveway of his brother's condo, but he left the engine running as he swiveled in his seat to stare at her with a distracted gaze. "But why would she kill anyone? Especially her employer? And she certainly wouldn't have run over her own son."

"Wayne told me that Drew's father was working construction at the meatpacking plant when he was injured," Lia said, belatedly recalling the conversation. "I didn't think anything about it at the time, but he said Drew's dad was hit with a load of steel pipes. That could have been when Ryan Burke was forced to build his new lagoon."

"That would connect them at the time Vanna was working as an EPA inspector."

Lia nodded. "Maybe he suspected what Burke was doing with the wastewater before they built the new lagoon. He might even have suspected Vanna was taking bribes to turn a blind eye."

"It's possible, but why would he kill her?"

"I don't think he did," Lia confessed, "but he might have tried to get his own blackmail payout. Especially if he was injured on the job, and then Vanna vanished. . . ." Her words trailed away as she tried to connect dots that didn't want to be connected. "He might have seen it as a warning to keep his mouth shut. At least until the bones were found."

Kaden considered her rambling hypothesis. "I suppose it's possible Drew's dad decided to try his luck again with the blackmail—"

"Or Drew's mom," Lia interrupted. "It could explain what Barb and Ryan Burke were arguing about."

Kaden nodded. "And either Burke or the judge, or even Tate, might have run down Drew in warning."

"It would certainly explain why Burke and the judge are dead. Drew's dad might be nursing an old injury, but he's a huge man who could easily overpower either of them. And if he thought they were responsible for trying to kill his son . . ."

They fell silent, exchanging a rueful glance. It was a stretch. Actually, it was way beyond a stretch. It was a leap across a gaping canyon.

Shaking his head, Kaden switched off the engine and reached over his shoulder to grab the bag of cookies and the stack of files he'd left in the back seat.

Lia shuddered at the sight of the cookies. The damned things were responsible for her brush with death. It was also a reminder that it had been Kaden's skill behind the wheel that had saved her life. If she'd been alone after eating the cookies . . . who knew what might have happened?

Grimly, she forced her gaze back to Kaden's face, discovering him studying her with eyes that had darkened to a steel gray. Was he remembering the frantic drive to Grange? Probably. It had been as stressful for him as it was for her.

"Have you heard how Anthony is doing?" she asked.

"I had word that he was discharged from the hospital this morning."

Relief blasted through Lia. "Thank God. I hate to think I'm responsible for making him sick."

Kaden's brows snapped together. "It was the poison that made him sick. It had nothing to do with you or your cookies."

"Still." She shrugged. The guilt she felt didn't have to make sense. It was going to haunt her for a long time. She nodded toward the plastic bag. "Have you decided what you're going to do with them?"

"I'm turning them over to the FBI, along with all the files we've collected," he announced without hesitation.

She sent him an approving glance. "We need professionals handling this." They'd been bumbling along for days. But it was one thing to investigate a death that had happened fifteen years ago. It was something else to try to outwit a maniac who was stalking through the streets of Pike at that very moment.

They were way out of their league.

"Agreed." His jaw tightened. "Although it's going to be hard to wait around for answers. I don't know much about the FBI, but I'm assuming it might take days or even weeks before they decide whether to open an investigation."

Lia started to agree with his frustration, only to have the words die on her lips. During her long hours trapped in a hospital bed, she'd had plenty of time to think about what they'd discovered. And the questions that were still waiting to be answered. Most of them would take investigators who actually knew what they were doing to solve. But there was part of Vanna's life they hadn't bothered to look into yet.

"We don't have to just wait around," she assured Kaden.

"What do you mean?"

"We've been assuming it was her habit of blackmailing people that led to Vanna's death. After all, that's the most obvious reason for someone to kill her. But from talking with her foster mom, we also know she spent time in Pike before she ever became an EPA agent."

"True."

"Vanna could have made an enemy during that time."

He paused, as if trying to imagine what she might have been doing as a young, eager college student living in a remote town.

"I'm not sure how we can find out what she was doing during that time," he finally admitted. "Or who she might have pissed off."

"We intended to speak with Professor Sanderson before Anthony called to say that Ryan Burke was dead," she reminded him. "I think we should go see her. Maybe Vanna told her she had an enemy. Or was afraid of someone."

"It couldn't hurt."

"I found her on the university website," she said. She'd spent last evening on her phone, searching for information on the woman. It wasn't like she'd had anything else to do. "She retired a few years ago, but it has an active email address where she could be contacted."

"Let's set up a meeting."

Chapter 23

Kaden held the files in one arm as he helped Lia out of the Jeep and led her toward the door. Logically, he understood she was capable of walking without his assistance. She might even prefer to have some space to move. But he'd spent a frustrating night walking the floor after his nightmare trip to Madison, aching to have her at his side.

Now he felt a surge of satisfaction as she entered the condo and sucked in a deep, appreciative breath. He'd known it would take time for her to be checked out this morning, so he'd kept himself busy making the condo as comfortable as possible for her arrival.

"What smells so good?" she asked as she pulled off her parka and draped it on a nearby chair. Next, she toed off her shoes and walked forward in her socks.

She looked like a woman who had arrived home. Kaden smiled with pleasure. The sight touched a place in his heart he hadn't known existed.

"I stopped by the local deli and picked up some chicken noodle soup and a loaf of bread this morning," he told her.

She released a low groan. "Can we have some? Now?"

Kaden ground his teeth as he gazed down at her eyes, which were dark with anticipation. He wanted those glorious green eyes smoldering with a hunger that had nothing to do with soup and everything to do with their naked bodies moving together.

That, however, would have to wait until he was sure she was 100 percent recovered.

"Absolutely," he assured her, heading into the kitchen, where he'd left the soup in a Crock-Pot to stay warm.

Taking a seat at the table, Lia planted her chin in her palm as she watched him efficiently fill two bowls with the soup before cutting slices of the crusty bread and adding a dish of butter to his tray. Was she judging his skills or just enjoying the view? Both were fine with him. He liked having her attention focused on him.

Placing lunch on the table, Kaden returned to the fridge to grab two bottles of water before settling in a seat next to Lia.

She was already scooping up the soup in large bites with low groans of pleasure. She paused long enough to butter a thick slab of bread she could dip into the rich chicken broth, but in a remarkably short amount of time she'd cleaned her bowl and eaten another slice of bread.

Taking a swig from her water bottle, Lia slumped back in her chair with a sigh. "Mmm. Just what I needed."

Kaden shoved aside his empty bowl and studied her flushed face and sparkling eyes with a surge of approval. She looked like she did the day he walked into the store and first caught sight of her. Young and vibrant and capable of taking on the world.

"Thank God."

He didn't realize he'd spoken the words out loud until she arched a teasing brow. "Thank God for soup?"

He leaned toward her, his gaze sweeping over the delicate lines and curves of her face. Each one was seared into his mind. And into his heart.

"For seeing you healthy," he rasped. "I've never been so afraid in my life."

A faint smile curved her lips. "Kaden Vaughn is fearless."

He grimaced. "That's what I would have told you until I was driving to the hospital at a hundred miles an hour." His hands instinctively clenched as the memory seared through his mind. Each second that ticked by had felt like an eternity. "I was certain my life was going to be over if I didn't get you there in time."

A flush stained her cheeks at the harsh intensity in his words. "Very Hollywood."

"No," he insisted. They both had a habit of deflecting their emotions with sarcasm and teasing. For once, he intended to plow through their mutual barriers. He reached out to grasp her hand, giving her fingers a squeeze. "I've never been more sincere. If something had happened to you, it would have destroyed a part of me."

She stilled, meeting his steady gaze. "Why?"

Kaden's lips twisted. She'd given him the opening he wanted. The question was whether he had the courage to take the leap.

He lifted her hand to his mouth, pressing a kiss against the back of her fingers. "I can drive a motorcycle through a wall of flames and rebuild a motor with my eyes closed, but I don't have any skill in sharing my emotions."

The color staining her cheeks deepened. "Neither do I. We're in trouble."

Kaden sucked in a deep breath. "I'll bumble my way through this first."

"Okay."

He threaded their fingers together, not giving himself time to think about his words. They would never be poetic or elegant. Which was fine. He wasn't poetic or elegant. He was blunt, and honest, and rough around the edges.

"From the moment I saw you, I knew there was something different."

She chuckled. "I believe that."

He leaned closer, breathing in her familiar scent. "It was as if I suddenly found the one person I hadn't even known I was searching for."

"Is that a good thing?"

"I wasn't sure at first," he admitted. "I came to Pike to discover what happened to Vanna, not to have my life turned upside down."

"And now?"

"Now I have no doubts that you are the most astonishingly, outrageously fabulous thing that has ever happened to me." He leaned even closer, smiling deep into her eyes. "And I don't ever want to imagine a world without us together."

She heaved a small sigh. "You're not so bad at this emotional stuff, Kaden Vaughn."

"Don't tell my business partner. He'd never let me live it down."

She reached up to cup his face in her hand. "Your secret is safe with me."

Silence wrapped around them. The sort of warm, comfortable silence that was only possible between two people who relished each other's company. But while Kaden could spend endless hours feeling Lia's fingers lightly stroke his cheek as they leaned close together, he needed the reassurance that she shared his hopes for the future.

"It's your turn," he said in unexpectedly gruff tones.

She wrinkled her nose. "Can't I just cook you a roast? Or bake you a pie? Oh, I could do your accounts."

He lowered his head to press a gentle kiss against her

mouth. He could taste the soup that clung to her lips, but beneath the rich broth was her natural sweetness, which stirred his ready hunger.

"I will happily allow you to do all those things, but right now I need to hear the words," he insisted, nibbling a path of caresses along the stubborn line of her jaw.

"I'm not sure what I felt when I first saw you," she reluctantly admitted.

Kaden nipped the lobe of her ear. "This isn't starting off well."

Her fingers moved to thread through his hair, as if she enjoyed the feel of it against her skin.

"Hush," she commanded. "You looked dangerous and reckless and arrogantly confident. Everything I'm not."

His lips moved to press against her temple. "Lies," he murmured. "You're a risk-taker at heart."

"Let me finish before I lose my nerve." She tugged his hair to punish him for the interruption. "But when we're together, I'm not afraid. Just the opposite. I was convinced from the beginning that I've never been safer than when I'm with you."

Kaden's breath hissed between suddenly clenched teeth. Twice Lia had been attacked and he hadn't been able to do a damned thing.

"I wish that were true," he growled.

"It is," she insisted. "And not just in the physical sense. I trust you with my secrets." She tilted back her head, as if trying to judge his reaction to her words. "And with my heart. I never doubt you'll be there if I need you."

Kaden grunted as her words slammed into him with shocking force. He understood just how hard it was for Lia to open herself to someone else. She was naturally introverted, and her father's rejection had increased her desire to keep others at a distance. It wasn't just a way to protect herself. It gave her a much-needed sense of privacy in a town that made a habit of prying into one another's lives.

"Always." He framed her face in his hands, willing her to sense the sincerity of his promise. There was nothing he wouldn't do to make this woman's life as happy and secure as it could possibly be. Pulling her forward, he scattered kisses over her beautiful face. "Always, always, always."

Kaden felt her shiver with pleasure as she wrapped her arms around his neck, her lips parting in blatant invitation. With a low groan of satisfaction, Kaden gave in to the inevitable. He'd assured himself that Lia was fully recovered, and that she understood he wanted more than just a fleeting affair, right? There was no longer any need to resist temptation.

He wanted Lia.

No. He *needed* Lia.

Rising to his feet, he bent down, and without giving her the opportunity to guess his intention, he scooped her out of the chair and cradled her against his chest.

"You know the doctor's last order was that you should spend the day relaxing?"

She snuggled against him as he headed out of the kitchen and down the short hallway.

"And that's why you're carrying me to the bedroom?" she teased. "To relax?"

He pressed a kiss against her forehead, his long strides never slowing. "I can give you a nice massage."

She allowed her hands to smooth down his back, as if eager to explore his body.

"That sounds lovely," she breathed.

Kaden entered the master bedroom and headed for the king-size bed across the pale ivory carpet. It wasn't a massive space, but the furniture was handcrafted of solid walnut and the walls were papered in a tan and ivory stripe. The stark, elegant style reflected his brother's taste.

Ignoring the tiny pang at the thought of Darren's wasted life, Kaden focused on the woman in his arms.

She'd never looked more beautiful, he acknowledged, as passion blazed through him. The sun poured through the window to bring out the burnished highlights in her pale, spiky hair. Her eyes shimmered liked the finest emeralds with flecks of gold. And there were tiny freckles dotted over her nose that emphasized the perfection of her smooth skin.

Better yet, she was warm and soft and blessedly *solid* as she snuggled in his arms.

"You're real," he murmured, leaning forward to gently place Lia in the middle of the bed before perching on the edge of the mattress. He reached to cup her cheek in his hand. "I've spent so many nights dreaming of holding you in my arms only to wake and discover you were no more than a figment of my imagination." His thumb brushed her lips. "It was a constant reminder I might never discover what I desperately want to know."

Lia gazed up at Kaden, savoring the stark features of his face as he bent over her. She'd worried that if they ever managed to get in the same bed, it would feel awkward. Not because she was inexperienced, although she had been extremely selective in taking lovers. But because she was certain Kaden had been with the most beautiful women in the world.

The thought was more than a little intimidating for an introverted, small-town girl.

But now that they were finally where she wanted to be, she didn't feel awkward. She felt . . . exhilarated. Probably because he was studying her with a smoldering hunger that assured her there was no lack of desire. It sizzled in the air between them.

She settled into the soft mattress, allowing a slow smile to curve her lip. "What are you desperate to know?"

His fingers drifted down the curve of her throat. "If you have any secret indulgences."

Lia tilted back her head, inviting him to continue his caresses. The mere brush of his fingers was sending jolts of sizzling pleasure through her.

"Secret indulgences?" she demanded.

She wasn't sure what she expected, but it wasn't for him to swivel on the edge of the mattress until his broad back was turned toward her. Her eyes widened as she felt him gently peel off her socks.

"You know. Secret indulgences, like sneaking off to the spa when you're in Grange to have your tiny toenails painted."

Lia snorted. "It's the middle of winter and I live alone. Who would notice whether or not my toenails are painted?"

She watched as he bent forward; then her breath was trapped in her lungs as he nibbled the tip of her toes.

"A small treat that makes some women happy," he murmured, stroking his lips up the arch of her foot.

The soft touch tickled, but that wasn't why she shivered. It was the thrill of excitement that tingled through her as his breath brushed over her bare skin.

With a soft chuckle at her low groan, Kaden turned back to face her, his gaze lingering on her parted lips.

"I have more questions."

Her heart picked up speed as he reached toward the waistband of her jeans. "Somehow I'm not surprised." The words came out husky. Lia barely noticed. Her entire being was focused on Kaden. As if the world around them was fading away.

With obvious skill, Kaden unsnapped her jeans and pulled down the zipper. He held her gaze as he firmly tugged the heavy fabric down the length of her legs before dropping them on the floor. Then, cupping her legs in his hands, he messaged her sore muscles from her ankles up her calves and then her slender thighs. Lia sighed in pleasure. Kaden had a magic touch, she concluded. She didn't know whether to melt in a willing puddle of desire, savoring each caress. Or wrap her arms around him and drag him onto the bed so she could have her wicked way with him.

Her fuzzy thoughts were interrupted when Kaden made a strangled sound. "You do have a secret indulgence," he murmured, his gaze locked on her panties. They were a tiny triangle of black lace with red velvet ribbons that were tied into bows on her hips. "Very sexy, Lia Porter."

A ridiculous heat stained her cheeks. "They were a gift."

He stilled, his eyes abruptly narrowing. "A gift?"

Lia blinked at the hint of jealousy in his tone. Did he think she was wearing a gift from some previous lover?

"From Bailey," she revealed. "My best friend."

The tension eased from his face as his gaze returned to the frilly panties. "Bailey has excellent taste," he assured her, lowering his head to stroke his lips along the waistband. "Black satin." His tongue touched her bare skin, making her gasp at the fierce heat that darted straight between her legs. "Lace." He kissed and nipped his way to her hip. Then, grabbing the ribbon between his teeth, he gave it a quick jerk. Lia trembled, her breath coming in shallow pants as he moved to the ribbon on the other hip, easily dispensing with the bow in the same way. A second later, the fragile material slid from her body.

He straightened to gaze down at her, but Lia didn't feel exposed. Or vulnerable. Not with that hint of awe on his face. She knew with absolute certainty he wasn't judging her imperfections. He was cherishing her with every soft stroke of his fingers.

"Now I have to know," he murmured.

She blinked. Heat and passion pulsed through her, making it difficult to think. "Know what?"

"Does your bra match?"

Lia's breath lodged in her throat, her heart thundering as she battled against her instinct to glance away. In Kaden's bed she wasn't shy, timid Lia, she reminded herself. She was daring, take-charge Lia, who could create a financial empire that made her rich beyond her wildest dreams and still manage to keep her family's store open for business.

She eyed him with a bold challenge. "That's something you'll have to discover for yourself."

His smoky eyes darkened to charcoal as he sucked in a shocked breath. "There's my reckless Lia," he said in gruff tones.

Sliding his fingers beneath the hem of her sweater, Kaden gently pulled the fuzzy material up her body and over her head. A slow, wicked smile curved his lips as he dropped it over the edge of the bed and he studied the black lace bra with red ribbons.

"Perfection," he said in a voice that was harsh with need.

She reached up to thread her fingers in the satin softness of his hair, tugging him down. His gentle teasing was fun, and she would happily indulge in any games he wanted to play.

Later.

She'd desired this man since he walked into her store. Now her hunger had gone from a nagging ache to a raging need that refused to be denied. They could indulge in a slow, delicious exploration after she'd sated her desire.

Kaden readily gave in to her urging, claiming her lips in a searing kiss as his fingers stroked along the neckline of her lacy bra. Lia gasped as he located the clip between her breasts. A moment later, she felt the satin slip down her body, leaving her naked.

Still devouring her lips in a kiss she felt to the tips of her toes, Kaden cupped her breasts in his palms with reverent care. Lia tightened her grip on his hair, arching her back in silent invitation.

Kaden didn't hesitate. Using his thumbs, he teased the sensitive tips into hard nubs, growling deep in his throat as she shivered in anticipation. With a last lingering kiss, he swept his lips down the clenched line of her jaw, nuzzling the tender spot just below her ear before caressing a path down her throat.

Lia hissed as sensations stormed through her. Heat and hunger and a raw void that demanded to be filled.

"Kaden," she muttered, not sure what she was asking for until she felt his lips close around her nipple.

Oh . . . yes. That was what she needed. She squeezed her eyes shut as he stroked his tongue over the acutely sensitive flesh, each lap sending jolts of bliss to the center of her being.

She restlessly combed her fingers through his hair before lowering her hands to grasp his broad shoulders. Her palms landed against his flannel shirt and she reluctantly opened her eyes.

The material was soft beneath her palms, but she didn't want to feel flannel. She wanted to explore hot, male skin.

Sliding her hands down his chest, she struggled to deal with the buttons. She didn't have Kaden's skill in undressing her partner.

"Kaden, there's a lot of me exposed," she muttered.

Lifting his head, he allowed his silver gaze to sweep down her naked body. "Yes, indeed. Exquisite."

She shivered, but she wasn't going to be distracted. She tugged at the collar of his shirt.

"I want to see you."

He chuckled at the impatience in her voice that she didn't bother to hide. "That can be arranged," he assured her.

Rising to his feet, he held her gaze as he kicked off his boots before stripping away the flannel shirt and the heavy jeans. She wasn't surprised to see the loose silk boxers or the heavy knit socks. In some ways the two of them were the same. They both preferred comfort over fashion. Not that he didn't look sexy as hell in whatever he was wearing.

Once he was gloriously naked, he settled back on the mattress, his expression difficult to read as she abruptly sat up to press her hands against the hard muscles of his chest.

"Oh," she breathed in wonderment.

He arched his brows. "Is everything okay?"

Lia's mouth went dry at the sight of his sculpted chest, which narrowed to a slender waist and long legs. She'd already suspected he was lean and muscular and hard as a rock, but seeing him in the naked flesh revealed the sheer perfection of his body. A perfection that was emphasized rather than marred by the scars from his numerous injuries.

It was his tattoos, however, covering his chest and arms, that captured her attention.

Keeping her touch as light as a butterfly, she brushed her fingers over the dazzling images that were imbedded in his flesh.

"These are beautiful."

He reached down to grasp her hand in his, pressing them against his chest. "They tell my story."

"The story of Kaden?"

"Yes." He tugged her hand down to the ridges of his

six-pack, which was inked with a large tree being struck by lightning. "This represents the chaos of my childhood." He slid her hand to the vibrant image of a golden sunset over a beach. "My escape to LA." He bent his head to kiss her fingertips before moving them to his upper chest, where she could make out the sleek motorcycle jumping through a circle of fire. "My journey from the streets to Hollywood." His features tightened as he moved her hand to his arm, where an empty road wound its way through the shadows of a graveyard. "My brother's death." He shifted so he could press her hand against his other arm. The tattoo wasn't as large as the others, as if he intended to add to the image of a money sign that was etched in the middle of the desert. "And, finally, Vegas."

Her fingers drifted down to the skin of his forearm, which was bare. "It's not the end of your story."

"No." Kaden abruptly wrapped his arms around her, urging her to lay back as he covered her with his naked body. Lia groaned as his weight pressed her into the soft mattress. Instinctively, she spread her legs, allowing him to settle in the perfect position. Lowering his head, Kaden nuzzled the pulse that was pounding at the base of her throat. "It's just the beginning. I intend to devote the rest of my life to pleasing you."

Lia wrapped her arms around his neck, relishing the sensation of his hot, bare skin rubbing against her.

"You're already doing a pretty good job," she assured him, arching her hips to press against his thick arousal.

"*Pretty* good?" He released a low growl, his lips sweeping down to the swell of her breasts. "That sounds like a challenge."

Lia chuckled. "I suspect everything is a challenge to you."

He slid his hands down her back, cupping her ass in his palms as his lips teased her nipple.

"I like to think I'm doing my best. Especially when it involves you, Lia Porter."

"I like your best, Kaden Vaughn." Lia released a shaky sigh, desire clouding her mind with a haze of pleasure.

Chapter 24

Kaden woke to discover Lia tightly wrapped in his arms. As if he was afraid she might disappear while he slept. Or maybe it was to reassure himself she wasn't a figment of his imagination that would disappear with the dawn. With a rueful smile, he eased his grip, running his fingers through the satin spikes of her hair. It was going to take time to accept that this magnificent woman had agreed to be a part of his life.

With a slow stretch, Lia opened her eyes, blinking at the morning sunshine that poured through the open curtains.

"What time is it?" she asked in a husky voice.

Kaden perched on his elbow to gaze down at her sleep-flushed face. His heart slammed against his ribs. He'd never seen anything so beautiful in his life.

"Does it matter?"

She reached up to stroke her fingers through his hair. Kaden shivered in pleasure. Her touch was more addictive than any drug.

"I suppose not." She wrinkled her nose. "Which is strange."

He bent his head to sweep his lips over her brow, savoring the taste of her skin. Her touch wasn't the only thing he was addicted to.

"Why is it strange?" he asked.

"I've been working since I was old enough to hold on to a broom. It's always mattered what time it was."

Kaden didn't doubt Lia was expected to pull her weight from a very early age. Being the daughter of a single mother who struggled to provide for them meant she would have to take on duties and responsibilities that most kids would find unbearable. He'd been just the opposite. While Darren had shouldered the responsibility of keeping the house running—since his father couldn't be trusted to get dinner on the table—Kaden had run wild. His one contribution had been handing over the money he earned in underground fight clubs. His thick skull had been good for something.

It was one of a thousand reasons he adored her.

"This morning, let's pretend we're two people with no job and no worries." He brushed his lips down the narrow length of her nose. "Nothing but each other."

She chuckled. "Hollywood dreams."

"The dreams of a man in love."

He felt her stiffen at his words. "Oh," she breathed.

He lifted his head, frowning down at her flushed face. "Does that frighten you?"

"It astonishes me." She shook her head "I'm so . . . ordinary."

Kaden snorted. As far as he was concerned, no one was ordinary. Everyone had a story that made them unique and interesting. And this woman was more unique than most.

"Never ordinary. You're gloriously down-to-earth," he corrected in stern tones. "I've spent too many years in Hollywood surrounded by fake and shallow people who are willing to play whatever role will give them an advantage." He nipped the lush curve of her lower lip. "You might have your secrets, Lia Porter, but you are who you are."

She arched her naked body against him, tugging on his

hair. "I suppose that's true. I don't know how to play games. I never did."

"Thank God." A shiver of anticipation raced through Kaden. It didn't matter that he'd spent hours sating his ravenous hunger the night before. He was already eager to continue exploring the various ways to please this woman. "I've never feared you wanted anything from me."

She tugged his head down so she could press a soft, lingering kiss on his lips. "That's not entirely true."

He nuzzled the corner of her mouth, pressing his aching erection against her hip. "Anything I wasn't ready and eager to give," he growled. "And just as importantly, I never feared you were going to use me to gain some sort of advantage. You didn't need an advantage. Instead, you treated me like I was an annoying intruder you were forced to allow into your home to help solve the mystery of who jumped from the railroad bridge."

She clicked her tongue. "Not exactly annoying."

"Pushy?"

"Dangerous." Her eyes shimmered like emeralds in the morning sunlight. "I still think you're dangerous. But only in the best way."

He swept his lips over her cheek to discover the sensitive spot just below her ear. "That sounds like a challenge."

Lia wrapped her arms around his neck, melting against him in blatant invitation. "Not everything has to be a challenge."

He nipped the lobe of her ear. "Do you know me at all?"

In answer, she lifted her leg to drape it over his hip. "Not as well as I intend to."

Kaden groaned in approval, tugging her so close, nothing could get between them.

"A challenge," he insisted.

Lia kissed a path along the stubborn line of his jaw. "A promise."

"Yes." He slid his hand down the curve of her spine, his touch boldly possessive. "You were never getting rid of me. The moment I walked into Porter's Grocery Store, my fate was sealed."

She shivered, but she tilted back her head to send him a worried glance. "You know, we haven't discussed what we're going to do."

He allowed the tip of his erection to penetrate the entrance to her body. They both shuddered in pleasure. "I prefer action to words. That's why I was a stuntman and not an actor."

"I'm talking about our future."

Kaden captured her lips in a demanding kiss. There was no doubt their lives together would be complicated. And not only because they lived two thousand miles apart. But he refused to accept they couldn't find a way to be together.

"We'll figure it out," he murmured against her lips.

"But—"

"It won't be easy," he interrupted her protest. "But we'll work together to share each other's burdens, which includes you revamping my accounting system and me renovating your store into the twenty-first century." He narrowed his gaze with determination. "Plus, we'll scale back our businesses, we'll hire more staff, we'll learn to delegate, and we'll make a vow that nothing is more important than our happiness."

Lia studied him in surprise. As if she hadn't expected him to have spent so much time contemplating their future.

"That all sounds . . ." She appeared lost for words.

"Yes?" he prompted.

She smiled as she pressed herself onto the hard length of his arousal. "Like paradise."

* * *

Lia was floating in a delicious haze of bliss when a vibrating sound jerked her awake. At first she thought it was a fly buzzing around. Then she grimaced, remembering that it was the dead of winter. There were no flies.

Forcing open her eyes, she glanced around the bedroom in confusion. It wasn't until her gaze swept over the nearby nightstand that she realized the sound had come from her phone.

With a low groan, she pulled herself out of Kaden's arms and wiggled into a sitting position so she could grab it. Her muscles were stiff, but she savored each ache and pang. She'd loved every second of making love to the man snoozing next to her. And she had every intention of repeating the experience.

At the moment, however, her attention was focused on the text message that flashed across the screen.

"Kaden." She reached out to grasp his shoulder and give him a small shake. "Kaden."

"Yes, please," he muttered, flopping over to wrap his arm around her waist.

She gave him another shake. "Wake up."

Her sharp tone managed to penetrate the sleep fogging his mind, and with shocking speed, he was shoving himself to a sitting position to study her with a clear-eyed concern.

"Is something wrong?"

"No, for once it's good news," she assured him. "I sent an email to Professor Sanderson, asking if we could meet. She just sent a text that says she'll be available at one this afternoon."

"Where?"

"She has an office in her home." Lia hit the address to plug it into her map app. "It's only a few blocks from here."

Kaden nodded. "Let her know we'll be there." He tossed aside the covers and slid off the bed. Then, lifting his hands over his head, he stretched, emphasizing the lean perfection of his body. Lia openly ogled his raw male beauty, her hands twitching with the desire to reach out and touch him. Easily sensing her awareness, he sent her a wicked smile. "Shower?"

She pulled the covers up to her chin. "You go first."

He arched a brow. "We could save water if we shared."

"No way. We'll never get to talk to the professor," she said, her stomach abruptly rumbling in protest. "Plus, I'm starving."

Kaden laughed. "Rejected for a bowl of soup."

Lia heaved a sigh at the memory of the delicious chicken and noodles, unreasonably happy they had some left over. "It's really good soup."

Kaden chuckled on his way into the attached bathroom and Lia felt a momentary pang of regret as he shut the door, but she resisted temptation. Instead, she headed for the spare bedroom to take a quick shower and change into clean clothes. Then, entering the kitchen, she warmed up the soup and sliced the last of the bread.

Less than an hour later, they were out of the condo and driving the short distance to Dr. Sanderson's house, arriving exactly at one o'clock.

"This is it." Kaden parked the Jeep next to the curb and they both studied the red-brick bungalow that was surrounded by neatly trimmed bushes that were laced with Christmas lights. On one side, a small brick building was attached to the house by a covered breezeway. Presumably, the professor's office. Kaden reached out to squeeze her hand. "Ready?"

"I'm not sure," Lia admitted, her mouth dry and her stomach churning with nerves. When she'd decided to reach out to the professor, she hadn't considered how she was going to approach the woman. Or exactly what she hoped to learn. Now she felt incredibly awkward. "This is kind of a long shot," she muttered.

Kaden shrugged. "It's the only shot we have."

"True."

Squaring her shoulders, Lia grabbed her purse and pushed open her door. Climbing out, she grimaced at the frigid breeze that whipped through the quiet suburban street. Kaden was swiftly at her side, wrapping his arm around her shoulders as they walked up the driveway to the attached building. They sidestepped the plastic Santa Claus that waved toward the street and halted in front of the glass door.

Before they could knock, it was pulled open to reveal a woman in her early sixties. Lia's lips twitched, silently acknowledging the woman looked exactly like a college professor should look. She had fading red hair that was pulled into a knot at the nape of her neck and a pale face that was more handsome than pretty. Her eyes were dark and snapped with a restless intelligence behind a pair of wire-rimmed glasses. She was reed thin and wore a red sweater and casual black slacks.

"Hello." She smiled, holding out her hand. "You must be Lia Porter."

"Yes." Lia shook the offered hand. "And I assume you are Professor Sanderson?"

"Please, call me Mary." The woman turned her attention to Kaden. "And of course I recognize you." She stepped back. "Please come in."

Lia entered the building, closely followed by Kaden. They paused to slip off their jackets and left them on the coatrack before following Mary into a large office. Glancing around, Lia felt a pang of envy. The room was at least twice the size of her own office, with built-in bookcases that reached halfway up the walls, leaving ample room for the towering windows that allowed the afternoon sunlight to spill across a Persian carpet.

"Can I get you anything?" the professor asked. "Coffee? Tea?"

"Nothing for me," Lia said as Kaden shook his head.

"Have a seat." Mary pointed toward the high-backed leather chairs that were arranged in front of the desk. Waiting until they were obediently settled, the older woman took her place behind the desk and studied them with a stern expression. Suddenly Lia felt like she was sitting in a principal's office, waiting for her punishment. Was it deliberate? Or had the woman been a teacher for so long she instinctively took command of any encounter?

Lia cleared the lump from her throat. She wasn't a misbehaving teenager. She was there with a purpose, and the sooner she got to the point the better.

"Thank you for agreeing to meet with us," she said.

Mary placed her palms flat on the desk. "You said you wanted information about Vanna Zimmerman?"

"Yes," Lia agreed. "Her foster mother mentioned the two of you were close when Vanna was in college."

"I'm not sure what I can tell you. I haven't heard from Vanna since she disappeared fifteen years ago."

"No one has," Kaden told her. "And now we believe we know why."

The woman stiffened in shock. "You found her?"

Kaden held up a hand. "Nothing's confirmed, but we suspect the skeleton that was discovered near Pike, Wisconsin, is Vanna."

Something that might have been hope died in Mary's eyes. "I remember the headlines in the newspaper about a

body being discovered. I didn't bother to read the story."
She shook her head. "How tragic. I'd always hoped . . ."

"So did my brother," Kaden murmured as her words
trailed away.

"Yes." She squared her shoulders, as if trying to gather
her composure. She was clearly disturbed at the thought of
Vanna's death. "I spoke to him several times over the years.
I was so devastated when I read his obituary in the newspaper."

Kaden grimaced. "He never stopped looking for Vanna.
Or loving her."

Mary leaned forward, her stern expression softening as
she sent Kaden a sympathetic smile.

"Vanna was a different woman after she met your brother.
A *better* woman."

Kaden nodded. "Darren was a rock for a lot of people.
Including me."

There was a brief silence before Mary pushed herself
back in her seat, tapping a finger on the arm of her chair.

"Where did you say the skeleton was discovered?"

"Pike," Lia answered. "It's a tiny town—"

"I know where it is," Mary interrupted. "I used to visit
the college's extension office just outside of town. I was responsible for the interns who worked there."

Lia and Kaden shared a quick glance. Perhaps this meeting wouldn't be a waste of time.

Lia returned her attention to the older woman. "So, you
knew Vanna spent a summer in Pike?"

Mary pinched her lips. "Unfortunately."

"Why unfortunately?" Lia demanded.

The older woman glanced away, as if considering her
words. Or maybe she was deciding whether or not she
wanted to talk to them at all. The old-fashioned clock on the

wall ticked off the seconds, the wind rattling the windows. At last she heaved a faint sigh and turned back to meet Lia's curious gaze.

"Let me start at the beginning," she said.

"Please," Lia murmured. She was desperate to discover any information about Vanna's time in Pike.

Mary slowly leaned forward, placing her forearms on the desk as if she was preparing to share a long story.

"I met Vanna when she took my freshman botany class. It was obvious from the beginning that she was there on fellowship and that she had a chip on her shoulder that annoyed her classmates. She sat by herself in a corner, and even though she could have answered every question I asked, she refused to respond." Mary clicked her tongue. "It was almost as if she was daring me to kick her out."

"I'm sure as a professor that bothered you," Lia said.

"More than that, she reminded me of myself at that age," Mary surprisingly confessed. "Sullen. Defiant. Too smart for my own good."

Lia arched a brow, suddenly understanding why Vanna might have felt a connection to this woman.

"You knew how to reach out to Vanna," she said.

"As much as she would allow."

"Including an internship in Pike?" Kaden abruptly asked.

Mary sent him a startled glance. As if surprised he knew about Vanna's time in Pike.

"Yes. Vanna was ambitious and she was genuinely interested in protecting the environment. But I'd discovered over the years that for many students, the desire to save the world was one thing and spending your days testing landfills and spill off from sewers is another." A rueful smile curved her lips. "I wanted her to understand what fieldwork would entail before she committed to a career in the EPA."

"Smart," Lia said. She'd gotten her degree with no genuine knowledge of what she wanted to do when she graduated. Luckily, she managed to discover a career that was perfect for her.

Mary made a sound of disgust at the compliment. "As I said, I'm sometimes too smart for my own good."

Chapter 25

Kaden sensed the edge of bitterness in the older woman's tone. Along with a heavy sense of guilt. Emotions that were all too familiar. He'd carried them since his brother's death.

But while he sympathized with her regrets, he was more interested in just how close she'd been to Vanna. And whether she could reveal any conflicts Vanna might have had during her time with the extension office.

"Did something go wrong during her internship?" he asked.

Mary grimaced. "At first she complained about the town, the locals, the endless boredom."

"Anything specific?"

"No. Just the tedium of a young, attractive woman being buried in the middle of nowhere."

Lia smiled wryly. "She wasn't the only young woman to complain."

Mary nodded, as if she agreed it wasn't easy to be stuck in a small town with no entertainment.

"It's what I expected, but surprisingly, she didn't lose her interest in her career. In fact, she was more determined than ever to join the EPA."

Kaden absorbed her words. Vanna was a weirdly complex

woman. Ambitious and greedy and immoral. Yet devoted to his brother and worried about the environment.

"That seems like a good thing," Lia said.

"It was."

Lia frowned in confusion. "What happened?"

"After the first month, she stopped coming back to Madison so often. She said she was busy, and I let it go for several weeks. Then I became worried and decided to travel to Pike to check on her."

"Why would you be worried?" Kaden demanded, genuinely interested. "I would have assumed she'd made some friends and preferred to stay in Pike rather than make the two-hour drive every Friday."

The professor looked away, as if she didn't want him to see her reaction to his question.

"I was concerned she might have bailed on the internship and was too embarrassed to tell me that she quit," Mary grudgingly shared her fear. "Vanna was ambitious, but she also battled a self-destructive impulse."

Ah. Kaden belatedly understood the woman's unease. He didn't have any trouble believing Vanna would walk away from a commitment she'd decided wasn't going to be beneficial to her career. Or her bank balance.

"But she hadn't quit?"

"No."

"Did she tell you why she stopped coming home?" Lia asked.

Mary paused, heaving a harsh sigh. "She didn't have to. When I arrived at the extension office I discovered it was already closed for the day, so I went to Vanna's private apartment in the back and knocked on the door." She grimaced. "There was no answer, but I could hear voices inside. I knocked again, and Vanna finally pulled open the door far enough to tell me to go away. She was wrapped in a sheet and her hair was a mess. It didn't take a genius to know there was a man in there with her."

Kaden jerked, his lips parting at his sheer stupidity. Why the hell hadn't he considered the possibility that Vanna was in a romantic relationship during her time in Pike?

"A boyfriend?" Lia asked, sounding equally startled.

Mary held up her hands, as if warning them not to jump to conclusions.

"I'm not sure it was a traditional boyfriend," she told them. "At the time I was concerned because Vanna never had an interest in relationships. At least not the sort of relationships most girls her age enjoyed."

Kaden waited for the soft words to continue. When she remained silent, he sent her an impatient frown. "What does that mean?"

"She preferred picking up guys in bars, or better yet, having affairs with married men." Mary grimaced. "There were one or two incidents at the college that had to be covered up."

Kaden nodded, not bothering to probe for details. It was obvious that discussing Vanna's poor choices was painful for the older woman.

"Did she give you the name of the man in her apartment?"

"She didn't say anything. She slammed the door in my face."

Frustration flared through Kaden. Trying to discover the truth of what happened to Vanna was always one step forward and two step back.

"I don't suppose you ever discovered who it was?"

"No." There was a tense pause before Mary cleared her throat. "But I know what happened to the relationship."

Lia leaned forward. "What?"

The older woman surged to her feet, as if she couldn't sit

still a second longer. Then, pacing toward the nearest window, she gazed absently at the waving Santa next to her driveway.

"I've never told anyone what I'm about to share with you. Vanna swore me to secrecy, and I honored that promise. Even after she disappeared." Slowly, she turned back to face them. "Now that I know she can no longer be hurt . . ."

"It might be important," Kaden assured her.

Mary slowly nodded in agreement. "Vanna unexpectedly showed up in my office two weeks before her internship was scheduled to end. She said she was done and refused to go back to Pike."

"Did something happen?" Kaden asked.

"It took a while for me to convince her to tell me what was wrong, but she finally admitted the truth." Mary gripped her hands together, her face flushed. "She was pregnant."

Lia's breath hissed through her clenched teeth, as if the air was being squeezed from her lungs. At the same time, the earth seemed to shift beneath her feet.

It wasn't just shock. It was the realization that they had been so focused on Vanna's work as an EPA inspector and her nasty habit of making extra income with blackmail, it hadn't occurred to her that her connection to Pike might be far more intimate.

"Pregnant," she breathed, her gaze locked on Mary's tense expression. "Did she have the baby?"

"She did. Honestly, I was shocked," Mary confessed. "It was obvious the relationship with the child's father was over, and Vanna had always been compulsively obsessed with her career. I couldn't believe she would be willing to risk her future with a baby she didn't want."

Lia couldn't believe it either. Raising a baby alone when you were still a college student would be a daunting task. And everything she'd heard about Vanna Zimmerman indicated she didn't have a nurturing bone in her body. Not to mention the fact that no one seemed to know about the child. Not even her fiancé.

There was only one potential explanation.

"Did she give the baby up for adoption?" Lia asked.

Mary hesitated, her jaw tightening as if she was struggling against her instinctive urge to protect Vanna, who'd obviously been more than just another student to her.

"That's what she told me," Mary finally conceded.

"You didn't believe her?" Lia was confused. Why would Vanna lie about giving her baby up for adoption?

"I did. At least at first." The older woman lowered her head, as if she was studying the tips of her leather shoes. Or, more likely, trying to hide her expression. "But then I discovered she'd received a fellowship that paid off her college loans in full. And that she'd moved off campus into her own apartment in a neighborhood that was nicer than where I lived."

"I don't understand." Lia shook her head. "What does her fellowship have to do with . . ."

Abruptly turning her head, she met Kaden's smoldering gaze. He nodded before he glanced toward Mary.

"Let me guess," he said, his voice harsh. "The Burke Fellowship Award."

The older woman made a strangled sound, clearly caught off guard. "How did you know?"

"She told her foster mother the same story," Kaden said.

Something that might have been relief flashed across Mary's face. "Maybe it was real."

"Doubtful," Kaden said in dry tones. "The businessman

who wrote the check wasn't the sort of guy who would willingly hand out money to anyone."

"You know him?" Mary clung to her vague hope. Perhaps she blamed herself for sending Vanna to Pike. "You should ask him about the fellowship—"

"I'm afraid that's not possible," Lia broke in before Kaden could respond. He had many fine qualities, but he could be blunt to the point of rudeness.

"Why not?" Mary asked.

"He was found dead a few days ago."

The older woman widened her eyes. "Oh my God. What happened?"

"It's being investigated," Lia said, keeping her answer vague.

"We think he was murdered. And the killer was there to steal files that revealed Ryan Burke was blackmailed by Vanna fifteen years ago over dumping toxic waste from his meatpacking plant into the Pike water supply."

Lia frowned at Kaden. Okay, that went beyond bluntness. Was he hoping to shock the older woman? Did he think she was hiding more information? Or just wanting to see her reaction?

Mary shivered, wrapping her arms around her waist in a protective gesture.

"Meatpacking plant? Why is that familiar?" she muttered, speaking more to herself than Lia or Kaden. She sent Lia a startled look. "I think I remember Vanna mentioning that place."

"What did she say?" Lia asked.

"She didn't say anything directly to me, but when she returned to Madison, she let me read through the notebook she intended to include in her final report for her internship," Mary revealed. "She was scathing in her opinion of the meatpacking plant's waste disposal, although she didn't go into detail, and she didn't include the fact that he was potentially poisoning the citizens of Pike. I would have taken action if I'd suspected anyone was in danger."

"The fellowship might have been a bribe to keep the notes out of her final report," Kaden suggested.

Mary nodded, her expression distracted. "In part."

"You suspect something?" Lia demanded.

"I've hated myself for thinking this. . . ." The older woman's words died on her lips and suddenly she looked older. As if she was weary of the secrets she'd been carrying for years. "But the news about the fellowship arrived a week after she gave birth. The same day the baby was adopted. It was hard to believe it was just a coincidence."

Lia sucked in an audible breath. "She sold the child?"

"No." Mary shook her head at Lia's accusation. "In Vanna's mind, it would have been a business transaction."

With an effort, Lia battled back the urge to argue. The professor's memories of Vanna had already been tainted. Why cause her more pain?

Besides, Vanna's motives didn't matter. Lia was more interested in what happened to the baby, and if it was somehow connected to her death.

"Then there's no way to know who has the child," Kaden said, pointing out the obvious.

Lia wasn't so sure. She had friends who'd gone through the adoption process. It was lengthy and expensive and the adoptive parents drowned in red tape, including background checks and character references. If Vanna was dealing with a legitimate agency, it would be difficult to keep it a secret. At least from a woman who'd been as close to her as Professor Sanderson.

"The most obvious guess would be that she handed it over to the father," Lia suggested. "That would avoid any paperwork or investigations by the authorities."

Kaden nodded in agreement. "Her lover in Pike."

Lia considered the options. It was possible the father was someone who'd moved away from Pike years ago. Or even someone who'd never lived there. Vanna could have met him in another town and invited him back to her apartment. But it was also possible the father was someone they'd already connected to Vanna and her death.

"It couldn't be Ryan Burke," she finally said. "He doesn't have any children."

"True." Kaden paused, then his jaw tightened as he muttered a sudden curse. "Tate Erickson."

The name smacked into Lia like a punch. Not because she was surprised by the suggestion but because it was so ridiculously easy to imagine the arrogant, self-obsessed man seducing a college student.

"I know that name," Mary said without warning. "He's from Pike, isn't he?"

"Yes," Lia answered. "He's the mayor."

"The mayor." Mary pressed a hand against the center of her chest, as if her heart was suddenly beating too fast. "Right."

Kaden stepped toward her. "What is it?"

"It's possible I saw them together in Madison," she told them.

"Where?"

"I was invited by a friend to the opening of a new, very expensive restaurant on the outskirts of town and happened to run into Mayor Erickson as I was entering. I'd met him a few times during my visits to Pike, so I easily recognized him, although he pretended not to notice me until I actually spoke to him." Her lips pinched, revealing Mary's obvious distaste for Tate Erickson. "I asked him what he was doing in Madison and he claimed he was in town to visit with some state officials, but I could tell he was uncomfortable."

She shrugged. "I assumed he was using his night away from home to meet with a woman who wasn't his wife."

Kaden clenched his hands and Lia swore she could feel the tension vibrating through his rigid body.

"Did you see who he was with?"

"Just a glimpse." Mary's voice held a hint of apology, obviously aware she was going to disappoint them. "After I was shown to my table, I glanced out the window to see him bundling a brunette into a sports car. It seemed to confirm my theory of an affair, but at the time I never suspected it might be Vanna. Now . . ."

Lia didn't allow the older woman to finish. In her mind, she was already convinced Tate was the father of Vanna's baby. It would explain why he'd pretended he'd never met her. And why he was willing to kill anyone who might know the truth about his relationship with the younger woman. He hadn't been concerned about an ancient blackmail scheme. He was concerned his daughter might discover the truth about her birth.

"If Tate was her lover and he was responsible for handing over the fellowship money, that means Sunny is Vanna's daughter," she spoke her suspicions out loud.

"Not for sure," Kaden attempted to reason with her. "Even if he was her lover, he might have paid the fellowship to keep her mouth shut about the baby."

"Then what happened to the child?" she challenged him.

"The baby might have been put up for adoption, just as Vanna claimed."

Her brows snapped together. "You don't believe that!"

His lips parted, as if he intended to insist they keep our minds open, only to heave a sigh.

"No."

Their eyes locked and held, but before Lia could speak,

a loud chime echoed through the air. Together, they glanced to the empty desk.

"That's my alarm," Mary explained. "It's time for me to take my mother to her therapy session. I'm afraid I have to leave."

Lia instinctively moved forward to grab the woman's hands, giving them a small squeeze.

"Thank you so much for speaking with us."

Mary heaved a harsh sigh. "I have a lot of regrets when it comes to Vanna. She was a troubled soul who was searching for something that remained just out of reach. I'm not sure she would ever have found peace."

The mention of Vanna's seemingly unquenchable thirst for money reminded Lia that they still had no idea where her considerable wealth had gone. She didn't think Vanna would have shared that information with her professor, but Mary might be able to give them a lead on someone who might know.

"We have reason to believe Vanna had a secret bank account," Lia said, releasing the older woman's hands as she stepped back.

"I'm sure she did," Mary said without hesitation. "She would have craved the sense of security of having her money spread in several locations."

"Do you have any idea where she might have kept those funds?" Lia pressed. "Perhaps a bank she used when she was in college? Or a friend who was willing to let her use her identity to open another account?"

"I'm sorry." Mary shook her head. "I really wouldn't know."

Lia shrugged. "It was worth a try."

Turning away, Lia halted when Mary reached out to touch her shoulder.

"Wait." Glancing back, Lia met the older woman's worried gaze. "I don't know if this is connected, but shortly before she disappeared, I had lunch with Vanna." A wistful smile touched Mary's mouth. "I don't think I'd ever seen her so happy. She was excited about the wedding and the honeymoon she was planning with Darren. At the time, I remember thinking she was glowing. I decided to use the opportunity to ask the question that had been on my mind for a while."

"What question?"

"I wanted to know if she'd seen her mother. Her real mother."

Lia was confused by what Vanna's real mother had to do with her bank accounts. Vanna was way too smart to give a junkie large amounts of cash. Still, Mary seemed to think it was important.

"What did she say?"

"A weird expression crossed her face and she told me that she hadn't seen her mom, but that Lisa was allowing her to live the life she'd always desired."

Okay, that was strange, Lia conceded. "Did you ask her what she meant?"

Mary nodded "She said that for once the worthless bitch was giving her something she really needed." The older woman held up her hands as Lia arched her brows. "Her words, not mine. I asked what that was, and Vanna said, 'Her name.' That was it. I didn't understand, but I let it go."

Her name. Lia sucked in a sharp breath. "I think I do."

Mary firmly headed toward the door, bringing an end to the meeting. "If that's all, I really should go."

Chapter 26

"A baby. That's a plot twist I didn't see coming," Kaden muttered as he drove out of the quiet neighborhood and headed north.

Lia nodded, feeling almost numb as she struggled to comprehend what they'd discovered. It was more than a plot twist, she silently acknowledged. It had shaken up everything they thought they knew about Vanna Zimmerman and her connection to Pike.

"I'm not sure if I'm more shocked that Vanna had Tate's baby or that Tate managed to disguise the fact that Jolene wasn't Sunny's mother." The words held an edge of bitterness. "Everyone in Pike knew my dad fled town rather than be a father and that his parents refused to acknowledge my existence. But I never heard so much as a whisper that Sunny might have been adopted."

Kaden reached out to give her hand a comforting squeeze. "Thankfully, you were raised by a loving mother who believed honesty and decency were more important than pride," he said. "Tate Erickson, on the other hand, is a man who would be willing to go to any extreme to cover up his sins. The last thing he'd want is for his citizens to discover he'd been having sex with a college student and then purchased her baby after he got her pregnant."

Lia grimaced. "Not the best reelection platform."

"No shit." He returned his hand to the steering wheel, but the warmth of his touch chased away the unwelcome memories.

Trying to imagine Tate bargaining for his baby, Lia was struck by a sudden thought.

"Do you think Jolene knew about Vanna?"

"How could she not?"

"Tate might have told her that he bought the baby on the black-market. It's something he would do."

"True."

"And if Jolene was desperate enough for a child, she wouldn't have asked awkward questions." Lia wrinkled her nose. Just talking about Jolene Erickson left a bad taste in her mouth. The snobby woman treated everyone in town as if they were beneath her. "And honestly, I can't imagine she could be as devoted to Sunny as she is if she knew the baby belonged to Tate's lover."

Kaden nodded. "The baby black market would certainly be the easiest way to explain why there was a large amount of cash missing from their bank account."

Lia sighed. It was impossible to speculate exactly what Jolene did or didn't know about Sunny's real mother. Always assuming Sunny was Vanna's daughter. And it didn't really matter.

"The more important question is whether the baby has anything to do with Vanna's death." She turned the conversation back to more important matters.

"It's possible, but I can't see the connection. She died . . . what?" Kaden paused as he considered the time lapse between the birth of Vanna's baby and her death. "Three, maybe four years after she gave birth? If you wanted to get rid of her, why not do it when she announced she was pregnant? Or after she first handed over the child?"

Lia considered the question, remaining silent as they hit heavy traffic clogging the streets. She didn't want to distract Kaden from his driving, even if he was a professional. It wasn't until they reached the highway that she at last swiveled in her seat to study his sculpted profile.

"I agree, it doesn't make sense. Why go through the farce of creating a fake fellowship if he intended to kill her?" She made a sound of frustration. "Or let her blackmail him and his buddies when she came back as an EPA inspector?"

"Blackmail." Kaden spoke the word softly, as if he was tasting it on his tongue. "When I confronted Tate with proof he'd been paying off Vanna, he mentioned that the judge had to get involved because he was the president of the Chamber of Commerce and they needed the funds. They obviously reached the end of what they were willing to pay to avoid being exposed."

Lia nodded. "You think she was demanding more money from them?"

A hard smile curved his lips as he merged onto the highway and pressed his foot on the gas. "No. I think Vanna was smart enough to realize she'd squeezed all she could from Burke and the town of Pike," he conceded. "But now that we know about the baby, I suspect she found another target."

Lia frowned. "Tate?"

"I'm pretty sure he would pay anything to keep his dirty little secret. . . ." Kaden's words trailed away as his fingers tightened on the steering wheel. "Damn."

"What's wrong?"

"The picture."

"Picture?"

"The one with Tate and Vanna in front of the extension office," Kaden clarified. "I sensed there was something different about his reaction when he saw the photo. Until that point he'd been defensive, but he had an answer for every accusation I made." He grunted in disgust. "A true politician."

"What was different?"

"He looked genuinely concerned. As if he was worried I'd seen it." Kaden's jaw tightened, clearly angry at himself for missing an important clue. "At the time, I assumed it was because it was undeniable proof he was paying Vanna large sums of money. Now I wonder if he was worried I might discover he wasn't being blackmailed to keep her mouth shut about the violations, but to keep it shut about a baby."

Lia nodded. The theory would certainly explain Tate's reaction. And why he'd risked doing his dirty business in broad daylight when anyone might have seen them.

"But why then?" she asked the question that nagged at her. Or one of the thousands of questions that nagged at her. "Why choose that moment to demand the money?"

"Why not?"

"Unless Vanna had some hidden addiction that was costing her thousands of dollars, she had to have a small fortune stashed away in overseas transfers. Why continue to press her luck when she didn't need to?"

Kaden shrugged. "Maybe she was addicted to money."

It was possible, of course, but Lia couldn't shake the premonition there was a tangible reason she'd been so insatiable in acquiring as much money as possible in a short period of time.

"Or she thought she was going to lose her ability to make more," she hesitantly suggested. "Was it possible she planned to leave her job after she got married?"

Kaden snorted. "No way . . . wait." His brow furrowed, as if he was searching through his memories. Lia remained silent, allowing him to think in peace. At last, he released his breath through clenched teeth. "That's it," he said in harsh tones. "The wedding was just a few weeks away."

"Was she going to take time off for a honeymoon?"

"Just a few days, nothing that would have interfered with her blackmail scheme." He sent her a quick glance. "But my brother was constantly complaining he hated that her job meant they spent so much time apart. He told me that after they were married, he intended to travel with her so they could be together."

Lia smiled. Obviously, the Vaughn brothers had a lot in common. Not only did they have enough confidence in their masculinity to admire strong women, they were willing to do whatever was necessary to make sure they could acquire their dreams.

Lia's heart melted.

Clearing her throat, she resisted the urge to reach over and run her fingers through Kaden's silky hair.

"What about his job?"

"He did most of it online. He only went into the office a few days a month unless he was called into court."

Which meant it wasn't just a hopeful wish to spend more time together, Lia silently acknowledged. It was a plan in the making.

"Vanna must have realized her ability to bully and blackmail the people she was inspecting would be threatened by his presence."

"It's a theory."

Lia reluctantly nodded, settling back in her seat. "What now?"

"We go back to the beginning."

* * *

Tate snapped shut his briefcase, glancing around the shabby office with a grimace. He was done playing sheriff. In fact, he wished now he'd never insisted on taking the job. Or at least that he'd had the sense to head out of town when that damned skeleton was found.

Of course, he'd always been overly confident in his ability to manipulate any situation to his advantage. He'd been doing it since he convinced his mother he deserved twice the allowance as his younger sister because "boy" toys cost more. And he'd been certain that once he had the bones hauled away, any danger to himself would be over. Not the most sympathetic means to deal with his former lover, but it wasn't like she hadn't tried to screw him over. More than once, right?

Everything would have been fine if it wasn't for Kaden Vaughn and that bitch, Lia Porter.

What right did they have to stick their noses into his business? Vanna was dead. Their interference wasn't going to bring her back. Not to mention that if they'd just left well enough alone, Burke and the judge would still be alive. Tate happily stoked the flames of his self-righteous indignation, thinking of the shit show that had plagued him over the past week. The anger helped to mask the terror that was humming through him like an electric charge.

A shame, really.

Thankfully, he was always prepared.

Whether it was paying a small fee to the receptionist at the local news station to let him know whenever the cameras would be out so he could be sure to get his face on TV. Or creating fake awards he could frame and have presented to him at the Lions Club. Only a fool left their fate to chance.

Which was precisely why he had a suitcase filled with

clothes, a stash of cash, fake IDs, and keys to a cabin in Colorado he'd secretly purchased years ago. Better yet, he kept it hidden in a location his overly inquisitive wife would never discover.

It was time to get the hell out of Pike.

Chapter 27

Kaden's nerves were on a razor's edge by the time they reached Pike. The mere thought of taking Lia back to the place where she'd been deliberately poisoned was terrifying. Then again, there was no way he was leaving her alone in Madison. It seemed unlikely anyone could sneak into his brother's condo but not impossible. It didn't help that night had fallen during the long drive and snow had started to fall. No shocker, that. It was December in Wisconsin. At the moment it was just a few flakes lazily drifting through the air, but that could change to a full blizzard without warning.

Bypassing the first exit, Kaden drove until they were north of town before he veered off the highway. Not only was it closer to his destination, it allowed him to avoid being seen by the locals. The fewer people who knew they were back the better.

Especially tonight.

As he slowed the Jeep, Lia stirred next to him, stretching her arms with a wide yawn. Kaden smiled as a shiver of awareness raced through him. She'd been dozing off and on for the past two hours, clearly exhausted by their previous night together. He'd done his best not to disturb her sleep. He had plans to do more exhausting tonight.

Thankfully unaware he was already imagining the pleasure of stripping off her heavy sweater and jeans, Lia glanced out the windshield in confusion.

"Where are we going?"

"To the beginning," he repeated his earlier words, turning onto a narrow lane that was packed with snow.

"I don't know what that means."

Kaden swallowed a sigh. He wasn't entirely sure himself. He just knew the answers were in Pike.

"We've established motives for Vanna's murder," he said.

"A lot of motives. And a lot of suspects." Lia grabbed the console as they rattled and skidded over the icy road. "Too many."

"Exactly," Kaden agreed. "Which would probably be great if we were cops who had the training and authority to question them."

"Instead of amateurs fumbling in the dark?"

Kaden chuckled at the painful accuracy of her words. "Not exactly how I was going to put it, but yeah, fumbling in the dark."

"What else can we do?"

He slowed to a crawl as the lane continued to narrow and the snow began to fall in earnest. It was becoming increasingly difficult to see more than a few feet in front of him.

"If we could discover *why* Vanna was running down the road the night you saw her, we might be able to narrow the list of suspects." Kaden cautiously tapped the brakes as they reached the railroad bridge. Once they stopped, he shoved the gearshift into Park. "This is where she jumped, right?" He waited for Lia's hesitant nod. He hated putting her through the events of that night, but he didn't know what else to do. He pointed toward the road that stretched in front of them. "And she was running from that direction." Lia nodded again and Kaden glanced around the isolated spot. "Why here? The most likely explanation is that she was coming from town."

"But?"

"Why was she running?"

Lia glanced toward him, as if surprised by the question. "I assume because someone was chasing her."

Kaden shook his head. "No, I mean she had to drive to get to Pike. Why not get in her car if she wanted to get away?"

"Yes," Lia breathed. She glanced out the passenger window, as if looking at her surroundings with the eyes of an adult instead of a terrified teenager.

"Plus, she was familiar with this area. She would have to know there was nothing out here but empty fields once she was past this bridge."

"And if was in town, there would be no need to run." Lia added. "All she had to do was scream for help. There would have been a dozen people rushing to see what was going on. Even if they didn't intend to help, they wouldn't dare miss the opportunity to be part of the action."

Accepting that Vanna's presence at the bridge hadn't been a random accident, Kaden turned his thoughts to how she'd gotten there.

"It seems more likely she was brought to this area by someone else."

Lia glanced back in his direction, her expression difficult to read in the shadows of the night.

"But was she lured or kidnapped?"

"A good question."

"I have more."

He didn't doubt that for a second. She probably had a

hundred more questions. Just as he did. For now, however, he wanted to concentrate on Vanna's reason for running down this particular road in the middle of the night.

"We've determined the closest locations to the bridge are the meatpacking plant. The Walsh farm. And the extension office."

Kaden hesitated as he considered the various options. It didn't take long to decide. The meatpacking plant was probably empty, but it was surrounded by security cameras. He didn't want to get caught poking around a place where there'd just been a murder. Not if the FBI was going to start an investigation. And they could hardly barge into the Walsh home and ask to look around for evidence.

There was really only one choice.

Putting the Jeep back into gear, Kaden slowly bumped his way along the frozen road, painfully aware he had no real plan. He was just trying to feel as if he was doing something to solve Vanna's murder and make sure Lia was safe.

Rounding a sharp curve, Kaden caught a glimpse of the decaying building. From a distance, it looked like a haunted house on a Hollywood set. All it needed was a . . .

"Kaden." Lia's voice sharply intruded into his aimless thoughts.

On instant alert, Kaden swept his gaze over their surroundings, at last spotting the sleek sports car parked at an odd angle toward the back of the building.

Giving the steering wheel a jerk, he pulled to the side of the road and hastily switched off the headlights.

"I see it."

Lia unhooked her seat belt and leaned forward. "That's Tate's car."

"Yeah, hard to miss," he said dryly. "And for once, I don't want to barf at the idiot's narcissistic need to show off. He just made sure we know exactly where to find him."

"True." Lia shook her head. "Why on earth would he be out here at this time of night? It's freezing."

Kaden unhooked his belt. "I'm going to find out."

Without warning, Lia reached out to grasp his arm. "How?" she demanded. "You can't just go up there and ask him."

"Until I know what's happening, I'll have to improvise."

She rolled her eyes. "Because that's worked so well for us in the past?"

"Sometimes." Kaden leaned forward, sweeping his gaze over her upturned face. "I have a vivid memory of your improvisation when you discovered the tattoo on my—"

"You can't risk confronting him," she sternly interrupted his teasing. "Tate Erickson might act like an idiot, but he's cunning and selfish and probably armed. If he feels threatened, he's going to pull the trigger."

Kaden stilled. She was genuinely worried. A strange warmth spread through him. He'd grown up with parents who didn't give a damn whether he was safe or not. Only Darren cared.

And now this amazing woman.

He reached out to cup her cheek in his palm. "I'm not going to do anything stupid, I promise."

She narrowed her eyes. "I wish I believed that."

"Lia, I know you think I'm impulsive."

"You are."

Kaden sighed. He couldn't argue with that. He did tend to act first and think later. Like packing a bag and heading to California. Or opening a business he knew nothing about. Or rushing to Pike when he heard a skeleton was discovered.

"I can be . . . reckless on occasion." Kaden didn't give her a chance to interrupt. "But when it came time for a dangerous stunt, I can assure you that it was meticulously planned to the tiniest detail and I practiced it a hundred times. I have no intention of getting shot. In fact, I don't intend for Tate to even know I'm here."

"Good." She suddenly smiled. "In that case, I'm coming with you."

Kaden cursed as his attempt to reassure his companion backfired in spectacular fashion. He'd meant to comfort her, not encourage her to put herself in danger. Dammit.

"Lia."

"You just said Tate wouldn't even know you were here."

Before he could continue the argument, Lia was out of the Jeep and headed toward the building. More curses flew from Kaden's lips as he quickly joined her, not bothering to shut off the engine. He wanted a quick getaway if things went sideways.

And they were bound to go sideways . . .

They reached the front of the building in silence, carefully bypassing the deteriorating porch and rounding the corner. It was only then they could see light spilling from the back window to reflect against the layers of snow. Kaden frowned, briefly confused by the glow. Surely the electricity wasn't still turned on? The place had been abandoned for years. It wasn't until the breeze swirled around them that he caught the smell of smoke coming from the chimney.

Whoever was inside had started a fire to combat the frigid temperature.

Lia quickly pressed herself against the side of the building, no doubt aware the light would cause shadows once they got closer. She didn't hesitate, however, as she continued to inch toward the back window, her face set in lines of grim determination.

Kaden was content to follow behind her. He'd seen enough movies to know the bad guy always snuck around the house to ambush the good guys. He intended to be prepared for any sneak attack. Of course, he'd be a lot more prepared if his feet weren't freezing and he'd put on his stocking hat, he wryly admitted, relieved when they at last reached the window.

When he returned to Vegas, he was going to spend the next month lying in the sun by his pool. It was going to take that long to thaw out.

Leaning to the side, Lia peered through the grimy panes of glass. Kaden pressed close behind her, using his superior height to see over her head. Not that there seemed to be much to see. It looked the same as it had the last time he'd peeked through the window. An old kitchen that doubled as an apartment, with bunk beds, a desk, and a dresser. The only difference was the fire that blazed in the old-fashioned iron stove, spilling a weird orange glow through the space.

And the man lying in the center of the floor, blood dripping from the hole in his forehead.

"It's Tate." Lia breathed in horror. "He's hurt."

She took a step forward before Kaden could wrap his arms around her. There was no way either of them was going inside. Everything about this situation screamed of a trap.

"We need to get out of here," he warned, pulling her backward.

"But—"

"We'll call the ambulance on the way to town," he promised.

"There's no need for an ambulance." A voiced drifted through the air before a shadow appeared from behind the building. "I made sure he's dead."

Kaden hissed in shock, narrowing his eyes as he tried to peer through the darkness. The form was small enough to be a woman. Or maybe a teenager. It was impossible to say for sure. Why the hell wouldn't they step into the light from the window?

Thankfully, Lia knew her neighbors well enough to guess the identity even in the darkness.

"Jolene," she muttered.

Kaden made a strangled sound, the air squeezed from his lungs as the woman stepped forward, and he could see the cloud of blond hair and the face that might have belonged to an angel. He could also see the handgun she was pointing at his heart.

"It's too cold to chat out here," Jolene said, despite the fact that she was wearing a heavy parka and knee-high boots. "Let's go inside."

"Actually, we were just on our way—" Lia started to protest, only to snap her lips shut when the gun swung in her direction.

"I'm afraid I'm going to have to insist."

Kaden stepped to place himself in front of Lia. He didn't even consider trying to rush the woman. This wasn't a movie, where a villain could shoot a hundred times without hitting a damned thing. Jolene held the weapon as if she knew exactly what she was doing. Not to mention that he wasn't about to put Lia in the line of fire.

As if sensing his sizzling concern, Lia grasped his hand to give his fingers a reassuring squeeze.

She might be scared, but she wasn't going to panic.

Together, they climbed the rickety steps, and Kaden pushed against the door. It swung inward with a loud creak that made him wince. The grating sound was a reminder they were in an abandoned building in the middle of nowhere. Just as the sight of the dead man lying in the middle of the floor was a bleak reminder not to underestimate the woman who was closing the door behind them.

Steering Lia away from the body, he was caught off guard when she abruptly released a loud sob and wrapped her arms tightly around his neck.

"Kaden!"

Unnerved by her unexpected burst of emotion, he held her tight against his body. But the storm of tears he was expecting never came; instead, she pressed her lips against his ear.

"There's a gun under the suitcase on the bed," she whispered so softly he had to struggle to catch the words.

Kaden stiffened, glancing over her shoulder. Sure enough, there was an open suitcase on the lower bunk, filled with clothes and stacks of money that had spilled onto the filthy mattress. And peeking from beneath the case was the unmistakable muzzle of a handgun.

"I see it," he whispered back.

"Keep her distracted and I'll get it."

"Lia . . ."

"Trust me," she chided.

He did. Completely and utterly.

"The good Lord didn't intend for us to be pawing each other in public," Jolene's sharp voice intruded into their private discussion.

Kaden sucked in a deep breath, using the skills he'd developed as a stuntman to calm his shredded nerves. A clear mind and steady composure were the only way to look death in the face.

Untangling himself from Lia's arms, he slowly turned to face Jolene. She had moved to stand by the fire, as if trying to absorb the warmth. Despite the bright flames, the room was as cold as an icebox.

Pretending a nonchalance he was far from feeling, Kaden strolled to stand next to the body. As he hoped,

Jolene's wary gaze was locked on him. She considered him the threat, not Lia.

A mistake.

"Not that I blame you for killing your husband. I wanted him dead five minutes after I met him, but was there a particular reason you put a bullet through his forehead?"

"There were a thousand reasons, but I ignored them." She deliberately paused. "Until tonight."

"What made tonight different?"

"After years of turning a blind eye to his cheating and lying and neglect, the bastard was going to walk away and leave me to face the scandal he created on my own." Jolene nodded her head toward a gaping hole in the floorboards near the kitchen cabinets. "I found that unacceptable."

Kaden arched his brows in surprise. A trapdoor? Why the hell would that be there? It took a second for Kaden to realize Tate must have built it to hide his getaway suitcase.

Slowly, he turned back to meet Jolene's hard gaze, trying to act confused. He had to keep her attention on him.

"What scandal was he leaving you to face?"

Jolene clicked her tongue. "Don't play dumb. It doesn't suit you."

Kaden's lips twitched. She obviously never met his dearly departed father. He claimed Kaden was dumb as a stump. Whatever that meant.

"Well, there's just so *many* scandals," Kaden drawled. "You could be talking about Tate's habit of paying off officials to protect his wealthy business friends even when it put the citizens of Pike in danger. Or covering up crimes, including murder." He deliberately paused. "Or seducing innocent college students."

"Vanna Zimmerman," Jolene spat out the name as if it

was poison. "There was nothing innocent about her. For God's sake, I knew she was going to be trouble the second she arrived in town. It was obvious to anyone with a brain that she used her looks to manipulate people." The woman's gaze shifted toward the corpse that stared sightlessly at the ceiling, her lips pursing in disgust. "Not that men ever use their brains, do they? Not when it comes to a pretty brunette who's willing to spread her legs."

"You were jealous?" Kaden prodded.

"Me? Jealous of that gutter dweller?" Anger flared through her eyes, but it was a cold anger. As if her emotions were as frigid as the Wisconsin winter. "I knew when I married Tate he would never be faithful. All I asked for was a comfortable home and an allowance that would keep me in the luxury I deserved." Her pale features tightened. "And discretion."

"Ah, yes. Hard to be discreet when your lover announces she's pregnant."

Jolene flinched, as if Kaden hit a raw nerve. "When Tate came to me to confess, I considered . . ." She waved her gun toward the dead man. "This."

It wasn't an unreasonable reaction, Kaden silently acknowledged. Anyone would consider violence if they discovered their significant other was expecting a baby with their secret lover. Thankfully, most people managed to control their furious impulses.

"Obviously, you didn't go to such extremes," he murmured.

"No. After I had time to consider my various options, I realized I could use the revolting situation to my advantage."

Kaden didn't have to ask what she meant. The fact that Sunny was an only child suggested Jolene either didn't want children or struggled to conceive. He was betting on the latter.

"You wanted a baby."

"Yes. I'd tried to become pregnant." She grimaced. "Not very hard, to be honest. Tate is as selfish and incompetent in the bedroom as he is in everything else." She paused, her gaze once again flickering toward the corpse. "I suppose I should say *was*."

Kaden suppressed a shiver of disgust. Not only was the dead man creeping him out but Jolene's cold indifference to murdering her husband was adding to the horror movie vibe. She acted as if she committed murder every day. And maybe she did, he realized, as memories of the past week seared through his mind. The citizens of Pike had been dropping like flies.

"It didn't matter it was the child of your husband's lover?" he forced himself to ask.

Jolene widened her eyes in outrage. "The baby might have come out of Vanna's body, but she belonged to me," she said in fierce tones. "From the moment I held Sunny in my arms, I knew she was mine. I was destined to be her mother. To love her unconditionally. And to have her love me."

Kaden didn't doubt for a second that Jolene loved her daughter, regardless of the fact she hadn't given birth to her. But he suspected it was a sick, obsessed love. The sort of emotion that could destroy any sense of morality.

"And no one questioned how you managed to acquire a baby that looked suspiciously like your husband's lover?" Kaden asked, casting a covert glance over his shoulder. Lia had managed to inch her way closer to the bed, but she was still too far to make a grab for the gun.

"No one ever suspected Sunny wasn't mine." Jolene

laughed, the harsh sound echoing through the empty building. "People in this town are as blind as they are stupid. They share the most absurd gossip without ever seeing what's happening beneath their noses. All I had to do was say I was pregnant and the doctors told me it was high risk. Obviously, I would need to live in an area with a large hospital. Just in case of an emergency." She shrugged. "So I disappeared for a few months and returned with a baby. Simple."

Had it really been that simple? Maybe. People did tend to see what they expected to see. Motivated perception, or something like that.

"So what went wrong?" he demanded.

Jolene looked confused. "Wrong? Nothing. Everything was perfect."

"If it was perfect, Vanna wouldn't be dead, would she?"

Jolene hesitated, clearly caught off guard that he'd managed to figure out she was responsible.

"You really are too clever for your own good."

"Why did you kill her?"

Jolene regained command of her composure, sending him a mocking smile. "Because she became engaged. To your brother, I believe."

Kaden jerked as the unexpected words bit into him. Like tiny shards of ice. "You murdered her because she was engaged to Darren?"

"Yes. It made her greedy."

He struggled to understand what she was implying. "Vanna wanted more money?"

"No." Jolene looked exasperated by his question. "I would have given her money. She wanted her child back."

Kaden's mouth dropped open, his brain trying to grapple

with the shock of Jolene's revelation. No, it wasn't shock. It was whatever was beyond shock.

Of all the reasons for Vanna to be in Pike, the very last one he would have guessed was that she wanted the baby she'd bartered away.

"Christ," he finally breathed.

Chapter 28

A silence as thick as the winter snow settled around Kaden as he stared at Jolene in disbelief. His words felt stuck in his throat as the woman abruptly tilted back her head to laugh. Was she amused by Vanna's death?

"The stupid bitch showed up one morning with a suitcase of money claiming she changed her mind," she said, shaking her head in disbelief. "She said she was getting married soon and she wanted her baby."

Kaden cleared the lump in his throat. Had Darren's gentle devotion touched a thread of decency inside Vanna? Did she finally realize her child wasn't an asset to be sold off?

With an effort, Kaden shoved aside all thoughts of his brother and what might have been. Later, he would sort through his tangled emotions. Right now, he had to keep Jolene distracted.

"What happened?"

"Exactly what you would expect to happen," Jolene said dryly. "Tate burst out of his office and promised he would take care of it. As if I would ever trust him. They drove off before I could tell her exactly what she could do with the money."

"Do you know what happened between them?"

"Of course I do. I'm not stupid." She tossed her golden curls. "I followed them to this very spot."

Kaden glanced around the room, a niggling alarm sounding in the back of his mind. There was something he should remember. Something that had to do with Tate whisking away his pregnant lover to this place.

It took a moment, but at last he dredged up the memory of the envelope stuffed with evidence, and the picture that revealed Tate and Vanna standing in front of the building. That explained why they'd been there, standing in the snow. It also explained the piles of cash, although Kaden had jumped to the conclusion that Tate was giving it to Vanna. It'd never occurred to him it might have been just the opposite.

Kaden blinked, hit by another realization. "You took the picture."

"Yes." She tilted her chin to a defiant angle, as if she wasn't quite as confident as she wanted him to believe. "I needed evidence that Vanna and my husband were in the habit of trading cash for their own child. Like she was a piece of property. If there was ever a custody case, I wanted proof I was the only fit parent."

Kaden had to admit the woman was smart. A crazed lunatic but smart. The most dangerous kind of killer. Kaden cast another covert glance toward Lia. She was near the bunk bed. A couple more minutes and she would be in position to grab the gun.

"How did Burke get the picture?" he asked. Not only to keep Jolene distracted but because he was genuinely curious.

"I gave it to him. Ryan and I have been . . . close over the years." Her lips twitched, the dimples deepening as she confessed to her affair with the businessman. Kaden grimaced.

They called Vegas "Sin City," but obviously small-town America was seething with its own dirty secrets. "I knew he'd keep it safe. Then I warned my husband I had the means to destroy him and his career if he tried to take my child away from me."

"Wait." Kaden held up his hand, sensing he'd missed something important. "Did Tate take the money from Vanna?"

"Naturally." Jolene glared at the corpse with blatant loathing. "My husband was nothing if not predictable."

"He was going to give Sunny back?"

Kaden narrowed his eyes. He didn't doubt Tate Erickson was a sleazebag. But he found it hard to believe he would rip a child from the arms of the woman who'd been her devoted mother for over three years and hand her to a complete stranger.

"He swore he was just pretending to concede to Vanna's demands to get her out of town, that he had the means to ensure she would never bother us again," Jolene retorted.

Okay. Now Kaden was convinced the woman was exaggerating Tate's depravities to excuse her inexcusable behavior.

"Are you trying to say he was responsible for Vanna's death?" His tone made it clear he knew she was lying.

"Tate?" She released another one of those creepy laughs. "He didn't have the balls. My dearly departed husband was all talk and very little action. As usual, I had to take care of our problem."

Kaden could see Lia out of the corner of his eye, inching ever closer to the bed. He stepped in the opposite direction, drawing Jolene's gaze away.

"How?"

Jolene appeared eager to reveal just how clever she was. No doubt she'd spent her married years forced to pretend her husband was superior in every way, including intelligence.

"I used Tate's phone to send a message to Vanna. I told her that she could pick up her daughter at this location that evening."

That explained why Vanna would be here that night, Kaden silently acknowledged. "Why here?"

"I knew Vanna would feel more comfortable at her old apartment than at my house." A bitterness edged her voice. "Sunny was conceived here, after all, and in her mind it would be the perfect place to purchase the child she'd bartered away three years earlier."

"But instead of her child, she found you waiting for her."

"Exactly."

Kaden felt a pang of sympathy for Vanna. She might have been greedy and manipulative, but she hadn't deserved to be judged and condemned to death by the cold-blooded bitch currently pointing a gun at his heart.

"I'm guessing things didn't go as planned?" he said.

Jolene appeared confused by the question. "What are you talking about?"

"Vanna escaped, didn't she?"

Jolene's jaw tightened, as if she was still pissed at the memory. "I'll admit she was more wary than I expected. I'm not sure if she suspected it was a trap or if she was always on guard, but as soon as she caught sight of me, she turned to run." She glanced down at her gun, her expression easing, as if the weapon was some sort of security blanket. "Thankfully, I managed to pull the trigger before she could escape."

"Did you hit her?"

Jolene sent him an offended glare. "I never miss my mark, but she was already fleeing, so it wasn't a kill shot. Unfortunately, that meant I had to . . ." Her words stumbled to a halt, as if she had nearly revealed a secret she didn't intend to share. "To pull on my coat and boots to track her down and finish the job," she smoothly finished.

Kaden could easily imagine this elegant woman setting up an ambush to destroy her enemy. She had a chilling lack of concern for anyone other than herself and her daughter. But it was more difficult to picture her racing through the night in pursuit of Vanna.

"You chased her in the dark?"

"It wasn't that hard. She was bleeding like a stuck pig. It left a convenient trail for me to follow." The older woman clicked her tongue. "Still, it was annoying that I had to wade through the snow and ice, especially when I was wearing my favorite Dior boots. Do you know how much they cost?"

Kaden shrugged. "Too much?"

She ignored his mocking question. "I was still too far away to take another shot when I caught sight of her jumping off the bridge." Jolene shook her head in disgust. "Naturally, I was furious."

Kaden understood why Vanna was running down the road. And why the sight of Lia walking in her direction had made her panic. She would have been scared and disoriented and in agonizing pain. Plus, she was losing blood. No one could think clearly under those circumstances.

"You were furious the woman you were trying to murder in cold blood had the audacity to try to escape?" He didn't hide his disgust at her lack of empathy.

She shook her head, as if he was being unbearably dense. "I had to walk all the way back to my car to get a flashlight, and then climb down that stupid hill. I almost broke my neck."

A shame she hadn't, Kaden silently told himself, even as he realized why Lia hadn't seen Jolene when she'd made her quick search for the stranger who'd jumped off the bridge. Lia had no doubt already headed home by the time Jolene returned with her flashlight.

"Did you find her?" Kaden asked, not wanting Jolene to recall that Lia had been a witness.

"Eventually. She had crawled beneath a thick clump of bushes to hide, which meant it took forever. But in the end, it was a lucky break for me."

Kaden shuddered at her blunt words. "Why lucky?"

"She was dead by the time I located her. The fact that she was already hidden meant I didn't have to try to drag her body somewhere."

Kaden clenched his teeth at Jolene's blunt explanation. Was she deliberately trying to evoke his disgust? Did it give her pleasure to reveal her psychopathic lack of simple decency?

"What about Vanna's car?" He abruptly changed the direction of the conversation, refusing to play her sick game. "She had to drive out here."

Jolene smiled, as if smugly pleased with her talent for concealing the evidence of her crime.

"I parked it in the woods. The next day I called a wrecker from Grange and had it towed to my grandfather's farm. He was in the nursing home by then and no one ever bothered to go out there. When I eventually sold the land, I had it hauled away, along with the old equipment to be scrapped. Yet another problem solved."

Out of the corner of his eye, Kaden could see Lia had at last reached the bunk beds.

"Actually, your problems are just about to start," he drawled.

The words had barely left his lips when he heard Lia abruptly call out, "Kaden!"

With a confused frown, Kaden started to turn in her

direction. It was only then that he heard the footsteps directly behind him.

Too late.

The pain exploded in the back of his head as something hard smashed into his skull. He had enough time to curse himself for not having searched the rest of the building to make sure there weren't more bad guys hiding in the dark before he was tumbling forward to land face-first on the wooden floor.

Rookie mistake . . .

Chapter 29

Lia had been reasonably confident in their chances of surviving the encounter with Jolene. As long as Kaden was with her, she felt strong enough to face any demon. Including one with a puff of blond hair and deceptive dimples. Plus, she'd taken the opportunity to dial 911 on the cell phone she had tucked in the pocket of her parka while the older woman was distracted. She'd been forced to turn the sound down so Jolene couldn't hear the operator. And because she couldn't risk pulling the phone out of her pocket to explain what was happening, she had to hope they hadn't already hung up, assuming it was some sort of prank call.

Now, she wasn't nearly so confident as she watched in horror as Kaden crumpled to the ground. Dammit. She'd been so focused on inching her way toward the bunk beds, she hadn't noticed Sunny enter the room until she was swinging a heavy board toward the back of his head.

Why hadn't they searched the building . . . no.

Lia shoved aside futile recriminations. What was the point? Nothing was going to change the fact that Kaden was knocked out cold and it was up to her to keep them alive.

And there was only one way to do it.

With a rush of adrenaline, Lia dove toward the bunk

beds and knocked the suitcase aside. The pile of money spilled onto the floor as she grabbed the gun, along with several passports and a burner phone. Clearly, Tate Erickson had prepared for the day he might have to go on the run. His only mistake was marrying a woman with more brains and bigger balls than him.

Wrapping her fingers around the grip of the weapon, she pointed it directly at Jolene, hoping no one could tell she didn't know what the hell she was doing.

"Put your gun down," she commanded, her voice remarkably steady as she kept her gaze trained on Jolene. She had to assume Sunny would have shot Kaden if she had a weapon.

"Don't be a fool," the older woman chided. "I'm willing to pull the trigger. Are you?"

It was a direct challenge. Like a deadly game of chicken. Lia instinctively understood she had no choice but to play.

"Let's find out. On the count of three." With a cold smile, Lia swung her arm until the gun was pointed at Sunny. "One, two—"

"Don't!" Jolene cried out, the word sharp with genuine horror.

Lia swallowed a sigh of relief. Certainly, this was far from over, but even if the cops weren't coming, Kaden could wake up at any moment. And the Jeep was outside running, she reminded herself. It wasn't that late at night. Someone might come along and see the vehicle. They would be certain to stop to see if they needed help.

She just had to stay alive until then.

"I'm confused," she forced herself to say in mocking tones. If Jolene had time to think, she might realize that the longer this encounter went on, the more chance there was of her being caught. "You came here to murder your husband and you brought along your daughter?"

"It's not the first time she brought me to a murder," the younger woman drawled.

"Sunny, hush," Jolene snapped.

Lia turned her head to study the teenager. She was wearing a heavy coat with a knit scarf wrapped around her neck, but there was a dark flush staining her cheeks. Was she cold? Or excited by the sight of her father's dead body? Maybe both.

"It's true." Sunny ignored her mother, flashing a smug smile in Lia's direction. "Not that I recall much. I was only three. But I have a vivid memory of seeing my mother's body curled under the frozen bush."

Lia gasped, her stomach clenching into a painful knot as she realized the extent of the perverted relationship between the two women. Jolene had not only invited her daughter to witness the murder of her father, she'd brought her to this place when she was just a baby to watch her mother being killed.

What sort of psychopath did that?

Jolene made a sound of annoyance. "She wasn't your mother."

"No," Sunny hastily agreed, as if anxious to avoid provoking Jolene's temper. Lia didn't blame her. "You have always been my true mom."

"That's just . . ." Lia shuddered. "Sick."

Sunny hissed in outrage. "Shut up, bitch."

"Sunny!" Jolene called out, her gaze on the gun clenched in Lia's fingers. "Be careful."

With an effort, Lia bit back her words of disgust. She wanted them distracted, not angry.

"It makes sense to kill your husband." Reluctantly, Lia forced herself to glance toward the dead body just a few feet away. Bile rose in her throat, but she managed to maintain her composure as she returned her attention to Jolene. "Why run over Drew?"

Jolene shook her head. "I didn't."

"I did," Sunny announced in proud tones, shrugging as her mother clicked her tongue in warning. "We're going to kill her, aren't we? Who cares if she knows the truth?"

Lia hissed in shock. "You ran over Drew?"

"I did."

"Why?"

Sunny tossed her dark curls, her expression defiant. "He came to our house a few hours after he found the skeleton. I assumed he was there to brag. That was the only thing he was good at. Well, that and ramming his head into players on the football field, I suppose."

Lia ignored the girl's disgusting lack of guilt for nearly killing Drew. She was more interested in why he would go to Sunny's house. It wasn't like the two of them were friends.

"He wasn't there to brag?"

"He did that." Sunny curled her lips in disgust. "But he found something on the skeleton."

"What was it?"

"A leather satchel that held a picture of me." The pale blue eyes shimmered with sudden anger. Unlike Jolene, this girl was filled with fire, not ice. Lia, however, didn't doubt she was equally dangerous. "Along with my official birth certificate, signed by Tate Erickson and Vanna Zimmerman."

"He knew Jolene wasn't your mother," Lia breathed.

"I am her mother," Jolene reprimanded her in frigid tones.

Lia ignored her. "What did Drew want?"

"Money, of course." Sunny lifted her hand to stifle an exaggerated yawn. "So predictable."

Lia grimaced. She had no difficulty imagining Drew Hurst searching the skeleton for valuables. Or using what he'd discovered to try to make some extra cash. He obviously didn't have a clue he was dealing with a family of liars, psychopaths, and cold-blooded killers.

"So you hit him with your car?"

"What else could I do?" Sunny looked disgusted. "I knew he'd never keep his fat mouth shut. He'd be blabbing all over town that the skeleton was my mother. It's a pain in the ass he didn't die like he was supposed to."

"A loose end we need to tie up," Jolene drawled, as if Drew was a piece of trash, not a young man she'd known since he was born.

"Yes," Sunny agreed, an ugly smile twisting her lips as she glanced down at Kaden's unmoving form. "When we're done here."

Lia shuddered. She'd always wondered whether it was nature or nurture that formed the personality of a child. After all, she didn't have any connection to her father's family. Did that mean they had no impact on who she became as a person?

Now she knew without a doubt.

Sunny didn't have any blood ties with Jolene, but she'd developed her psychopathic tendencies.

Imagining the girl's pleasure when she rammed into poor Drew with her car, Lia abruptly recalled a question that had been nagging at her.

"Did you steal Drew's pocketknife?"

"Yep. I gave him five hundred dollars to get him to hand over the birth certificate. I wanted it back," Sunny readily admitted. "After I ran him over, I got out of the car and pulled the money out of his pocket. I didn't know I had his knife until I was driving away."

Lia was still puzzled. "Why did you use it to vandalize Kaden's Jeep?"

"I wanted your boyfriend out of town."

"How could slashing his tires get him out of town?"

Sunny shrugged, as if she hadn't really given her impulsive decision much thought. "I hoped it would scare him."

"Is that the same reason you threw a rock at me?"

Without warning, Sunny released a high-pitched giggle. As if the memory of hitting Lia with the rock was hysterical.

"I was hoping it would bash your head in."

Lia felt another shudder race through her. It was no wonder the sporadic attacks had all seemed so strange and childish. Sunny was a spoiled, immature brat who wallowed in her unstable emotions.

The question now was what other crimes she had committed.

"Did you kill Judge Armstrong?"

"Of course I did." Sunny glanced toward her mother, as if seeking the older woman's approval. It was only when Jolene offered a small nod of her head that the girl returned her attention to Lia. "I overheard a meeting he had with my dad. It was obvious he intended to squeal like a pig to whoever would listen to save his own neck. As if he had anything to live for, the senile old shit." Sunny stuck her finger in her mouth, as if she was gagging. "I couldn't risk having anyone with actual brains poking their nose into our business."

Lia narrowed her gaze. It wasn't much of a reason to kill the old man, she conceded. As Sunny had pointed out, the judge wasn't as sharp as he'd once been and few people took him seriously. It was doubtful he could have done much damage.

Had Sunny decided to murder him simply because she *wanted* to? That seemed the most reasonable explanation.

"So you hid in the garage and bashed in his head," Lia said, using Sunny's own words. "Then you placed something on the accelerator to make it look like an accident, right?"

"Very good. Cord taught me that handy-dandy trick."

"He knew what you were doing?" Lia's brows snapped together. Cord Walsh could be a troublemaker, but he was usually following Drew's lead. And she'd never heard that he was violent.

"That idiot? Hardly." Sunny rolled her eyes. "We were at a pizza party together and he was telling some kids that he was going to ram his truck into a tree to get the insurance money. He said all he had to do was wedge a brick against the gas pedal and put it in gear. It seemed simple enough. Not that the loser ever did it. He's still driving around that piece of shit."

"If he's such a loser, why spend time with him?" Lia demanded.

"Because he did anything I asked. And I mean *anything*. The stupid idiot is like an eager puppy, falling over his own feet to make me happy."

Ah. That certainly made more sense than Sunny being interested in a boy who was destined to be a dairy farmer.

"You used him. . . ." Lia's words died on her lips as she realized Cord wasn't the only boy Sunny had manipulated to get what she wanted. "You were driving his truck when you threw that brick at me."

"I wasn't sure what I was going to do, just that I wanted you hurt. Or dead," Sunny confessed with a shrug. "But I couldn't risk being spotted by one of those nosy bitches who are always roaming around town, so I told Cord I wanted to go buy a bag of weed and I didn't want to take my parents' car." She laughed. "Guys are so easy, aren't they? Especially guys in this town. One smile and I have them wrapped around my little finger."

Lia couldn't argue with that. She didn't doubt for a second that the boys in Pike were willing to do whatever Sunny asked.

"Why would you poison me?" she demanded instead.

Sunny's smile faded, a hint of irritation darkening her eyes. "You kept digging into the past. You and your boyfriend had to be stopped somehow. I noticed your vehicles were missing from the alley and it seemed the perfect opportunity to get rid of both of you. After all, Wayne conveniently left the key to the shop where I could find it. Such an idiot."

Lia ground her teeth as fury blasted through her. She wanted to reach out and slap the little bitch. Anyone could have eaten those cookies. Even Della, who was in the store every day. At her age, there was no way she would have survived.

Wisely, Lia bit back her words of condemnation. She wasn't sure Sunny had the moral capacity to understand what she did was wrong. Besides, she still had more questions.

"Is that why you killed Ryan Burke?"

Waiting for Sunny to brag about yet another murder, Lia was caught off guard when Jolene interrupted the conversation.

"She didn't. I did."

Lia glanced back at the older woman, a combination of shock and horror and disbelief making her feel nauseated.

"Quite the murderous tag team, aren't you?" she accused, her voice harsh in the frigid air. Jolene arched a plucked brow, her expression indifferent. "Why kill him?"

"It was becoming increasingly obvious that someone was going to be blamed for killing Vanna," she pointed out. "Why not my faithless husband?"

"You intended to frame Tate for the murder?"

"It was easy enough. All I needed was the proof of Vanna's blackmail and the picture of Tate and Vanna I'd given him."

Lia blinked at the woman's cunning. She didn't know what was scarier. The fact that Jolene was a psychopath. Or the fact that she was clever enough to avoid getting caught.

"You put the envelope in Kaden's Jeep," Lia said, speaking more to herself than Jolene.

The older woman glanced down at Kaden. "He kept threatening to go to the FBI. I assumed he would eventually get around to handing the evidence over to the authorities. I followed him from the hospital in Grange, and when he went into the store, I dropped the envelopes into his vehicle."

"Why bash in Ryan's head?" Lia asked, her voice louder than necessary. She wanted Jolene's attention on her, not the unconscious Kaden. "I'm sure he would have handed it over."

As she'd hoped, Jolene looked up, her expression puzzled. As if she didn't understand why Lia was asking the question. Obviously, in her mind, it was perfectly reasonable to murder anyone who might be a threat to her role as mother.

"He knew I didn't give birth to Vanna. He was . . ."

"A loose end," Lia finished for her.

"Exactly." Jolene stepped forward. "Just like you and your lover."

Kaden swallowed a curse as he felt a cramp twisting his calf muscles into a painful knot. He'd been alert for several minutes, watching the situation from beneath lowered lashes. He was waiting for the right time to make his move.

Annoyingly, he didn't know what his move was going to be. Or when he would know the time was right.

His body, however, had just made the decision for him.

The freezing temperature in the building combined with the hard floorboards were causing his muscles to stiffen. Soon it would affect his mobility. If he was going to do something, it had to be now.

The thought was still forming in his foggy mind when he heard the distant sound of sirens blasting through the night air. They were growing louder with every second, and Kaden allowed himself a tiny spark of hope they were the calvary riding to their rescue.

At the same moment, there was a loud creak of the floorboards. Obviously, Jolene had heard the sirens as well and was instinctively turning toward the window.

A grim smile curved Kaden's lips. At last the bitch had made a mistake. Not only had she taken her attention off Lia, she'd lowered the gun to her side. Now it was up to him to make her pay.

Planting his hands flat on the floor, Kaden used his considerable strength to shove himself upright in one smooth motion. Or at least as smooth as possible, considering he was cold and cramped and amped on adrenaline.

Sensing his movement, Jolene whirled back in alarm, but she was too late. Kaden was already lunging forward, lowering his shoulder to jam it into the center of her chest and using his leverage to lift her off her feet. It wasn't a trick he'd learned as a stuntman. This was pure street fighting.

Barreling forward, Kaden slammed the smaller woman into the wall with enough force to crack the decayed paneling and dislodge a layer of dirt from the exposed rafters.

Kaden, however, barely noticed the cloud of dust and debris that clogged the air. He was far more concerned with the deafening boom as Jolene managed to pull the trigger.

The shot wasn't unexpected, but he wasn't prepared for the shocked scream that immediately followed the blast.

Shit. Kaden had been convinced that Jolene was at an angle from which she couldn't do any damage, even if she did get off a shot. With his heart lodged painfully in his throat, he jerked his head to the side. A second later, relief surged through him as he caught sight of Lia. She appeared shaken but unharmed as she stared down at the floor.

Lowering his gaze, he discovered what held her horrified attention. A startled curse was wrenched from his lips as Kaden caught sight of Sunny, crumpled next to her dead father. Blood was pouring from a bullet wound in the center of her chest and her face was unnaturally pale in the fire-light.

There was another scream that threatened to burst Kaden's eardrums as Jolene realized what she'd done.

"No!" she wailed, collapsing against Kaden as if she'd lost the will to live.

Outside, the flashing lights pierced through the grimy windows, revealing that help had arrived. Kaden grunted in exhaustion, continuing to keep Jolene pinned against the wall. He was quite certain those flashing lights were the most beautiful things he'd ever seen in his life.

Epilogue

Four weeks later

Lia stepped out of the courthouse and sucked in a deep breath of the crisp air. She'd been inside the building for hours. Not only to go over the official statement she'd given earlier about the events that occurred during Jolene and Sunny's reign of terror, but to chat with Zac, who'd thankfully returned to resume his job as sheriff. It had been beyond comforting to know he was back in charge; plus, she'd wanted to hear about every detail of his honeymoon.

Well, not every detail . . .

Once her eyes adjusted to the bright afternoon sunlight that reflected with a blinding intensity against the newest layer of snow, Lia headed down the steps. She knew Kaden would be waiting for her.

Sure enough, the gleaming red Land Rover he'd bought in Vegas the week before to drive them back to Pike was parked next to the curb. He'd insisted he needed a dependable vehicle for when they were in Wisconsin. And it was true. His vast collection of motorcycles and sports cars would be dangerous to use during the winter. But he hadn't been thinking about snowy roads when he at last decided on this SUV. He was a man obsessed with his favorite hobby. Collecting expensive vehicles.

Her lips twitched as she pulled open the passenger door and climbed into the high seat. Kaden was going to be an interesting addition to the town.

Waiting until she tugged the seat belt across her body, Kaden pulled away from the curve and did a U-turn to head north.

"How did it go?" he asked.

"Not bad." Lia settled back in the soft leather seat, savoring the warm scent of his aftershave. Her heart skipped a beat, warmth flowing through her. She would never get used to sitting next to this glorious man. Not ever. "Thank God Zac is home."

"Maybe Pike can return to normal now."

"Don't jinx us," she protested. "We've had enough troubles."

Kaden chuckled, turning onto a side street that headed out of town. "Did you give him the account numbers?"

"I did." Lia had taken the stack of offshore accounts connected to Vanna that she'd managed to uncover, as well as the code on the back of the map Kaden had found in his brother's files. "He's going to turn them over to the EPA investigators."

"That's probably for the best."

Lia grimaced, remembering Zac's words of warning. "If word of Vanna's blackmail scheme happens to get out, I doubt they'll be able to keep her name out of the papers."

Kaden snorted. "I can't imagine the EPA or any other government agency would willingly admit they employed an agent who was taking bribes to turn a blind eye to illegal activities. And, more importantly, they won't want to expose the businesses willing to pollute their communities for the sake of profit."

"True." Lia hadn't told Zac that she'd found the bank account Vanna had been using under her mother's name. Or the fact that Kaden had discovered her last will and testament in his brother's office. Vanna had listed her foster mother, Sharon Bradly, as her beneficiary. No doubt Vanna and Darren intended to change their wills after they were married, but once Vanna was officially declared dead, her assets would go to Sharon. It seemed the only good thing that could come from so much bad.

"Did you go to the hospital?" she asked.

Kaden nodded. "Drew regained consciousness a couple weeks ago and the nurse said he's able to walk on his own now. Hopefully, he'll be released soon."

"What about Sunny?"

Lia was certain the girl was dead after her mother had put a bullet through her chest. But, remarkably, she'd managed to hang on while an ambulance arrived and loaded her into the back. A hysterical Jolene had been cuffed and taken to jail by a grim-faced Anthony.

"She's in stable condition. Or at least she's physically stable. Mentally . . ." Kaden shook his head. "I assume she'll be transferred to a secure facility as soon as she's strong enough to be moved."

Lia shuddered. She still had nightmares of Sunny's evil smile as she described her violent attacks.

"It's so twisted. And awful."

"Too awful." Kaden turned onto a narrow path as they reached the edge of town. "Let's not spoil such a beautiful day with the past."

Lia agreed. She'd done her duty. She was ready to concentrate on something else. Or rather *someone* else.

"Where are we going?" she asked, not really caring as long as she was with Kaden.

"I have something I want to show you."

"Out here?" She glanced toward the rolling hills that spread toward a distant valley. She'd been out this way with her grandfather when she was young. "I'm pretty sure this road is a dead end."

"Trust me."

Lia arched her brows. "You said that in Paris and then you shoved a snail into my mouth," she reminded him.

Just days after they'd escaped death, Kaden had whisked Lia off to Paris to enjoy their Christmas holidays in peace. She'd been acutely thankful that she always had her passport updated just in case she needed to travel. It had been a glorious two weeks.

"It was escargot, and many people consider it a delicacy," Kaden chided.

"It was nasty," Lia insisted, even as a smile of remembered pleasure curved her lips.

Until Kaden crashed into her life, she'd been content to spend her days in Pike, never daring to expand her horizons. Now she never knew if she was going to be in Paris or Vegas or whatever other place captured Kaden's interest.

It was like being caught in a constant whirlwind. And she never wanted the adventure to end.

"Lesson learned," he assured her. "No more snails."

She reached over to touch his arm. "Everything else in Paris was sheer perfection," she assured him.

Kaden pulled to a halt as they reached a cattle gate that blocked the road, indicating they'd reached private property. Glancing in her direction, he sent her a mysterious smile.

"Including our discussion about our future together?"

Excitement fluttered in the pit of her stomach. Kaden had taken her to a dinner on a private balcony that overlooked the Seine. There had been candles and roses and champagne that made her tipsy. It was there he'd asked her to spend the rest of their lives together.

Lia hadn't hesitated. She nearly tipped him off the balcony as she rushed into his arms. She was always smart. She knew a good deal when she found one.

And Kaden was a good deal.

"That was the best part," she assured him.

"Good." Kaden waved his hand toward the nearby fields. "Because I think I found us the perfect plot of land to build our house."

Lia leaned forward, studying the landscape and picturing the image of a house angled to overlook the valley. "It has a stunning view."

"It's not too isolated?"

"No. I like the idea of living in a place where I can wander outside without having nosy neighbors watching my every move."

She glanced toward Kaden as she recalled the chaos of the hours after Jolene's arrest. Not only had a horde of reporters set up camp outside her store, there'd been a shocking number of strangers who were determined to make a movie about the sordid events. With Kaden playing the starring role, of course.

After a couple of days of being harassed, Kaden had endured enough. They'd packed their bags and disappeared to ___. And even when they'd returned to the States, they'd ___ past week in Vegas. Not only to check on his busi-___ or Lia to meet his best friend, Dom Lucier.

"___," he agreed, reaching out to stroke his fingers ___ cheek. "So, what do you think about this place?"

"___'s a lovely area, but this used to be a farm," she ___rned him. "It probably comes with more acreage than we want."

He shrugged. "Just three hundred."

"*Just* three hundred? How big a house do you intend to build?"

"Average size."

Lia narrowed her gaze. "Pike average or Hollywood average?"

"Average average."

"Kaden," she murmured. She loved Kaden, but she would never be comfortable in a lavish monstrosity of a house.

"We'll need space for a garage so I can work on my motorcycles," he interrupted her dark thoughts. "And you'll need an office. An official office, where you don't have to worry about interruptions."

An office without interruptions? Lia returned her gaze to the land that seemed to spread out forever. There was a lake somewhere on the property, she distantly remembered. Her grandfather had let her fish while he was visiting with his friend. What a perfect location for an office.

"That would be nice," she murmured in dreamy tones, already picturing a small cottage surrounded by a lush garden nestled next to the water.

"And, of course, we'll have to have enough acreage for the hanger and runway," he said.

She blinked, the vision she was creating abruptly shattered by his words. "The what?"

"If we're going to travel from Vegas to Pike on a regular basis, it only makes sense to have a small plane we back and forth," he pointed out in reasonable to

"You're a pilot?"

"Not yet." He smiled, leaning forward to p kiss against her lips. "I thought we'd learn together."

"Together," she breathed.

"Forever."